SOUL OF
TOLEDO

SOUL OF TOLEDO

—m—

Edward D. Webster

ISBN: 0997032006
ISBN 13: 9780997032000
Library of Congress Control Number: 2015957177
Dream House Press, Ojai, CA

TABLE OF CONTENTS

Dedicated to

Eleanor and Willard

In Loving Memory

During the period covered by *Soul of Toledo,* Iberia was composed of
these Kingdoms:

Portugal
Navarre- in the north center
Aragón- in the north-east, whose king also ruled Naples and
    several Mediterranean islands
Castile and León (referred to most often in the book as simply
    Castile) covering the greatest portion

And the Caliphate of Granada in the south

MAJOR CHARACTERS DURING THE PERIOD 1442-1449

—◊—

In Toledo

Viçente Pérez* (born ha-Levi): first deputy of Toledo until 1445

Diego Pérez*: Viçente's son, at university in Salamanca

Archbishop Juan de Cerezuela: archbishop of Toledo until his death in 1442

Archbishop Alfonso Carillo: archbishop of Toledo later in the book

Vicar Pero López de Gálvez: vicar of Toledo's cathedral

Marcos García de Mora: an attorney who despised and mistrusted converts, later first deputy

Sancho*: head of the Wool Carter's Union

Fernando de Avila: commander of Toledo's Calatrava gate in 1449

Pedro López de Ayala: Toledo's chief magistrate until after the Battle of Olmedo

Rabbi Benjamin*: Chief Rabbi of Toledo

Samuel*: a mute Jew

*Sangre Pura**: a band of insurgents formed to attack Jews and converts

In Castile's capital, Vallodolid

King Juan II of Castile and León: the king

Constable Alvaro de Luna: principal advisor (and some say puppet-master) to King Juan

Pedro Sarmiento: King Juan's Butler and later commander of Toledo

Philip*: courtier who assists Sarmiento

In Rome

Pope Nicholas V: pope beginning March 1447

Ralducci*: Viçente's old friend, now an advisor to Pope Nicholas

Ambassador Ortega*: King Juan's ambassador to the Holy See

Cardinal Juan de Torquemada: A cardinal in Rome (uncle to the infamous inquisitor)

Bartholomew Texier: master of Dominican order from 1426 to 1449

In Segovia

Prince Enrique: King Juan's son (who will become King Enrique IV of Castile and León after the book ends)

Juan Pacheco: Prince Enrique's confidant and advisor

Bishop Lope de Barrientos: bishop of Cuenca, advisor to Prince Enrique and King Juan

King Juan's opposition

The Royal Cousins

King of Navarre (major city Pamplona),

King Alfonso V of Aragón (major cities Zaragoza, Barcelona) and Naples

Master of Santiago: commander of a military-religious order with bases in León and Castile

In Naples

King Alfonso V: king of Aragón and Naples
Francesca*: a charming woman who lives in the court of King Alfonso
Penélope*: Francesca's attendant
Carlo*: Francesca's chaperone
Guido Tivolini*: King Alfonso's minister of state

* Fictional Character

PART I

THE REVELATION

Toledo, Castile—1404

—◊—

CHAPTER 1

BLESSING OR BLASPHEMY?

Trust or doubt?

How did Satan appear when he came to tempt you?

Viçente's parents had raved about this night for weeks, but they'd raved with nervous eyes. None of Viçente's friends spoke of a thirteenth birthday as extraordinary. Why in his family?

And now it was time. A strange brew of apprehensions set his pulse pounding.

Father entered the dining room, wearing his black suit and string cravat with gold-on-black etched medallion, finery he'd only worn for Uncle Santo's funeral and the time he'd gone to the courts to testify. Papa's dark hair was combed across the bald patch, his cheeks and chin scrubbed and shaved.

A knot formed in Viçente's stomach as his father took him by the shoulders and appraised him with serious eyes, but he couldn't help feeling pleased that this man who'd loomed so tall in his life was no longer a giant compared to him.

"Sit with me, son, and we'll see what luscious dinner your mama has prepared."

The table was set with their finest silver. Candles blazed on the pewter chandelier. Rosa brought a tureen from the kitchen and set it on the side table. While the servant ladled chicken soup into porcelain bowls, Mama brought in the family's huge copper platter, almost hidden beneath potatoes and legs of baby lamb, cloaked in sautéed onions and gravy. The scent of garlic filled the air.

"Oh, Mama, my favorite." It was nearly enough to make him relax.

She tousled his hair. He would talk with her about annoying motherly habits, but not on a day when she'd cooked baby lamb in garlic for him.

Rosa stood in the kitchen doorway, smiling over the scene. Father said, "Wish him happy birthday, Doña Rosa. Then go home to your family."

"But …" The woman glanced from one parent to the other, looking helpless. Viçente wanted to protest that Rosa should stay for his celebration, but his father's level gaze stopped him and sent Rosa out the door.

Father folded his hands on the table. "Tonight, son, I will pray as you have not heard before, and you will drink wine. After dinner, we'll talk, for you've reached an extraordinary age, the age of manhood. There are things you must know."

Viçente still wondered what was so magical about being thirteen. He listened to Papa's prayers, spoken in an alien tongue that made him squirm. These didn't feel like incantations that Christians said on a son's special birthday, but sinister prayers the priests warned of. He ate more lamb, potatoes, and carrots, more of the honeyed cookies than he would have thought possible. He drank two glasses of red wine and felt dizzy. Apprehension faded as he finished this most delicious meal ever, and his stomach bulged.

But Mama didn't hum as she brushed crumbs from the table, and Papa didn't smile as he led him to his compact study lined with bookshelves.

They'd never sat together in this room before, but now one of the kitchen chairs had been squeezed in. Father took it and gestured to the armchair. "Take my place."

As he settled, Viçente saw Papa's hands shake. Papa clasped them in his lap and cleared his throat. "I'm going to explain about our lives, your mother's and mine. Please listen, and try not to judge."

Papa's grimace sent Viçente's pulse pounding. Something horrid was coming; he knew from his parents' lack of humor, from those dinner prayers, and from so many other hints these past weeks. He knew, and he didn't want to know, what all of this was about.

"You were an infant when I made a dreadful decision about our faith, one that was wrong according to God. But ..."

Now that Papa had mentioned faith, Viçente could deny it no longer. "What do you mean, 'wrong decision'—about becoming Christian?"

"Please. Don't interrupt." Papa looked frightened in a way he'd never seen. "Your mother and I were Jewish until you were born. You've asked about that religion, and I avoided many times. When you were younger, you'd come home crying because the older boys called you names—'Jew boy' or 'pig' or 'Christ-killer.' I told you part of the truth then—that our family had belonged to that other religion, but we'd changed, and those boys were just confused. When you repeated bad things you'd heard about Jews, I tried not to defend them, but to help you understand that Jews have their own beliefs that make sense to them."

Viçente's stomach, so full from the meal, felt sick. How could Papa speak of converting to Christianity as wrong? There was no way to be silent. "They killed Christ. What sense does that make?"

Papa leaned closer, looking angry—a little—but more sorrowful. "I worry, Viçente, about the things they tell you in this new school. I'd like you to consider their words. Can you do that?" Viçente nodded, and Papa said, "No Jew who is alive today killed Christ, so how can you blame the Jews of Toledo?"

The priest who came to their school, what had he said? *Jews today deny Christ, which is as bad as killing him all over again.* He repeated this to his father.

"Is it possible that they don't believe Christ is God?" Papa asked.

"That's ridiculous. Everyone knows."

"Not everyone does." Papa looked flustered. "Let me say it this way. I changed my name years ago from Judah to Carlos, but I still think of myself as Judah."

Again Viçente's stomach wanted to give way, but he held it down. "Oh my God. You've lied to me."

"We let you believe untruths. We loved you and didn't want you hurt."

"You're still *one* of them? It's true what they say about Jews pretending to be Christian. You're ... how could you be?"

"We've raised you Christian to keep you safe." Papa's voice trembled now. "We disavowed our God, our *Yahweh*, even though he commanded us to die rather than deny him. Everyone here did." His father swept his arm in an arc, as if gesturing to the homes along the street. "We fled Christian swords, like mice from a burning granary, and we lived, but we also fled God, a great sacrifice. These bookshelves once held sacred volumes, all destroyed."

"Coward." The word was out before Viçente could question it. "If you believed you should die for this *Yahweh*, you should have fought them or let them lock you up or kill you. If you're a secret Jew ..." The words he wanted to say—*you deserve to die*—withered on his lips.

Visibly shaken, the man, this stranger who'd raised him, took a minute, drawing calmness into his face. He stood and placed a hand on Viçente's shoulder. Viçente would shuck it off, but old habits couldn't be shed so fast. The words his father had been speaking sounded almost like those of a man of conscience, but only a Christian had that.

Still, this man had taught him what morals were. He relaxed just a little to his father's touch.

"We had an infant son, and we loved him very much." Papa patted the hair behind his ear, and tears sprang from Viçente's eyes. How could this be happening on the day he was becoming a man? And what was this foolishness about becoming a man if not Hebrew sacrilege?

His father returned to his chair, his hair mussed, the bald patch above his forehead exposed, like so much else in his deceitful life. Tears emerged from the shadows cast by the candlelight around Papa's eyes and ran down his cheeks. "We felt our son should have a chance to grow up and taste this world. I beg you, don't hate us for preserving your life."

Holy God. Father was blaming his treachery on Viçente. He wanted to yell at this Jew who masqueraded as a righteous father, but his constricted throat wouldn't speak.

"It's easy to say we were wrong, but when these Christians attacked, we lived without defenses."

"I knew this was a nest of Jews," Viçente said. "All my friends know. But you'd converted."

"Let me tell you what Christians were to me. Men that broke down the gates of our refuge, slaughtered the defenders, and seized the first woman they found, one of your aunts, my sister, Rachel. They slit her throat." Father hunched in his chair, pressing his forehead between his palms. "They strung her upside down by the gate and yelled taunts at her lifeless body while her blood dripped to the paving stones."

My God, Viçente's aunt. Jesus, was this true? Jews were sinners, but you didn't slit their throats. Or was this the deceit of a devious Jew? And Mama, the mama who adored him and prepared his special dinner, was also a heathen Christ-hater? Viçente clapped his hand to his mouth, but he couldn't hold back.

His father grabbed a waste pot for Viçente's vomit, retrieved a towel and a mug of water from the kitchen. He waited for Viçente to rinse his mouth and asked, "Shall I go on?"

The vile taste choked him. The weight of this loathsome man's touch lingered still on his shoulder, and he understood now what they said about Satan's power to tempt the innocent. He would never allow this Satan to come so close again.

Viçente longed to fling open the door to the study and the door to the house and the door to heaven or hell and throw himself through, but he nodded.

"They *invited* us to become Christians that night. I detested them. I would have fought. I would have killed myself with one of their swords, like the martyrs of Mainz in the Rhineland. I hated *Yahweh* more than

I despised those men, for he had put me in a position where I could turn neither direction without transgressing. On one side, my wife and tiny son. On the other, the path heaven decreed. As I knelt and kissed the priest's cross, I cursed God for testing me and finding me wanting. I cursed myself, because I was wanting. I was weak, without principle—a *coward,* as you say."

Papa poured half a glass of wine and handed it to Viçente. "You were a baby. Our family name was ha-Levi, not Pérez, and you were called Moses. It was 'the year of our Lord 1391.' The words stick in my throat. In 1390, we didn't have this lord, just God. Please, son, don't hate me."

Viçente closed his eyes, feeling so very lonely. He took a breath and spat out the question: "What do you want from me?"

"You enter manhood today, and you'll make many choices. I hope you will continue to honor your mother and me. Continue worshipping this Christ, but don't forget your ancestors. Never speak of this, for your safety and your mother's, if not for mine. And remember: it is depraved and evil to harm another person for his beliefs."

PART II

THE FIRST DEPUTY

—꧋—

... Because we have heard it said that in some places Jews celebrated, and still celebrate Good Friday, which commemorates the Passion of Our Lord Jesus Christ by ... stealing children and fastening them to crosses ... we order that ... if ... anything like this is done, ... all persons who were present ... shall—be seized, arrested, and brought before the king; and ... he shall cause them to be put to death in a disgraceful manner...

—Siete Partidas, fourteenth-century
laws for the kingdom of Castile

CHAPTER 2

38 YEARS LATER

—⁓—

February 1442

WALKING TOWARD HIS OFFICE AFTER lunch, Viçente stopped at the cathedral construction site. A newly carved statue stood beside a small
mountain of planks, the likeness of a man with a bishop's bonnet—a
saint, no doubt, but which one? He gazed up at the cathedral's new
tower, wrapped in scaffolding, only half-finished but already rising im-
possibly high.

He allowed himself a moment of pride. This work had been fi-
nanced and managed largely through his efforts. But the irony still
pierced his soul, even this long after his parents' deaths; as a loyal
Christian raised by blasphemers, he could never believe enough, could
never prove his worth or his faith sufficiently.

A sound startled him, boards clattering. A boy of ten darted from
behind a crate and handed him a note. "From the rabbi," the lad said.
As the words knotted Viçente's stomach, the boy ducked around some
scaffolding and was gone.

Viçente unfolded the paper. *R. C. at dawn.* That was all it said, but
it was more than enough.

"What does the damned Hebrew want?" he muttered as he climbed
the stairs to his office. Maybe it had to do with the Jew who'd been arrested that morning for stealing a crucifix from the cathedral. *I don't
have to go,* he thought. *Don't have to jeopardize everything over some petty crime.*

When he reached his offices, an odor halted him, some foul excrement, which reminded him about his first afternoon appointment. He hustled past the two men waiting in his anteroom and entered the office.

His clerk, Flores, followed him in. "I sent that man to scrape his shoes, but there's only so much to be done. His trousers are foul, too."

"Thank you for trying," Viçente said. "Wait five minutes and send them in."

He settled behind his wide oak desk, needing to clear his thoughts, but instead the rabbi haunted him. If life were sensible, he'd charge to the Jewish Quarter to confront the problem, but he couldn't. He thought again of ignoring the Jew's summons. Inadvisable.

As first deputy of Toledo, many called Viçente the 'second-most-powerful man in the city.' Yet he felt helpless with the Jews. Their peril was self-imposed and worsened by their beards and black garb that flaunted their blasphemy, but Viçente was forced by duty to protect them.

Another thought made him almost laugh aloud. He might be the second-most-powerful man, but duty dealt him his next unsavory task—settling a petty quarrel between two oafs while tolerating the scent of pig manure.

—ɯɯ—

Opposite Viçente, in two of his guest chairs, sat the ruddy-faced pig farmer and the man's neighbor, a scrap dealer. The dealer, Ramos, sought redress for the stench he endured every night when the atmosphere grew still, a reek that Viçente could well imagine.

"Any fellow who can't abide a little stink got no plain decency," the pig man said.

Crude, rotund, and slovenly, the farmer resembled one of his livestock, and yet he wore that look of superiority when addressing Viçente. It still rankled, even after all these years, that a man such as this would disdain one who'd earned the right to govern a city. The reason, of course, was that the pig farmer's parents, grandparents, and great-grandparents, though all of them illiterate, had been born Christian. 'Old Christians' kept careful note of those who shared their respectable ranks and those outside them, who, in polite conversation, were called *conversos*.

Beside the farmer, Ramos looked plain scared. He gripped the arms of his chair as if prepared to rip them off.

"It's good shit." The rancher leaned as close to Ramos as the arms of his chair allowed, and bellowed, "A sensible man would buy some and put it to use."

Viçente's sword hung useless on the coatrack by the door. If the pig man attacked, he might jump up to aid Ramos, but he'd be better off shouting for the guard. "How much do they pay for that manure?" he asked.

"That's my business." The pig man leaned toward his neighbor again and cuffed his arm with a meaty hand.

Ramos was over fifty and skinny, no match for the brawny farmer. He slid his seat further away.

The farmer half-stood and moved his chair close to Ramos.

"Normal rate's two *maravedis* a cartload," Viçente said.

The pig man's eyes widened. "Don't always pay so well."

"Someone's cheating you." Viçente was glad to see the farmer's glare shift his way.

"What the hell someone like *you* know?"

Viçente ignored the tone. "You might have to cart the load further, but I know a man who'll pay that much."

Ramos surprised Viçente by speaking up. "You make this *pendejo* richer. How does that help with the stink?"

The pig rancher turned his snout toward Ramos. "To *government men* like Pérez here, bribes make pig shit smell like rosebuds." Again, the contempt.

Normally, Viçente would ignore the taunt—his goal was promoting peace in his city. But today wasn't normal, not since receiving the rabbi's note. He glared at the pig man. "There are some honest government men, Mr. Pig Farmer. I make sure that Toledo's government is full of them. And there are some converts who really believe in Christ. Almost all of us do. I'm trying to help you, if you'll let me."

Viçente turned to Ramos. "You may not think so, but we're making progress."

Back to the farmer, who'd turned to sulky silence. "Are you interested in two *maravedis,* or maybe you're too stubborn or too pious?"

"How far I got to take it?"

"The hills across the river."

"The bridge keeper will eat my profit in tolls." The pig man scratched his armpit.

"If I can free you of that—"

"What you want for it?"

"You pay no toll, and you get two *maravedis* per load. How many loads do you cart at once?"

"I hold on till I got a few, once every second month."

"You hold it in a big rotting pile, don't you, heaped beside Señor Ramos' fence? But you won't do that any more. Move it away. When you get one load, haul it, and you give Ramos here half interest in every fourth one."

The pig man grumbled, but relented in the end. He stood over a cowering Ramos and kicked the leg of his chair. Not likely that the scrap man would see any payment, but his life would be a bit less fragrant.

The stink remained in Viçente's office long after the men left, and it derived not of manure. Viçente swung open the wooden shutters to disperse the smell and to take comfort in viewing the cathedral.

A chill breeze drifted in, carrying the clatter of hammer and chisel, sculptors carving more saints for the new west entrance and gargoyles for the tower. His city had been at peace for some time now. Many Christians owned ranches or businesses, but others, the resentful ones, performed menial labor for scant wages. *Conversos* like Viçente, though Christian, were shunned by many of their fellows, so he used his position to assist when possible.

Muslims and Jews—much diminished from former times—were allowed to practice their trades within the limits of custom and to worship as long as they kept to themselves, but there'd been recent signs of trouble for the Jews—vandalism at a synagogue, a few beatings. Minor issues, but they troubled Viçente, whose role was to keep order and promote the city's fortunes; troubled him more because any aid he offered would be suspect.

And that report of the Jew stealing from the cathedral. Could the Jews be foolish enough to retaliate against the majority? Even if they had no such intent, the theft of a holy crucifix could incite more violence. He should have realized earlier; the rabbi's summons wasn't petty or unimportant. Viçente's resentment for the Jew had clouded his perception.

Damn the rabbi and double damn him! All of this was carrying Viçente's thoughts back to his father and the irony—that he, a jeweler's son, held the post of first deputy. That jeweler had been a secret Jew, while Viçente was a principal sponsor for construction of Christ's new edifice. His father, long dead, would have seen the incongruity, but they never would have discussed it; they'd never discussed much of anything after Viçente's thirteenth birthday. He'd reconciled with his mother, that last year of her life, and she'd praised his accomplishments, even accepting his work for Jesus.

And proudest of all had been Marta, who'd been born an Old Christian, but who hadn't hesitated to marry a *converso.*

Viçente's heritage was the stink that wouldn't depart with the afternoon breeze. It wasn't that his ancestors had been Jews. If they'd truly converted, the grace of God would have followed. The stench rose from the Old Christians' suspicion that converts secretly continued perverse pagan rites. Viçente would ridicule the thought, were it not for the shame of his own deceitful parents who'd done just that, and the fact that suspicion was all it might take to end his good works.

CHAPTER 3

—ᜍ—

NORTH OF THE CITY WALLS, beyond the orange groves, stood the ruins of a Roman Circus, where plays and animal shows had once been performed for the Empire's privileged citizens. What remained was a bare ellipse of standing gray stones, many broken in half or fallen and buried in sediment. The site lay near the city, yet obscured by a pine thicket. From the Jewish section, a person could stroll northwest along the curving bank of the Río Tajo, pass out of view, and then climb the hill into the grove.

Viçente took another route. As first light touched the western clouds that morning, he saddled his black Arabian, Amistad, and rode east to the Puente de Alcántara, his stomach wound in a hard knot. Waving to the guards on the gate towers, he passed through and rode across the bridge and partway up the hill toward the castle of San Servando. He halted to scan the road behind. Seeing no riders following, he recrossed the bridge, circled, and approached the Roman Circus from the far side. He tied his horse to a limb and entered the thicket.

The rabbi stepped from behind a boulder, looking like some Roman carnival act sprung to life, a homely, big-nosed demon in a wide-brimmed black hat and scraggly beard. The rabbi offered an unconvincing smile. "I see you so seldom, Viçente."

The man's familiarity, his arrogance, and his appearance rankled. Viçente made a dusting-off motion. Rabbi Benjamin looked down and brushed leaf fragments from his beard.

"You summon me here like a vassal," Viçente said. "You place me in danger and place the people who depend on me at risk, and then you speak as if we're old friends who miss one another."

"Just a little pleasantry. I've no need for secrecy, but your good Christians seem to impose it on you."

Viçente had wanted only to find out the problem and leave, but how could he let that pass? "I didn't ask to see you, so don't complain about the circumstances. Your people are persecuted for not coming to Jesus, and you know in your souls, he's God."

Rabbi Benjamin leaned against the stone. "I thought we were persecuted because we scratch out a living despite the Christians' oppression. I'd expect more tolerance from a Jew's son."

This rabbi was nothing like Viçente's father, shorter, bearded, wearing the absurd hat, but the rebuke stung like paternal censure. "I'm a Christian, bound by my profession to tolerate all our citizens. If it weren't for you stubborn Jews and the few who pretend, good converts wouldn't be treated as fakers."

"I've come about a serious matter, not these stale arguments. Your men seized an innocent ... a distant cousin of yours, in fact."

"No Jew's my cousin, and if he's the fellow who robbed the cathedral—"

"His name's Samuel, and if you knew him, you'd understand that he's no thief. He's too simple and kind-hearted to steal, and too afraid—like all of us—to approach a church. He lives with his parents and sisters and does chores for members of my congregation."

"He's created a serious problem. They'll make this an excuse to attack your people."

Rabbi Benjamin bristled. "Perhaps I didn't speak clearly. Samuel's innocent."

How many mothers or sisters, friends or priests, had approached Viçente, all claiming that a man was too good, too honest, too pious to steal or vandalize or injure, when the truth was clear as new raindrops? How many truly believed in the culprit's innocence, as the rabbi seemed to believe? "I don't exempt cousins from the law on some feeling about their virtue."

"He's also a mute, unable to defend himself against the charges."

"I can't order a Jew released, even an invalid. If he can't speak, someone will help with his defense."

"You're misinformed about his guilt, First Deputy, and there were two crimes involved, one an attempted rape."

Viçente took in a breath and eyed the rabbi—he'd never known the man to lie. "One of your Jewish girls?"

"A *Morisca*."

So she was a Christian of Muslim ancestry. "Why didn't her father come forward and accuse the man?"

"The family's not Christian enough to accuse this one."

"If they go to church, they're Christian. The Muslims converted centuries ago."

"You should understand this better than I, Viçente. Every Jew who converts, they question, do they not? You're a Christian, but Old Christians never trust. Though this girl's great-grandparents were Catholic, somewhere in the deep past there was a non-believer."

The words—though partly true—roiled Viçente's gut. He was tempted to slap this man. "You should sympathize with my position, Rabbi. I seek to advance my people, as you do yours. We need a world that respects us. My son and his children deserve this."

"But we're one people, Jews and converts."

"You're the source of these doubts about me and about all of us. If there wasn't a damned rabbi trying to subvert our faith—"

"We're one with the Muslims, too, and with those Christians who despise us." Rabbi Benjamin grimaced and shook his head. "Even the man who attempted rape—your vicar, Pero López."

Viçente gasped. "I knew the vicar was—" The word that entered his head was *vile*. "I know he preaches against Jews. His sermons may incite hatred, even inspire vandalism against your people, but ... What's his second crime?"

"Accusing that defenseless boy who rescued the *Morisca* girl from his assault." The infuriating rabbi waved his hands in the air as he spoke. "You may have seen him—Samuel, the mute, as I said, a relation of yours."

"Even if this is true, what arrogance permits you to demand my help? And again, why didn't the girl's family come forward?"

The rabbi stilled himself and looked Viçente straight on. "You know the reason. The church would tear this family down to defend their priest, accuse the girl as a harlot. Can her father confide in your civil guard? Can they trust your magistrate? The reason I approach you is—" The rabbi shrugged, still looking Viçente in the eye. "Despite being Christian, you're a just man."

Viçente took a moment to swallow his fury. "Rabbi, you insult my beliefs and praise me in the same breath, all the while seeking a favor."

"Is justice a token to be begged for? You're descended from the great Samuel ha-Levi, a man of conscience. Or perhaps you demand that I pretend to convert, as others have done, before I can speak with you."

"Pretend? I'm as Christian as any man." Viçente's pulse ran fast in his throat as he wondered how many *conversos* stole off for secret, profane meetings with this man.

"Then why must we meet like thieves devising a robbery?"

Because of the danger, Viçente thought. Because Old Christians would assume he was corrupt, and one day, given the chance, they'd act against him. If they deprived Viçente of office, others would lose their livelihoods, laws might be passed, recriminations.

"Christians are arrogant and covetous," the rabbi said. "They detest the fact that just when they're ready to confiscate a Jew's gold, he converts, and the church accepts him. When the kingdom is weak, prejudices become principles."

Viçente sighed. "They attack Jews, not converts."

"Behind your back, your fellow Christians don't call you '*conversos*,' do they? They say '*marranos*.' One day, they'll turn against those whom they refer to as 'swine.'"

Viçente's cheeks stung as if he'd been slapped. It had to be the cold morning air. The word '*marrano*' couldn't still hurt so badly. "You're wrong, Rabbi. If there's trouble, they'll come at you again, and I won't be able to protect you. Now, I have to speak with this *Morisca* girl and her father."

"His name's Gonzalo," the rabbi said. "The daughter's Ramona. He's a builder who has helped me renovate the temple. He's also working on your cathedral. But if you meet them—"

"I know. The meeting must be secret."

CHAPTER 4

—ɯ—

Pᴇʀᴏ Lóᴘᴇᴢ ᴅᴇ Gáʟᴠᴇᴢ, ᴠɪᴄᴀʀ of Toledo's cathedral, slid his desk near the window for light and hunched over it, recomposing Sunday's homily.

The door creaked open and Marcos García de Mora entered. Though Marcos was small of stature and practiced law from an obscure office above a butcher shop, he had mysterious connections that allowed him to achieve wonders.

"Some juice, Don Marcos?" Pero poured from the decanter and offered a glass.

Marcos took it and sipped. "Tell me about your sermon."

"This week, I'll neglect the Jews and discuss Muslim perfidy." Pero chuckled.

"Did you become dull-witted when I made you vicar? Muslims are weak. Focus on the damned *marranos*, the Hebrew dogs who feign Christianity."

Pero turned away, thinking of the praise Marcos used to bestow on him when he'd been a simple priest, before Marcos had found a way to raise him to the vicar's chair. It had been nothing less than a wonder, and Pero thanked God each night for this remarkable friend, but not for Marcos' sarcasm. "The Mother Church wants to encourage converts, not drive them away," Pero said.

"Then be subtle." Marcos sipped and set the glass on the windowsill. "You want to lecture about Muslims?"

"Yes. Listen." Pero located the passage and read. "'Muslims once ruled our beloved Toledo from their heathen mosques. Three-hundred-and-sixty years ago, the Lord brought us victory, but Muslim devils still control Granada to our south, their presence like gangrene in a foot.'"

Marcos glanced around the room. Was he losing interest? Pero went on. "'These wanton barbarians replace our blessed Savior with the camel-eating Mohammed. We must banish this evil from Iberia and make our Lord, Jesus, smile again.' Do you like it?"

Marcos scowled. "Did you miss my point about *marranos*? What does your lecture say about them?"

"Nothing, but the church forbids—"

"Why must I think for you? Speak of the Jew-converts without saying their name." Marcos poked a finger at the paper. "After this part about banishing them from Iberia, say, 'Beside you in these pews are men descended from those camel-eaters. How many, in their dark souls, fall back to the profane?'"

Pero swallowed, gathering his courage. "*Morisco* families are among our most devout."

Marcos snatched the paper and slapped it down on the table. "Haven't we discussed the treachery of these false converts—*Moriscos and marranos* over and over? You can use one to cast doubt upon the other. Remind the people that anyone descended from dogs can't help but bark at the moon. If you can't trust *Moriscos*, who converted from Islam centuries ago, what of *marranos*, Jews who'd slinked into the church this last generation?"

Marcos had lectured him before about false Muslim conversions, but how could Pero believe such evil of the *Morisco* families in his congregation? He couldn't agree with Marcos, but he'd learned not to argue. A pounding on the door saved him.

A brown-robed priest entered with a man in the black-and-gold garb of the city's *Guardia Civil*. The guardsman held a visored hat in his hand.

Marcos glowered at the intruder. "What do you want?"

The officer looked from Marcos to Pero and clicked his heels. "I'm Corporal Amayo of the city guard, assigned to First Deputy Pérez. He requests a meeting with the vicar."

"Next week," Marcos said. "We're busy."

"The request is for today, sir."

"Vicar López is an important churchman," Marcos said. "The first deputy is a … functionary."

"I honor you, Vicar," the guardsman said. "But I have orders."

Pero was feeling queasy, wondering if this concerned the *Morisca* girl and the mute. "Why does he want me?"

"It's a matter of—"

Marcos stepped close to Pero, raising a hand to quiet him. "As I said, *Corporal,* not today. Is next Wednesday possible, Vicar?"

The guardsman took in a breath, looking at the floor. "Sir, I'm afraid that's not soon enough."

"Are you one of those …" Marcos paused as the unfinished question hung in the air. "Have you no respect for the church, Corporal?"

"Señor, as I wanted to explain, this is a church matter, involving the theft of holy treasure."

So this did involve the mute. How could Marcos still look calm?

"Then the deputy can write one of his fancy invitations," Marcos said.

"Out of respect, I did not mention this, Vicar, but now I must." The corporal's lower lip quivered. "Two of my men await outside. We'll escort you now."

When they reached the street, out of respect, the corporal dismissed the other two guardsmen. As the corporal accompanied Pero and Marcos from the rectory to the *alcázar,* Marcos kept speaking in Pero's ear. The words entered—something about insisting on justice for the mute's heinous crime—but he couldn't comprehend with his hands trembling and the memories from two nights before flooding his thoughts.

He tried to remember just how it had happened and the words Marcos had spoken then.

It was just past dusk, Pero there in the rectory office, working on the same sermon, when Marcos arrived. Marcos peered out the window over and over again, turning back to inform Pero, "There's a Muslim convert I want to meet, a girl in your congregation. She walks through the plaza at this hour." Glancing out again. "You'll bring her here, introduce us, and leave us alone."

It took Pero a moment to think what Marcos could want with her, and then he said, "If she's Christian, I don't think I can—"

"She may attend your church, but you know these camel-eaters are not true Christians." Marcos beckoned him to the window. "There. That one. Bring her in."

Pitch lamps illuminated the street between the church offices and the new cathedral. Pero recognized the child, who had a mantilla covering her hair. He'd seen her before and known she was a *Morisca* by the bright swirls on her clothing, the cheap metal bracelets and necklaces she wore, the tone of her skin. He'd taken the trouble to learn her name: Ramona. God had ripened her, sent her past Pero's window each day, and brought her late and alone this evening. He'd never have approached her, but now his trusted friend demanded it.

She passed close below, the curve of her hip barely visible beneath that full skirt. In a moment she'd pass the rectory's side entrance and be gone. If he could delay …

"GO," Marcos shouted, and Pero ran for the stairs.

He burst through the door and confronted her. "Girl." She stood just a few steps away, taller than he'd imagined, her forehead at the height of his chin, her presence so tangible he could almost feel her against his chest. Yearning filled him, that and fear of the girl, fear of failing his friend as well.

She glanced his way and sidestepped.

"Do you know me?" he asked.

She nodded, keeping her eyes on the ground.

"I am vicar of the cathedral, sent by God. Look here, when I speak."

"It wouldn't be right." Her gaze flashed to his face, then away. For that instant, light from a pitch lamp glinted in her eyes, revealing the spark of womanhood, and also, he thought, a bit of the wanton Muslim. Marcos was right; she was still a heathen.

"Come. Someone wishes to meet you." He held out a hand. "This way."

Her body inclined toward him, as if she wanted to comply. Beneath her cape, her breasts were small but enticing. She shivered from the cold, or perhaps anticipation. He'd only had one woman, and her but a few times—an aging whore Marcos had arranged for him. What would an experienced man say to lure her? "God has given you a fine look."

Curse his clumsiness. She was backing away again. If she didn't want to go with him, he couldn't force her. But she was a non-believer, not a daughter of Christ at all. He had to succeed for Marcos. "Come in out of the chill so I can introduce you to him."

Her eyes darted to the side, and he knew he had to act. Leaping forward, he seized her wrist.

For a moment they stood frozen, but Pero was off balance. As he got his feet under him and straightened, his face came close to hers, and he saw terror in those dark eyes. She shrieked, and fear knotted his chest. The vicar of Christ's church could not be found this way. "Quiet."

He wrapped an arm around her chest and reached with the other hand to cover her mouth. She bit his fingers. Pero fought the need to cry out and the urge to strangle her as he succeeded on his second try. She squirmed, her buttocks pressing into him. He'd heard that harlots cried out when they were eager for it, and here was this ripe girl, driving herself into him, pressing her breasts against his arm. He lifted her and backed toward the doorway.

A grating sound. Pero turned to see a man emerge from the alley, moving toward him. Tall, long beard—a Jew. He dropped the girl and yanked her by the wrist. She twisted and screeched and dropped to her knees. He hoisted her upright. When he turned back, the Jew blocked the doorway, fists cocked against his side. Why was he silent? Now Pero recognized him—it was that mute who ran errands for the rabbi.

The *Morisca* girl stopped screaming and gaped at the intruder.

"Go away," Pero commanded.

The mute stood his ground, his eyes harsh in a face chubby with youth. He pointed at Pero's hand, still holding the girl's arm. Pero gripped tighter. "*Out of my way.* I'm taking this child for religious instruction." Pero looked down, hoping for a rock, a stick, any sort of weapon.

The Jew moved closer, looming over him now, huge, annihilating any hope of Pero defending himself.

From a window above the doorway came the hiss of Marcos' voice. "Fool. Let her go and get in here."

And now they were following Corporal Amayo up the stairs and into the deputy's waiting room. How was Pero to justify what he'd done that night?

CHAPTER 5

—ᔑᒲ—

WHEN HIS CLERK ANNOUNCED THE arrival of Vicar Pero López, Viçente let the priest wait in the anteroom for half an hour. He spent the time gathering his confidence, reminding himself that he was working for peace in his city, not bowing down to the rabbi; maintaining justice, not catering to the Jews. Remembering his meeting with the tearful *Morisca* and her protective father, he wondered how a priest, pledged to God, could attempt this foul act.

At a handful of previous encounters, including a repugnant sermon denouncing Jews and Muslims, Viçente had taken the measure of the vicar—a weak-spined bigot. To avoid the priest and his venom, Viçente attended Santo Tomé, halfway across town from the cathedral. If he had his way, the church would rid itself of the man; but the church was as powerful, political, and capricious as any government.

—ᔑᒲ—

Opening the door for the vicar, Viçente found that the anteroom bore the stink of the unwashed, and the stink entered with the hulking priest in his frayed black robe. *Still better than the pig man.*

Following the priest came a hawk-nosed, greasy-haired fellow, who introduced himself as Marcos García de Mora, counselor of the law.

They took seats in Viçente's office and García spoke. "Why have you invited us, Deputy? Perhaps there's a boon the church can impart for the city?"

The lawyer's syrupy speech annoyed Viçente, and the odiferous vicar appeared far too smug for a rapist. "I summoned the vicar because I've heard a disturbing report of his conduct."

García leaned toward Viçente, glaring. "Vicar López's honor is well known, but what of yours?"

"Then why bring his 'solicitor' instead of his prayer book?"

The vicar narrowed his eyes under Viçente's stare, but the lawyer seemed unfazed. "You, Viçente Pérez, are a *marrano*, who has no-doubt cheated your way to authority. Anyone visiting you would be well advised to bring a witness."

The term '*pendejo*' formed on Viçente's lips, but slurs would be futile. *Forget the lawyer. The vicar must recant.* "As a courtesy, I seek your account of some events involving you, Vicar López. I don't wish to arrest you, but I cannot ignore your transgressions."

"Absurd." The lawyer jabbed a finger into one of his nostrils. "What transgressions?"

"Bringing false charges against a man, for one." Viçente watched the priest flinch.

García fidgeted. "What man?"

"The mute, whom the vicar accused of stealing."

"Wrong twice, First Deputy." García made the title ring with sarcasm. "The mute's a Jew, not a man, and he pilfered a silver crucifix from the altar of the holy cathedral." García stood, paced to the wall, and examined Marta's picture.

Viçente's skin itched at the sight of the vile attorney so near his wife's portrait, but he kept his eyes on Vicar López. "I've heard an account in which you tried to rape a woman and were thwarted by the mute. Rapists go to prison, did you know?"

The vicar's leg jerked beneath the robe—a good sign. He clutched the leg with one of his meaty hands, but it twitched again.

"Would you like a glass of water, Padre?" Viçente asked. Would the damned priest concede the truth? If not, Viçente would have to intervene to free the mute, and word would spread among the 'faithful.'

García strode over and whispered in his client's ear. The priest's leg calmed. The lawyer turned on Viçente. "You should be torturing that thief in your prison." García showed his teeth, like a rat gnawing a bone. "Instead, you take the word of Jewish scum? You came from them, but you are now a Christian, are you not?" García grinned now and a muscle twitched beneath his eye. "Perhaps you're too old for your duties, with that gray coming into your hair. Perhaps the gray invades your mind." García had turned jocular, like a friend teasing over a glass of whiskey in a tavern.

This man was erratic, annoying, maybe dangerous, but his insults could be ignored. "I'm sufficiently qualified to accept the word of three Christian witnesses, including another priest." Viçente had only Gonzalo's daughter as witness, a *Morisca* girl, who was afraid to come forward. But it would require at least three Christians to challenge the head priest.

"What?" The vicar shot out of his chair, his face red. "Marcos, you have to—"

García moved between Viçente and López. "First Deputy, if you have these witnesses, they are liars. Just as likely, you're the liar. Bring them so I can get the truth."

The tic came again in García's cheek, and Viçente grew confident. One more bluff should pry the truth from the vicar. "I will present the charges to Archbishop Cerezuela, a worthy man who works with me on the cathedral construction. He'll arrange an inquiry."

"No!" Vicar López looked past his solicitor to Viçente. "I never hurt the girl."

"You assaulted her."

"Silence!" García ordered.

"I spoke with her," López blurted.

"You tried to carry her into your offices. Then you falsely accused the mute."

López nodded weakly. "You mustn't tell the archbishop."

With only the girl for witness, Viçente couldn't carry the matter further. It would ruin her father's business and damage Viçente's relationship with the Old Christians. "If you retract your charges against the mute, there'll be no need. But you, Vicar, will be in my debt."

"You are a mangy dog," García spat, but López pushed him aside with a bulky arm.

"Say it," Viçente commanded.

"I am in your debt, Don Viçente." Moisture glistened in the vicar's eyes and his hefty body trembled.

The lawyer's dark stare burned with loathing, but Viçente ignored it.

"And you admit you've done wrong to this mute man and the young woman?"

The vicar was nodding his head, but that wasn't enough. Viçente stared at López, until the priest said, "I h-have."

Viçente strode to the office door and summoned the corporal. "Vicar, would you explain to Corporal Amayo the error about your misplaced crucifix?"

That afternoon, alone in his office, it wasn't García's furious glare that nagged Viçente. It was the attorney's malevolent smirk as he'd marched out of the office.

CHAPTER 6

—ⱴⱴ—

THE THURSDAY EVENING AFTER THAT miserable encounter with Viçente Pérez, Marcos headed to the Wool Carters Guild meeting in the stale back room of a local inn. He arrived early and ordered three earthenware crocks of wine brought to the meeting hall. The first two were emptied before the meeting, and Marcos watched from the back of the hall as Sancho, the balding, nearsighted guild leader, plodded onto the stage.

These gatherings of malodorous, rambunctious guildsmen were familiar now. Marcos understood the men's needs and their anger. After the meetings, he joined them in taverns, where conversation turned naturally to hatred for Jews and *marranos*, who prospered without shedding their sweat. Which brought his thoughts back to the *marrano* merchant who'd condescended to hire Marcos' mother as a maid all those years ago, and to educate Marcos with his own children, the merchant who lorded his power over them and thought himself better than Marcos and his mother, better than true Christians because of his indecent wealth—a merchant who very much resembled Viçente Pérez in his grand office.

Marcos could picture that *marrano*, Pérez, even now—sneering as he'd made God's vicar cringe and beg. The fury in Marcos' gut thrilled him. Fury he would use to rouse these slothful louts. He watched as Sancho mopped sweat from his brow with the sleeve of his coarse, brown tunic and shouted about the rich *pendejos* who set the price of wool in Flanders. The guildsmen cheered and banged flagons on the tables as Sancho declared that those who shipped wool to market deserved an ample share of profits. The men's gruff voices resonated in Marcos' chest. These were like the lads Marcos had sought out all those years ago, when he escaped the manor each day after his lessons—boys who shouted and swore, who liked getting dirty, who hated the rich swine who owned the mansion that Marcos' mother cleaned on her hands and knees.

He could spur these guildsmen to violence and use them, if he could find the words and the tone and the fury. Fury—that was easy.

Marcos took a long swig of wine, ignoring his disgust at Pero's pathetic weakness, focusing on Viçente Pérez with his smug conceit, forming the argument to rally these lads. He rehearsed in his mind, taking short, gasping breaths, building the hard knot of rage until he felt a slap on his shoulder. He jerked and looked up. A gap-toothed man stood over him, grinning and pointing to Sancho, up on the stage, gesturing to Marcos. Marcos joined him as the men formed groups and began to talk. "Wait, Marcos wants to speak," Sancho called, but the guildsmen didn't notice. Marcos jumped atop a chair and whistled. Nearby guildsmen looked up. "We're not finished," he shouted. Most of the men gazed at him as Marcos raised his glass. "*To men who work for a living.*" The Wool Carters cheered and drank.

"I am not a wool carter, but I've shared many drinks with you." Men laughed, and Marcos shouted still louder. "You're good and loyal Christians, but the powerful rob you." Perhaps there had been too much wine in those crocks. The din droned louder. Men turned away. "Toledo's government is riddled with Jew-lovers. Tyrants run Castile's royal house. We must end the tyranny."

If the crowd would pay attention, he would speak of First Deputy Viçente Pérez and his *marrano* tax collectors. He would tell them about God's will to destroy false Christians. Instead he bellowed, "*Listen!*" The commotion ebbed. "If you're not afraid, if you're willing to act against tyranny, stay with me in this room. Let the rest go get drunk." Marcos sighed and climbed down from the chair.

Wool carters shouted, nudged, and shoved their way from the room, leaving Marcos, Sancho, and ten others. They wore the filth of a hard day's work on their faces and their frocks. One muscular, thick-browed lad had lost his shirt in the antics of the other men's departure. All appeared sturdy, angry at the world, and eager to listen.

From the Wool Carters Guild and the Christian Stone Masons Union and the Sword Forgers Brotherhood, Marcos assembled a core of twenty-five men. Each knew how to use a knife, and each swore vengeance against Jews and thieving *marranos*.

But when he returned home that night, mind half-numb with drink, those shaming thoughts returned.

When Marcos had been fourteen, the *marrano* son-of-a-dog merchant had accused his mother of stealing household money, money that Marcos had borrowed for his own needs. The *pendejo* evicted them. His mother rushed him to the village church. They knelt together, praying—she with tears streaming down her cheeks, he with an uncontrollable fury burning in his chest. She pleaded to the padre for support and he advised her to leave the district, go somewhere where her crime would not be known. "But I stole nothing," she said. "Evil lie," the priest proclaimed. "Your master is so generous that he funded new stained glass in the chapel, so benevolent that he hired you and educated your son. Pray for forgiveness before you depart."

So many times before he'd prayed there with her, bowed down to this priest, so many communions they'd taken, so many free hours she'd spent on hands and knees scrubbing the church floor, coming home cramped with pain, but prayers and service meant nothing to this one. Marcos had heard of false-Christians, of *marrano* whores, of stolen communion wafers and sacrilegious rites—those lads he knew had told him. He'd not imagined that priests could be impure, that men with tainted blood would be allowed in God's service. This one betrayal shocked him awake. He would never see all priests or all men the same. He wanted to kill the master and the priest too, but his mother begged him to forgive.

Marcos rejected her, fled alone to Barcelona, and created the story of an aristocratic birth. He secured the patronage of a rich count. The count feigned Christianity and spoke noble words about shaping Marcos' intellect, but seemed more impressed with Marcos' lean, pubescent body. Marcos accepted his beneficence, accepted his sexual advances, accepted it all while it suited him. And then one night, the count's mother, a filthy Jewess, snuck into the house, and Marcos overheard her pleading for money, sounding as his own mother often had, beseeching him to follow her wishes. He'd recoiled at the realization—once again he'd been dependent on a *marrano*, and this time, the *pendejo* had sullied him.

Even today, his soul burned with hatred for that shallow, pampered count, who had hid his heretical lineage and his passion for boys. Marcos hadn't understood in those days, hadn't known how much Jesus despised the traitors who pretended to worship him. Now he had a chance for revenge; Viçente Pérez was as deceitful as the false count, with arrogance to match that lord of the manor. Marcos would destroy the *hijo de puta* and his brethren to gain the Savior's esteem.

In the morning he'd meet with Sancho and prepare to strike the first blow.

CHAPTER 7

—⁓—

How should one approach an archbishop—especially one whose half-brother was the most powerful man in Castile—about a problem with his vicar? Of course: Viçente would present good news first, news to bring them both great joy.

At three bells in the afternoon, the knock came on his office door. Archbishop Juan de Cerezuela entered, breathing heavily, his white robe loosely cloaking his spare body, revealing only his hunched shoulders and his pale face beneath a red-and-gold bonnet. Cerezuela was in his mid-fifties, half a decade older than Viçente, with angular features far too sober and meek for his lineage.

The priest dropped into a seat. "Your message promised important information."

"I have something good to tell you and something discouraging. I understand we're running out of construction funds for the cathedral."

The cleric grimaced. "The discouraging part—that's no surprise."

"I've arranged a meeting tomorrow with some merchants to seek contributions."

"Is there hope?"

"Would I invite you, otherwise?"

"I enjoy meeting with you, Viçente, but you always confound me with riddles."

Viçente chuckled. "The trouble is all that silver the church already collects, like the tolls from the bridges into the city."

"*Pontagos*. They pay to maintain our churches."

Viçente held up a hand and raised one finger. "And *portagos*." A second finger.

"For passing through the city gates." Cerezuela shifted in his chair, looking perplexed. "We must feed the priests."

"And *bartascos* from the ferry crossings on the Río Tajo, and revenues from your flour mills." Viçente raised a third finger and a fourth.

A scowl furrowed the archbishop's white brows. "We've many expenses, Viçente. Did you invite me here to torment or assist?"

"Archbishop, when I ask my rich friends to contribute, they speak of priests drinking imported whiskey and dining on venison."

Cerezuela snorted. "Surely you deny it."

"Of course, but what response can I give when they bring up the *bulas* your parishioners pay to shorten their time in purgatory and for the pleasure of eating meat on Fridays? Aren't those thousands of *maravedis* available for the cathedral?"

"Don't they understand? We commission artists to glorify God even as we hire stone masons to construct walls." Cerezuela looked pale. He wheezed, brought out a cloth from his pocket, and coughed into it. "I'll cancel the remaining statues." He spit into the cloth and coughed some more.

"Are you all right, Archbishop? Here, take a drink." Viçente poured a glass of water and waited. When Cerezuela recovered, Viçente said, "I told my rich friends that there were little *bulas* and huge *bulas*. If a few *maravedis* allow a bite of meat on Friday, mightn't a few thousand *doblas* gain God's special notice? The donor's name inscribed on the cathedral wall or his mortal remains buried within."

A crooked half-smile appeared on Cerezuela's lips. "Your friends are merchants. Only nobles occupy sacred ground."

"I haven't promised anything, but a merchant's name inscribed in the wall of a side chapel or in an obscure monastery couldn't offend the Savior. Here, look at these." Viçente removed four documents from a drawer and waved them.

"Don Viçente, stop grinning and tell me what you have."

Viçente lifted each paper in turn and said, "Eighty, ninety, eighty, one hundred."

"Tell me or I'll damn you to hell."

"Pledges from men who will attend tomorrow's meeting—350,000 *doblas.*"

The archbishop reached for the papers. "My son, your place in heaven is assured. We can go on building for two more years."

Viçente shook his head. "Not enough, your eminence. If you're skillful tomorrow, you'll be able to commission a new jeweled monstrance to parade through the streets on Easter."

"Should we be greedy?" The archbishop dropped the papers on the desk. "What must I do?"

"At the meeting, raise the specter of Toledo ridiculed for building a great structure without even a crucifix inside."

"We have many crucifixes, as you well know, Viçente. What then?"

"Each of my friends who signed will offer his pledge. You'll bless them and turn to the others. Start with the most prosperous businessmen who want to seem more pious than their well-born peers." Viçente paused a moment and said, "I hesitate to mention, your eminence. Your speech will be more effective if you offer something, too."

"Now you manipulate me." Cerezuela thumped a palm on the desk. "Without even a glass of fine wine." Cerezuela smiled again, but his expression lacked vitality, like a man seeking to overcome some internal lethargy. "Of course my family will contribute."

"Very good, Archbishop, and now for the other matter." Viçente lowered his voice. "It involves security in the city, which isn't the church's concern, but your vicar's implicated."

"He's less than I would have wished, but I inherited him." Cerezuela whipped out the cloth again, and Viçente looked the other way as the clergyman cleared his throat in a series of huffs and gurgles. "We've spoken of this before."

"He's committed a new outrage."

"Is it more than usual?" Cerezuela spit into the cloth again and whisked it back into his pocket. A dab of phlegm remained on his lower lip.

"I summoned him here to discuss an attempted rape, and—"

"My lord." Cerezuela seemed to grow pale again. "When I became a bishop, I wasn't ready for these little catastrophes, but that was in another place and many years ago. It seems the clergy has its share of evil-doers, rape among their grave offenses."

"The other problem concerns false charges against a Jew."

The archbishop frowned. "Something to do with the stolen crucifix that miraculously reappeared?"

"Never stolen. Your vicar lied to cause trouble for the Jew who protected the girl from him."

"Oh, very unfortunate." Still frowning, the priest shook his head. "But all turned out well."

If a city employee was accused, Viçente would know what to do, but he couldn't afford to offend the archbishop. "And you still can't act?"

"Regrettable, if true, but long years of disappointment have taught me to tread carefully. Priests and canons resent me, for I've risen through privilege, not by tedious years of supplication. The brothers selected Vicar López. Likely they share his prejudices and perhaps his other failings."

"Your brother, Archbishop, is so bold. It's hard to believe …"

"That I'm so meek, I know, but Alvaro's only my half-brother. If he were archbishop, he'd do something ruthless to Vicar López or cleverly banish him, but you've seen the trouble my brother gets into. Even the king exiles him now and again."

"Surely, it weakens the church to have a rapist and liar in that position. It casts a poor light on the church and drives away possible converts, even as it creates strife in my city. If you could discipline the vicar, if you could—"

Cerezuela raised a shaky hand. "Do you know that my brother, Alvaro, keeps strange animals at his castle? Giraffes and camels …

monkeys. His giraffes cannot grow humps like the camels, and his camels don't reach with long necks to meet the stars. I—I am not my brother. I can not become him."

The archbishop gave a half-smile as he worked to stand. "I guess I'm feeling my age, Viçente, but you're a marvel. Look at how you've come back from … from your misfortune. You're an asset to the city and the church." He walked halfway around the desk and leaned against it. Viçente rose to embrace him as he grasped the meaning of the archbishop's unfinished sentence. It referred, of course, to Marta.

After the hug and the priest's departure, Viçente approached the portrait on the far wall. Marta, vital and alluring in her red dress and ruby necklace. Other images filled him—Marta, slim and lovely, dark eyes twinkling beneath a white veil at their wedding; Marta sending their little son, Diego, off to school for the first time and sobbing in Viçente's arms; Marta, unable to rise from her bed days before she died; Archbishop Cerezuela wearing gold-threaded vestments, performing her funeral Mass. Only four years ago, lost forever. No, not forever—until the Savior took Viçente from this world.

With morose thoughts spinning in his head, he left the office and went out into the fresh air. As he walked, he realized he'd forgotten to ask the bishop to exempt the pig farmer from bridge tolls next year.

CHAPTER 8

—ᴡ—

By that year, 1442, Castile was an armed camp where each of the fifteen powerful noble houses kept a militia. To the far south, Muslims retained their last patch of Iberian soil at Granada. In the north, two of King Juan's cousins ruled the kingdoms of Navarre (Cousin Juan) and Aragón (Cousin Alfonso, who also ruled parts of Italy, including Naples), and a third, the master of Santiago (Cousin Enrique), commanded a private army to the south. They mocked Castile's King Juan, despised the king's constable, Alvaro de Luna, and sought any advantage against them.

The king's cousins disdained conversos and denied them government positions, while King Juan and his confidant, Alvaro de Luna, courted the wealthy converts.

The Ayala family had ruled Toledo for decades, with the (sometimes reluctant) sanction of Castile's sovereigns. Toledo's current ruler, Pedro López de Ayala, was a war hero who'd lost an eye fighting Moors at the battle of Higueruela. He held the titles of chief magistrate and ruler of the alcázar.

As Viçente waited for the stableman to saddle Amistad, he thought about his meeting with Archbishop Cerezuela, speculating about the clergyman's health, something he hadn't dwelt on for fear of offending.

He thought, too, about Chief Magistrate Ayala's message this morning, summoning him to Ayala's hacienda—the hacienda, rather than his palace in the city or his castle, a less formal setting and a shorter ride. Ayala traveled half the distance to accommodate Viçente. He had something disagreeable to discuss.

As Amistad ascended the road between dark boulders, Viçente glanced back. Sunlight sparkled on the Río Tajo, meandering in its canyon, skirting three sides of the noble city—a patchwork of brown-hued walls and buildings, crowned by the mighty *alcázar* and the cathedral, its new tower swathed in scaffolding.

They moved through the small forest into grasslands fragrant with ripe Castilian wheat. Ayala controlled this country—the fields and olive groves from here to his stronghold at Guadamur and on to the distant mountains. His hacienda lay ahead, a complex of low structures inside a protective wall, spanning a hilltop in gleaming white and sunburnt orange.

A servant brought Viçente into Ayala's salon, with its alabaster fireplace flanked by mounted antelope and boar heads.

"It's a glorious day, Deputy." Magistrate Ayala strode in. A white-haired, seventy-year-old man with a black leather patch over his left eye, Ayala poured glasses of Madeira and smirked. "Have a seat, my friend. How are things in the city?"

Viçente took the drink and settled in a brown armchair. "You have informants, Magistrate. You'll already know what I have to tell you: the vicar preaches hateful sermons about Jews and slanders converts by implication."

Ayala waved the back of his hand at an imaginary gnat. "And you summoned him to your office to humiliate him."

Viçente felt blood rise to his face. "Not over his sermons, but for false testimony."

"Against a Jew, Viçente." Ayala wrinkled his nose. "Helping them renders you suspect."

No use mentioning the attempted rape or that the accused was a helpless mute. Ayala had as little sympathy for women and cripples as he did for Jews. "You've directed me to act in the city's interest. A new band is forming to attack Hebrews. False accusations against any Jew fuel the violence."

"I let you fill the city offices with *conversos*, Viçente, and the nobles ask me why."

"I hired some Old Christians, too, but the converts have fewer opportunities outside. They're excellent, well-educated bookkeepers. You'll notice that *Moriscos* dominate the civil guard, which is their tradition. Our administration is above reproach."

"Some say converts are always suspect."

"Damn it, Magistrate. You know I tolerate no hint of sacrilege, not even innocent jokes about Jews. We are Christians, all of us. You should defend us instead of goading me." Viçente saw the hint of a smile on Ayala's lips. "I know your game—put me off balance and then ask me to do something disagreeable."

Ayala sipped wine, hiding his grin behind the glass. "I'm lighthearted today. Don't try to douse my flame."

Viçente was used to Ayala's condescension and to his rapid shifts of mood. When Ayala's spirits soared Viçente grew wary.

"King Juan's weak and his opposition is growing," Ayala said.

"The king's a good man."

"Devotion to weaklings is a flaw, Viçente. The master of Santiago visited me yesterday."

Viçente's stomach knotted at the mention of one of the king's powerful cousins—cousin and foe. "What does that man want?"

"My friendship is all. And you don't need that fool of a king, Viçente." Ayala was headed toward one of his favorite topics, the notion of how grand life would be if King Juan should fall from his throne.

"The good people of Castile need him," Viçente said.

Ayala gave him a sideways glance. "You mean the *conversos*."

"Yes, *conversos*. King Juan protects our rights."

"The king wouldn't be a problem if not for his damned constable. Alvaro Luna's unscrupulous and foul, and the king doesn't scratch his *huevos* without his approval."

"Constable Luna's wily and practical," Viçente countered. "He possesses the *cojones* to govern Castile, playing the noble houses against one another while courting the church's favor."

Ayala glowered. "My noble house despises him. He tramples cities' rights. You'd agree but for your bias."

Viçente spread his hands, palms up. "My bias is natural, Magistrate. Without the king and constable, *conversos* like me would be persecuted. Jews would be slaughtered. In Navarre and Aragón, the Royal Cousins have banished *conversos* from government."

"You have my protection, Viçente. You don't need the king's. And who cares about Jews, damn it?"

"I shouldn't have mentioned them. I just couldn't watch my fellow *conversos* persecuted, if the king fell."

"I might test your loyalty, Deputy." Ayala stood and stretched. "These old bones crave adventure."

Ayala was a few words short of declaring himself a traitor to the regime. Viçente searched for some way to head off this lunacy. "You joined a failed rebellion twenty years ago."

The magistrate prodded his eye patch with a knuckle. "The opposition's stronger now."

"If you crave adventure, take on a new mistress, jump on a sailing ship for India, challenge some other old fellow to a duel." Ayala offered only a crooked smile, letting Viçente finish. "Castile's King Juan is stronger too, and you can't ignore his son. Prince Enrique's raised his own army."

Ayala shook his head and smirked.

Viçente's chest tightened. The last time he'd seen Prince Enrique, the prince had been a naïve lad of fifteen. Had three years turned him to bold betrayer? "I couldn't be part of such a thing," Viçente said. "These factions sap the king's power and prevent him from acting for the good. Do you care about nothing but yourself?"

"*Stop.*" Ayala glared. "Don't test my tolerance."

Viçente took a slow breath and lowered his voice. "My lord, I'm a simple first deputy who wishes to keep his magistrate from reckless peril."

"Then don't help the damned Jews, all right?" Ayala paused a moment, as if waiting for Viçente to argue, and then went on. "No matter what happens, I require your support."

Viçente stared into the fireplace, wondering what the master of Santiago had proposed and fearing that the rumored insurrection might be more than idle fantasy.

Ayala wrapped an arm around his shoulder. "When I gave you Amistad, I gave him out of friendship. When I taught you to hunt with the falcon, I didn't teach a first deputy. I taught a man I cared about. Promise you won't divulge my relationship with the Royal Cousins, and we'll discuss this again."

Viçente felt touched by Ayala's words—this magistrate, so ruthless with others, yet tender with him. "I'll pray you find your senses and discover another outlet for your ... restlessness."

"No, no. No need to pray. I'm testing you, Deputy. All of this is mere ... speculation."

Ayala's high spirits offered ample reason for prayer.

—⚉—

MARCOS ANSWERED THE KNOCK ON his office door, and Sancho, the wool carter, plodded in with three fellows who smelled almost as bad as the vicar. But odor was irrelevant. The group Marcos had formed, *Sangre Pura*, had grown to fifty men, and tonight they'd consummate the holy mission.

The men sat around the table. Sancho hunched forward, light from the pitch lamp reflecting on his dirty forehead and pudgy cheeks. He pointed to the others. "These two are from my Wool Carters Guild. This other's from the Sword Forgers. Better we not mention names."

The recruits sat straight, nervous lads, fidgeting, one no more than sixteen, the others perhaps twenty. Marcos eyed them. "Look me level on. Tell me if you're ready to kill a Jew."

One fellow with a strong face and jutting brows smirked. "Only *one* Jew?"

Marcos glanced at Sancho, and they broke into laughter. "We'll start with just this one," the wool carter said.

"But Sancho, you promised we'd rid Toledo of Jews and *marranos*."

"Silence," Marcos commanded. "We don't use each other's names. If you can't keep secrets, all three of you—" he looked to each recruit "—then get out. Do you understand?"

Each of them nodded. Marcos had their full attention; no, more than that—their devotion. He felt a strange giddiness, the euphoria of a natural leader. "Obey each command without question. Our enemy who dies tonight may seem unimportant, but he has trod upon Mother Church. Killing him will recruit heroes to the cause, and when we're stronger, we'll take them all down." He focused on Sancho. "You know where to find the Jew? And where to meet me?"

"Aye," Sancho said.

"Bring him at ten bells, and serve him up alive."

—⁊⁊⁊—

Marcos paced the dim alley near the old Muslim Quarter. Ten bells chimed, and Sancho didn't appear. The bells rang again and again— half an hour late, damn them! Finally, footsteps and the sound of something dragging. The four men approached, and Marcos asked, "He's still breathing?"

Sancho nodded. "He fought hard. We had to pound his noggin."

"Keep your voice low. Lay it in that patch of moonlight."

They set the body down, and one of the men slipped a cloth sack off its head. Marcos knelt, touched the bloody spot at the side of its head, then ran his fingers through the long, scraggly beard. He bent close to listen for the Jew's breathing. "You've done well, men. Each of you will have a chance to spill Jew blood and something to boast of after." The Jew's head moved, and Marcos flinched. Soon the beast would wake. Marcos slipped his knife from its sheath and waited. When he saw moonlight glint in the Jew's eyes, he said, "You're going to hell for what you did. Do you recognize me?" The Jew's eyes opened wide, and Marcos drove his blade into its stomach, all the way to the hilt. The creature writhed.

Marcos yanked the knife out, yearning to drive it home again, but he'd promised the men a chance. He stepped away and let them in. Holding his hand up, seeing the moonlight gleam on the dark liquid and savoring the sticky feel of it, imagining how red it would be if this were daylight. He listened to the men grunt and stab and laugh as he kneaded blood between thumb and forefinger, touched his tongue to a fingertip, tasted the saltiness, smelled something metallic, felt the light from heaven shroud him.

The lads finished and stood. Marcos saw the gleam of their teeth and eyes as they beamed at him. He gestured for them to come together and wrapped an arm over two of the men's shoulders. The others joined in a circle.

"It's begun, men, and you're the lads who've started it. Tell everyone you know that Jews have begun to die, and soon the false ones will die, too. Good Christians will hold their heads high and rule again."

They fell silent in the magic, heaven-lit circle. Finally, Sancho cleared his throat and asked, "What should we do with the corpse?"

As Rabbi Benjamin approached the synagogue to begin his morning labors, he saw a high-sided wooden cart in the dirt roadway and a man pounding on the temple door. From the vest and the chin-beard and the posture, he recognized the master builder, Gonzalo. The craftsman had finished his restoration work on the temple, and he'd been paid. What made him so intent on getting in now?

"Be patient. I'm coming."

Gonzalo stepped to the cart, bent as if he were going to gather something from it with both arms but halted and looked up, a miserable grimace on his face. "What they've done," he said. "Rabbi, I'm sorry."

Benjamin, seeing something black—hair, a head, a beard—rushed forward. *Oh my God. Samuel.* There was dirt and black ooze caked behind his ear. Gonzalo stood aside as Benjamin tried to raise the boy's head. But the neck was stiff, and the body, in a filthy black vest and trousers, was twisted and rigid. These weren't his normal clothes. Benjamin remembered that the lad often went on Tuesday evenings to hear a choir that sang in a school just inside a nearby Christian neighborhood. He loved the singing, and he always wore his good clothes.

There must have been an accident last night, and now he was stiff and dead and distorted, and *Oh my God, why?*

Benjamin sagged onto the cart with his forehead touching the dead boy's shoulder and his fingers on the chest. He felt a crusty substance there, black, shiny—blood. And holes in the vest. Knives had been jabbed in. Samuel had been murdered, he realized. As Benjamin sobbed, Gonzalo rested a hand on his shoulder.

After a while, Benjamin opened the synagogue doors, and Gonzalo wheeled the cart inside. They stood in the entry, staring down at Samuel as Gonzalo explained that children had found the body in a seldom-used alley. The *Guardia Civil* had been summoned. From the wounds and marks in the dirt, they knew Samuel had been dragged to the location, stabbed several times, and his skull crushed on one side. Gonzalo's cousin in the *Guardia*, remembering something about a debt Gonzalo owed to the lad, had sent a runner to his house.

Gonzalo clenched a fist. "He was a fine young man, this mute of yours. Only Vicar López had reason to do this. He tried to rape my Ramona, and Samuel rescued her virtue. I owe him everything, and you, Rabbi. You spared Ramona the horror of testifying."

The builder's ferocity worried Benjamin. "We don't know who's responsible."

Recent incidents had foretold something like this. Broken gravestones in the cemetery, milk jugs kicked over on doorsteps at dawn, rocks thrown at children outside the Jewish Quarter. As rabbi, he couldn't indulge the grief and rage that boiled into his throat. *Shove the anger down. Guide your kinsmen to safety.*

Gonzalo swallowed and looked away. When he turned back, his chestnut eyes blazed. "It was the vicar. We must go to the first deputy."

"He can't bring a dead boy to life."

"Samuel saved my family's honor. His murder will be avenged."

Benjamin raised his hand for silence. "Samuel must be washed, wrapped in a white shroud, and prayed over. His parents will sit with their rabbi. Later, if you wish, we'll go to the first deputy." Benjamin wheeled the cart to the preparation room, thinking that Viçente Pérez would pay a heavy price for the aid he'd already given. Though Pérez—Viçente—rejected Judaism, somehow he seemed part of the congregation.

Later, Benjamin would accompany Gonzalo, but not to seek the first deputy's aid.

CHAPTER 10

—⚭—

VIÇENTE'S HOUSEKEEPER, CONSTANCIA, LIT CANDLES in the library and added logs to the fire in the granite fireplace. He poured a glass from the
decanter of Madeira and surveyed the volumes of literature on the oak
shelves without interest.

A few days before, he'd been summoned to Archbishop Cerezuela's
bedside. Cerezuela, lying helpless, had barely ceased coughing into a
large towel full of bloody phlegm. He'd thanked Viçente for his fine
work and told him to prepare for a 'new regime.' What had he meant?
New regime in the church? Or did it have to do with that horrible
discussion with Chief Magistrate Ayala—Ayala playing the friend and
mentor, coaxing Viçente to what? Join in treason against their king?
Abandon his fellow converts?

And this morning, news of the archbishop's death. Deaths summoned all those memories—of his papa, the man who'd become
almost a stranger for so many years; his mother, with whom he'd reconciled that last year; and then Marta, always Marta …

The tart scent of this wine brought memories, too—his thirteenth
birthday, the taste of becoming a man, the aroma of anger and betrayal. He held the vessel near the candelabra, seeing light sparkle in the
tiny air bubbles in the glass. Thinking of the way the Old Christians
referred to converts as *marranos*—pigs—he swirled the glass, traces of
crimson receding down the sides and fading, like the traces of hope
he'd once felt that he would be accepted in the true religion. If Marta

were here, she would find his slippers and robe, coax him to rest his head against her breast, stroke his cheek. He would feel better knowing that she'd share his future no matter what. But she wouldn't. Jesus hadn't granted enough time with her.

Still, a bit of her love comforted. And he had his son, Diego, at the university in Salamanca. In the summer, Diego would come home for a few weeks, but that was too long to wait.

A shout from the entry hall—Constancia—and a man's voice. In the hallway, he found the housekeeper blocking a man. Black hair, intense dark eyes, neatly clipped black-and-gray goatee—the builder, Gonzalo, the man whose daughter had been attacked by the vicar, and who managed workers at the cathedral construction site.

Gonzalo looked past the housekeeper. "Señor Pérez, it's important."

Viçente gestured for the maid to leave, fearing this had to do with the man's daughter and hoping it was something else. "Has there been an accident at the cathedral?"

"You must come," the builder said. "I mean, if you please, First Deputy." Gonzalo lowered his voice. "The rabbi awaits you at my home. It's not far, on the Calle San Pedro."

"What does the damned fellow want?" Viçente regretted the words, but he hated the thought of meeting the rabbi.

The builder frowned. "Rabbi Benjamin is a man of respect. He'll tell you."

Viçente took his boar-hide coat and green wool scarf. Outside, the street was lit by moonlight and an occasional pitch lamp. Smoke poured from vents in rooftops and permeated the stinging-cold air. Shadows blanketed sidewalls, doorways, and corners of the market plaza. Shadows could hide observers, men interested in the activities of a *converso* first deputy sneaking to meet the rabbi.

Gonzalo stalked into an alley, through a dark courtyard, into a home—a plain room lit by oil lamps, with two cushioned chairs and a settee, whitewashed walls with one picture. Viçente peered at it and saw Jesus preaching on a hillside. The scent of roasted meat and savory herbs provoked his empty stomach, until he turned to see Rabbi Benjamin standing in a doorway. In the dim light, his beard looked less bedraggled than before, but the wide-brimmed black hat was still absurd.

"Thank you for coming, First Deputy. Has Gonzalo informed you of the calamity?"

Calamity. Viçente shook his head.

"They murdered Samuel last night," Rabbi Benjamin said.

Samuel. That Jewish mute who'd been falsely accused. Until this moment, his story had been part of a growing list of minor persecutions. Now it was something else. "How?"

The rabbi grimaced. "Stabbed and stoned. You may recall that Samuel saved Gonzalo's daughter from attempted rape."

"Rape by Vicar López, yes, I recall." An inane comment, but what was Viçente to say?

Gonzalo slapped a hand against the wall. "You must arrest the vicar."

Viçente's heart pounded. A year, even a few weeks ago, with his friend Archbishop Cerezuela leading the church, Viçente might have summoned the vicar for questioning about the murder. But Archbishop Cerezuela could no longer help, and Magistrate Ayala would stand with the church. "I'd need evidence."

"Question him. Force him to confess," Gonzalo said.

"You don't understand. The royal government—" Viçente halted, unsure why he'd mentioned that, his thoughts moving too fast for him. "You must recognize the church's influence, the fact that we're dealing with a Jew, the effect this could have on selection of a new archbishop."

Viçente saw the rabbi step toward Gonzalo, but the builder didn't notice. He glowered, moving closer to Viçente. "If he was one of my bricklayers, you'd arrest him and then decide."

"I wish he was a laborer, or anything besides vicar—but I can't." Viçente shook his head, repulsed by his own words. What sort of administrator knew so well what he couldn't do, but had so few abilities to offer?

"He's a *murderer*." Gonzalo stopped as Rabbi Benjamin touched his arm.

"Enough," the rabbi said. "First Deputy, even if you were sure, you couldn't act."

Gonzalo gaped at the cleric, who still held his arm.

Rabbi Benjamin went on. "Because Samuel was a Jew, the *Guardia Civil* won't investigate his murder without a special order. Because Señor Pérez is a *converso*, he can't command it."

Gonzalo opened his mouth to protest, but Viçente spoke first. "Don't say what I can't do." The rabbi had expressed Viçente's own misgivings, but the man was so damned pompous. "You're a helpless Jew."

Benjamin smiled sadly and eased himself into a chair. "Yes, we are helpless. We are chosen by God to be his people, and he would have us suffer and still believe in him. Are you not suffering, First Deputy, as if you were one of us?"

Viçente clenched a fist and moved toward him. "Damn you."

Gonzalo stepped between them and pressed his palm against Viçente's chest. As the builder pushed him back, Viçente was tempted to shove past, to take the rabbi by his jacket and shake him. Why? For telling the truth, or for implying he was still Jewish? He gave in to the builder and let himself drop onto the settee.

"Rabbi," Gonzalo said. "He won't help because he hates you."

"Señor Pérez isn't furious with me, but with his Christians, who won't accept him."

"I am *not* a Jew." Viçente stopped at the sound of the quiver in his voice and the mass of frustration in his gut. Damn it, if he could only ignore the rabbi's taunts and *think*.

Rabbi Benjamin shook his head, his shaggy, black beard brushing his thighs. "Perhaps there's enough of the Jew in you that you sense danger, Viçente. Perhaps you know that when vandals destroy our gravestones and hurl rocks at our children, they shout, 'Death to Jews' and also 'Kill *marranos*.'" The rabbi sighed and lowered his voice. "Possibly you've heard stories about the first deputy who freed a Jew who'd stolen a holy crucifix. So you understand. You are despised for this."

Viçente would proclaim his authority, but if he did, the tremor in his voice would put the lie to it.

The rabbi reached under his frock, produced a thick volume, and passed it to Viçente. "This is sacred to me because one of my ancestors toiled over it."

Viçente opened the cover and saw a painting, a seductive Eve offering an apple to Adam as a serpent watched from a tree branch. He turned the page, and his breath caught as he recognized the strange writing of the Hebrews on the left side, Latin to the right.

"My great-grandfather scribed the Hebrew," Rabbi Benjamin said. "He translated the words into Castilian, and a monk wrote the Latin. I give this to you because you helped Samuel."

"Keep it." Viçente tried to hand it back, but Rabbi Benjamin raised his hand. "You can not refuse a gift when it's the most precious thing the donor owns. This will remind you that in your blood and in your soul are generations who were exiled from our Promised Land and cast to slavery. We never had power, only the determination to follow God's will. We learned to be meek in perilous times. It is time to be meek, Viçente Pérez. You can not afford to act."

"He can arrest the depraved priest," Gonzalo said.

Rabbi Benjamin scratched his bearded cheek, his eyes sorrowful. "Our first deputy is in more danger than any Jew, because he can't believe that he is. Look at him. He still believes in justice."

Viçente swallowed his rage, still struggling to comprehend the labyrinth of ever-changing powers that boxed him in: the shifting church hierarchy, the royal intrigue threatening the king, Magistrate Ayala's whims. "I seek justice in Toledo. I do. I seek peace. I want your daughter to be secure and my people to prosper, and I even want the Jews to be safe. I would punish the killer. But my power has limits. If I reach too far, I'll have none."

The phrase 'second-most-powerful man in Toledo' gnawed the inside of his throat until it ached. Second-most powerful wasn't enough. A *converso* would never be first. "I'll find ways to investigate this murder."

"No," the rabbi said. "Acting against the church will imperil us all."

"Silence, Rabbi. I'll order patrols near the Jewish Quarter. We'll catch the vandals and question them. If their confessions lead to the vicar, we will arrest him."

Rabbi Benjamin sank back in his chair. "I'm afraid I've pushed you to this rash decision. I don't doubt your motives or question your power or challenge you in any way, but please reconsider."

Gonzalo touched Viçente's shoulder. "You're an honorable man, First Deputy. My cousins and nephews in the *Guardia* will help."

The rabbi pushed himself up from the chair and faced the builder. "This morning you said you owed Samuel a debt for protecting Ramona and that you owed me for saving her from having to testify. Samuel's gone, and I liberate you from your pledge. Deputy Pérez put himself in peril to free Samuel, and now he plans to again by investigating the murder, all because Samuel saved your daughter. Whatever loyalty you owe me or Samuel, double it and render it unto Señor Pérez."

Viçente took a deep breath, his mind already devising orders for the *Guardia Civil* to patrol certain areas at night without making it obvious he was trying to protect the wretched Jews. Question those caught destroying property or harming others, without mentioning Hebrews. Without even implying that they were considered people.

CHAPTER 11

—⚞—

A year later

THROUGH THREE DAYS OF HARD riding with many changes of mounts, Viçente puzzled over this strange mission and the sealed message in his saddlebag. Magistrate Ayala disdained Prince Enrique, but he'd sent Viçente all the way to the prince's stronghold in Segovia. Ayala had handed the message to Viçente, saying, "I simply cannot tell you what's inside," which told Viçente quite a bit but not quite enough. Could it involve anything other than rebellion? The magistrate hadn't mentioned treason in a year, but his silence made it no less likely. And his other instructions: "Take Rodriguez and Baez with you." The magistrate's favorite civil guards would happily spy on Viçente and report back. "Do not open this and hand it personally to the prince. Wait for a reply. Wait a week or a month, if you have to."

Viçente felt a nervous flutter in his chest as he left the civil guards outside the *alcázar*. Royal soldiers showed him to a spacious salon with mullioned windows and a view of the river valley. Viçente recognized the tall, strapping prince, and his advisor, Pacheco, who rose to meet him. He blinked, looked again, and chuckled—the prince and his counselor wore the red silk robes and golden turbans of Arabian potentates. The prince's smashed nose, broken in a childhood fall, completed the farce. Prince Enrique grinned and embraced Viçente. "Pacheco, do you remember my hunting partner from three years ago? Señor Pérez."

Pacheco was six years older than Enrique and a hand's width shorter. He and the prince returned to their gold-embroidered armchairs. "Enjoy a s-seat," Pacheco said, gesturing.

Viçente had forgotten Pacheco's halting speech—a disarming trait.

The prince sat back in his chair. "Señor Pérez, Viçente, I remember our adventure fondly."

"I do as well, Prince, and the pride the king showed when you presented your stag." Viçente watched the prince's reaction at the mention of his father.

"We were expecting you, Viçente. I believe you're carrying a message from your disagreeable magistrate."

Viçente passed the packet to Pacheco. "Correct, and I'm curious about its contents, if you don't mind revealing them."

"Ayala didn't tell you?" Enrique shook his head.

"Doesn't trust his first d-deputy?" Pacheco echoed.

Pacheco broke the wax seal, opened it, and turned it over. Nothing fell out. He handed it back to Viçente—empty.

Both men grinned. "You see, Viçente, *you're* the package," Enrique said.

Viçente wanted not to appear foolish, but his mouth had dropped open. "I don't understand."

"The true message arrived last week with a courier, requesting that I offer you my hospitality."

"What? Why?"

"We're to keep you here," Pacheco said.

"Against my will?" Viçente's heart hammered.

"It seems you and your magistrate disagree about some important matters," Pacheco said.

Viçente swallowed and said, "Involving a conspiracy against the king."

"I'm shocked, Señor Pérez." Enrique wagged a finger at him and turned to Pacheco. "Have you heard of a plot, Juan? If our friend Viçente's involved, we'll have to arrest him."

Viçente's stomach clenched. He saw amusement in the young prince's blue eyes, a conspiratorial shared pleasure between prince and counselor. But a threat also that came with the words *arrest him.*

He remembered that last meeting with the fifteen-year-old prince: the evening before the hunt, the lad had watched, wide-eyed, as the king, wearing an ermine cloak and jeweled crown, knighted five warriors. Viçente joked with the lad, and in Enrique, he had seen something sweet hiding in that thicket of arrogance. The next day, hunting together, Enrique, took down a stag with a perfect shot from his crossbow. The prince ran to the beast, slit its throat with one quick thrust, and stood over his prey, grinning, his shirt bloody and a crimson smear across his mouth. The lad was three years older now, possessed of a formidable army.

Something sweet about the lad, and also something that delighted in the blood of an innocent beast.

Pacheco shook his head, smirking. "No plot that we can speak of, Prince. Shall I summon the guard?"

The prince gave Viçente a disarming grin. "We're amusing ourselves with your discomfort, Viçente. I apologize. My uncles are plotting against my father again, and this time, they've enlisted some proper allies, Pacheco and I among them."

"*You mustn't,*" Viçente blurted. He saw Enrique's frown and lowered his voice. "I mean, there are reasons—"

"Too late. The insurrection's begun," Enrique said. "Magistrate Ayala sent you here because you disapprove. Even now, he disposes of my father's loyalists in Toledo."

The lump in Viçente's stomach grew heavier as he wondered which of his friends would be expelled—expelled, or killed, or ... And what of Viçente, himself? "So I'm to be imprisoned?"

Pacheco waved a hand like a man shooing a fly. "Not imprisoned. Protected."

"Your scruples are in the way," the prince said. "Ayala's a foul *pendejo,* but he has the good sense to value you. He asked us to—what were his words? 'Watch over him and help him understand the prudence of this action.' My father's a weak fool, Viçente. His constable's an evil *cabrón*. Why not support the rebellion and reap the rewards?"

Viçente bristled at the prince's lack of scruples. "Without concern for the people the cousins will hurt?"

Enrique turned to his advisor. "I don't think I care about that, do I, Juan?"

"Then how about gratitude to your father?" Viçente asked. "The king who gave you this lovely city for your fourteenth birthday?"

The prince chuckled, but his eyes were not amused. "Señor, such bold statements could set you choking in a noose."

"I apologize, Prince." Viçente paused, weighing the term 'noose' and Enrique's demeanor. "You remind me of my son, so I tend to speak freely. I imagine how I would feel if Diego supported my enemies."

Enrique pointed to his misshapen nose. "I doubt that your son looks like me. Nor do you resemble my father. Though Father gave me Segovia, your son's the fortunate one."

"When last I met you, you struck me as a decent lad. If you join the Royal Cousins, they'll destroy the *conversos*. You'll have that on your conscience."

Enrique stood and glared at him. "Did you not understand when I told you the rebellion's already begun?"

Pacheco was shaking his head. He gestured toward the guards at the back of the room. "He's a spy. We'd b-better lock him in the dungeon so he can't escape."

"Wait." Viçente felt his stomach turn.

Enrique laughed again, but this time his eyes danced. "If he's a spy, he's the most inept I've seen." The prince stepped close to Pacheco and whispered.

Viçente watched, confused, as Pacheco nodded and spoke into the prince's ear, then turned to Viçente. "Follow me, Señor Pérez. We'll find you an agreeable dungeon."

"So you are …"

"Commanding you to accept the royal hospitality," Pacheco said. "And not try to leave until we allow it."

Viçente was confined in a fine bedchamber in Enrique's palace a short walk from the castle. He visited the chapel each afternoon to pray and took dinners with the prince and Juan Pacheco in a huge dining hall. They discussed hunting and swordplay and the ladies at court.

The 'royal hospitality' was indeed grand … and frustrating, continuing day after day. How long before Viçente could return to governing Toledo? But aside from those official duties, there was moral duty—to stand up for *conversos*. For this, confinement meant opportunity.

One evening, in the middle of a roasted pheasant dinner, Prince Enrique looked Viçente straight on and said, "My father's visitors at court used to indulge me with false affection, but you respected me, Viçente. It took courage for you to lecture me about gratitude to my father, and again you respected me by speaking of 'my conscience.'" He pulled off his emerald turban and tossed it on the floor. A maid gathered it up and scurried away.

"A conscience. I don't want to offend you, Prince, but each night I pray that you discover one." Viçente watched Prince Enrique for signs of anger but saw only an incredulous smile. "To my magistrate, overthrowing the king's an adventure. At the Royal Cousins' bidding, he'll banish blameless nobles from Toledo because of their loyalty to King Juan. Does it bother no one that the cousins will usurp the rightful king and subject converts to ruin?"

Pacheco spread his hands, palms up. "Perhaps a few priests and converts care. The Royal Cousins offer Enrique five of his father's castles. Unless you tender six, Señor Pérez …" Enrique screwed up his mouth. "My father's butler says that *conversos* are well-shaved Jews who run the treasury while stealing from the king."

"Jews have always been good with money," Pacheco said. "Of course, we've forbidden them other trades."

"About the Jews." Enrique took a bite of roasted potato and chewed. "Magistrate Ayala wrote that you can be blinded by your sympathies, not only for converts, but also for Hebrews."

"I've little compassion for them, but—"

"Be clear, Viçente. Converts are your people, not Jews. It can only hurt you to—"

"What kind of kingdom are we, if we let them be slain?"

"Ayala thinks you went too far to protect them."

Damn this discussion about Jews, and damn Ayala for airing this grievance to a powerful stranger. Viçente shoved his plate forward. "*You need to understand.*" He saw Pacheco shaking his head and lowered his voice. "Thousands of *conversos* like me have known only Christianity. Many are city officials around Castile. If the Royal Cousins dismiss them, who'll support their families? Who'll protect them if the rabble attacks them, as they do the Jews?"

Enrique took a bite from a pheasant leg and grinned at Pacheco. "Viçente, you're much too somber and a bit repetitious-repetitious."

"Please be serious, Prince. *Conversos* help administer this city. They perform vital tasks in the national treasury, in the royal army, and—"

Pacheco gave Viçente a warning frown. "Enrique and I would rather the cousins were more enlightened, but—"

The prince held up a hand. "We received word this morning, Viçente. My uncles captured Father at Medina del Campo. Queen María and the Royal Council sent Constable Luna home to his estates."

"And now you'll treat Segovia's converts as dirt under your feet?"

Enrique set down the bird's leg and raised his wine glass. "I'll not be the cousins' puppet. You've convinced me of this, Viçente. *Conversos* who work for me will stay."

"Thank you, Prince," Viçente said. "But other cities and royal offices employ my people, too. If you'd stood with your father against the cousins—"

"*Don't,*" Pacheco commanded.

Enrique grimaced and stood. "This talk of loyalty bores me. Have a servant bring the spice cake to my chamber." He strolled out.

Pacheco leaned toward Viçente. "It was foolish to embarrass him with talk of m-morality. I counsel him to support the Royal Cousins and expand our realm. You undermine the effort. Accept what you're offered."

That night in bed, Viçente pondered Ayala's treacheries that had sent him to this 'agreeable prison.' What other acts of distrust had Ayala perpetrated? The *Guardia Civil* hadn't discovered the mute's murderers this past year, and now Viçente understood: Ayala had countermanded his order to investigate.

He thought back to times when he'd asked Don Ricardo, making sure to speak casually, if there had been any word about the mute's murder? *No, sir,* the commandant would say. Increasingly frustrated, Viçente couldn't demand more action, not for a Jew.

The culprits would have gone to a tavern and bragged about slaughtering a helpless cripple, and guardsmen could have heard, if they'd opened their ears. Ayala had ordered them closed.

At least Ayala hadn't revoked the order for patrols near the Jewish Quarter, which had no-doubt saved lives this past year.

Around dawn, sleeping little, Viçente came to believe that Ayala had protected him from his own impulsive actions, protected again with this gentle exile. Damn the protection. Damn the magistrate. Damn the Jews and the Jew-haters all.

—◊—

Viçente refused to sign a loyalty oath to the prince as long as Enrique was in league with the king's enemies, but the prince and Pacheco continued to treat him as a friend. On the sixth day, neither prince nor advisor appeared at breakfast, and then half a dozen royal soldiers escorted Viçente and his guards back to Toledo.

CHAPTER 12

—⁓—

THE PRINCE'S WARRIORS HALTED THE party atop a bluff within sight of Toledo. The soldiers turned back as Viçente and the two civil guards rode to the city. Arriving at the city offices, Viçente found three sentries at the main door—three instead of one. Why and by whose authority? There was only one possibility.

In his anteroom upstairs, he found Don Ricardo, commander of the *Guardia Civil*. Viçente listened for the footsteps of other guards come to arrest him, but heard none.

Standing a forehead shorter than Viçente with thick, black brows and hair, Don Ricardo wore the red stripes of a commander on his black-and-gold tunic. He held his black visored cap against his chest with his left hand and saluted with the right. "Good day, First Deputy. The sentries informed me of your arrival and I rushed here with an invitation to Magistrate Ayala's palace."

Viçente swallowed. "You mean 'an order for my arrest?'"

"No, my lord."

No one followed as Viçente and the commandant strode the city streets. But two guards stood at the corner of Calle San Salvador, where there should be none. Tears of anger welled in Viçente's eyes. By posting these guards, Ayala was usurping Viçente's command once again, sending a personal message as he embarked on the treason that destroyed Toledo's standing in the realm. A pulse of fear in his chest mingled with the beat of suspicion, the rumbling of disappointment, the throb of betrayal.

He paused before Ayala's *palacio*, with its carved stone emblems on either side of the entrance—two wolves on each crest, predators like the Royal Cousins. Viçente thought back four years to Marta's funeral. After the Mass, Ayala had been one of eight who bore her coffin. Every week after that, the magistrate had reserved half a day with Viçente, ending in a quiet dinner at this palace. One Saturday, Ayala led him on a pheasant hunt in the forest with falcon and dogs. He gave Viçente a falcon and patiently helped him train it. This mentor had trained Viçente, too, trained him to live a bit past his sorrows week by week.

Making this betrayal all the more humiliating.

Don Ricardo led him up the wide, marble stairway to the open courtyard at the heart of Ayala's palace. Two levels of square, white, fluted pillars, and gray, carved capitals supported a covered portico. Don Ricardo gestured to a table and chairs in a sunny corner and departed.

Ayala strode toward him, his eye bright and happy, mustache glossy, glistening white hair arranged neatly over his furrowed forehead, a yellow cloth eye patch over his missing eye.

Viçente stood rigid as Ayala wrapped him in a tight embrace. "You've heard, haven't you? We've succeeded, Deputy."

Viçente wanted to pull back, but Ayala held firm, exclaiming in his ear, "It's perfect, Viçente. The Royal Cousins control his palaces and the treasury. Surely now you see the prudence of this course." He released Viçente and studied him with that one good eye. "Was the prince a good host?"

"I appealed to his conscience, because yours has abandoned you."

Ayala frowned. "What was Enrique's attitude?"

"He mocked me."

Ayala chuckled and patted Viçente's shoulder. "The absurd pup likes you. We may yet need his help."

Viçente knew he looked miserable. "And now, for the sake of revolution, you've ejected the best men from Toledo."

"Not all. You and I are still here."

Viçente heard a sound and started. It was only a maid, setting fruit juice and pastries on the table.

Ayala gripped his shoulders. "I'm not insensitive to your position, Viçente. I proceeded with the expulsion to relieve you of the distress you seem to feel over this."

Viçente pulled free. "You expect me to acquiesce as you expel innocents whose only crime is to support the king?"

"*Still your tongue.*" Ayala glowered and Viçente glared hard into his eyes. "No man's innocent, Deputy, though you pose a good pretense." He wrinkled his nose. "You'll want a bath. The maid will arrange a tub. Then come, and we'll talk."

"We'll talk now."

"Then sit over there, where the wind can disperse your scent." Ayala settled and took a paper from his back pocket. "Have a bit of cake and see who departed Toledo last week."

Viçente felt the sickness return to his stomach as he sat, preparing to see which of his friends had been ripped from their homes. "If treason is a triviality, my resignation will be, too."

Ayala jabbed a finger at the page. "I make this palatable. Look."

Viçente snatched the paper. Printed in large letters at the top was 'Marcos García de Mora.' He read on, finding mostly men from the Council of Governors who'd opposed Ayala, and only one of Viçente's friends, Don Antonio, a close associate of the king's treasurer. He looked to Ayala with a mixture of anger and befuddlement. "Don Antonio's a fine man, but the rest—I'd expected to see nobles and *conversos* who support the king."

"I couldn't avoid Antonio, but I've spared the rest. I presented this to the master of Santiago with my offer of Toledo's cooperation against King Juan. The master reconfirmed his pledge to provide a generous land grant."

"You altered the list for me?"

"You'll continue to manage the city, but, naturally, you can't represent Toledo at the Royal Cousins' court."

Viçente's stomach felt like a pile of wet clay. Blood pounded in his temples. "You shame me by thinking I could support this." He pushed back his chair, bumping the table as he rose.

The magistrate grabbed his cup of juice to keep it from toppling. His eye narrowed, white eyebrow bulging. "Don't end our bond out of vanity, Viçente. I'll bribe you to stay."

"Money to betray my king?"

Ayala smirked. "Gold and whores are most men's currency, but not for my righteous deputy. Stay with me, and I'll let you keep your staff."

Viçente blew out a breath. "Keep them because they're capable. You'll need their help."

"The cousins urge me to eliminate converts from office. If you leave, I'll accommodate them."

"Why do you even want me, damn it?"

"You can be contrary, but you achieve marvelous results, Viçente." He shrugged. "And the Jews," he went on. "You commanded the *Guardia Civil* to protect them. I wouldn't be so benevolent if you were gone."

"I asked for a quiet investigation of the mute's killing."

"A mistake I corrected. Any other magistrate would have dismissed you."

Viçente winced. "I don't care about Jews. I'm a Christian. But we have to keep peace."

"If you leave, I'll run the city according to *my* conscience. You'll stay, Viçente, because you believe in justice." Ayala's sneer was too damned confident.

"*Christ* believes in justice. Can't you simply do what's right?"

Ayala shook his head. "You can't make me angry today, my friend. How can I convince you?"

Blessed Jesus, what was Viçente to do? If he remained first deputy, he could protect Toledo's *conversos* and do what little he could for the lowly Jews. Damn them. He could say he didn't care, he could despise their beliefs and the rabbi's impudence. Their presence was a blight, but their murder would be the most unholy of sins. He'd received Enrique's assurance about Segovia's converts, but how quickly might that young man renege? "Make me the city's liaison with the prince."

"An excellent thought, Deputy. That could strengthen our role with the Royal Cousins." Ayala beckoned. Viçente hesitated and then walked around to him. The magistrate took his hand. "I've always felt affection for you."

Viçente couldn't let his mentor's touch distract him. Nor could he abandon his staff and leave the Jews to the zealots of *Sangre Pura*. He pulled his hand free, despising himself for following this manipulative man so far beyond reason. If he had a chance, Viçente would help return the king to power, but for now, nurturing the prince might be his best course. "When I meet the prince, I'll seek his help restoring *conversos'* rights."

The magistrate's look grew distant as he gazed toward the upper portico. "A dead Jew or two, a few men sent down the road—a small price to pay. We'll have land grants and wealth beyond our dreams."

Viçente told himself that desperation drove him to this awful choice—conspiring against his king, as the prince betrayed his father for power, as Ayala befriended the *conversos'* enemies for property.

Convenient, wasn't it, for Viçente to keep his comfortable position out of loyalty to his fellow converts and chief magistrate? Convenient for Judas to think that Jesus was a false prophet as a sack of silver slipped into his hand.

Viçente sipped his juice but couldn't swallow.

CHAPTER 13

—⚏—

January 1444—A year later; Viçente's third visit to Segovia since the coup

VIÇENTE STROLLED WITH HIS TWO companions beside the Río Eresma, swelled by winter rains to a muddy, roiling tumult. Prince Enrique still wore his special hat—a miniature castle with two square towers—made by the servants for his nineteenth birthday. Juan Pacheco clung to the prince's arm, the two forming one mutually sustaining, drunken torso.

Thickets of bare willows clustered along the river, their trunks submerged. Beyond the river, dark conifers filled the rise to gold-orange canyon walls. Thirty paces back, a dozen of the prince's soldiers followed, their armor raising a banging, clanking rattle, just audible over the river's dull thunder. Two of Viçente's Toledan guards in their gold-and-black uniforms strode with them, looking slight compared to the armored titans.

"You take life too seriously, Viçente." Enrique wore a foolish grin, made more comical by his smashed nose. "Always going on about *conversos*. Am I right, Pacheco?"

Juan Pacheco nodded. His hair, the color of a dark cork oak, danced about his cheeks. "We know you're a true Chr-Christian, Viçente, really, but so many *conversos* are secret Jews. How can one judge?"

"And Jews will always be ... they'll be Jews," the prince added. "People will throw stones and call names, a healthy outlet for the populace.'"

Mentioning *converso* rights had been a mistake with the prince so drunk. But the prince's loose tongue presented an opportunity. "What news have you from Constable Luna, Your Highness?"

Enrique picked up a stone, hurled it in a high arc, and waited to see it land in the trees across the river. "The Royal Cousins keep Luna isolated in his castle."

"The cousins' agents annoy us all," Pacheco said. "You've seen the ugly pair lurking here in Segovia."

"Viçente, we've become such comrades. Don't you feel silly saying 'prince this' and 'highness that?'" Enrique gave Viçente a crooked smile. "Especially with this paper castle on my noggin. Call me Enrique, damn it."

Viçente felt honored and a little embarrassed, though the privilege might dissipate with the alcohol next morning. The prince touched Viçente's arm. "Pacheco and I talk about you, Viçente. We note that you are guileless in certain ways and clever in others. We trust and respect you, and we reward our friends."

Sounds of horses approaching. Viçente turned to see the two cousins' informers riding up to the band of soldiers. They halted, gestured, and shouted. The men at arms massed to block them. One of the horses lurched forward. Soldiers drew swords and hoisted spears.

Pacheco shrugged at the prince. "What do you suppose they want?"

"I can't imagine." Enrique smirked.

"Viçente," Pacheco said. "Did you invite them?"

Viçente chuckled and shook his head.

The two interlopers dismounted, and moments later, one of the soldiers ran to Pacheco. "Sir, they wish to join the prince's party."

"Send them back to the castle," Enrique snapped. But then he raised a hand. "No, bring them."

The cousins' men came forward—one large, muscular, and angry-looking; the other shorter with graying hair, a sour expression, and a large, blotchy mole on his chin. They stopped a few paces from the prince and bowed. The older fellow said, "No disrespect, Your Majesty, but you should not meet alone with this *marrano*."

Pacheco wrapped an arm around Viçente's shoulder. "His name is Viçente Pérez and he's our friend." Pacheco let go but kept standing shoulder to shoulder with Viçente.

The larger of the interlopers scowled as the other said, "This man could be a heretic. It appears badly for you." Enrique spat on the ground. "Your king promised a handful of my father's fortresses if I supported the coup. Instead he sends two repulsive spies."

The larger man stepped to the side, his stare fixed on Viçente. Viçente moved away from Pacheco, preparing to defend himself. Two of the prince's soldiers drew batons from their belts.

Enrique stepped around Pacheco, heading toward Viçente. "Tell your master I resent his deceit. His next emissary had best bear good news. You two are dismissed."

The man with the birthmark said, "Your Highness, we must stay and observe."

"You heard me. Get away."

The larger intruder snarled, "You turn us away and consort with this blasphemer." His older comrade moved to block him, but the brute stepped past, moving fast toward Viçente.

Viçente clenched his fists as the two soldiers pursued the man. Prince Enrique jammed a fist into the brute's side as one of his soldiers whacked his baton on the fellow's back. The other soldier leapt forward, driving the intruder to the ground near the prince's feet. The big man tried to wriggle free, but the first soldier jammed a knee into his back.

Prince Enrique hauled back and booted the man with a glancing blow across his ear. He kicked again. The brute's head jerked. Blood spurted from his mouth. The prince raised a foot high over the fellow's head.

"NO," Viçente grabbed Enrique's shoulder. Enrique paused and gave him a curious look. "Please, Prince. Don't make enemies of the Royal Cousins over me."

Enrique eased off and looked around, spotting his birthday hat in the mud. Pacheco picked it up and smirked. "Got some bl-blood on it."

The soldiers lifted the oaf and dragged him away. Enrique glared at the man with the marked chin. "Get him out of Segovia. Tell your king I'll tolerate no more."

"I apologize, Prince, but the King of Navarre commands me to stay."

"GET AWAY." Enrique stomped his foot and the cousins' man spun and ran after the soldiers. "*Hijo de puta* ruined my bonnet," the prince grumbled. He grinned at Viçente. "I hope he didn't hurt your feelings, old man."

"You hold the highest office of any convert in Castile, Viçente," Pacheco said. "You're a symbol to them."

The prince and Juan Pacheco lurched to a seat on a boulder by the river. Viçente settled on another stone, thinking of his mission to seek information for Magistrate Ayala. "Why haven't the cousins given you the castles they promised?"

"If Enrique controlled those fortresses," Pacheco said, "with the pledges he holds from the noble families, he'd have the power to return his father to the throne."

"You'd support your father after conspiring against him?" Viçente asked. "What of consistency?"

"Consistency?" Enrique slapped Pacheco's knee. "What the hell is that, Viçente?"

"Dominion is a dance," Pacheco said. "If you're driven to control land and money and power, you shift a-allegiances to the one who'll grant them. The more you change partners, the more fun. The Royal Cousins made an offer, so Enrique opposed his father. If the cousins renege, we'll try another pairing for the *seguidilla*."

Viçente looked from the river to Prince Enrique's fortress atop the cliff, golden in the afternoon light with its slate-roofed towers and newly constructed, turreted keep, those weighty, massive walls rooted in Castile's bedrock. That stronghold sheltered scores of men at arms.

In the countryside, hundreds stood ready to set aside hammers or hoes, don helmets, and fight for Enrique. Nobles throughout Castile had pledged him fealty. This lad with the crooked nose and foolish hat might truly be able to tip the throne from uncles back to father. "The cousins promised my magistrate they'd give him land," Viçente said. "But their pledges are *mierda*."

"*Pendejos*." Enrique shielded his eyes from the afternoon sun and squinted at Viçente. "Did Ayala believe that nonsense?"

"Your father kept his word by giving you Segovia."

"*Pendejos* had better do something for me soon." Enrique spat on the ground.

—⚬⚬—

CHAPTER 14

VIÇENTE SPENT THAT NIGHT IN a high-posted bed in an opulent room of
the *alcázar*. The next morning, he rode with his Toledan guardsmen
into the lower city to negotiate purchase of a boarding house, his second investment outside Toledo.

Later, he composed a report for Magistrate Ayala.

> *From my meetings with the prince I gather two important facts: first,
> Prince Enrique is disappointed in the Royal Cousins. They've failed
> to keep their promises to him as they have to you, Chief Magistrate.
> Second, a growing number of nobles have joined the prince's Loyal
> League. I suggest that you enlist in the league to cement our relation-
> ship with this important ally.*

Viçente went on to discuss the Royal Cousins' men at Enrique's court
and describe his discussions with the prince, omitting any reference
to King Juan's return to the throne. It made Viçente queasy, scheming
against his mentor, but he couldn't risk Ayala's interference.

In the evening, he donned his brushed lambskin jacket over a
pine-green tunic and headed to the ballroom—that night's event a
reception for Prince Enrique's Aunt Francesca. In the hallway, he saw
Bishop Lope de Barrientos lumbering toward him, wearing a pale
blue-and-yellow robe and yellow bonnet, his white hair clipped close
above his ears, his pale, round face beaming. Barrientos, ten years

Viçente's senior, had been Viçente's teacher years ago at the university in Salamanca. Until King Juan's ouster, he'd served as king's counselor and tutor to Prince Enrique. Viçente embraced him and they joined the line of distinguished citizens waiting to greet Lady Francesca. At the ballroom entry, he held the bishop back and murmured, "There's something I'd like to discuss."

"Later, my son. First you must gaze upon this." Barrientos gestured.

Viçente looked through the doorway and spotted Prince Enrique in a silk robe the soft yellow of a peach skin. A step beyond stood a lovely woman with black flowing hair. "I take it you don't mean the chandeliers."

Barrientos clucked his tongue. "I'm still a man beneath this fancy robe and pretty cap."

As they moved forward with the queue, Viçente caught glimpses of her. The curve of her back remained regal as she turned from one noble to the next, her bosom pressed against the beaded fabric of her long, emerald dress. Viçente reached Enrique. They clasped hands, the prince gave him a playful poke in the ribs, and then Viçente moved to the lady, noticing the way little creases formed, fanlike, at the corners of her eyes and disappeared. But a grim fellow with a narrow mustache and goatee stood just behind, scrutinizing her visitors. The red ribbon draped across his white jacket, a bit ostentatious.

Barrientos took the lady's hand in both of his. "Lady Francesca, it's an honor for this humble priest to see you again. I trust life in Naples pleases you and that King Alfonso is well."

"Bishop, a lovely man such as you should never be humble." The lady smiled into Barrientos' eyes, and Viçente felt as if she were beaming into his. But Francesca, Enrique's aunt, lived in Naples, and was somehow involved with King Alfonso, one of the Royal Cousins who trampled converts' rights.

The bishop was saying, "Rome is a swine hovel. Popes tear down palaces to build barren structures from the stones."

Francesca touched Barrientos' hand. "But Bishop, what of the delicacies they serve there? What of the people's hospitality?"

Her words brought a spark of remembrance, and Viçente said, "Superb villas in the countryside, balmy nights scented by sweet blossoms."

Francesca gazed at him, her mouth slightly open, eyes a soft brown, lighter and more golden than chestnuts. "You've traveled in Italy? I've not met you, Señor …"

"Pérez," Viçente said. "I spent a year there."

"And unlike the bishop, you found it agreeable?"

"I was young, visiting Rome to learn about church politics. I had leisure time to explore, to read and contemplate, to learn about life, too, I guess. I thought of becoming a priest, but—but I was diverted." Viçente felt his face redden.

"Then Rome brought different passions," she said. Francesca's smile reminded him of those Roman girls who'd seduced away his more pious thoughts.

"There are too many of that sort of priest." The harsh baritone startled Viçente, and he turned to see the cousins' dour emissary with the birthmark.

"I can't imagine what you mean," Francesca said. "No. Don't tell me—too many priests who admire women."

The man had clearly meant *converso* priests, and his words had destroyed the moment. Barrientos and Viçente moved separately into the ballroom.

Beneath golden chandeliers, women in low-cut gowns—reds trimmed in garnet jewelry, blacks with pearls or diamonds—and men wearing uniform jackets with golden medallions—informed Viçente of their interests and their importance. Most of the men had served King Juan in battles with the Muslims in the south, protecting the Portuguese frontier on the west or the borders with Navarre and Aragón to the north. Over drinks and tapas, a hundred wealthy Segovians raised goblets to Francesca's health—Francesca, radiant in her beaded emerald gown with diamond necklace, eyes flashing. He saw her speak with the cousins' man, who pointed at Viçente. She looked his way and frowned, and Viçente wondered how this woman was related to the King of Aragón and Naples and to the man with the pompous red ribbon.

When Barrientos had a free moment, Viçente pulled him aside. "Bishop, would you be as discreet as my confessor?"

"Certainly, my son."

"I've heard rumors about restoring King Juan."

The bishop pursed his lips. "You know the Royal Cousins captured me when they took King Juan, but they found me unpalatable and spit me out." The bishop nodded toward a group of women in lavish dresses, moving close. "What do you think of our honored guest?"

Radiant was the word that flirted with his thoughts. "I haven't decided."

Barrientos smirked. "She brings a touch of liveliness, don't you think? And the prince will feed us well tonight." Barrientos patted his stomach and winked, then lowered his voice. "She is a beautiful woman, as you full well have noticed."

"No doubt, but how is she related to King Alfonso?"

Barrientos raised a hand and pointed toward the ceiling. "The royalty marries to gain alliances. Kings wed each other's siblings. Enrique yoked himself to his cousin two years ago, so they have no shame about these things. Yet everyone's vague about Francesca's place in the royalty. I don't choose to speculate."

The women moved on. Viçente stepped closer and said, "There can be no justice while the cousins rule. Juan's the true monarch, but I don't know if it's possible."

"If God wills it and if good men like you are determined ..." Barrientos folded his arms and gazed at the party-goers.

"Bishop, speak plainly. What can I do?"

"As you've done for your cathedral, Viçente. Bring me bags of money."

Viçente had many questions, but guests began filing past, bidding the bishop *adios*. A servant summoned the remaining company to dinner. *What would the bishop do with bags of money?*

In the dining hall, two tables held large, silver candelabra, fine plates and goblets. But the tables had been moved far apart. Three of Enrique's house guards, in green-and-gold uniforms, patrolled the space between.

"Aunt Francesca and Viçente, Bishop Barrientos and Pacheco, this way," Enrique called.

"PRINCE." Viçente turned to see the Royal Cousins' man blocked from joining them by the house guards. "You mustn't dine with that *marrano*." Behind the cousin's man, Francesca's three ladies-in waiting and the fellow with the red ribbon seated themselves.

Pacheco touched Viçente's arm. "Don't let him worry you, my friend. Have a fine dinner and get to know our guest."

But what would the man with the marked chin report to his king?

Enrique settled at one end of their table and Pacheco at the other. Barrientos and Francesca shared a side as Viçente sat across. They ate partridge soup and artichokes sautéed with garlic and drank red wine. Servants set steaming copper platters of roasted venison to either side of the candelabrum. As Viçente savored the scent of meat and fine spices, Enrique explained that the vegetables were grown in greenhouses set south of the palace to catch the winter sun.

"Enrique," Francesca shot a mischievous glance at Viçente as she spoke to the prince. "You speak of legumes in their plant houses, but where is Princess Blanca enjoying the winter sun?" The lady was either close with Enrique, remarkably audacious, or the wine had taken her to dangerous excess. Viçente had yet to encounter Blanca, whom Vincente had heard Enrique refer to as 'my deformed bitch wife.'

The prince bit into a chunk of venison and chewed it, looking toward his plate. "My princess is with her father, the King of Navarre. She'll return soon enough."

"How thoughtful of her father to send that solemn man with the dimpled chin to keep you company." Francesca nodded at the other table, where the cousins' emissary sat, scowling. "When I chatted with him, he was lamenting the fact that you'd sent his comrade away."

"They're fools," Pacheco said. "He didn't b-bother you?"

"No, he was quite informative, full of talk about farm animals. He spoke constantly of *marranos*."

Viçente tensed at the mention of that hated word. But seeing her bright eyes and fine lips holding back a grin, fascination ruled. Elements within him, desiccated and dormant these past years, felt the pulse of buoyant nectars.

Barrientos thumped his wine cup down. "Evil nonsense. We priests labor to convert people, and once they come to Christ, men like that harass them."

"But Bishop, haven't you heard how these former Jews steal the holy bread from the church and say heathen prayers over it?" Her words were abhorrent, but her voice intoxicated. Her half-smile allured and worried Viçente all at once.

"*False.*" Barrientos glared at the table.

"Bishop," Francesca said. "I'm just repeating what that man told me. '*Marranos* poison Christians' drinking water.'"

The bishop blew out huge gasps of air. This mysterious woman had managed to confound both prince and bishop within a few minutes' time. "I think she's teasing you," Viçente said. "But I'd feel better if I were sure."

Francesca turned to him, eyes dancing. "That man, who speaks for the Crown, warned me to avoid you. You must be quite sinister."

"Preposterous," Barrientos grumbled. "They don't represent the legitimate Crown of Castile."

Francesca inclined her head toward the other table. "Now he's filling Carlo's head with the same nonsense. First Deputy, Carlo will be unbearable for a week because I'm talking with you."

Viçente felt that lustful energy ebb. Carlo, the man with the goatee and red ribbon, had to be her husband.

"When they told me you were a *marrano*, I was amazed." Francesca looked Viçente straight on, her smile agitating those nectars despite all reason. "I said, 'But if he's a swine, where is he hiding that great, pink snout?'" Laughter bubbled up in her, and she covered her mouth with a hand. How did she possess the magic to insult and entice at the same instant, and how dangerous the result?

After dinner Barrientos marched toward the other table. Viçente stepped beside Francesca to follow. Maybe he shouldn't walk with her while Carlo and the cousins' spy observed, but he was a man, and he'd not yield to them. She was taller than he'd thought, the top of her head level with his eyes. She took his arm, and the touch sent a shiver through him. "You worried me with that talk of *marranos*," he said.

Francesca pursed her lips. "When they speak that way in Naples, I leave the room."

"I was relieved when you turned it into a joke."

"You looked like you wanted to scream at me. It was quite comical."

"Who would dare shout at you? You have the protection of kings."

"Do you think I might cut off your head?" Still keeping pace with him, she released his arm, whirled, and skimmed her hand in front of his neck like a scythe slicing wheat.

His mind recoiled at this powerful woman, blithely swiping an arc of death through him. "You're playing, Francesca, but I fear your game. And your husband, why was he seated at the other table?"

She laughed. "Carlo? He's one of my chaperones. When I departed Italy, I had eight soldiers, my three women, and Carlo. Do you imagine I need so many?"

His heart raced. "A dozen escorts might have trouble keeping pace with you."

She stood so near he felt her warmth. He glanced toward the other table and saw Barrientos, red-faced, jabbing a finger at the Royal Cousins' man. "We'd better stop the bishop," Viçente said. "He may strike."

As he turned back to her, Francesca raised herself on her toes. Instinctively he bent toward her, and she brought her face beside his. The delicate scent of spice roses carried sensations of those long ago Roman nights. A wisp of hair tickled his cheek. "I'd like to see those eyes of yours in full daylight," she whispered. "Are they truly green? We must meet after breakfast."

Viçente couldn't speak, could only breathe her scent, savor her presence, and feel the others staring. Why was this mistress of royalty flirting with a man fifteen years older, a mere first deputy? "You want them to kill me?"

She brushed his cheek with a fingertip. "Let's go rescue our bishop." She strolled toward the others, and he stood alone, relieved and disappointed.

CHAPTER 15

—ᴍᴍ—

Lʏɪɴɢ ɪɴ ʙᴇᴅ, Vɪᴄᴇɴᴛᴇ ᴘɪᴄᴛᴜʀᴇᴅ Francesca's soft brown eyes as she laughed, covering her mouth with a delicate hand after speaking of the pig's 'great, pink snout.' How juvenile to feel such ... infatuation. He drifted. Images of the sneering cousins' men mixed with his dreams. One grabbed Viçente's throat. The other jammed a dagger into his chest. He woke sweating, knowing with the certainty of death that he must flee. He stood to put on his clothes but realized he'd exaggerated the danger beyond reason.

Back in bed, drowsing, Francesca approached him in a cloud, shrouding him in her warmth, whispering, "Come see me in the morning, if you dare."

—ᴍᴍ—

As he had the last time he visited Prince Enrique, Viçente planned to travel on to Salamanca to see Diego at the university. He looked forward to the two-day ride, accompanied by his favorite Toledan guards, good horsemen who kept him company on the ride through the rolling hills of western Castile. But after breakfast that morning, he strolled out to the battlement wall, looking to the Río Eresma running fast in its canyon, its roar faint from this high perch. Sometime before midday, Juan Pacheco joined him. "You'll not see her today."

The words stung. "Why not?"

"You and Francesca are subjects of much chatter." Pacheco nudged a knuckle into Viçente's arm. "I see why you're attracted, my friend, but be wary. She flirts to demonstrate in-independence she doesn't possess. The cousins' man ranted to Carlo about *marranos* corrupting women, and Carlo ordered her confined."

Viçente pounded the side of his fist against the wall and wheeled on Pacheco. "I'm not a damned heathen. Francesca and I are barely acquainted ... They won't harm her?"

"They're protecting her from 'irrational whims.'" Pacheco slipped a folded page from his pocket.

"She sent a note?"

"I was tempted to read it and share the gossip." Pacheco smirked.

Viçente snatched the paper.

Viçente,

How embarrassed I feel, locked away in my room, unable to see you. That terrible man convinced Carlo that he'd be executed if he didn't protect me. Protect me from you—how foolish. All we did was share a pleasurable moment.

Please don't hate me, and don't blame Carlo. He thinks he's doing King Alfonso's bidding.

You love Italy, and that's part of your charm. If you ever come to Naples, please visit. I'll guide you to the most romantic places, and don't worry; there at home, I can have any friend I want.

Fondly,
Francesca

The word, 'fondly' lingered in his mind. Then the other words: *All we did was share a pleasurable moment.* Was that truly all? Or was she writing this note, as Viçente had written to Ayala, revealing only part of the truth?

—m—

Viçente sat in an armchair in a dark corner of the busy tavern in Salamanca as Diego maneuvered through a crowd of university lads toward the bar. The scent of fermented spirits emanated from the earthen floor. Raucous male voices reminded Viçente of his youth. An amorous lad nearby ogled his female companion—one of the few women brazen enough to come here—and the sparks dancing between them touched Viçente, too. But none of the girls, with their innocent allure, nor the bar maids who carried trays of alcohol and sexual insinuations, could touch the fascination Francesca had conveyed with one passionate glance.

Diego headed back with two pottery mugs, pausing to converse with one of his fellows. "Spiced wine for you, stout for me." Diego clunked them down and beer slopped onto the rough wooden table. "Doesn't that sweet wine make you sick, Papa? I invited my friend Alberto over. Is that all right?"

A tall, fair-haired fellow ambled to their table, and Diego introduced them. They chatted about challenging courses and disagreeable professors. "We call our finance teacher 'the mad man,'" Alberto sneered. "He shouts and pounds the table."

"Passion for a subject isn't bad," Viçente said.

"Papa, this one's dangerous."

Alberto gulped from his drink. "Your son hasn't told you? Sorry, Diego."

"What's this about?" Viçente asked.

Diego looked away as Alberto answered. "He says that we *conversos* have too much power and we've pilfered Castile's wealth."

Viçente took a swallow of wine, feeling a hard knot form in his stomach. "This is wrong. I'll speak with the department master."

Diego held his palms up in a restraining gesture. "No, Papa. The master knows, and he'll protect our standing. But some of the teachers say there's no place for us in government now that converts have been banished. Well, most, but—"

"But not your father who governs Toledo." Viçente set the mug down hard. "Alberto, do these professors ridicule Diego?"

"Some admire you, Señor Pérez, for confounding fate. One professor calls Toledo a well-run city. But this finance teacher implies that you've connived for your position."

Viçente watched his son shift uncomfortably in his chair. "Diego, we can enroll you in another school."

Diego slapped the table. "Papa, did you raise me to run from hypocrites?"

"Have you thought about law or commerce?" Viçente said.

"After university, I'd like to study in Rome, as you did, Papa. By the time I return, Castile will be sane again."

Could things really turn around by then? Would Castile ever be as noble as it once had been? "You should at least consider a different—"

Diego's face colored, and he clenched the mug tightly. "Respect me, and let me decide." After a moment, Diego gave him a crooked smile. "You're still running a city, Papa, despite bigots and Royal Cousins' decrees. When they speak of you that way, I'm proud."

A minute before, he'd bristled at Diego's blunt words. Now the lad's pride touched him. His son's independent spirit brought him both hope and worry. Pride and self-reliance could spark success or destruction in a hostile world.

He sighed. "All right, I'll accept your autonomy, if you'll grant me leave to the latrine."

When he returned, the lads were deep in conversation, but they ceased as he arrived. Diego said, "Papa, you worry too much about me."

Alberto clapped a hand on Diego's shoulder. "Your son's sensible, Señor Pérez. When we go to Rome together next year, we'll watch out for one another."

"You fret about everything, Papa. Your letters are full of wicked sermons, royal politics, and murdered Jews. You need diversions."

"Since we're all good Christians," Alberto winked, "I remind you that being serious is a mortal sin."

That wink annoyed Viçente. He'd not tolerate a clerk who made light of Christian values. But the boys were right; he needed to drink and lighten his heart.

Diego patted Viçente's forearm. "What you need, Papa, is a woman."

"Your son's right, Señor Pérez," Alberto said.

Viçente laughed. "You two conspire against me."

"A toast to conspiracy." Diego raised his glass. He and Alberto gulped.

"That barmaid's a lusty specimen." Alberto gestured.

"Maid, over here," Diego cried. He and Alberto waved until the woman sauntered over.

"More drinks, lads? What are you having, sir?" The woman's barely-concealed breasts bobbed close to Alberto's bulging eyes.

"This isn't a call for liquor." Alberto stood and put his arm around the maid's waist. "My friend's father here, he needs companionship."

Diego nodded. "If you could find it in your heart, modest señorita."

"Is this really your son?" The woman sneered. "Aren't you ashamed?"

"Utterly." Viçente chuckled.

"Then you're a decent man." She looked Viçente over. "And well turned-out. Meet me at the back door when we close." She twisted free of Alberto, pinched Viçente's cheek, and marched away. Diego and Alberto collapsed in laughter. Viçente laid his head on the table and thumped it with his hand. The boys had done him in.

The crowd in the tavern thinned. Alberto departed. Viçente's heart swelled with warmth for Diego, warmth and reminiscence and heartache. He'd never had a congenial drink with his papa, never shared feelings or forgiven Papa's covert Judaism. But how could he?

Outside, they strolled, guided by moonlight and the silhouettes of dark buildings. Crisp air stung Viçente's cheeks. "Do you really think I need a woman in my life?"

Diego nodded, keeping his gaze on the path ahead.

"I've wondered how you'd feel about it. A son might resent such a thing."

Diego halted and looked Viçente in the eye. "I told you, Papa, you worry too much. Make your life enjoyable."

"I think about what your mother would feel."

"She'd want you to. It's been long enough. Too long."

And then, although it made no sense, Viçente told his son about Francesca.

—⚏—

CHAPTER 16

MARCOS DRUMMED HIS FINGERS ON the window frame. Outside, in what passed for a street in the village of Simancas, a wagon bogged in the mud and tipped on its side. Clay pots dropped off. A barrel rolled out, smashing the vessels. Oil from the pots oozed into the muck. Workmen shouted and pulled along with the beasts, trying to right the cart. Marcos spat out the window, disgusted at the filth and the events that had brought him down. The killing of the mute was almost two years past. The *pendejo*, Pérez, had connived with his fellow Jew-lovers, Magistrate Ayala and Archbishop Cerezuela—at least that pathetic old fool was dead and gone—and managed to have Marcos exiled from Toledo. Pérez had exposed his evil soul by sending *Guardia Civil* patrols at night to protect his Jew blood brothers, and still they kept him in office!

Jew blood wasn't pure; it was slime, and someday it would run in the streets like oil in the muck. Marcos would reenter Toledo, and *Sangre Pura* would take Pérez.

He spotted Philip now, carrying a cloth sack and treading on tiptoes through the mud. Philip was an imbecile, but he'd served Marcos' purposes. When Philip had been a courtier to King Juan, he'd provided access to the king's palace and to government officials. In those days, the thin, effeminate courtier had worn velvet jackets with lace collars and irritating jasmine cologne that lingered in the palace corridors. He'd introduced Marcos to Pedro Sarmiento, the king's master butler, a butler with power. Sarmiento had overseen the king's palaces, ordered provisions, and arranged to move the court when King Juan traveled. The king trusted him like no other man, except the constable. But now the king was captive, Philip was reduced to wearing workmen's garb, and Marcos lived in exile in a dirty little town called San Marin.

Outside, Philip slipped in the mud, regained balance, and approached. Marcos opened the door. "Stop there or you'll get dirt on—"

Philip traipsed to the center of the room, pulled off his coat, and tossed it on the bed. Gobs of muck marked his path across the floor.

Marcos swallowed his anger. "When and where will I meet Sarmiento?"

"Simancas Castle, tonight." Philip leered at Marcos like a woman he wanted to bed.

"Go stare out the window," Marcos said. "Look anywhere but here. With the Royal Cousins' guards patrolling, why does Sarmiento choose such a dangerous place?"

"He's a funny fellow. Relishes danger one minute and abhors it the next. You'll wear these." Philip upended the cloth sack, dumping burlap clothing onto the bed.

So Marcos had fallen to this; lodging in this dung hole and sneaking into a palace dressed as a servant to meet the butler of an imprisoned, disgraced king.

Marcos sat across the battered table from Pedro Sarmiento in the servants' kitchen in the castle basement. The light from a smoking torch revealed pots and racks of wooden spoons hanging over cook stoves. The king's butler wore a leather jacket. His dark hair glistened in the torchlight, his face indistinct in shadow.

Behind Marcos, a row of granite pillars supported the ceiling with storage alcoves beyond. There would be wooden cartons and barrels of provisions back there—a place to hide if the Royal Cousins' men came searching.

Sarmiento leaned forward, speaking softly. "The last time we met, we discussed your hatred for *marranos* and my loathing for Constable Luna. You sang the praises of a group you called *Sangre Pura*. Has your little band accomplished anything since killing that mute boy?"

"Our brotherhood destroys blasphemers, while your impotent king sits in prison."

"And you've been exiled from Toledo." Sarmiento slammed his hand on the table, making Marcos twitch. "But I'm interested in your sheepherders. How many men do you command?"

Marcos glanced at the door. "I thought we were to be quiet."

Sarmiento grunted. "Are you going to tell me about your pure bloods or fret like a girl? Philip's in the hall to warn of trouble."

If Sarmiento played a game of nerves—first whispering to feign danger, then half-shouting to frighten him—Marcos could deceive, too. "Though I'm exiled from Toledo, *Sangre Pura* robbed the *marrano* tax collector and killed his guard. We spread the loot among the men to recruit more."

Sarmiento smirked. "I suppose your lads boast of the adventure as if they hadn't let the tax man escape. How many pure bloods did you say there are?"

Marcos couldn't deny that his men had botched the raid, but he could exaggerate their numbers. "Two hundred."

Sarmiento fixed him with a hard-eyed stare. "I'm deciding if I should trust you."

"And I'm wondering why I came. You serve a deposed king and lack plans to return him to power."

Sarmiento smiled. "I'm thinking you may support the cousins. They persecute your *marrano* enemies, after all."

"The cousins leave Viçente Pérez to rule Toledo."

Voices outside. Marcos jumped up and followed Sarmiento into an alcove.

"There's no one in there." Philip's voice.

"I heard something." A gruff male: one of the cousins' guardsmen.

Marcos saw torchlight beneath the door. He slipped his dagger out of its sheath and ducked behind a barrel.

Outside, Philip spoke again. "I heard something, too—further down the hall."

"What's your name?"

"Philip. I'm one of the servants."

"Come, Philip," the gruff man said.

The torchlight retreated, and Marcos whispered, "We should go."

Sarmiento left the alcove, drew his sword, and leaned it against the wall. "They'd see us." The butler seemed far too calm for a sane man, but at least he whispered now. "I was asking why you support King Juan—or is that a pretense?"

Marcos moved close and murmured, "I told you why."

"You reject the cousins over a grudge against one *marrano*, this Pérez fellow." He brought out a glove and pulled it onto his right hand. "They'll come back, of course."

Marcos felt a twinge of fear. He wanted to search for a better hiding place among the crates, but he couldn't show weakness. "The *marranos* revere Pérez. He's bribed his way to power so he can protect Jews."

Sarmiento wrapped an arm around his shoulder. "This is what I'm thinking, Marcos. I will raise a force to return King Juan to power. The king will reward me with Toledo. Once I'm magistrate, the damned constable won't be able to tell me how or when to wipe my ass. But I'll need fighting men, like your Toledan sheepherders."

"See, there's light under this door." The gruff voice, just outside.

Marcos darted back behind the barrel. Sarmiento disappeared with his sword into the shadows near the entry. The door creaked open. Marcos ducked.

"The kitchen's empty," Philip shouted.

"Then why's this torch alight?"

Marcos switched his knife to his left hand and explored with his right. Boxes blocked him from moving further back. Slow footsteps, light fluttering overhead. He returned the dagger to his right hand.

"Stand and show yourself!" A huge man, dark-featured and un-shaven, glared down at him. The man held a sword in one hand and a torch in the other, but he wore no armor. Marcos rose, seeing another fellow almost as large, and behind them, Philip, looking meek and puny. Where in hell was Sarmiento?

"Drop the knife."

As Marcos lowered the dagger toward the barrel top, he saw movement in the shadows. Light glimmered on metal—a sword. Just visible in the darkness, a form darted toward the cousins' men. Marcos heard no sound as Sarmiento swept out of the shadows and rammed his blade into one soldier's back. The point emerged from the man's chest with a spurt of dark liquid. Sarmiento slammed into the fellow. The man grunted and crumpled. Sarmiento landed on top. The fellow with the torch spun toward them.

Marcos was frozen. He saw Philip lower his shoulder and charge the man with the torch. The giant shouted and lurched toward Marcos, with Philip bearing into him. The man tripped. The torch, hot and flaming, flew at Marcos. He ducked as the soldier crashed into him, knocking the breath from his lungs. Marcos felt the dagger in his hand and thrust with all his strength. He felt it ripping, warmth gushing. Stabbing. Stabbing. Stabbing into the man's back and side. Then there was only warm liquid flowing and terrible weight pressing down.

CHAPTER 17

—◊◊◊—

MARCOS LAY GASPING ON THE frigid floor with the warm body. Strange, this dead thing seemed like an old friend or a prostitute he'd bought for the evening, or maybe Marcos was still that adolescent, sleeping with the *marrano* count in Barcelona. But the count had rolled on top of him and wasn't waking up. The closeness that had comforted at first now repulsed him.

He was looking up at a dark ceiling in a cellar somewhere, hearing a voice: "Let us get this piece of *mierda* off you." Sarmiento. That was it; he was in Simancas Castle. Marcos released the body. Sarmiento and Philip rolled it off and helped him to a seat. Sarmiento patted his back. "Well met, Marcos, my friend. You're good with a knife."

"Philip." Marcos hated the way his voice trembled. "He shoved that man at me, almost got me killed."

"Philip saved you," Sarmiento said. "A knife doesn't stand against a sword."

"No. I could have—"

Sarmiento squeezed his shoulder. "We don't have time. Philip, rummage in the servants' closet and find new clothes for our friend and rags to mop up this mess. Fetch an empty barrel, too." Philip departed and Sarmiento said, "You struck a blow for King Juan tonight, and he'll be grateful."

Sarmiento could act casual, but Marcos had slain this man—not just a simpleton Jew, but a warrior. He'd killed, and the soldier's blood had covered and warmed him. His fingers were sticky from it, and his tunic and trousers were wet and cold and growing stiff. He put aside his queasiness to bask in the triumph. He would kill again for the cause, not just men. All false Christians—men, women, children—would be destroyed. But to have the opportunity, he had to impress the butler.

Sarmiento led him near the cook stoves to warm. "You said the king would give us Toledo," Marcos said. "You and I will govern together?"

Sarmiento smirked. "You're a presumptuous knave."

"We'll rid the city of Viçente Pérez and his *marranos*, and you'll become very rich," Marcos said.

Sarmiento didn't respond, but the gleam in his eye answered well enough.

Philip arrived with the clothing and the barrel in a wooden workman's cart with four wheels, four sidewalls, and thick, oak handles. They set the barrel on the floor, lifted the larger man and dumped him in headfirst, then jammed and twisted his legs until he fit. "Bring another barrel," Sarmiento said. "And there's a spot on my trousers. Find me new ones, Philip."

"Wait," Marcos said. "When the men are missing, they'll search the barrels."

Sarmiento prodded his chin with a knuckle. "Right. We'll remove them from the castle."

"The guards will search the barrels on the way out," Philip said.

"We'll cover the bodies with meat," Sarmiento said. "When they look inside, they'll see beef, not boots."

Philip departed. Marcos stripped off his dirty clothes and tossed them on top of the corpse. He donned new burlap garments, knowing that even this indignity was bringing him Pedro Sarmiento's trust. "Sarmiento, there's a flaw in your plan. Men don't break into a fortress to steal meat."

"Go on, Counselor."

The term *counselor* sounded perfect. "Have Philip bring some good silver. We'll stash it with the corpses. Then no one will doubt that burglars murdered these two."

"Good." Sarmiento cast him another fond look.

Philip returned with a barrel half full of beef. They dumped its contents and stashed the other body inside. As the courtier went to search for silver candlesticks, Sarmiento and Marcos wiped the mess from the floor and tossed the bloody rags atop the bodies in the barrels. When Philip came back, they arranged candlesticks on the rags and cuts of beef over top, and set the lids in place. They wrestled the barrels upstairs, and then the cart, arriving at the portal to the main courtyard. Sarmiento clasped Marcos' forearm. "Your work isn't finished, my friend. Now you'll escort these barrels from the castle."

Marcos' heart raced. "Your jest doesn't amuse me."

"You entered as a servant," Sarmiento said. "No one here knows you, am I correct?"

"Of course," Philip said.

"I killed that soldier." Marcos pointed at the courtier. "Philip hasn't dirtied his hands."

Sarmiento dug his fingernails into Marcos' arm. "If you're going to work with me, you'll heed. You will wheel this barrel out through the gate and down to the river. Return for the second. Dump them in the river and take the silver, as any robber would."

There had to be another way. "The gate must be closed for the night."

"Philip can deal with that," Sarmiento said.

With a self-satisfied grin, Philip reached into a jacket pocket. "I've brought stationary and a quill from the lord of this castle." He waved some papers at Marcos. "When the guards halt you at the gate, say, 'Master's special order to the guard.'"

"Excellent, Philip." Sarmiento chuckled. "Write the note. 'You're to rush two barrels of beef to the river warehouse … It's to be ferried to Valladolid for a feast tomorrow.' Take the paper and pen, Marcos."

"Philip can write it. He's your damned underling."

"Do as I say, unless you want us all hanged."

The noose of subservience tightened around his neck as Marcos dipped quill to ink and wrote. "Now sign it for his lordship," Sarmiento said.

"If we're going to collaborate, you should know—I don't like commands."

Sarmiento sighed. "A suggestion, then."

Marcos scribbled a signature and shoved the pen at Philip. Sarmiento swung the big door open, and Marcos rolled the cart into the moonlight. The wheels clacked on the stone pavement, wagon heavy with the beef and the other meat. He ground his teeth at the thought of the damned courtier sipping whiskey by a warm hearth.

Two soldiers leaned against the wall beside the gate. One stepped forward. "Gate's closed."

What was a guard but another lackey, like a courtier? "Open it. I'm taking this meat to the warehouse."

"Of course, Your Majesty." The guard took a belligerent step forward, one hand on his sword.

Marcos' heart pounded as he pulled the paper from his pouch. "Sorry, Your Honor. I should have said, 'Master's special order to the Guard.' His lordship gave me this."

The other sentry snatched a torch from the wall and examined the paper. "Says here you've got two barrels of beef."

"I'll get this to the warehouse and come back for the other."

"Pretty scrawny fellow to be wheeling that big cart." The soldier snickered, but called up to a man on the ramparts and then strained to turn the windlass. The gate began to rise. When it was high enough, Marcos eased the cart through. He took the fork toward the river, the road lit by occasional oil lamps and moonlight, moving faster, past a block of two-story residences.

Cursing, he glanced over his shoulder. Good, he was out of sight of the battlements. Sarmiento had set him this chore, which would mark him as a murderer. Did the butler think him dispensable? Cool air helped him keep down the nausea that wanted to rise, helped him think. If he left the second barrel in the palace, what would the Royal Cousins' men think? The robber had been frightened and decided to forego the rest of his loot, he decided. As long as they suspected a thief from outside ... His anger at Philip propelled him, though he was careful not to move too fast. The hill steepened and his speed increased. Philip wasn't the cause. None of this would have been necessary but for that filthy, God-hating *marrano*, Pérez, who'd expelled him from Toledo. When Sarmiento ruled the city, they'd hoist the *marrano's* head on a pole in Zacodover Plaza.

He was running now, faster than he should, the barrel shifting forward. The cart vibrated hard against his hands. He tried to slow it, but all he could do was direct it right or left and lean down hard on the handles against the barrel's weight. Cold air burned his lungs and he was running faster than he'd ever run, but the cart flew quicker still. The lid flipped off the barrel and flew past his head. His boot heels skimmed and bumped and dragged over rough stone pavement, pummeling his feet. "OH ... AH ... AYYI ..." Somehow he kept the cart upright and the cargo inside all the way to the bottom. As it rolled across a roadway, the ground leveled for a moment, and he jammed his heels in to slow it. A lightning bolt of pain shot up his legs. The wheels hit curbing stones and upended. Marcos soared over the cart.

He covered his head with his hands and pulled in his legs, flying off the bluff toward the river below. Behind him, the cart and the barrel—and the body—were flying, too.

CHAPTER 18

—⟋⟍—

VIÇENTE'S DAYS WERE TROUBLED, TRYING to maintain the city's peace with what powers Chief Magistrate Ayala allowed him.

At night, images assailed him as he tried to sleep. Thugs leapt at a young, bearded Jew—Samuel, the mute. They stabbed him to death and then jumped on horses and galloped at the taxman, hacking his guard to bits. The tax collector fled, and Viçente was relieved.

Sangre Pura. Damn them.

The episode with the mute was years ago, yet still it haunted him. Why was he so bothered by the fate of a Jew?

Viçente sat up, trying to clear his thoughts.

His head back on the pillow, he saw Vicar Pero López pinning an innocent girl under his fat, smelly body. And the new archbishop of Toledo, nodding his approval.

Almost awake, seeing a pattern to it all and wondering.

Why had Toledo changed so? Two hundred years ago, when King Alfonso X ruled, the city had been a center of learning. Muslims wrote Arabic poetry. Jews sat at tables with priests, translating sacred books and philosophical works from Greek or Hebrew to Castilian and Latin. Christians, Jews, and Muslims studied here, created jewelry and art. Muslim architects designed churches and synagogues—all of this because the king, residing in Toledo, mandated peace among his peoples. But hatred had emigrated from northern lands, along with wild stories of Jews defiling churches and poisoning wells. The royal household had departed Toledo and fallen to disrespect under this weak, well-meaning king.

Viçente rolled onto his side. There had been poetry once, but no more. There had been love—Marta—but her memory faded day by day. Marta ... Francesca. It had been many months since he'd met Enrique's lovely aunt. They knew each other so little. Yet he imagined himself holding her as he fell back to sleep.

—m—

In the morning, he took a piece of fruit bread, threw on his black wool coat, and rushed out. He finished the pastry as he walked to Calle Comercio, a narrow street with shops on the ground floor and residences above. He knocked at the side entrance of the Joyería del Ciudad. The door opened an arm's length, and Don Hidalgo, the stoop-shouldered merchant, appeared in his nightshirt with curly gray hairs filling the opening, neck to stomach. Hidalgo scanned the street and admitted him.

Standing in the vestibule, the jeweler scowled.

"You've considered my request, Don Hidalgo?"

The merchant grimaced and scratched his side. "I don't give to charities."

"It's not charity. The funds would help create a more favorable climate for *conversos*, like yourself."

"Say it plainly. You plan to overthrow the Royal Cousins."

Viçente shook his head. "I haven't said that, but if one were to support King Juan, he'd need to raise an army."

"Why should I care how they run Castile?"

"Some ignorant men don't care that the cousins strip converts' rights, as the new archbishop divests *converso* priests of church rank. Did you realize that? This royal government and this church deprive our people of their incomes and positions."

"I'm not a first deputy or a priest. Give the king money, if you're fool enough."

Viçente swallowed the words this man deserved. "You're not a fool, Don Hidalgo. You're a businessman with *converso* customers. Their livelihoods suffer under the cousins, and your business withers."

"If the Royal Cousins find out I give to the king, I'll be burned in the square."

"If King Juan were to benefit, he'd count you as a friend, and your customers would, too. If you don't care to prosper, other jewelers do."

"Stephan, the jeweler on Calle Tornerias, has he given?"

Viçente let a cat's smile cross his lips. "If I answer, you'll not trust me with your confidence."

Don Hidalgo poked at his abdomen and glowered. "If I donate this diamond, will the king be more inclined to favor me or Stephan?" From inside his nightshirt, he produced a gem half as big as the tip of his small finger.

Viçente's pulse quickened. The stone was larger than any he'd received. "It's a sizable stone, but Don Stephan also possesses high-quality gems, some perhaps larger."

"You are a scheming whore dog, Viçente Pérez." Don Hidalgo bit his lip and brought out a second stone, smaller than the first but still a good size. "Take both. If King Juan succeeds, make sure he hears of Don Hidalgo. If he fails, I never saw you."

Sitting in his office, Viçente fingered the diamonds in his pocket and contemplated a life with King Juan back in power. His clerk dropped the afternoon mail on his desk, the first envelope bearing the name *Lope Barrientos,* and below that, the words *Bishop in Christ.*
He ripped it open as the clerk departed.

My Dear Viçente,

I hope this letter finds you well and prosperous and your soul at peace. If you rush to Prince Enrique's palace, we can talk about your ethereal growth. Summon all your spiritual resources to enable the fullest discussion.

You'll find someone of interest here, should you not delay.

Lope Barrientos

Intriguing but full of riddles. 'Spiritual resources' could refer to the funds Viçente had been raising. If others were as successful, the king would have a mighty war chest.

'Someone of interest' could be a messenger from the king or Constable Luna carrying battle plans, an inspirational monk to aid Viçente's spiritual growth, or—he dared not hope—Francesca. His pulse livened at the thought.

CHAPTER 19

—◁ω▷—

As Viçente and his two Toledan guards crested a hill, he sighted the golden spires and towers of Segovia. Dusty and tired from four days' riding, he spurred his horse on, anxious to resolve Bishop Barrientos' riddles. They splashed through the Río Clamores and ascended the hill through the dusty-brown Puerta de San Andrés into the city.

Inside Enrique's palace, Viçente found an alarming quiet. As a servant led him toward the guest rooms, Viçente gripped the handle of his sword and pulled the satchel close against his chest. The man gave a nervous smile and said, "The prince's other guests board in the *alcázar*, but the bishop requested that you stay here in the palace."

"Do the Royal Cousins still have men in the city?"

"Two, sir, both at the *alcázar*."

The knot in his shoulder muscles eased just a bit at the news.

They entered a room with a canopied bed and polished floors inlaid with ivory roses. The servant lit candles and pulled the shutters closed. He handed Viçente a note and departed. Viçente bolted the door and checked in the dressing cabinet and under the bed before reading.

Viçente,

 Better you not be seen, so I've arranged this discrete accommodation. The servants will prepare your bath. When the bells sound the sixteenth hour, take the back hall to the chapel.
Lope

—m—

Viçente had come to love this chapel during his visits to Prince Enrique's palace, so full of brilliant stained glass it seemed as though one wall was made of jewels. He set his satchel down, knelt, blessed himself, and looked to the image of Saint Miguel in a dazzling ruby robe, poised high upon his rearing horse, aiming his lance to the heart of the beast. The beast in Castile was the illegitimate rule of the cousins. But it was a many-headed monster—another of the heads, simmering hatred against converts. How much easier to fight a dragon than a band of treacherous schemers.

Viçente heard a sound and spun to see Bishop Barrientos in a white robe, pacing down the right aisle. He beckoned to Viçente and disappeared behind a carved wooden partition. Viçente followed to a confessional, a wooden booth for the priest with kneeling benches on either side. He knelt, and heard the bishop's murmured prayers from inside.

Barrientos ceased praying and whispered, "You are in God's presence."

"Father, please bless me. I have sins to confess."

"Proceed, my son, but don't be too solemn."

"Speak softly, Padre. We mustn't be heard."

"We're safe. Loyal Dominicans guard the entrances."

Viçente felt light-headed. He had raised more treasure than he could have hoped, and now his revered bishop was playing a game with him—priest and penitent, the real sport being counterrevolution. "I don't know which to confess first," Viçente said. "I've collected funds and thus deceived my superior, Magistrate Ayala, and—"

"Deception?" the bishop interjected. "Sometimes circumstances demand it."

"Padre, Magistrate Ayala forbids me to act against the Royal Cousins. I agreed to use words, not actions, to support the king."

"Your magistrate would do well to join the king's side while the monarch has need of him. Tell me, son, about these funds you've raised."

The bishop's playful tone encouraged Viçente to mischief. He fingered a bag of coins in his satchel, making them clink. "There's something even more troubling, Bishop. I must also confess the sin of lust."

Barrientos' voice rose. "Wait, one sin at a time."

"Lust for a woman whom I barely know."

"We all have desires, my son. Tell me how much you deceived your magistrate." The bishop chuckled, but his voice was edged with frustration.

"The lust weighs my conscience, Padre. And your letter increased my burden. Tell me—what interesting person has come to Segovia?" Viçente raised his eyes to heaven, praying that it was Francesca.

"You torture me by not answering my query. It's a sin to antagonize Christ's bishop."

It *was* Francesca; Viçente was sure of it and Barrientos was taunting him. He jiggled the coins again. "I confess the transgression. Tell me my penance, and after you name the person who's come, I'll comply."

"You may be damned doubly for desires of the flesh and for torturing a holy man. The visitor is Prince Enrique's aunt, Francesca."

Viçente beamed, though he knew his joy was foolish. He was likely one of Francesca's many flirtations, easily dismissed by such a woman.

Barrientos cleared his throat. "If you seek forgiveness, speak about these funds you've brought for the king."

"I have this satchel, and if there's some good place—"

The metal screen between them swung back, and Barrientos' large head in its white skullcap filled the opening. "Show me, my son."

Startled, Viçente took a sack from his satchel. "This bag contains sixty thousand gold *doblas*. It's heavy." The bishop pulled it in through the window.

"This little one holds diamonds, five rather large and some smaller."

The bishop snatched it. The window clapped shut, and Barrientos' voice chanted in a priestly resonance. "These offerings will please the Lord Jesus. They will help restore our God-given monarchy. I absolve you of your sins and command you stay in the confessional to contemplate until I depart. Then may Jesus bless you further. Amen."

Viçente waited until he heard the chapel doors thump shut before peering around the partition. Near the front of the chapel, a figure in a blue cloak knelt in prayer—a woman or a monk; no other would wear a hood in God's presence. But a monk could not choose blue. The figure seemed slight, the posture regal. It had to be her, but was she lovely, as he remembered, or some fantasy created out of need? He settled behind her, his body tense, blood pounding in his ears. Watching so close, he thought he saw her shoulders tremble.

She made the sign of the cross, slid back in her pew, and turned. "I was praying for a miracle: that you not be a fool like other men."

He laughed, and at the same time, observed her fine forehead and cheeks, the fan of tiny lines by the corners of her eyes, the contour of her shoulder and swell of her breast beneath the blue shawl. His memory had not deceived. "Can we dine together this evening?"

She frowned. "Bishop Barrientos didn't tell you? My king, the king of Aragón and Naples, has ordered us kept apart. If he knew of your presence, Carlo and the soldiers might attack, and that would wound me, too."

She watched him with eyes the color of brown honey, an intimate gaze that thrilled him.

"Why care about me, if men are such fools?"

"When we met last year in the *alcázar*, you treated me like a person, not a bridge to royal power. When the cousins' lout insulted you, you didn't charge after him to avenge your 'honor,' like an impulsive man I knew."

Viçente wondered about that man, but he said, "Small clues, hardly enough to judge me worthy."

She smiled, her eyes never leaving his. "And you're uncomfortable with my compliments—another good quality."

"You may spend too much time with kings and fools."

"Now there's a bad thing about you." She frowned. "Interrupting when I praise you."

"You encourage me with that lovely smile."

She placed a cool, slender hand on his. "We have little time, so I speak plainly. I do encourage you." She stroked the back of his wrist and looked into him with honey eyes. Hunger pulsed in him, as though she stroked the inside of his thigh beneath his breeches. "I'm not sure you have feelings in return," she said.

"I've thought of you often; not just your beauty, but the way you seemed ... sympathetic about the Royal Cousins' abuse, amused by everything we talked about over dinner. You challenged Prince Enrique, the bishop, and me, and you charmed us. You charmed me."

She blushed and looked away. Had he said too much?

"How did you get away from Carlo?" he asked.

"We're staying at Enrique's *alcázar*. You're here at the palace, a fifteen-minute walk, so they've no notion of you. If they inquire, 'her ladyship' is receiving her bath and plans a nap."

"Did you?" he asked. "Take a bath?"

"One of my ladies, Penélope, occupies the tub. I borrowed her shawl, and Prince Enrique's servant escorted me through a passage from the *alcázar* cellar to a path along the cliff and then to this delightful chapel. How surprised I am to find *you* here." Francesca laughed, swung around the end of her pew, and stood. Viçente rose to meet her. "I haven't finished divulging what I like about you," she said. "Do you remember when I joked about *marranos*? Even though my family has harmed converts, you saw the humor in it. You defended me to the bishop. And best of all, when Bishop Barrientos maligned Rome, you defended it. You see past the rubble to things nobler and more romantic." Francesca stepped close and reached toward him.

Viçente took in a quick breath. She brushed fingers across his cheek and turned aside. "You know you can't kiss me in God's house." She took his hand and led him toward the altar. "Bishop Barrientos told me the history of this fascinating little church. The first two alcoves on the side are consecrated to saints Peter and Paul."

"Saints are fine, my lady, but I'd rather learn about your life in Naples."

"Patience, dear man." She held tight to his hand and swiveled, pressing her side against him as they turned. "These two are for the Virgin and Saint Mary Magdalene." She led him toward the back of the church, smiling like a nymph. "Did I leave anything out?"

"These last two niches, but you don't need to ..." In one alcove, Viçente saw a portrait of Moses holding the tablets. The opposite recess lay in shadow.

She led him to the dark corner and faced him. "But I do. It's a curious fact. These two sanctuaries were added during the palace renovation. The rest of the chapel was consecrated years ago, but this chilly spot has never been blessed at all." She shivered as she slipped her hood back and ran a hand beneath her hair, sending a black cascade over her shoulders.

The words, her flowing hair, and her eyes, now magically turned a deep chestnut in the shadows, thrilled him. He wrapped his arms around her and she beamed. He pulled her close and felt her body press into him. She rose on her toes and kissed his cheek. "Another lovely thing about you: you take care when a woman needs protection from the cold."

Viçente took in the scent of spice roses and felt her firm body. He nuzzled his lips into her silky hair, across her cheek, to her mouth. He caressed her shoulders, her waist, the bulge of her buttocks; he would touch every part of her. Better hold back and not frighten her away, but they had only these moments. Ardor kept his mouth exploring hers, though he longed to know her thoughts, her taste in art, details of her solitary moments at home in Italy. He pulled back to look at her, but Francesca pressed moist, insistent lips into his neck. "Do you have a garden at the palace in Naples?" he murmured. A foolish question, but he wanted to know so much. "I picture you wandering among the roses."

She laughed. "Better your hands wander my skin." She set his hand on her breast and rose to kiss him again.

Their mouths opened to each other, her tongue devouring all questions. How could this passionate woman be so confident, yet vulnerable? How little he knew, and so much he wanted. For now, he could only hold her here in this cold corner of the chapel, hold and caress and want her fiercely.

Pounding at the chapel door. She eased back and sighed. "I knew they'd interrupt, but this is *much* too soon." She sulked, then brightened. "How lovely this has been. I really will go take a tub now."

"Can you get away this evening?"

"Alas, no, but you won't be alone. Prince Enrique will entertain my party in the *alcázar* while our bishop keeps you company here in the palace."

"I know so little about you."

"I don't want to leave." Her voice was plaintive and her eyes glistened. She stepped toward the door, paused, and turned back. "This is better, Viçente. If a man knows too much about a woman, he loses interest. And here's something to cheer you—the bishop has granted me solitary time in this chapel every afternoon this week. My prayers could be brief, and I could visit this corner, if a gallant man came to warm me."

PART III

THE DESCENT

—ⱳ—

*And what will it profit our lord and king to pour holy water
on the Jews, calling them our names, "Pedro," or "Pablo,"
while they keep their faith like Akiba or Tarfon ... Know,
Sire, that Judaism is one of the incurable diseases.*

— Solomon Ibn Verga, *Shebet Yehudah*

CHAPTER 20

—ᵐ—

AT FIRST, VIÇENTE THOUGHT HIS feelings absurd, a fifty-three-year-old man infatuated with a woman in her thirties, born of royalty. But after spending secret time together in the prince's chapel each afternoon that week, receiving confidences, kisses, and intimate touches, he could think of nothing else. Her body had drawn him, of course, but what most wound through his thoughts as he rode back toward home were the three times, three scant hours, when they'd foregone the physical to share their tales—hers of kowtowing visitors who courted her pudgy king, pretending he was a delightful host; his about that night in the tavern with Diego. Her joyful hours in her rose garden, his mocking Magistrate Ayala who cared so little about justice but kept Viçente on for some unfathomable reason ... Their conversations kept coming back to him now; she was so joyful and witty that every second delighted, and their parting each afternoon seemed to wound her as much as him.

Arriving at Toledo, Viçente dismissed his guards and rode to the cemetery. Tying Amistad to a fence post, he stepped between the carved pillars and walked along rows of gravestones. Marta's was a simple rectangular stone bearing the details:

Born Marta Ramirez March 28, 1399
Died April 15, 1438
Devoted Wife of Viçente Pérez
Loving Mother of Diego Pérez
Eternal life through Jesus

He knelt and laid a hand on the stone. "I love you, Marta." The words brought tears, as they always did. "I will always love you. If you're watching from heaven, you know that I've met a woman named Francesca. She possesses a sense of humor that matches mine, sympathy for all people ... and such beauty—attributes that remind me of you, can you imagine? Do you see those things in her, too, or am I dreaming?

"I've been so frustrated, losing faith in my ability to accomplish anything against the tides of adversity and hatred. Diego's away, and there's no dear Marta to share my disappointments and praise small victories. Francesca brings hope of something beyond the day's futile efforts. She's younger, of course. Does that make me foolish? You were always good at keeping me from rash actions."

He looked up to the sky. "If you see me, see my pain. Try to understand. Try to forgive. I will come to you in heaven and love you there when it's time, but this life without you has been unbearably long. I need this bit of joy."

Trudging home with Amistad trailing behind, thoughts of Marta turned to introspection about the empty place in his heart, which dissolved to longings for Francesca.

He settled at his desk, took a piece of paper, and dipped quill to ink.

5 May 1444
Lady Francesca
Royal Palace
Naples

I hope you are in good health and high spirits.

A dreary opening for a note to the lovely Francesca, but the letter might pass through the hands and beneath the eyes of her chaperones. He had to write as if he'd met her only that one time.

It seems such a long time since I've seen you, but I send good news. My son, Diego—did I mention him to you? He's following the path I took as a young man. Now finished with his government courses in Salamanca, he goes to Rome to learn church law and church organization. He'll meet other young men studying to become government or church officials and form relationships to enhance his future.

Now I ask humbly for a favor, my lady. If you should go to Rome, could you look in on him? A cheery face would mean a great deal to a young fellow in a strange country. Once you meet Diego, I'm sure you'll want to help him. He's gifted with youthful insights and news from Toledo that might possibly brighten your day.

Perhaps you could introduce Diego to some church officials, and thereby assist this worthy young man?

In any case, I am in your debt for reading this letter and granting your consideration.

Viçente wanted to rip the letter up, but if he started again, he'd still have to write inanities for fear of scribes and censors. Would Francesca think he'd become one of the fools who sought royal favors, or would she recognize his purpose and visit Diego? He added a flowery closing and drew another sheet of paper.

Diego Pérez
Spanish Students' Residence
The Vatican, Rome

My Dearest Son,

Are you settled comfortably in Rome? I miss you even more now that you're further away.

I know you'll study diligently, as always, but please take time to explore Rome and the rich countryside nearby. Enjoy the wine, but not too much. Sample the superb cuisine—I still long for the Italian veal with mushrooms and garlic, even after all these years. Of course you'll admire the women, but remember: our Castilian girls await your return.

I've such warm memories of the night we spent in that tavern in Salamanca. We seemed more like comrades than father and son, and it touched me to feel that way. I fear you had more than your share of brew, for I recall you encouraging me to seek female companionship. I shared your affliction and confided to you about the Lady Francesca.

She resides in Naples. I've written and asked her to seek you out and help you meet church officials. But my request was a ploy.

This must sound odd. How do I explain? First, about her family— she's related to one of the Royal Cousins, the King of Aragón, though I'm not sure precisely how. Her family has been unjust to converts, but she disapproves of their actions.

When I wrote to her, I couldn't be candid for fear her chaperones would intercept the letter. As you must guess by now, I'm fond of her, more fond than I'm comfortable revealing even to you. If she calls on you, tell her that, and ask if there's a way for us to write each other with privacy and without jeopardizing her safety.

Diego, I pledge to visit you within the year, and I plan to see Francesca then, too. Tell her it's my fervent desire to spend time with her—a great deal of time, if she desires it.

Enjoy the Italian life, but please be prudent, and write soon. I love you.

Papa

One more point, son: Arriving back in Toledo, I stopped by your mother's grave. I wanted to explain to her about Francesca, but how can such a thing be told? I only hope that she can understand from her vantage point in heaven.

Their time together had told Viçente more about Francesca's passion than her reliability, but he believed in her with a depth that startled him. He smiled to himself as he took the letters to a trusted priest who'd deliver them to Bishop Barrientos in Segovia for dispatch on to Italy.

CHAPTER 21

—m—

VIÇENTE OPENED HIS OFFICE DOOR and welcomed Raul Castro with a grand gesture. "Have a seat, Señor Castro."

Castro settled in one of the chairs, and Viçente sat behind his desk. "I understand you're doing good work at the city building department."

Castro nodded, looking pleased. "Thank you, First Deputy."

Viçente tried to keep his tone neutral as he said, "I've invited you to discuss an administrative issue."

Castro's smile faded.

Viçente waved a hand. "Nothing significant. I just need to clarify. There are so many rumors about city staff members, and now one about you. Could you have made remarks that sounded as if you're not—not Christian?" He forced himself to give the man a broad grin.

"I wouldn't—" Castro said.

"Maybe something about lies a man tells to survive—raving over the taste of pork to make people believe you eat it."

Castro eyed him. "I might have given the wrong impression. Did that fellow from treasury say ..."

Viçente swallowed his disgust and chuckled. "You understand it's no matter to me if a man's a Jew in his heart, but we have to keep an appearance of Christianity. People want to believe that city employees follow the accepted beliefs."

The man gaped at him, and Viçente lied, "Of course, I protect my workers either way, but still I need to know the truth."

"Then you're ..."

Viçente nodded, hoping the fellow would take him for a vile pretender. "Did you really joke about worshiping a holy bastard? Ha! That's pretty good."

Castro seemed to relax. A sickly smile crossed his lips. "I am a Jew, naturally. Maybe we all are. You understand. It's a shame we have to cover it up."

Viçente stood, his blood running angry in his veins and his heart heavy with disappointment. "I have to dismiss you, Castro. Thank you for your service to the city."

"But—"

"If we allow one pretender, we're all suspect."

"But you said you're—"

"I'm a Catholic, Señor Castro, and I hope some day you'll accept Jesus, too. Please leave before I have to call the guard." He watched Castro depart and dropped into his chair. Anger melted away, replaced by frustrated sorrow. How many had he dismissed this way?

As he looked from his office window this bright June morning at the troubling image of a Toledo mired in church corruption and bigotry, he wondered if he deserved to govern. His efforts came to so little now—forceful suppression of potential violence by his police, counteracting the hateful sermons that promoted it. The royal intrigues disheartened him, too. And yesterday, he'd had to dismiss another clerk, the man now out of work, his family affected. How many impostors were hidden within these walls, employed because of Viçente's favor? Was anyone loyal to any truth? But, as frustrated as he might be, through this office, Viçente had been able to protect so many of his people, the true *conversos*.

"First Deputy." A man stood at his open office door, wearing chaps and holding the wide-brimmed hat of a *caballero*. Viçente beckoned, and the fellow brought him an envelope.

Pedro López de Ayala
Chief Magistrate and Ruler of the Alcázar
City of Toledo

Viçente

Tragedy has befallen us.
Hurry to the hacienda.

P. L. A.

Another of the magistrate's contrived 'emergencies.' How tiring they'd become.

—⟁—

Entering the magistrate's study, Viçente was shocked to see his mentor unshaven and without his patch, his eye socket raw and shriveled, as though someone had jabbed a corkscrew in and twisted out the eye. Ayala paced the Persian carpet, muttering. He stopped beneath the stuffed head of a wild boar near the white stone fireplace and pointed at an armchair. "Sit, goddamn it."

Viçente dropped into the chair and let his attention drift to the boar's head that stared down on Ayala, as if admiring the purity of the magistrate's white hair and slender mustache. "Perhaps, if you tell me what's happened," Viçente said.

Ayala's eye bore into him, and he clenched a fist. "*Perhaps* nothing. There's been a coup. King Juan's free, and Constable Luna raises an army to support him."

At last. Viçente's heart raced, but he sighed in feigned sympathy.

"You've always been clever, First Deputy. Tell me how to protect our position."

"Forgive me, but—"

"Don't say that I shouldn't have supported the Royal Cousins." Ayala strode to a side table, poured brandy into two stubby glasses, and thrust one at Viçente.

"You thought the cousins would give you land."

"*Pendejos* didn't give me horse manure." Ayala grimaced, and for a moment Viçente pitied this reckless fellow who'd treated him well when he'd most needed it.

"Chief Magistrate, there's something I want to say before we argue." Viçente stood and grasped Ayala's hand. "I know it's been difficult having a *converso* first deputy. The cousins wanted you to dismiss me, and I'm grateful you didn't. You let me keep my staff, against their wishes. And you made me your liaison to Enrique."

"You're an able man. You deserved—"

"All over Castile, converts were cast out of positions they deserved. You defended me, even when I defied the cousins' men at Prince Enrique's palace. All of this must have been difficult." Of course, Ayala had acted the fool in challenging his king, had threatened to dismiss Viçente's staff, but it was necessary sometimes to discard a bit of one's pride to gain cooperation.

Ayala gulped his drink and poured another. "I told you to cultivate the prince. Now let's hope you succeeded."

"You guessed, of course, that Enrique and I spoke of restoring King Juan to power."

"*Silence.*" Ayala jerked a fireplace poker from the rack and pointed it at Viçente. "You did none of that. And if you did, I say, stop it now. We'll defeat the king. We have to."

Viçente took a calming breath. "You asked my advice, and I'll give it. Humble yourself to Prince Enrique. Give him ten thousand *doblas* and join his Loyal League."

"Hand a small fortune to that nineteen-year-old pup? Don't be *stupid*. The cousins wouldn't stand for it."

"Shouting isn't a tactic to try on me, Magistrate." Ayala clenched his jaw and glowered as Viçente went on. "The Royal Cousins deceived

Enrique as they did you, but this young prince is wise enough to offer fealty to both Royal Cousins and king. Now both court his favor."

Ayala scowled and banged the poker against the fireplace, sending shards of alabaster careening. But he looked more sullen than furious.

"So many nobles have joined Enrique's league that he holds the balance. If he sides with King Juan, the king will win. If the cousins want his aid, they must give him real power. Either way, if you join him, you gain."

"You think you're an authority on national intrigue." Ayala sneered. "You know only what the boy-prince tells you."

"I know you're in a dilemma of your own making. If you refuse, we'll lose Toledo. You won't have to kiss Enrique's feet, only swear allegiance. If the cousins find out, say the prince has assured you he's on their side."

"*Goddamn it*, Viçente. I sent you to the prince to cultivate him, and you've become one of the royal scoundrels."

"Is that your way of admitting you were wrong?"

A wisp of a smile stirred Ayala's lips. "My protégé thinks he's surpassed me, but your influence depends on my position."

Viçente refused to flinch at the veiled threat of dismissal. "My people and I are grateful for your faith in us."

The magistrate gestured to the decanter on the table. "Have another drink while I cover this hole in my face and get the money from my safe box."

As occasionally happened, when Viçente saw Ayala galloping headlong into folly, the flighty fellow had reigned in and turned to the safer path.

CHAPTER 22

—ɯ—

MARCOS SAT ON A BENCH on the porch of the miserable supply stoe in wretch-ed San Marin, trying to understand why such miseries plagued him. Each morning, he woke in the storeroom to see hams hanging from the ceiling overhead and feel lumpy sacks of grain beneath him. His back ached. He moved to sit and his left leg throbbed, as it did every damned day.

Every night he relived that horror fifteen months ago, when he'd wheeled the barrel from Simancas Castle, run out of control, and cata-pulted toward the river with the cart and its contents hurdling down behind him. The candlesticks, the beef, the body, and the cart failed to smash into him, but when he struck on his left leg, the loud pop pierced his brain. Pain gouged his calf like a burning knife. He longed for death, but death didn't oblige, so he lay on the cold earth, thinking this was God's punishment for failing to rid Toledo of blasphemers. Crawling to the nearby trees, he found a branch for support. Searing spasms shot up his leg with each lurching step, but he struggled to his rooming house, and then Philip helped him escape, back to this bug-infested little town.

The pain had eased over the months, but it always ached, and it prickled his bones as he walked. Without Pérez, he would never have supported King Juan against the Royal Cousins, wouldn't have gone to Simancas Castle that night. Each pang reminded him of his vow: Capture that *marrano* son of a pig who pretended to love Jesus. Pierce Pérez with the sword of Christ's vengeance, over and over and over again, as Marcos was pierced every minute by his wound.

Now, he turned to the sound of a horse galloping toward him and saw the supply store owner draw to a halt, puffing as if he'd run down from his mansion without the steed. The merchant pulled off his wide-brimmed hat, fanned his sweaty, bald head, and grinned down at Marcos. "The king," he gasped. "The king's free."

Marcos jumped up and lightning shot through his leg. "God curse it."

"Don't you support King Juan?"

"God curse it, my leg." Marcos pressed the heel of his hand into his thigh to calm it. "I do support the king ... what of the Royal Cousins' soldiers?"

"They retreat, thank Jesus."

"Loan me a horse and buggy. I go to aid the king."

At last Marcos was back in the seat of power, the royal palace in Valladolid, the walls of his ample chamber decorated with gold fabric and ornate mirrors. Servants brought cheese and fruit juice and prepared a steaming bath. He abhorred the royal gluttony. Still, he ordered buckets of hot water to soak his wounded limb, then dried himself and crawled beneath the feather-filled comforter. He drifted off to sleep, understanding in his soul that this comfort was Christ's way of honoring his loyalty.

He woke to a touch on his shoulder. Philip stood over him, wearing a ruffled purple tunic. Marcos flinched and Philip moved aside, revealing Master Butler Sarmiento in a blousy white shirt and superior frown. Marcos gasped.

Sarmiento stepped close, shaking his head. "We had a plan that night in Simancas. You were to drop the body in the river and take the silver."

Marcos tried to clear the sleep away and think of a reply. The truth—that when he'd shattered his leg, he didn't care if they were all caught and hanged—would obliterate Sarmiento's trust. "The cart you gave me was defective."

Sarmiento shook his head. "Then you were to come back for the other body."

Beside Sarmiento, Philip smirked.

"Philip, get me that chair." The master butler flicked his hand toward the corner, and the courtier slinked in that direction.

Watching Sarmiento bully Philip pleased Marcos, but he had to make it clear; he wouldn't be treated that way. "Didn't Philip tell you? I broke my accursed leg that night. I had to make new plans."

"You?" Sarmiento snapped.

"Master Butler Sarmiento makes the plans, not you." Philip set the chair beside Sarmiento and poked Marcos' elbow. Marcos forced himself to ignore the jab.

Sarmiento chuckled as he sat. "Your plan, if we pretend it was one, worked out only because I sent Philip to your rooming house that next morning to help you escape." Sarmiento winked. "Stop scowling, Counselor. The king's in control, and you sleep on silk."

Marcos pulled himself to a sitting position. "It means nothing until we cast the slime out of Toledo."

"I've broached that issue with the king," Sarmiento said.

"About destroying Viçente Pérez?"

"Hardly. The king's partial to your friend, Pérez, who brought sacks of jewels to aid the counterrevolution."

"Discredit him, Sarmiento. Pérez is a secret Jew."

Sarmiento grinned. "I'll do my part with the king, but we'll need your two hundred fighting men to support the war."

Two hundred. Had Marcos promised so many? *Sangre Pura* numbered less than a hundred. Perhaps they could find other lads who'd fancy a chance to slaughter the king's enemies. But how was he, exiled and destitute, to find them?

He took a slow breath and forced himself to smile.

C H A P T E R 2 3

—⋙—

June-August

HOW MISERABLE THE WAITING. VIÇENTE had written to her so coldly, but he'd had no choice. His hopes for a reply turned to worries, to resignation.

One day in mid-August, he returned home, and Constancia handed him a solitary letter. It bore a woman's handwriting and smelled of spice roses. He rushed to his study.

Viçente,

I am overjoyed!

When I received your letter, I almost tore it up. How impersonal and distant it seemed, but still I held it against my bosom, because it came from you. The paper, touched by you, spoke to my heart, but my pride resisted. Finally, I traveled to meet your son as you asked. He showed me the letter you sent him, and everything came clear. You do care!

I'm here now, in Diego's apartment in Rome. You were right. He's sweet, serious, and charming, like his father. The apartment's simple, with paint peeling from the walls. He lives in two rooms with three other students. One, a bold fellow named Alberto, asks that I send you his regards and his congratulations. I don't want to ask what he means.

Diego seems delighted with his arrangements, cramped and meager as they are. Who can understand the young?

As I told you once, my life in Naples is much freer than when I travel. You can write to me without fear that the letter will be destroyed. Still, you'd best keep your most passionate thoughts for our time together. I hope you have those feelings. I certainly do.

I long to see you! Hurry to Italy to visit Diego and me!

Fondly,
Francesca

Viçente's heart soared. He breathed in her scent, reread the letter, and pressed the page to his cheek.

—ᴍ—

Had it been six months since his magical time with Francesca, here in Segovia?

He'd received several letters now, filled with news of Italy, tender sentiments and hints of desire. The most recent included open mention of passionate kisses, of feeling his ribs with her fingers, of his sweet earnestness regarding his son. Was she somehow certain that no one would intercept those letters, or did life in a protected palace eliminate all cares? Every day and every night, her magic embraced him, especially here, near the scene of their private moments.

When a servant brought Viçente's breakfast to his room in Prince Enrique's *alcázar*, another servant followed, bearing armor. "My lord, you're to arm yourself and meet the prince in the courtyard."

Viçente thanked the man, but rather than feeling grateful, he was mystified and nervous. At dinner the previous night, the prince had accepted Magistrate Ayala into his Loyal League with a surprising lack of argument. Enrique and Pacheco had spoken of the coming war, but had made no mention of Viçente fighting in it.

He pulled his sword from its scabbard and felt its weight. He jabbed at the air—awkward but exhilarating. He jabbed again, thinking back to more of last night's conversation—Prince Enrique insisting that, if Ayala joined his league, it obligated Viçente as well, reminding Viçente that Segovia's *conversos* had remained employed despite the Royal Cousins' demands.

Implications, obligations, and heavy armor. Viçente strapped it on as the bells sounded ten times. He slid his sword into its sheath and carried the shield and helmet out to the main courtyard. A two-level arcade towered over three sides of the yard, marble arches below and square pillars on high, supporting a dark tile roof. In a duel, the arches could act as shelter or trap an unwary swordsman.

He stepped from under the portico and saw Bishop Lope de Barrientos leaning on the railing above, his broad chest draped in a sackcloth frock, a brown skullcap covering all but a fringe of white hair. The bishop waved and Viçente called out, "Bishop, when did you arrive?"

"This morning, my son. Have you heard of the royal decree?"

"Not so soon." Enrique sauntered into the courtyard with Juan Pacheco. "Men duel before they discuss." The prince slashed his sword at an imaginary opponent.

Viçente gave a half-hearted chuckle. "My debt to you involves combat?"

"Your debt to the king." The prince spun and pointed his blade toward Pacheco, who jumped back, laughing.

"You look out of shape, Viçente," Pacheco said. "Enrique and I have already bloodied our swords capturing the cit-citadel at Peñafiel on the Río Duero."

"Viçente, you've bragged of your swordsmanship as a young man," Enrique said. "It's time for a test."

Viçente felt his pulse quicken as he pulled on the constricting helmet. The faint wind that swirled in the courtyard whispered to him, and he thought it might be saying, *You're quite old for this game.* As he bent to grasp his shield, the sound of scraping armor grated in his ears.

At the center of the yard, Enrique challenged with his blade, and Viçente met it with his own.

Enrique pressed his sword against Viçente's. "Viçente, how would you respond if the king dismissed Ayala and offered you Toledo?"

Viçente looked for a smirk but saw none. "My magistrate joined your league. He merits your protection." The idea was at once absurd, repugnant, and intriguing. But he had no time to consider it with his sword crossed against the prince's. Perhaps that was Enrique's aim; distract him with a tantalizing dream and take advantage. *Focus!*

His arm ached, but he held steady. The pressure dissolved. Enrique slipped his blade beneath and slapped Viçente's sword from the other side. The weapon flew and clattered on the cobblestones. Viçente felt blood rise to his foolish face.

Enrique looked him in the eye. "Tell your one-eyed *cabrón* of a magistrate to beg clemency of King Juan. Do it now. Do it humbly, lest he lose Toledo, and perhaps his head." The prince picked up Viçente's sword and examined it. "Toledan artisans make fine blades, best wielded by true hands." He handed Viçente his weapon. "I may be too young for you. Duel Pacheco. At least he's half your age."

Viçente clutched the weapon, humiliated but feeling a touch of the old exhilaration from his university days. Pacheco came forward, poking his weapon at Viçente's chest. Viçente deflected and retreated a pace. Pacheco was gauging him, the first jab easy. Now he slashed upward toward the top of Viçente's head. Viçente ducked, and it swished over.

Bishop Barrientos called down, "Careful, Pacheco."

Juan Pacheco grinned. "Don't dodge. Block and attack." He swung at Viçente's head again. Viçente parried, heard an angry clang. A shock ran through his forearm. Pacheco attacked again. Viçente defended with his shield, almost falling. Pacheco whacked the flat of his sword against Viçente's chest armor. "Ha."

Viçente's heart beat wildly. At the side, he saw Enrique cupping his hands around his mouth to shout, "Don't go too far, Juan. Viçente isn't used to this."

"N-Nonsense. His skills are coming back." Pacheco rested the tip of his sword on the paving stones and eyed Viçente. "Ready?"

Viçente gulped air, reminding himself to watch his opponent's eyes. He raised his weapon, and Pacheco swung at Viçente's head again. Viçente blocked, withdrew a pace, and circled right, hearing Enrique call out, "Too predictable, Pacheco. Go for some other body part. Stab him in the toe." Pacheco slashed toward Viçente's left side, and Viçente blocked. Pacheco spun and hacked from the right. Viçente defended, alternating between sword and shield, backing to his right with each assault, avoiding the trapping pillars.

The rhythm grew familiar—clanging metal, sunlight glinting on steel, the camaraderie of friends testing each other. Struggling to conserve energy, Viçente looked for an opportunity to strike, but Pacheco was quick. Viçente blocked another onslaught, arms aching, lungs burning, feeling the urge to surrender. *No. Find a ploy to catch him up.*

Pacheco attacked, and Viçente stepped left this time, drawing his opponent close, hastening his next strike. He blocked and let his sword quiver in his hand, as if he were about to lose it. Pacheco slashed down, but Viçente jerked the weapon back. Pacheco's sword clanged on the paving stones. Viçente tromped the side of the blade with his boot. Pacheco teetered, and Viçente rammed him with his shield. The prince's favorite tumbled. Viçente pinned his chest with a foot. Panting, he pointed his blade at Pacheco's throat. Pacheco watched the wavering sword with wide eyes.

Viçente gasped, feeling the old elation. "Now, Enrique, can I learn the bishop's news?"

The prince howled with laughter. "After you dispatch Pacheco. I think he means to kill you, Juan."

Viçente laughed, too, and sheathed his sword, keeping his foot on Pacheco's chest. Enrique took Viçente's shield. "Come inside. Lope will explain."

Barrientos called down to him. "Viçente, my son, let Juan Pacheco up."

———✲✲✲———

They sat around a circular table on the upper gallery overlooking the courtyard. Enrique sipped from a mug of juice and said, "Your debt to my father is more than you know, Viçente. You must fight for him."

"I'm no warrior. I disarmed Pacheco by trickery ... And what of the king's debt to me? I handed him a fortune."

"You're a symbol to the *conversos*. We fight for their freedom, too."

"You didn't care about us when you helped the cousins strip our rights." Viçente swigged juice, hoping it would calm his fluttering stomach.

"I kept my converts working, as you asked. Now the king restores their pride. Bishop, tell him about the *cedula*."

Barrientos waited for a maid to put a small cake on his plate and then set both hands on the table. "It's a marvelous proclamation, though you'll think me vain to say. It took me a week to write, with Constable Luna demanding changes all the time."

Viçente's pulse quickened. "When will it take effect? Will *conversos* be returned to their offices?"

Barrientos nodded happily. "The document speaks of God's ecstasy at the conversion of each Jew to Christianity, promising converts equality and affirming their dignity."

Enrique stopped chewing and pointed at him. "The king risks much with this. He angers noble houses, and they'll subvert him. To recruit converts for his army, we'll spread the word: Viçente Pérez will fight beside King Juan. You'll enlist a force from Toledo, and others will come from all of Castile."

Viçente swallowed hard, his thrill at the wonderful news turning to a knot of worry. He'd taken Toledo's merchants' gold; how could he demand their sons as well? "Then your motivation isn't to protect *conversos*, but to gain warriors."

"*Conversos* get what they seek with the *cedula*," Enrique said. "It's meaningless without soldiers to defend the kingdom."

A chill entered the base of Viçente's spine and seeped upward. There was no way to avoid this duty.

"*Goddamn it, no*," Ayala shouted. A stuffed antelope's head beside the hacienda's fireplace watched over him, indifferent to the magistrate's anger.

Ayala wasn't stupid, so his refusal to meet the king stemmed from stubbornness. Viçente sat back in his chair. "Give in or lose Toledo."

Ayala jabbed at his cheek beneath the black eye patch. "I gave you ten thousand *doblas* to join the prince's League. Now you want me to bow down to that fool king and despicable constable. Don't just occupy that chair looking bored, Viçente. I'm talking to you."

Viçente's heart should have been racing. Instead, he imagined himself in the antelope's place, no longer concerned with trivialities. He owed this composure to Francesca; knowing her and longing to go to her freed him. "Things have changed since you gave me the funds," he lied. "The prince is firmly with King Juan now. The cousins' position is untenable."

"You tricked me to get the money."

"A small sum well expended if it gains the king's forgiveness."

Ayala glared, his eye dark and malevolent. "Forgiveness! Damn it. If I meet the king, what will he demand?"

Viçente's hand shook, but only a little, as he poured a glass of water. "Would a pledge of support stick in your throat?"

"What else, Deputy?"

"If there's a battle, and there might not be—"

"Of course there will. The king's soldiers capture one after another of the cousins' fortresses, as the cousins muster troops. I'm seventy. You expect me to fight for the *pendejos?*"

"Say what the king wants to hear. Isn't that how the cousins persuaded you to join their coup?"

Ayala went to Valladolid to meet the king late that month. He traveled with only four guardsmen for protection and returned alive, but taciturn. He shut himself in his castle at Guadamur, and Viçente left him to boil in a stew of his own obstinacy.

CHAPTER 24

—𝓂—

VIÇENTE VISITED SEGOVIA OFTEN THOSE next months, sparring with Prince Enrique, Juan Pacheco, and some of the prince's men, advancing from dueling to mounted combat, training both Amistad and himself to face charging warriors. Back home in Toledo, he had armor fashioned for Amistad's face and fore-chest. As the blacksmith toiled, Viçente lifted the heavy forge tools over his head again and again, strengthening his limbs, becoming more fit than he'd been in decades.

March 1445
My Dear Lady Francesca,
   How long since we've seen each other, and how terribly I yearn to travel to your side!
   Surely, you're unhappy with me, because I promised to visit, and I've been delayed so often, but critical affairs prevent me. I'm sure you're aware of the crisis here in Castile, and

Viçente took out another piece of paper and recopied the beginning, omitting the 'crisis in Castile.' He couldn't mention fighting against the Royal Cousins. Francesca was related to them and lived at one of their palaces. No matter how much he trusted her—he *did* trust her—there would be spies who could open his letters and reseal them artfully.

"You're a fool," he muttered. "She's beautiful, enchanting, *simpática*, passionate, but you hardly know her." He remembered the feel of her those days in the prince's chapel, mouth open to his, lips pressing, firm breasts, thighs moving against him, the scent of spice roses.

He took up his quill and wrote of his life—his frustration at the lack of progress on the cathedral construction, the excellent new Moorish inn where they could dine together on honeyed lamb and couscous, if she visited Toledo. He told her of spring flowers sprouting in the square near his home.

And then he decided to take a chance. Her letters to him had become so ardent lately, and she swore that her chaperone never saw his. He was tired of writing frivolities.

> *I notice these things, Francesca, since meeting you. The scent of your letters brings thoughts of you strolling in your rose garden. I see the stars more clearly. I watch the moon rise and imagine I'm in Naples, sharing these sensations with you.*
>
> *I shouldn't let myself feel this way, shouldn't put it on paper, but when you write of embracing me and spending long afternoons together in the Italian sun, how can I refrain? I promise to come to you. We will sit together in your garden, sip wine, and hold each other close.*
>
> *If it takes months before I'm able, they'll be months filled with joyous dreams.*
>
> *Affectionately,*
> *Viçente*

At least he'd written something of his feelings. If her chaperones read the letter, let them be shocked or irate or titillated.

But how would *she* react? Would she see him as foolish to feel so much or timid to say so little after her bolder declarations? His heart and her letters told him she shared the folly. He hoped these words would suffice.

—w—

His saddlebags were packed with changes of clothing, knives, punches, and leather straps for saddle repair, paper and lead for writing. Two burlap sacks held his shield and chain mail and Amistad's new armor.

In his sleep, mounted men in spiked helmets screamed battle cries and charged, swinging swords and clubs. Blades hacked into his body, and he bolted upright to find himself snared in sweaty bedclothes. Could he wield a sword intended to kill? He'd have to, or he'd die and never see his son again, never touch Francesca or know her passion. He needed to dream of killing rather than dying, had to fight for the dignity of converts, and then, no matter what, he'd go to her.

A courier brought the summons: Viçente and his recruits were to join Prince Enrique's soldiers at Segovia. Viçente sent runners to fifty *converso* homes. The heads of these households had pledged their swords, their sons, or their servants to King Juan. Viçente's housekeeper added dried meat, biscuits, and cheese to his travel bags. Viçente filled the water skins. The groom saddled Amistad and secured the armor and provisions to a packhorse.

The sun shone bright in a cloudless sky as Viçente and his hundred volunteers crossed the bridge over the Río Tajo and climbed the bluff. Hooves thudded on dry earth, raising a troubling cacophony, as if the hearts of all those younger men pulsed inside his chest. They traversed hills of ripe wheat and olive groves, arroyos strewn with wild grasses and black boulders. Ahead in the distance, he saw the hazy forms of the Montes de Toledo.

They traveled south, away from their destination, on a mission of little hope.

Viçente spotted the great granite tower and six turrets of Ayala's castle, Guadamur. The mid-level battlement came into view with its rounded towers and finally the lowest outer walls, brown-and-gray rock set in mortar. He saw armed men between the pointed merlons atop the lowest wall, and a man with a yellow eye patch holding a cup in his hand. Ayala wore a dressing gown the color of heavy cream and a scowl of slate.

"You've heard the news?" Viçente shouted.

"I told you. I'll not fight for this king."

"You're too aged to lead these men of Toledo?" Viçente gestured to his comrades, regretting the words.

"Say what you wish." Ayala yawned.

"I'd like to enter and speak with you."

Ayala gave an impatient swipe of the hand.

Viçente rode alone to the gate, dismounted, and led Amistad past the sentries into the courtyard. Ayala waited at the base of the stairs.

As Viçente embraced him, he hoped Ayala couldn't detect his trembling. He stepped back. "Magistrate, I beg you to come with us." Ayala didn't reply, and Viçente added, "At least send a token force to support our king."

"King Juan's acts are contrived by that mongrel, Luna. I'll send no one."

"You could lose everything."

Ayala's face reddened and his eye turned fierce. "'No one' includes you. Stay to manage Toledo, or lose your post, Deputy."

Viçente had hated his role more often than not since Ayala had betrayed the sovereign, but all Castilians knew of the one *converso* who still administered a major city. *First deputy* had been his vocation, his love, and his strength. It had allowed him to save people's lives and sustain their families and it had disappointed so often. "My post is with the king."

The ends of Ayala's thin white mustache darted upward but stopped short of a smile. "I might reconsider if King Juan triumphs."

"How benevolent." Viçente's breakfast churned in his stomach as he turned from the man who'd lent him Toledo's reigns. He felt as if his father had beguiled him, and finally he'd come to see the deception ... again.

—m—

Viçente and his warriors joined the prince's troops and traveled north on dirt roads through simple brown-brick villages—Santa Maria la Real, Montuenga, San Cristobal. The land leveled to colorless, low hills, wheat fields, and empty spaces with occasional clusters of round-topped pines, lonely ranches surrounded by poplars. At each village, armed recruits joined in, most on foot with scant armor and shovels, scythes, or pitchforks for weapons.

Coming together with the king's forces near the hamlet of Olmedo on a plateau above the Río Adaja, they found a hundred tents already standing. Soldiers raised new enclosures for the nobles and officers, including one for Viçente and Barrientos, but most wrapped themselves in tight-woven fabric and slept on open ground. Each evening, the smoke of thirty blazing fires covered them with ash and filled their nostrils with aromas of roasting game. Each morning, men practiced battle skills in a vacant field. Viçente encouraged his recruits and felt touched by the way their bright faces looked up to him, the way they called him 'sir.' As he lay on his cot at night, he realized these young men gave him more than respect. They offered hope and certainty. True and loyal *conversos* still fought for their principles and would fight in coming generations. True converts—he'd wondered lately how many there were.

He prayed that these bold lads fared well in battle. But if they did, how would life treat them? If Ayala still governed Toledo and appointed a new first deputy, would that man hire converts? Would he stand for their rights? And what of the Jews?

Ayala had hinted that Viçente might regain his position. How much would he have to humble himself to reclaim it?

A pavilion tent, large enough for a meeting of a hundred men, was erected near one end of the field. Heads of noble households arrived, the magistrates and commanders of every important city, summoned by the king for the Cortes de Olmedo. Viçente stayed away but prayed that Magistrate Ayala possessed the good sense to attend.

CHAPTER 25

—⁓—

MARCOS WHIPPED THE HORSE, DRIVING the carriage along the rutted road, his forty mounted men galloping behind. Lousy nag and run-down buggy, borrowed from San Marin's storekeeper. Marcos passed pathetic groups of men walking to battle with farm tools for weapons. Sweat streamed down his sides, but if he stopped to drink, dust and the damned flies would descend.

He cursed the flies and the *pendejos* that boasted of bravery as they joined *Sangre Pura*, only to hide when it was time to fight.

Smoke rose ahead. The battle? If they arrived during combat, he could claim he'd recruited the promised two hundred men, but scores had died for the cause. He whipped the beast, careening around a bend. A field of tents spread before him, campfires smoldering, men carrying pots, others dragging tree limbs. He let the carriage slow, but his mind whirred on. An idea evolved. He'd tell Sarmiento that most of the recruits had been held up back in Toledo. But, damn it, why were these imaginary warriors delayed?

Marcos reached Sarmiento's encampment and found dozens of men clustered near the master butler's oversized tent. He heard Sarmiento's booming voice and stepped to the circle of soldiers, all wearing tan tunics with no sleeves. Marcos nudged his way among them.

"Back off, you skinny clod," a big man muttered.

Marcos pushed past, catching a glimpse of Sarmiento sitting on a stump.

The men around him reeked of sweat and filth. Did they all sleep with mules? Marcos eased between two others, and he saw recognition enter Sarmiento's blue eyes.

"Ah, Marcos, my solicitor." The king's butler spread his arms in a welcoming gesture. "Rather slow to arrive, aren't you?"

"I had business to attend."

"Señor García's business is more urgent than war." Sarmiento laughed and his soldiers chuckled.

If Marcos said he'd been rounding up warriors, Sarmiento would ask how many. "As you know, Master Butler, Toledo's leaders practice treason, and I struggle to defeat them."

Sarmiento grinned. "You've laid siege to the city?" The soldiers guffawed.

One of the louts jabbed Marcos in the ribs, but he ignored it. "Toledo's Chief Magistrate Ayala and his *marrano*, Viçente Pérez, love their Jews, so I organized a force to stay in Toledo and harass them. Now Ayala and Pérez keep their guardsmen home, protecting rabbis." An inspiration! This one lie excused Marcos' tardiness and his lack of recruits.

Sarmiento sat on his stump, rubbing his chin and smirking. He'd know part of it was false, but Marcos' tale supported Sarmiento's ambition to depose Ayala.

"Counselor, aside from leaving these valiant men behind, you've brought some warriors, have you not?"

"Certainly, Master Butler."

"Then we welcome you."

CHAPTER 26

—m—

May 19, 1445, outside Olmedo

WARRIORS CLOGGED THE CLEARINGS BETWEEN pine trees by the bluff and overflowed onto the bare hills to the rear. The Río Adaja and the cliff beyond were cloaked in fog, but Viçente could imagine who was there.

He marveled at the variety surrounding him: mounted soldiers in full armor from helmet to toe-guard, with sword and lance—including a thousand sent by the king of Portugal. Men in chest armor and short breeches with crossbows and quivers of arrows; farmers grasping pitchforks and scythes, wearing leather vests or quilted jackets and narrow-brimmed cloth hats. Their mounts ranged from mules to nags to fine armored stallions. The world smelled of dust and sweat, worn leather, and manure. The odor attached to the soldiers and drifted in the morning breeze. But nowhere among the multitude did Viçente see any sign that Magistrate Ayala had changed his mind and brought a force from Toledo.

He looked toward King Juan and Prince Enrique, sitting atop their steeds thirty paces away. Their stallions were fitted with metal face-plates and draped in thick leather mantles. Nearby, knights held gold flags bearing the king's red lion and castle. Viçente recognized Juan Pacheco and the powerful figure of Alvaro de Luna, the king's constable. The king and Luna conferred and pointed at various parts of the army. King and prince alone sported red plumes on their helmets.

The prince gestured to Viçente. He climbed down from Amistad and made his way between the mounted soldiers, hearing the snorting of the horses and the murmur of a dozen conversations. The king stared down with vivid blue eyes, steel helmet covering all but his thin face and a bit of light brown curly hair.

Enrique bore a strong resemblance to his father but for the bridge of his nose, broad and uneven, beside the king's perfect nobility. "Father, this is Toledo's first deputy, Viçente Pérez."

"My lord." Viçente bowed as low as his chain mail allowed. The steel clinked.

"Don Viçente." King Juan's voice sounded higher pitched than Viçente recalled. "I remember you from a meeting you attended with your magistrate years ago. Was it the Cortes of Valladolid? You recall, Alvaro?"

Constable Luna cleared his throat. "I recall Señor Pérez making a point, and Magistrate Ayala interrupting to claim the argument as his own."

"You honor me," Viçente said. "Magistrate Ayala's far more articulate than I."

"And you're more diplomatic," Luna countered.

"And now you've become illustrious," King Juan added. "The only convert who managed a city when my cousins usurped the throne."

Viçente felt the blush of pride, pride and shame. The king might know he'd since lost his post.

King Juan leaned forward and spoke confidentially. "You raised substantial sums on my behalf. We pardoned your chief magistrate out of gratitude to you." The monarch straightened and his horse stomped. "I didn't see Chief Magistrate Ayala at the Cortes yesterday."

"He came," Luna said. "Signed the loyalty oath and marched out."

Thank God. Ayala had given them a token. But where was he now?

King Juan grimaced. "Without offering me the courtesy of a greeting."

"The magistrate grows older, Your Highness, he—" Viçente stopped mid-sentence, realizing how foolish it seemed, defending the man who'd put him out of office.

"If you were going to say he left to take a piss, don't bother," Luna snapped. "He and his men are not on this bluff today."

"There are old men here, and priests," the king said. "There would be small boys, if we allowed. The gray-headed ones, like your magistrate, ride in the rear or sit upon this high ground to observe. When it's time for war, you rally for your country. You say no words but those that praise the king." The king was right. Signing the paper and leaving before battle was indefensible.

"Ayala's judgment is the thing that's decrepit." Viçente turned to the source of this comment, an energetic-looking fellow on a gray stallion just beyond Enrique. He spoke a polished baritone and held his helmet in the crook of his arm, leaving his wavy brown hair perfectly arranged. "Ayala still supports the betrayers."

"He's right," Enrique said. "As I told you, Father, my friend, Viçente Pérez, is best suited to govern Toledo."

"Viçente has m-managed the city for years," Pacheco added. "Ayala received the credit for his good work."

The stranger chortled. "My lord, your son and his assistant may not understand that some are bred to rule while others are fortunate to serve. That's why you have experienced nobles to advise you."

Ayala's power was slipping away, and Viçente's birth didn't qualify him to assume it. He tried to keep his expression steady as he asked, "Which noble advisor are you?"

"Pedro Sarmiento, at your service." The man inclined his head toward Viçente, while keeping his eyes on the king. "Steadfast master butler to his majesty."

CHAPTER 27

—⚊⚊—

MARCOS HADN'T MOUNTED A HORSE since his wounding in Simancas, hadn't worn armor in a decade, but he ignored his throbbing leg and climbed upon the smelly nag. He and his men joined Sarmiento's troops. The others dismounted, but Marcos' sorry limb had grown numb. There was no point rousing it.

Sarmiento rode up and halted near the soldiers. "Platoon leaders, get your men together. Marcos, round up your sheepherders. Ready to march in five minutes. We are honored to fight between king and prince."

Leather scrunched as men climbed into saddles. Lances and battle-axes pierced the air. Marcos' mind went back to that night in the Simancas Castle, when he and Sarmiento had killed the enemies, the weight of the soldier's body, sticky, warm blood running down his chest. Sarmiento's look of approval.

A distant bugle sounded.

"All right, brave sons of God, follow me." Sarmiento slapped his reigns against his horse's neck and led them on a meandering path between groups of foot soldiers. At the edge of the bluff, Marcos caught a glimpse of the fog-shrouded river valley and the hint of the ridge on the opposite side.

To his left, he spotted the king's banners, falling slack on their poles in the morning calm. Seventy paces right, he noticed a patch of scarlet—that fancy *marrano*-loving bishop who hobnobbed in royal circles. Near the bishop, he saw the young prince, wearing a red plume on his helmet. The bishop spoke with a man, and as the man turned, Marcos' heart raced. It was the *marrano*, he and the unholy bishop groveling their way to princely favor. "Sarmiento," he called. "Look there. It's Pérez."

"I know." Sarmiento seemed indifferent. Didn't he understand?

Marcos kneed his horse closer to Sarmiento. He watched the *marrano* strap on a helmet, a different shape from the soldiers' head protectors. "This is our chance to be rid of the pile of *mierda*."

"It's *my* opportunity to lead men in battle. A few minutes ago, King Juan was all but offering Pérez the keys to Toledo."

Marcos stifled an urge to whip Sarmiento with his reigns. "You're the king's confidant, damn it. Use your influence."

"If you'd brought more fighting men, I'd be in a better position."

"I told you what happened."

"You told a tale about leaving your men in Toledo to harass Jews. How many men would that take? Your *Sangre Pura* isn't half of what you told me."

"That's Pérez, the enemy." Marcos would remind him of Pérez's humiliation of the vicar, but Sarmiento would only mock him again.

"To me, he's just another *marrano*."

"If the king considers him to run Toledo, he's your rival. But an accident might occur in battle ..."

"Can you make better work of it than you did disposing those corpses from Simancas?"

"Again, you give me the thankless job, Master Butler."

"I've given you no job, Counselor. I will lead my men to slaughter the foe. If you and I both succeed, I'll rule Toledo, and you'll be my second."

At last! Sarmiento had pledged it. Marcos maneuvered his mount through the soldiers to Sancho, the wool carter, who was already wiping sweat from his bald head. "Sancho, select your three best men."

Sancho ordered three forward—lads of low birth, who wore only leather vests for protection. "They're able horsemen and well tested. This one was on the mission that took the mute."

Marcos addressed the largest. "Take a sword from that man." He pointed to a fellow near the back of the squad. "Which is the fastest rider?"

Sancho nodded to a lanky lad.

"Get him a ball and chain," Marcos ordered.

Sancho obtained the weapon from one of the men and gave it to the lad.

"You'll be the first to reach our enemy," Marcos said. "Bash him in the head."

CHAPTER 28

—ʍ—

VIÇENTE SAT ATOP AMISTAD, FACING his Toledan recruits. They looked up to him with eager eyes as he shouted, "Men, we fight for our king today, the king who restores our rights. We fight for our people, to show we are strong and willing, honorable and pious." He paused, looking from man to man, feeling pride and fear for each of them and discomfort at what he needed to say. "Prince Enrique has asked me to ride with him, so I won't be beside you in battle, but I *will* be with you. Pray with me now. Pray to Jesus for bravery. Pray that all will behold our valor and grant us the respect of equals. Bring honor to your families, and survive to return home. Pray for me, as I pray for you. Let God guide your hand. May he keep you safe."

As the men prayed silently, he thought he should say more before sending men to their fates. He yearned to fight among them, but riding with the prince did more to protect them in a world of royal politics.

They joined the prince's force on the army's right shoulder, the farthest northern flank at the bluff's edge. He maneuvered Amistad between Bishop Lope de Barrientos and Juan Pacheco. The bishop wore a scarlet robe and held a staff topped with a golden cross. "Fine morning for victory, Viçente."

"Then damn it, let's begin. My apologies, Bishop." Viçente buckled on his helmet.

A bugle sounded from their left. The king's banners advanced above the throng. A dozen horns blared along the line.

"*God be with you,*" Barrientos shouted. "*God be with you all.*"

Prince Enrique led them forward, mounted men followed by archers and foot soldiers, moving single file down trails to the river bottom. Viçente followed Prince Enrique, the sounds of clomping hooves, creaking leather, and clanking metal echoing inside his cramped helmet. He felt the sureness of his horse and the damp mist on his face, watched the white backsides of the prince's stallion jolting downward, dry summer grass and prickly-looking bushes brushing against his horse's flanks and his boots. His horse snorted and drool spattered his leggings. He prayed to Jesus that he be allowed to live to see his son and Francesca, and then he prayed for the king's victory and for his soul.

The fog had drifted high enough that he could see the river bottom, the opposite ridge, and some trees to the right. The opposing army—hundreds of cavalry and scores of foot soldiers—descended in human streams down that bluff. Navarre's red banners with golden chains waved.

The enemy formed ranks by the base of their cliff as Castile's force moved forward to the muddy stream. Archers and foot soldiers formed up in knots between the cavalry. Someone shouted, "Do you see any troops from Aragón?" All down the line, the shout rose, and replies of "No. No. No. No." Viçente's pulse beat faster. If the third cousin, King of Aragón—Francesca's king—hadn't sent troops, King Juan should prevail. But the rows of enemy knights stretched so far. Their armor, their spears and battle-axes, gleamed dark and deadly. Viçente felt their might in the marrow of his bones.

And they waited.

Prince Enrique shouted to the archers, "Loose your arrows as soon as the enemy comes in range. Shoot as long as you can, but not so long that you skewer us in the buttocks." Murmurs and guffaws rose from the men.

The rattling of weapons subsided. For long moments, there was only the gurgling of the stream, as if God was speaking.

Horns blared from the opposite side. The enemy cavalry unsheathed their swords, swung them in the air, and charged. Men all around pulled their blades and roared as Castilian bugles answered, and Viçente's heart pounded. He screamed, sliced his sword through the air, and whipped his reigns across Amistad's rump. They hurtled into the river, water splashing all around.

Viçente's horse galloped out of the stream and up the other bank. Cold water trickled down his legs inside the armor as he wondered, *what had God meant to say?*

A buzzing sound, like bees darting overhead—the archers had unleashed.

"*Cover up, men,*" someone shouted. Viçente rode low, protecting his stallion's long neck with his armor, clutching his shield above his head.

Thumping, like heavy rain spattering—enemy arrows showered down. One careened off the shoulder of his chain mail.

Men screamed. Horses balled. A brown mare reared, arrow sticking in her hindquarters, the rider thrown. Soldiers on their beasts veered past. Ahead, the prince's red plume bobbed. Arrows pelted them again. The first of the enemy soldiers charged into their cavalry to the left, metal smashing metal, swearing, hollering, screaming, balling.

No more arrows. Enemy soldiers hurdled toward him. That one—galloping, furious, lance aimed at Viçente's face. *Oh, God.* He ducked, raised his shield to fend off. A terrible blow struck the shield and the sound made his head throb. The enemy's horse grazed by. Viçente was past him. Another mounted soldier broke between the riders, sword flying at Viçente's head. He blocked, swung his weapon wildly. Gripping the stallion between his thighs. Swinging, defending, clanging, metal screaming. Big, clumsy man; too strong. *Fend off. Jab at the face, drive again. Force him off.* The enemy leaned back. Viçente thrust his blade up under the man's arm. The soldier screamed, toppled into the mass of men and horses. Between the beasts, Viçente saw only a bloody arm.

But he was off balance, leaning over the enemy's horse. He let his shield drop, caught the other horse's saddle and shoved, straining, grasping with his thighs. Thank God, he was up.

He looked for enemy foot soldiers, but saw none. But there, a mounted foe dueled with one of theirs—black helmet, tan horse. Pacheco. Pacheco's horse wheeled, and Viçente saw a foot soldier try to get close enough to stab Pacheco. Pacheco swung at the mounted soldier then the man on foot. Viçente kicked Amistad forward.

The foot soldier whirled to meet him. Viçente bent low, aimed his sword at the space above the man's leather vest. Amistad jouncing. *Concentrate. Steady sword.* The enemy swung his blade, but Viçente's weapon grazed by it and struck. The man's neck burst in a red geyser. Viçente turned back to see Pacheco dispatch his mounted attacker and glance around. "Well struck, Viçente. Where are the rest of the *cabrones?*"

Gasping for breath, lungs burning, Viçente turned to see dozens of enemy soldiers running back toward the bluff. Behind him, one of the Castilian farmers jabbed a bloody pitchfork into a wounded man's face. The farmer looked up and saluted Viçente with a nod and a gap-toothed grin. But there were few bodies on the ground. The king's foot soldiers were looking around for someone to fight.

From his left came a banging, screaming, whinnying commotion. A torrent of enemy soldiers charged to the center, trying for King Juan. As he turned, Viçente caught a movement in the corner of his eye— enemy cavalry circling hundreds of paces away beyond those clusters of trees in the river bottom, heading to cross the stream, scores of them, moving around the right flank to attack the king from behind. "Pacheco, where's Enrique?"

Back toward the center, Viçente saw the red plume as Enrique raised his sword and slashed an enemy foot soldier's arm.

Bile rose in his throat, but he swallowed and screamed, "*Stop, Enrique!*" He urged his stallion towards the prince with Pacheco just behind. Enrique turned his horse. "*They're going around!*" Viçente shouted.

Enrique gaped at him and then to the place where Viçente pointed, the enemy crossing the river. "Intercept them!" The prince spurred his horse and raced past Viçente, leading his men past the dead and wounded warriors, back to the river.

CHAPTER 29

—ɷ—

MARCOS AND THE *SANGRE PURA* fighters descended to the river plain and halted well back from the prince's force. In the distance, he picked out Prince Enrique by his red plume, and near the prince, the *marrano* with his unusual helmet.

Sancho wiped sweat from his forehead with a dirty cloth. "We should move in close."

"*Fool,*" Marcos snapped. "We lie back to await opportunity."

"More chances when swords fly," Sancho muttered.

The wool carter was too dumb to comprehend; in battle, blades would fly at them, too.

Foot soldiers and archers passed them on their way to the front. Not far behind, Marcos spotted the red-robed bishop, riding his gray mare closer to the battle. Bugles blared. Ahead, the king's cavalry unsheathed swords and charged through the river. Archers let fly their arrows, and Marcos felt his heart soar. Foot soldiers ran after the horsemen. Mounted knights sped forward from opposite sides, crashing into each other, roiling like mad dogs eating one another alive, a splendid, bloody sight.

Years ago in Pérez' office, the *marrano* had turned Pero, Christ's vicar, into a quivering, pleading ass. He'd used the *Guardia Civil* to protect the evil ones. Today God would have revenge.

He led his men closer to the battle. Ahead, the fighting ebbed. Enemy soldiers fled up the bluff. Masses of fighters rushed toward the center. Marcos saw the prince with his plumed helmet, and the *marrano,* peering side to side and then galloping toward the prince. "Sancho, you see him?"

"Aye."

The prince, the *marrano,* and a troop of soldiers galloped back now, crossing the river, coming toward Marcos and his *Sangre Pura* men. He clutched his sword handle.

The prince's men veered to his right and Marcos saw that the *marrano* was behind, still coming out of the river. A pulsing rage drove Marcos' heart. "Quick! Follow along the base of this hill. When you get close, charge down at him." His men turned their horses, and he called after them, "Cripple him with the ball, but keep him alive." He kicked his nag and the beast moved forward as Sancho and the others galloped ahead.

The *Sangre Pura* mounts had better footing and moved faster than the prince's force near the river. And then—God be blessed—the *marrano* cut away from the stream, alone and closer to the *Sangre Pura.* "*See him!*" Marcos shouted. "*Move!*"

—⚊—

Viçente spurred Amistad, trying to catch up with the prince's soldiers. He urged the stallion into the river upstream of his comrades, striving to cut the distance. But the water here rose to the horse's chest, flowing over Viçente's feet. The stallion drove against the flow and emerged, still further back from the prince's force. Viçente cut away from the river behind a stand of trees—better footing for Amistad—bounding forward, galloping behind the thicket.

Sounds of riders coming—reinforcements. Someone shouted Viçente's name. One of his Toledan recruits? "*Pérez.*" Viçente slowed to look. "*Pérez.*" The man wore a leather vest—not one of the Toledans, but yelling his name. Two more riders behind the first, and another.

"We're losing time," Viçente shouted. "Follow me."

The newcomer raced toward him from higher ground, about to collide. Viçente yanked his reigns and Amistad reared. The stranger swung something on a post—a ball and chain. The sphere hurtled toward him.

No shield. He ducked, but it came fast. A deafening crack, ripping pain. He thudded onto the dirt, ears ringing, throbbing. *My head, is it there?* No sword, helmet caved in. The stranger dismounted and charged, his sword flying at Viçente's face. He rolled. A thump beside him. Dirt sprayed.

"I'm for the king," he shouted. Echoes bounced inside his head, but only ringing came from his ears. He dodged.

The man turned and barreled at him, fury blazing in his dark eyes. Another man dismounted, moving to block Viçente's escape.

"Don't you understand? I'm for the king." He took a half step and fell to his knees. *Keep moving. Crawl.* A sword slashed. Searing agony in his shoulder, a scream—whose scream? Red fire burning.

Ahead, Marcos' men flew at the *marrano*. He beat the horse with his fist. The beast snorted and trotted on.

Something bright caught his eye—the stout bishop, his scarlet robe flapping, riding toward the *marrano*. Marcos let out a yelp of joy. Once again the Lord was showing him the way. They would take both of them down.

But from the heart of the battle, more royal soldiers had peeled off, galloping toward the *marrano* and the *Sangre Pura. God Jesus, let them turn away.*

The first man struck Pérez with the ball. The *marrano* toppled and rolled on the ground, but the soldiers were closer than he'd thought. Scant time to kill the enemies and flee.

Two of Marcos' fighters attacked. The third dismounted. Sancho was almost there. But now the cursed red bishop galloped from behind the trees, straight into them, staff raised high, gold cross gleaming.

A *Sangre Pura* thrust his sword at Pérez. The bishop swung the cross like a mallet. Blood spurted. The *Sangre Pura* fell.

Sancho yanked his horse up short and looked to Marcos. "It's a God bless-ed priest," he shouted.

A dozen royal soldiers were closing on the fight. Marcos yanked the nag to a halt. His chest tightened and tears came to his eyes. "*Kill Pérez!* Kill the damned bishop. And get out." He turned his beast and jammed his boot into its ribs, searching the hillside for a path to escape.

CHAPTER 30

HAS THERE BEEN A BATTLE? *Or just a dream. Someone had cut a man's throat open.* Floating in the air above him, smiling sadly, a lovely woman—Francesca. She whispered. "Why do you fight? I fear for you." He should tell her he hadn't been in a battle, had only dreamt of one, but speech didn't come.

Familiar voices, the sound of a crackling fire. He strained to open an eye and saw only sand. So he was lying facedown. A patch of scarlet, like his last vision before the blackness. The scarlet rippled and swayed like cloth. He reached for it. Pain ripped his shoulder. He gasped.

"Viçente, my son, don't move. You've been injured."

The scarlet cloth spread on the sand. Hands appeared and a head—white hair and a pudgy face. Bishop Barrientos leaned on the ground and scrutinized him.

"Bishop." The sound of Viçente's voice ignited a fire that ran from the crown of his head into his eyes. "I heard Francesca."

"You were imagining, son." Barrientos pressed a damp cloth to his forehead.

"The battle?"

"The king prevailed," Barrientos said.

It hurt to speak, but Viçente had to know. "My young men from Toledo?"

"They're here," Barrientos said.

"They proved their honor, didn't they?"

Barrientos nodded.

"Make sure the king knows."

"Don Viçente, it's Luis." A pair of brown boots stepped into view. Luis knelt and his face appeared near the bishop's. "They killed the baker's son, Tomás. Two others were injured, not so badly as you. But we bloodied our share." Luis seemed too cheerful for one who'd lost a comrade.

Barrientos frowned. "The men who attacked you?"

"Enemy soldiers."

"No, from our side," the bishop said.

Viçente remembered a rider heaving a metal ball at him. "The battle's won. Now I can go to her. Help me up, Luis. I can't seem to—"

Barrientos touched his arm. "We must sear your shoulder wound. And one side of your head is swollen like a melon. I had to cut one of them down to save you."

"You, Bishop?"

A hiss like water thrown into a hot kettle.

"I'll pray, while the soldiers close your wound." The bishop pushed himself up and disappeared.

"Be strong, Don Viçente," Luis said. The young man held Viçente's arm as other lads pressed him to the ground. A loud crackling sound. His shoulder convulsed, burned, exploded in agony. He smelled the stench of burning flesh—his flesh—and then it ended.

Burning, piercing, scraping agony, the smell of dusty hay, movement, sunlight broiling his face, creaking wood, the grating of wheels on earth. He was a person ... Viçente Pérez, traveling in a wagon. He heard others groaning. Each bump tormented his shoulder and head. He was tossed in the air and thudded down, and then it ended.

Dreaming, remembering, wandering in and out of the void—

Viçente's sixteenth birthday. They tried to tempt him with another lamb dinner. He stepped to the side table, savoring the scent of garlic and meat, wanting a taste, but needing to defy them. His mother took a plate from the table, spooned on potatoes, carrots, and lamb. The year before, he'd taken his plate to another room. That's what they'd expect him to do. His father, sitting at his place—not dressed in finery, but in a plain brown shirt—gave a sorrowful grimace. "Stay and eat with us, son." His mother—"Please, Vicentito." Father—"It's been three years, son. Even if you can't forgive, at least we could talk." He needed them for subsistence but not company, shouldn't even be living here. His stomach turning over, leaving the plate on the sideboard, running into the street and away.

A hot, dull ache filled his head. Fever blazed inside him … no sound, no movement, no warmth from the sun. He fell asleep and woke to tapping footsteps, the whisper of cloth against cloth, the feeling that someone was bending over him. Footsteps moving away, the room fading.

Standing at the altar, Marta lovely in the lacy white veil. Seeing Mother at the back of the church, crying, crying for so many reasons. He yearned to go to her—to hug or to denounce? Turning away, he tried to pretend that only his bride mattered.

Viçente, a young city official living with Marta. Mother at the door, begging him. Viçente relented. He followed her through those familiar streets to the house of his birth. Father lay in his casket in the parlor. Grieving, crying, stomach boiling with bile, wanting to pound the body with his fists, wanting to lay his head on the dead man's chest and say, 'I love you.' Joining with Marta in the deceit that next day at the Christian funeral in Santo Tomé. Not attending would imply what Viçente, an ambitious city employee, could not afford—a hint of family discord, a hint that something stank in his heritage. The benign look on the priest's face, his white robe and skull cap, the scent of candles and incense, all of it scorching his senses.

He opened his eyes to see a bare plastered ceiling and a plain wall. He turned his head and a lightning bolt spewed hot fire inside his skull. Minutes passed. His vision cleared. A different patch of wall and a simple wooden cross. Jesus was here to comfort him.

The tapping returned. Something wet touched his lips. Cool water dripped into his throat. A cover lifted from his body. A moist cloth grazed his chest. The cloth ran up his side, stroked down the arm. He jumped. The moisture enveloped his scrotum. His eyes shot open to see a wrinkled old monk in a brown frock gazing down with compassion and curiosity.

—m—

"Viçente?"

He opened his eyes to see Prince Enrique frowning. He tried to say 'Enrique,' but his mouth was dry.

The prince produced a terra cotta cup, slid a hand under Viçente's head, and raised it. His head and shoulder throbbed, but he sipped.

"Don't try to speak. You've been in delirium, so let me explain. We're in the Priory of San Martín, near my palace. After they seared the wound, your shoulder blew up like a huge red beet. My physicians drained it many times, and it's begun to heal. It's June. The Royal Cousins fled Castile, but they're mustering for another try. I hope to convince my father to make you chief magistrate, but he's considering that rascal, Sarmiento."

How could Enrique even imagine that Viçente, a commoner, a *converso*, could be appointed? But if he allowed himself to imagine— governing the great city, protecting all its citizens without interference … no. He'd still be a *converso*, and therefore suspect. Viçente preferred not to admit it, but Ayala had not only restrained his efforts, but also shielded him from the Old Christians' resentment. "He should retain Ayala."

Enrique touched his hand. "Ayala and Sarmiento are knaves, and both will fail. I'll secure the position for you, and you'll be indebted to me."

Viçente moistened his lips, swallowed, and said, "Wisdom, Enrique, you must learn to see more than one side. Ayala—"

"You're a wounded hero, and I can make my father favor you." Enrique's voice was husky, and as he bent close, Viçente saw moisture shimmer in his eyes. "Have another drink, my friend. I'm sorry I let this happen to you."

—⁂—

Bishop Barrientos led four young monks in brown, hooded robes into the room. The four helped Viçente raise head and shoulders so they could mound pillows behind. They carried the bed through a long hall and out to a courtyard.

He drew in the crisp, fresh air. Birds chirped. The breeze whispered. He heard water trickling. Sunlight too bright—Viçente shielded his eyes with his good arm and squinted, discovering a gallery of perfect arches that ran around a yard, and there—the source of the trickling— a Moorish fountain. From its center, a copper shaft rose to a pinnacle, with a ball near the top from which four spigots dribbled water to a metal bowl, cascading then to a stone basin. Simple and lovely.

Viçente tried to push himself up, winced, and eased back. Barrientos touched his arm. "Be gentle with yourself." The bishop turned at the sound of voices approaching. "It seems you have a visitor, my son."

Diego strode to him and kissed his forehead, then cupped Viçente's cheek in a hand. "What have they done to you, Papa?" Diego pulled a stool close and sat.

Barrientos beamed. "You'll do more for his healing than any medicine our physicians conjure. I'll leave you to it."

"Papa, on my journey here, the ship stopped in Naples."

"You saw Francesca?"

"In the grand sitting room of King Alfonso's palace." Diego shook his head. "A surly chaperone named Carlo watched over us."

"Is she furious with me for fighting?"

"Far more worried and confused." Diego took an envelope from his pouch. "She sent this."

Viçente took the packet and sniffed the scent of spice roses, but he couldn't read the writing. "It's blurred. Did it get wet?"

Diego stood and looked over Viçente's shoulder. "It says clearly 'To my Darling Viçente.'"

"But I ..." Viçente looked at his son and back to the letter. "This is the first time I've been out of my dim room. My eyes aren't used to the light." Viçente broke the wax seal and ripped it open, then held it out to his son. "Please."

Diego unfolded it to read.

"Dearest Viçente,

"Bishop Barrientos wrote to tell me the terrible news. How sad I am for your wounds, for your pain, for missing you, for the thought of men killing each other and for the death of my cousin who fought against you."

Viçente took a long breath, relieved by Francesca's sympathetic words.

"Her cousin?" Diego asked.

"Prince Enrique told me. One of the Royal Cousins, the master of Santiago, was injured in the battle. His wound festered and killed him."

Diego nodded and went on.

"Bishop Barrientos wrote that you feared my letters would be read by palace spies, so you dared not write of your plans to fight. I try to accept this, but the notion persists, the feeling that you didn't trust me. The feeling makes me want to weep.

"*So many of the ones I loved have lost themselves to war. How miserably I sob for them and now for you!*

"*I would run to you, but my king, Alfonso, forbids me. He commands my guards and chaperones and he will not relent. I would write about the beauty of Italy and urge you to recover and come to me. But I can't allow myself to think of life's pleasures while I'm filled with lethal questions. Does your shoulder heal? Are you able to walk? Can you come, or do you still wish to? Are they holding your funeral Mass as I write?*

"*I wait in anguish for this news.*

"*With love,*
"*Francesca*"

Diego shifted the pages. "She wrote that before I came, but she added this while I was with her."

"*Diego has come, and his visit cheers me. Do you know how much he resembles you? Now that this letter will travel in trusted hands, I'm free to be candid. I feel a passion for you that I haven't known in years. I know a lady shouldn't write these words, and I must be mad to feel this way, but my desire grows in your absence. Since those tender moments in the chapel, I've longed to write about kissing and touching you and divulging our secret dreams to one another. Please come as soon as you can. Love me, dearest. Prove that I am right to hold you dear.*"

Diego paused and looked away, but Viçente caught the smirk on his lips. "You can read the rest to me later." He savored her words and her love and the stirring in his loins that gave him hope of recovery. But he and Francesca knew each other so little and cared so much. When he found her in Italy, would she take him into her arms or recoil at the sight of his wounds? And who were the loves she mentioned?

CHAPTER 31

—ɯ—

Valladolid

MARCOS LOATHED THIS ROOM, THIS soft bed in King Juan's palace, the coffered wooden ceiling painted crimson with swirling leaves of green and gold. The artists had been sons of Muslim dogs. Ornate ceilings, baths prepared in a man's bedchamber, dining in an elegant hall with courtiers and ladies. Frivolous.

He washed his face in the basin, thinking of the weaklings who governed this land. Ayala had refused to fight for the king two months ago. Yet he still ruled Toledo, while Marcos and Sarmiento waited like curs for scraps from his majesty's table. He strode out through the hall of mirrors to the meeting room where he and Sarmiento took breakfast. The master butler was lounging at the mahogany table, wearing a blousy white shirt, shaved and groomed to perfection, a half-eaten roll and chunks of cheese on his plate.

"Can't you even arrive on time to breakfast?" Sarmiento scowled. "Luna will be here at any moment."

Marcos took a sugared roll from the basket and poured tea into a porcelain cup. "I thought Luna hated you. Now he's bestowing a private audience?"

"As usual, you have it turned around. I hate Luna, but I treat him as my brilliant benefactor."

"You grovel before them all," Marcos observed.

"We wouldn't have this problem if you'd killed Pérez."

"If it wasn't for me, that *marrano* would be sleeping in Toledo's *alcázar*, Jews dancing in Cathedral Square."

Sarmiento speared a cube of cheese on a knife and waved it. "*Marranos* promote Luna's power and pay him tribute money. In his presence, we'll respect them."

"Christ. You want me to act the whore, too."

"We're all whores here. Accept it or get out."

The door creaked open and Luna stepped in. His graying brown hair fell to his shirt collar. Balding at the temples, Luna's straight nose and hollow cheeks made him look austere, but he wore the knowing smile of authority and the cashmere of prosperity. Today's jacket was a high-collared Oriental, sapphire blue. Luna took a chair. Sarmiento handed his knife, with the cheese still on it, to Marcos and poured tea for Luna.

"The king agrees," Luna said.

Marcos pressed the knife against the bottom of the table, cheese dropping onto his trouser leg.

Sarmiento regarded Luna with narrowed eyes. "To appoint me chief magistrate?"

"Your ambition becomes you, Master Butler, but King Juan hasn't chosen yet."

"Agrees to what then?"

"He *will* cast Magistrate Ayala aside. We just haven't chosen the means."

"Don't you execute traitors?" Marcos asked.

"Wait, Marcos." Sarmiento shook his head. "We must trust Constable Luna's judgment."

Luna glanced at Marcos, pulled a raisin off one of the rolls, and stuck it in his mouth. "Señor García, you fail to grasp the subtleties of governing. No matter what wrongs Ayala committed, he's head of a prominent family. Castile's nobles would resent a harsh resolution."

Marcos felt blood rise to his face. He jammed the knife into the bottom of the table and tried to match Luna's tone. "That sounds … judicious."

Sarmiento frowned at Marcos and sprang to his feet. "This means Ayala's posts in Toledo will be available. I stand before you, a loyal officer of the king, a war hero who mortally wounded one of the Royal Cousins in battle."

Luna chuckled. "Thirty men claim to have slain that cousin."

"I'm the one." Sarmiento pointed to his chest. "I drove him off his horse with my lance. I deserve the king's beneficence."

The constable smirked. "Haven't you heard? The cousin who was master of Santiago died from a festering wound to his hand. And we have a true hero to consider, Viçente Pérez, who averted disaster and who yet lies wounded."

Marcos jabbed the knife upward so hard the table quivered. Sarmiento and Luna eyed him. "Why consider a mongrel for the position?" Marcos said. "Even Ayala threw him out."

Luna compressed his lips in a look of impatience. "Señor Pérez is admired by his people. He raised substantial funds for the war."

Sarmiento winked at Luna. "Make me magistrate, and I'll increase Toledo's contribution to your estate."

"Pérez might as well," Luna said.

Marcos slapped the knife down on the table. "Constable Luna, Viçente Pérez and Magistrate Ayala plotted with the Royal Cousins."

"You challenge me a bit too much, Señor García. Prince Enrique assures us of Viçente Pérez' loyalty. And here's an amusing fact." Luna's gaze danced from Marcos to Sarmiento and back. "The prince favors Pérez to control Toledo, and opposes you, Sarmiento." Luna sipped his tea and poked a finger toward Marcos. "Now, in case you misunderstand, be aware that we value our *converso* supporters."

The *pendejo*. The enemy! Luna was the enemy. Marcos clenched his fists beneath the table and took two long breaths before speaking. "That's wise, Constable Luna. *Conversos* play an important role." He almost retched on the words, but he continued. "Still, Pérez is mortally wounded. Everyone would understand if the king appointed another."

Luna tore his roll in half, plucked a raisin from the center, and examined it. "They'd accept Señor Pérez' appointment, in the unlikely occurrence of a recovery."

Marcos looked to Sarmiento, but the fool placidly scrutinized the tabletop. As usual, it was left to Marcos. "I mean no disrespect, Constable, but how long will you and the king wait for this son of a Jew to either die or hobble into the Toledo *alcázar* and take control?"

To Marcos' surprise, Luna burst out laughing.

—ɯ—

In the morning, Viçente asked two monks to support him as he stood. His head felt like bursting, and he retched on the red tile floor of his room, but the next day they helped him take several steps. By the following week, he was walking with Diego along rectory corridors, skimming fingers along the wall for balance, stretching his muscles, forcing himself upright. Soon he walked unaided.

At night he dreamed of Francesca, but he woke to ponder Prince Enrique's tantalizing offer—Toledo. The prince had first mentioned it casually, then more seriously, and now Enrique had gone to the king to press the matter. Viçente hadn't encouraged him, but he hadn't refused. If the king offered, what did duty demand? What did the pain in his shoulder and in his head and in his heart require? He'd gone to war feeling like a young man—foolish conceit— and come back crippled and discouraged. Must he be a slave to this imaginary thing called 'justice?' To his fellow *conversos*?

But what would it feel like to govern again, to fully control the city's fate, without an overlord? Perhaps not very good. Without Ayala's restrictions and protection, he'd have to really decide how far to go to protect the Jews. He'd be a ready target for *Sangre Pura* and the vicar.

One morning he found Bishop Barrientos seated with Diego in armchairs beneath the courtyard arcade. Viçente eased into a chair and addressed the bishop. "You must know that the king might grant me Toledo."

Barrientos nodded. "Enrique asked me to encourage you."

"You observe the royal intrigues, Bishop. Castile is weak and immoral. Nobles trample people for power while the impotent king looks on. Do positions like chief magistrate serve anything more than our arrogance?"

"Don't say that, Papa," Diego blurted. "Now that I've studied to become like you, you can't declare governing futile."

"Not for you, son." How was Viçente to explain? "You're young. Over your lifetime, perhaps—"

"You made a difference in Toledo, Papa. You protected everyone, even Jews. You organized it all and employed the best men to govern." Diego spoke with startling intensity, and his pride pleased Viçente.

"I don't think I have the will anymore."

"Tell him, Bishop," Diego said. "His injuries make him timid."

Barrientos wagged a finger. "Viçente, God demands that we strive for the righteous." The cleric scrutinized Viçente and his look softened. "But don't do this for Prince Enrique or for your son."

"Mightn't God judge us for simpler things?" Viçente said. "Like respecting others or loving a woman?"

"You made a difference, Papa. You governed for the common good."

Barrientos chuckled. "Your father's not thinking of service, young man, but of the lady. Your desire overwhelms your senses, Viçente. Take time to consider. Let Jesus reveal the path."

Viçente didn't need time, but his son did, and he'd already spoken to Jesus. "As you said, Bishop, it's not just Francesca. How many false Christians was I forced to dismiss from their jobs? How hard did I fight for the king, who speaks noble words about protecting converts but vacillates between action and indecision? I can't move this one arm. Shall I give another? And if I help to build a cathedral, how pleased should I be when denunciations echo there for me and my people?"

He shook his head. "If I choose her and not this damned duty, how can I explain to my headstrong son and power-hungry prince?"

"You can't, because it's a mistake," Diego said.

Barrientos leaned toward Diego and grasped his hand. "You've been away, so you haven't witnessed your father's discontent with the political intrigues that brought us war. If you saw him blessed with happiness, wouldn't it please you?"

Diego opened his mouth to speak, but shook his head and halted.

"Your son will accept your decision," Barrientos said. "Enrique won't. For him, love is a new mistress to warm the space beneath his blanket. Duty is to his next new castle that earns tribute for his treasury."

"That's another reason, Padre," Viçente said. "If Enrique puts me in power, he'll demand far too much of my soul."

—⟋⟍—

No matter whether Viçente sat in light or shade or surrounded himself with lit candles, he couldn't make out the words of Francesca's letters. The bishop gave him a magnifying lens and said it was normal for a man his age. He kept trying to read without it, holding the letters at arm's length, but could decipher few of the characters.

Enrique strode into the priory dining room one day, interrupting Viçente's breakfast. The prince, well tanned, wearing a calfskin vest over his blue tunic, summoned him for a carriage ride. They rolled past the old cathedral, down the long, gradual slope to the *alcázar*. As they reached the narrow gorge that protected the castle and stepped out of the carriage, Viçente heard moans. Looking over the stone wall, he saw three large brown bears standing on hind legs on the chasm floor. Smaller ones lurked nearby. The prince gestured to a soldier atop the tower, who shouted, "The prince will feed the beasts." Bears growled and clawed the rocks.

Two soldiers wheeled a cart across the drawbridge and settled it near Enrique. "Join me in the sport, Viçente." He lifted a crate of apples from the cart. Viçente took two apples before Enrique tipped the crate over the wall, sending fruit flying into the gorge. The bears caught a few and the rest splattered on the ground. The larger beasts chased the others away, and Viçente tossed his apples to those lesser animals. Enrique said, "You're recovering, my friend."

"I feel alive, thank Jesus, but not sturdy."

"Do you remember my nineteenth birthday, walking with Pacheco by the river?"

"You wore a paper castle on your head." Viçente chuckled, picturing Enrique with his drunken, watery eyes, flattened nose, and his arm draped around Juan Pacheco.

"We defended you from the Royal Cousins' spies."

"The cousins' men had reason. We spent that afternoon conniving against their masters."

Enrique's blue eyes blazed. "Pacheco and I risked much for you. Now my father indulges me by awaiting your recovery. We made my father king again because we crave power, and now you'll play a role. Every day I await word that you're ready to govern Toledo, to approach my father for the right."

Viçente looked down at the bears standing on hind legs, begging. "Power was your reason. Mine was *conversos'* rights."

"You'll forfeit if you delay." Enrique dumped a tub of vegetable scraps over the side without looking down.

"I can't accept, not any time soon."

"Damn it, stop playing the invalid." The prince yanked Viçente's arm, sending a spasm through his shoulder. "If you can take a carriage across Segovia, you can ride to Valladolid."

"Be content, Prince. You've gained great influence with your father."

"When he's comfortably in control, he'll scorn my counsel." Enrique paced to the drawbridge and turned back. "I must have might to enforce my will. I must have you in Toledo."

Of course, Enrique's support didn't involve friendship or confidence in Viçente's ability, or anything close to morality. "If you labor against your father, conspiracies will paralyze our land. You do this for vanity? For power? I don't want to be part of that."

Enrique scooped a mound of meat scraps from the cart and heaved them into the chasm. The bears snarled, but neither man looked down. "These beasts understand, Viçente—strength sustains. You resist out of devotion to Magistrate Ayala?"

"No, Enrique. This is personal." Viçente felt a grin tip up the ends of his lips. It didn't arrive solely at the thought of going to Francesca, or of freedom from the burden of governing, or the idea of denying Enrique's whims this one time, but all three together. He fought it back, but too late.

"*It's a woman.*" Enrique bellowed. "Why didn't you say so? Have her and be chief magistrate. Have a score of them."

"I'll be voyaging to Italy."

"Italy? You know an Italian woman?" Enrique's mouth dropped open. "My aunt, Francesca. Viçente, you're mad."

"It's much more than that, Enrique. I have to get away. For once in my life, I'm following a nonsensical impulse."

Enrique glanced around as if searching for something. "The women in my family are deformed, you know. Did I tell you about my wife? You'd go to my father and tell him a woman is more important than duty?"

"I don't seek the king's blessing."

"*Coward.*" Enrique charged Viçente, his face red, eyes bulging. He poked a finger into Viçente's chest. "Goddamn it, I sponsored you, and now you make me a fool. I *order* you. Report to your king."

Viçente stepped back and swallowed to control his churning stomach. "No, Enrique. I gather my strength for the voyage to Naples."

The prince shoved him. Viçente fell back, sprawling on the paving stones, stifling a cry at the spasm shooting from his back up into his skull. Enrique pulled out his sword, grimaced, and rammed it back into its sheath. He seized a hunk of meat from the cart and hurled it onto Viçente's chest. "Eat this, Viçente. You're one of the beasts—the kind with feathers on your tail." Enrique whirled and crossed the drawbridge to his fortress.

The young man, his friend. Viçente longed to call after him, but he lay there, smarting from his pain. He was squandering what influence he had and now perhaps this affection. His yearning for Francesca—how irreparably it changed his life.

But he wasn't choosing this only for her. He truly wasn't.

CHAPTER 33

—⚉—

BACK IN TOLEDO, VIÇENTE PREPARED for the journey to Italy.

After Constancia departed one evening, he bolted the door and stepped into the kitchen. He pried up the floor panel beneath a cupboard, removed four bricks, and brought out two metal boxes. From the first, he took a sack of gold coins. On an impulse, from the second container he removed the leather-wrapped parcel bound in thick twine. In his study, he poured a glass of Madeira and untied the packet. Years before, that night at Gonzalo's home, Rabbi Benjamin had insisted he take this testament. Viçente had ignored it ever since, but tonight irritation surrendered to curiosity. As a Christian, he cherished the words of the Savior in the newer scriptures. As a convert, he avoided this older text.

Inside the book, he saw a drawing of Adam looking with the love and lust of mankind into Eve's eyes. The serpent lurked, but the lovers saw only desire. Viçente sat transfixed, feeling a bond with Adam but fearing the serpent that could entwine a man's heart. Turning pages, the odd ancient script on the left side, Hebrew, brought thoughts of the rabbi, Viçente's parents, and forebears he'd never known, a lineage bewitched by falsehood. He ran a finger over the Latin on the right side, then continued to another picture—in crimson, green, and golden yellow, Noah rode high above the flood in his ark, surrounded by beasts. Viçente smiled.

Half a sack of gold would suffice for his journey, but why did he feel the urge to bring this old Bible? If his relationship with Francesca flowered, he might give her the testament, but would she want such a book, exquisite as it might be? What had the rabbi said? That it was his most precious possession, and it was certainly the most unique Viçente could offer. But how would her protector, the monarch of Naples and Aragón, look upon the gift from a man of his ancestry?

The impulse was absurd, he knew, but since his wounding, absurdities often made the most sense.

After returning a portion of the gold, he sealed the hiding place. He sipped the last of his Madeira, considering the dangers of his journey. He was no longer first deputy, with city guards to accompany him. His thoughts returned to Gonzalo. The master builder had nephews in the *Guardia Civil*, and he employed brawny young men in his construction crews.

—ɯ—

The door swung open and Gonzalo held out his hand. "Welcome, First Deputy. How long has it been?" The builder appeared as he had before—dark features, the black-and-gray goatee, and that quiet, sure look.

"Too long, Don Gonzalo."

"Such a terrible evening that was after the mute was murdered." Gonzalo shook his head and led Viçente inside. The plain room, too, seemed familiar, but somehow changed. He settled on the settee and Gonzalo took a chair. On the table between them sat a decanter of pomegranate juice, goblets, and plates with olives, flat bread, and dates stuffed with roasted partridge. Gonzalo poured juice. "I don't suppose you've come to tell me the Vicar will finally pay for his crime."

"I'm sorry. No."

"Too bad, but I've accepted that truth. If this is a friendly call, I'm honored."

Viçente chuckled and glanced at the picture of a Moorish archway on the wall. "Actually, I seek lads to accompany me on a journey."

"I'll happily arrange it, as long as you don't offer money."

Viçente took a stuffed date. "I can afford it."

"And I refuse payment. You remember my daughter, Ramona? She was married last year. That couldn't have happened if the mute hadn't saved her from that priest. You risked your position for the mute, and I swore to honor you for it."

How odd it was for Gonzalo to abide by an oath based on such meandering logic, even after Viçente's failure to capture the killer. "I merely sought justice," Viçente said.

"Señor Pérez, my people have been Christian for generations, but we abide by a code still more ancient. You must allow me this favor, which honors Samuel's memory and Rabbi Benjamin's wishes."

"With gratitude, Don Gonzalo."

They shared the savory morsels, sipped juice, and spoke of Gonzalo's children and Viçente's son, Diego, who planned to seek a position with the king's administrators in Valladolid. Then Viçente headed home to prepare for the journey.

—⊗—

He sat with Gonzalo's nephews, Nacio and Jaime, on the verandah of a rooming house by the harbor in Cartagena, at the southeastern edge of Castile. Down in the harbor, men rowed brightly colored fishing boats with high, curved prows to the wharves, unloaded, and made way for other vessels. On the docks, workmen in canvas jackets took crates from the boatmen. As they dumped the cargo into carts, silver fish fins glittered in the sunlight. Dock men wheeled the carts away and returned for more.

He inhaled salt air and, with it, a deep breath of freedom.

On his last visit to Cartagena, he'd been twenty-three, returning from his studies in Rome, idealistic and eager to begin his government career and to return to his sweetheart, Marta. So little he'd known of life's pain, of loss and grief, of treachery and malevolence, of this body's frailty.

His companions sipped from goblets of malt and watched the fishing boats. Nacio gestured toward the two-masted ship at the end of the quay. "Are you certain you don't need protection on the ship? We'd be happy to travel on with you."

Viçente laughed. "The crew will take care of me. You two can go on home." But as he spoke, Viçente felt for the gold coins sewed into his jacket and reached to touch the valise beneath his chair.

"Señor Pérez, please excuse this impertinence, but you saw how they watched as we rode through those small towns, a wealthy man and his guards. Men are covetous, always seeking a chance to steal what you possess." Nacio assessed Viçente with reluctant eyes. "Your ship will stop in other ports."

"Mallorca and Sardinia, before I arrive in Naples."

"Mallorca and Sardinia are full of scoundrels and thieves. We two can fight them off." Nacio punched the air with his fists.

Perhaps it was a good idea, but Viçente had imposed too much on Gonzalo's kindness. "The captain will protect my valuables."

"I'm reluctant, Señor Pérez, because I must now mention your ancestry," Nacio said. "It puts you more in danger."

"What?" Viçente's pulse pounded in his throat. He stood and glared.

Nacio fidgeted as Jaime murmured, "We saw the strange Bible in your satchel."

"You go through my belongings like robbers, and then try to scare me so I'll take you along?"

Nacio's mouth dropped open and his eyes moistened. "Please. We would never offend. Our uncle respects you most highly."

"It was not right of us," his brother added. "But we saw the way you watched over it and thought you might be in danger because you carried some treasure."

"Seeing the language of Jews in that book, we worry still more," Nacio said. "What if the ship captain discovers it?"

Viçente stared at them, realizing they were right. If robbers ambushed him along the way and found the book, they'd quietly slit his throat or quarter him publicly in the town square. Viçente took a glass of malt, told them he would appreciate their continued company, and settled back in his chair.

Watching the boats in the harbor, the warm sun lured him back to reverie—Cartagena, this portal to new life dreams. Was this another spring of opportunity? Or a futile attempt to snatch back his youth? He knew so little of Francesca, hadn't seen her in two years. Still he craved her company, cherished the thought of her, and ached with the lust of a sailor to bed her.

CHAPTER 34

—◊—

SATISFACTION. WAS THAT THE PECULIAR feeling that lightened Marcos' chest? Or just the brawn of the brown gelding beneath him as he rode near the head of a force over a hundred strong. Beside him, Master Butler Sarmiento kept pace on his gray stallion. Ahead, only a half-dozen soldiers separated them from King Juan, ruler of Castile, in his gold embroidered cloak and fur-lined crown. Pedro Sarmiento had procured this mount for Marcos from the royal stables, procured for himself the appointments of high magistrate, warden of the *alcázar* and commander of Toledo's city gates.

As they descended from the pine forest to the Río Alberche, Marcos spotted a citadel on a high bluff. "Escalona," Sarmiento said. "Luna's stronghold."

Closing in along the river, the enormous castle loomed. But now what monstrosities loped down the hill toward them? Two horrific beasts, one bearing a rider in a crimson, flat-topped hat with a tassel. Camels. Marcos had seen them years ago at a carnival. The rider was visible now: Alvaro de Luna, grinning. The column halted. Luna advanced to greet the king, who dismounted. The second camel dropped to the ground. The creature brayed like a donkey from hell as the king mounted. It rose, jerking the monarch to and fro. Luna maneuvered his beast close and handed the king another hat. The monarch tossed his crown to a servant and put the stupid thing on.

Cackling like oafs, Luna and King Juan led them up a broad curving trail beneath high arches, across a drawbridge, and onto a parade ground within the fortress. Stairs from the yard climbed to a viewing gallery that ran across the top of one wall. This citadel was mightier, its yard larger, than King Juan's at Valladolid.

Marcos was thinking that Luna was the luckiest man in Castile. He'd come upon the king when the ruler had been a child, gained his trust, and taken control. Now King Juan was almost forty and Luna past fifty. Yet they played with animals and silly caps. What perverse relationship bound these masters of Castile, and for how long could Luna retain his head, flaunting such riches?

As Marcos dressed for dinner in the pathetic downstairs room he'd been assigned, a servant brought instructions to bring a coat for the cold night air.

Minutes later, Marcos entered a gilded ballroom adorned in tapestries of battle scenes and windows made of remarkably even, clear glass. Fires blazed on twin hearths in opposite corners, and hundreds of oil-candles shone on chandeliers. Black Moorish servants, barechested but for gold satin sashes from shoulder to belt, served morsels on silver platters to fifty guests dressed in their frivolous finery, strutting and bowing like mating peacocks.

He strode toward the king's circle. Luna, the only noble without a coat, had on a silk tunic the color of emeralds. The king wore an embroidered crimson cloak. Sarmiento and an army captain, both in brushed leather coats, stood by, laughing at something Luna had said. Luna spotted Marcos and held up a hand. The conversation stopped. The constable looked him over and turned to a servant. "José, find a better coat for our friend García. This one's wretched."

The guests gawked as bile rose in Marcos' throat, but he had to play the chief magistrate's counselor. "Alvaro, my friend, I see you're in high spirits tonight." He strode to the king's constable, hugged the *pendejo,* and whispered, "We're alike. Let's try to get along."

As Marcos backed away, King Juan chuckled and Sarmiento yielded an approving nod. Luna regarded his guests, clapped, and shouted, "Come outside and be amazed." Two Moors opened the doors, and Luna strolled—arm in arm with King Juan—out to the gallery that had been transformed. Black servants in heavy cloaks stood beneath blazing torches mounted on the walls. Hoops hung from rafters overhead. Here and there, braziers of hot coals blazed along the parapet, and the women gathered near.

Luna's silk shirt fluttered in a frigid wind as he and the king gazed over the railing to the dark parade grounds below. Luna beckoned to Marcos. "Señor García, don't huddle by the fire with the women." When Marcos came close, Luna muttered, "We're different animals, Señor García. Like a camel, you require beating to keep you faithful. I'm a stallion, bred to carry my master to glory."

"You'll be lucky to carry him into Toledo," Marcos snapped.

Luna smirked and muttered, "Our hundred warriors dressed as laborers will accomplish that. When Ayala accepted the king's request for a visit, he sealed his fate."

Luna turned his back. "Look, everyone." He pointed to the parade grounds, where more braziers glowed, casting light on phantom forms. Drums beat in the darkness. Men touched torches to the coals and the flames revealed figures—Moors pounding drums, soldiers atop camels. As the camels loped past, men at the braziers handed each rider a flaming torch. They circled the parade ground, more and more of them, arriving, receiving torches, a circle of rippling fire around the yard.

Men and women on the gallery applauded as servants led new beasts into the yard, tall apparitions that rose above the camels. Giraffes! The camel riders halted, allowing the strange creatures into the circle of fire. Marcos saw Luna beaming. The *marrano*-loving scoundrel wasted energy impressing the ladies, when he should be planning their attack on Toledo.

"The beat of Africa," Luna shouted. "Ladies, Your Majesty, my beasts are at your disposal." The camels formed into a row across the center. Slaves led the giraffes close to the gallery, their horned heads appearing below the railing near Marcos. He jumped back. Moors on the porch handed bunches of dry grass to the ladies, who giggled and bent over the edge to feed the beasts. "Don't let them lick you," Luna called. "Their tongues are slimy as eels."

Women squealed and pulled back their hands. *Foolish creatures, dumb as the camels*, Marcos thought.

"One more trick before dinner," Luna sang. "Light the hoops." Slaves removed torches from wall brackets and touched fire to the rings suspended along the gallery. A row of burning rings whooshed to life, their hot breath warming Marcos' cheeks. Slaves unlatched chains, lowering the hoops to waist height. More rings were set alight, suspended over the stairway running from the courtyard up to the gallery.

A door opened in the courtyard wall and Marcos heard dogs yapping. Small ghostly forms dashed in front of the camels—speeding, one after the other. Sleek and lithe, they raced to the stairs, bounded up through the burning hoops, flying, leaping, flying. They hurtled past the king's party, through the fiery rings, thin and agile. And now Marcos wasn't at all cold. But what were they? He'd never seen such creatures. The constable leaned toward him and said, "You're no greyhound, Señor García."

CHAPTER 35

—⚍—

AN OBSERVER TO THE KING'S party entering Toledo would see that His Majesty had only eight soldiers for protection, but he'd brought a score of laborers and sixty scribes. Sixty! Each of these muscular fellows carried a long scroll containing a short sword. The 'laborers' held similar weapons beneath their baggy jackets.

Marcos mounted and joined the last group heading to Toledo. The sergeant in command had ordered him to the rear, so he watched the ass ends of a dozen horses jouncing ahead. Luna's plan—did it have a chance?—called for the king to occupy the *alcázar* with the eight armored soldiers and a larger group of 'scribes.' If they succeeded, the king's party would seize the fortress and Sarmiento would control the city. It had to be!

But if Luna was so confident, why hadn't he come?

The brown stone towers of the Puerta de Bisagra came into view. Yellow banners with the king's red lion flew above the towers, along with the twin wolf crest of Magistrate Ayala. Now at the gates, he saw royal soldiers, masquerading as courtiers, with the Toledan guards in the towers. City guards in gold-and-black tunics stood with six of the king's fake scribes at ground level. The king's men had thrown their scrolls to the ground and held their short swords at the ready as Marcos' party passed.

The *alcázar* was a high impregnable block of a building, invincible but for the fact that a half dozen of the king's men—a mixture of uniformed soldiers and 'scribes'—stood with city guards at the gate. Dozens more occupied the inner courtyard, all displaying their weapons.

Marcos ran up three flights and along a corridor, occupied by masqueraders, to a chamber where the king lounged on a settee. Sarmiento stood with four uniformed soldiers by a wall hung in Persian rugs.

"Your Majesty, this isn't the best room in the *alcázar*," Sarmiento said. "As your master butler, I'll demand better."

The king smirked. "Your last act as butler will make you magistrate."

Marcos followed Sarmiento into the hallway. Sarmiento nodded to the fake scribes. "You stallions, come with us." They marched to a large office with a wide oak desk. Oil lamps burned in wall sconces. Chief Magistrate Ayala sat behind the desk, flanked by two city guardsmen.

Ayala frowned with his one good eye. He rose and offered a hand to Sarmiento. "Master Butler, the king brings a larger contingent than I'd expected."

"We plan an extensive stay," Sarmiento said. "I trust you won't find it inconvenient to remove your belongings from the building."

"*Inconvenient?* I suppose you, Master Butler Sarmiento, will take up residence, and this crude-looking fellow. Who in hell are you?" Ayala scowled at Marcos. His eye glared beneath the wispy white brow and the black patch over his missing eye bulged. His *Guardia* men clutched the handles of their short swords, nervously watching Sarmiento, Marcos, and the 'scribes' along the back wall.

"Marcos García de Mora. I'll take your *marrano* underling's office in the city building."

Ayala turned on Sarmiento. "I'm expected to slink off to the country?"

"Better accept. A man with no head finds slinking difficult."

Ayala whipped a sword from under his desk. The room echoed with the sound of blades coming unsheathed. Marcos found his weapon in hand without realizing he'd pulled it forth.

The old one-eyed man said, "You bring lions dressed in lamb skins to my house. Have them stand back, and my men will do the same. We'll see whose head falls."

"Stand ready, men," Sarmiento called. As he turned back, the magistrate charged, blade aimed at the butler's chest. Sarmiento parried off-balance and staggered. Ayala stopped short and swung at Sarmiento's head. Sarmiento ducked, stumbled, and grasped a windowsill for balance. He recovered before Ayala had a chance to follow and faced the magistrate. He tapped his blade against Ayala's, chuckling. "No more sneak attacks. Give way, or ..." He struck Ayala's sword, harder this time.

"You should ... reconsider this ambition of yours." Ayala pulled in deep breaths between his words. "You have grand skills for a chief butler ... but controlling a city, you choose men's fates. People covet your position."

"No stalling. Put your weapon down."

The old man's eye moved from Sarmiento's sword, to his face, down his body. He was going to attack. Marcos called, "Watch out!"

Ayala lunged, his sword aimed at Sarmiento's gut. Not much of a stroke, but Sarmiento flew backward. *Holy God, he's been speared.* But then the old man squealed and fell, losing his sword. Sarmiento had somehow tripped him. He pounced and stood over Ayala, prodding his throat with his blade. Ayala gasped. One of the city guards advanced with his short sword. Marcos took a step forward, but Sarmiento had the advantage of a full-length weapon. He flicked his sword, as if swatting a gnat, and slashed the guardsman's thigh. The guardsman screamed and Sarmiento returned the bloody shaft to the magistrate's neck, laughing. "You're a wily old *cabrón*, but not so brazen now."

"*Enough.*" Marcos whirled to see King Juan stride into the room. "We can't kill off the head of a noble house."

Sarmiento withdrew his weapon. Ayala slid backward and managed to stand beside the desk. "Your Majesty," he wheezed. "Don't replace me with this *hijo de puta*."

King Juan shook his head. "Magistrate, you were able to duel with my master butler, but unable to support me at Olmedo. It was a battle most rewarding. Constable Luna, for example, has been given the Order of Santiago, once held by my deceased cousin. You will cede this office to another of my faithful warriors."

"You expect me to resign?"

King Juan drew his blade and sprang toward Ayala, who cowered but didn't retreat.

The king dropped his saber on the desk with a terrible thud and stood nose to nose with Ayala. "Constable Luna and I have devised a way for you to keep your dignity, Citizen Ayala. I will compensate you and you will sign an agreement ceding this office. The other noble families will conclude that I was honorable and generous."

Ayala slumped into his chair. Tears flowed from his eye.

Sarmiento chuckled low in his throat. King Juan glanced at Sarmiento and covered his mouth. He bent at the waist, laughing and slapping Sarmiento on the back. Finally, the king composed himself and turned back to Ayala. "We shouldn't make light of your misfortune."

Marcos wanted to spit at this weakling king who put off decisions and apologized to traitors.

Ayala took a long breath and stood, his eye locked on the king. "By your leave, Highness. I'll be off to Guadamur to supervise my estates." He stalked out.

The king settled in a chair and gestured for Sarmiento to take the one behind the desk. "Do you like the city throne?"

"It's comfortable, Your Majesty. Thank you." Sarmiento nodded to Marcos. "And I'm pleased to see my new first deputy smiling at last. What are you thinking, Marcos?"

What Marcos had in mind, he couldn't say in the king's presence. The king's darlings, the *marranos*, had much in store for them, including the demise of their benefactor and hero.

PART IV

FRANCESCA'S GARDEN

—ᴍᴍ—

*No force or compulsion shall be employed in any way against a
Jew to induce him to become a Christian; but Christians should
convert him to the faith of Our Lord Jesus Christ by means of the
texts of the Holy scriptures, and by kind words, for no one can
love or appreciate a service which is done him by compulsion.*

—Sɪᴇᴛᴇ Pᴀʀᴛɪᴅᴀs, ꜰᴏᴜʀᴛᴇᴇɴᴛʜ-ᴄᴇɴᴛᴜʀʏ
ʟᴀᴡs ꜰᴏʀ ᴛʜᴇ ᴋɪɴɢᴅᴏᴍ ᴏꜰ Cᴀsᴛɪʟᴇ

CHAPTER 36

—◊◊◊—

PERO'S HEART SWELLED WITH EXCITEMENT when he learned Marcos was back. By some amazing turn of God's will, the king had evicted Magistrate Ayala, and Marcos was to become first deputy. What great works they could accomplish, vicar and deputy together! And now Marcos summoned him to the *alcázar*.

As he pulled on a fresh black frock, however, Pero began to fret over the questions Marcos would ask: 'What did you accomplish in my absence?' *I preached sermons against the Jews.* That was true, but only during those first few months, before a darkness of spirit overtook him.

Pacing through the Plaza Magdalena, he considered Marcos' next likely question: 'Did you do anything original, anything beyond what I directed you?' Pero had no answer. And then: 'Are you and your priests still giving those sermons?' In truth, Pero had ceased advising his priests, had hidden in his cell, sleeping the days away. Now, like a bear leaving his sheltering cave, he was blinded by daylight, not eager for worldly exertions.

He halted at the sight of six huge men in polished black boots, with battle-axes and helmets that gleamed in the morning sun. A lump formed in his stomach, but he stepped between them into the *alcázar* courtyard. A courtier led him upstairs to find Marcos pacing a dark hallway, glowering when he saw Pero. "Why so slow arriving? Come to the chapel and say Mass for His Majesty."

Pero's stomach turned upside down, but he followed.

—◊◊◊—

The monarch departed with most of his soldiers, but all through the week, Pero thought back to that thrilling event, holding Christ's chalice in his hand, the Sovereign, bareheaded and humble, kneeling before him to receive the might and mercy of God. If nothing else happened in his poor life, that moment would fill Pero's eternal cup.

When the king departed, Marcos assigned Pero another breathtaking duty—to preach Sunday High Mass, and not only preach but lead the church on a new course: open confrontation with *marranos*.

Now he stood upon the altar in a white robe and golden bonnet. Worshipers filled the cathedral's pews and spilled into the side aisles, more souls than Pero had ever addressed. How was he to deliver the words he and Marcos had written, which were the right words, but that would dismay so many?

The priests' chanting reverberated from the stone pillars and rose to the pointed arches on high. As one of his priests commenced a gospel reading, Pero looked over the congregation—nobles and prosperous families in front rows, laboring class further back. There, the Rodriquez family of *conversos*, father and mother with their daughters, and nearby the Flores family and the Santiagos, all listening to the holy words, as if they were pious.

Today, scores of unfamiliar men filled the rear pews and stood along the walls. They dressed like normal working-class worshipers, but Pero saw eagerness in their eyes, intensity, fury. And there was Marcos among them, standing by one of the stone pillars.

The reading ended. Pero moved to the lectern with his notes and looked upon the crowd. "Today, I will speak to those of you who are converts, sons and daughters of converts, and the sons of sons of converts." Señor and Señora Rodriguez stared. He had taken their confessions and baptized the girls. Their grandparents had converted from Judaism. What Pero must say to please Marcos, he could not. Better to create a compromise that would not destroy these people. "I challenge you today to become the most pious of men and women. For you must stand the natural suspicion of your fellow Christians." Pero knew his words had been too weak. He glanced at Marcos and saw his surprised anger. Marcos pulled a paper from his pocket and jabbed his finger at it, demanding that Pero follow the notes.

Two nights before, as they'd prepared, Marcos had questioned him about the convert parishioners, their eating habits and the scents in their homes. Pero realized he'd never seen any of them eat pork. Some burned perfumed candles. Marcos explained how secret Jews cooked with olive oil instead of pork fat and covered the smell with incense. Pero had been forced to concede that they might be—probably were—false Christians. Marcos was right, always. Delivering this sermon wasn't just to placate him. It was the moral path, but so very difficult with them gazing up at him.

Lay the truth in their faces now, or face Marcos later, with his furious, shrewd eyes. He stiffened his spine and said, "There are sons of Jews and sons of Muslims among us in this holy place. A small number truly believe, but I'm sad to say, most do not." Marcos nodded and Pero felt encouraged. He looked over the front pews to avoid the *conversos'* eyes. "In the Jewish Quarter, thousands of perverse, God-hating heathens make sacrifices to pagan gods and plot against Jesus."

Men in the rear stood, clenching their fists and muttering. A few of the well-off families at the front listened eagerly, while others stared with shock or looked away. They knew it, too, knew in their bones about the blasphemers.

He glanced at the notes. "We know that in other lands, Jews poison Christians' water." The angry voices grew louder, and Pero shouted. *"Even here in Castile, Jews pretending to be Christian steal holy wafers from churches and despoil them. Some among you pretend to take Communion and spit out the body of Jesus after Mass. We cannot tolerate these atrocities."*

The rugged men shouted, "No more!" "Not here!"

Pero raised a hand for calm. "Those Jews also poison your minds. They subvert those unholy, unbelieving converts who stand beside us here in God's cathedral." Pero pointed to the congregation and saw Señora Rodriguez and Señora Santiago sobbing, guilty. He didn't care any more that he'd baptized their children or that these men contributed to the church, didn't care, because he saw the truth on their faces. "The Jews of Toledo recruit you. They feed you lies so you'll betray our Lord. And now, the words that I am loath to say: Many of *you* conspire against Jesus." Pero pointed toward the Rodriquez family. "You poison the well of our spirits, you secret Jews.

"Now true believers, you and I will perform a sacred rite. You and I will root this evil out and destroy it."

More shouts erupted from men along the flanks. Pero waited and said, "Those who are true Christians will take Communion. Lamb of God, who takes away the sins of the world, grant us mercy."

Pero ended the Mass and walked down the central aisle. He saw women dabbing tears. Parishioners glared at him, even some of the Old Christians. But the rough men in the back waited as he passed, then followed. He stopped on the platform at the top of the cathedral steps and they filed by—round-shouldered, ruddy-faced fellows with fat bellies, lean young men erect as poles, all with keen, angry eyes—offering nods of approval or touching him as they passed. From the edge of his vision, Pero saw other parishioners scurrying away, like rats, these secret Jews. How could he have been so blind?

Marcos came close and whispered, "I thought you were going to fail, but it ended well enough." He moved a few steps away and shouted, "*Sangre Pura, assemble.*"

Pero marveled at the way these rough men obeyed, filing down the steps until he and Marcos stood alone on the platform with scores below. "You have heard God's word. We embark on a holy mission. We march to the Jewish Quarter to root out evil." Marcos gestured to Pero. "The vicar will give us God's words to chant."

Pero tried to remember the words Marcos had given him. He could only recall part, but other words from the liturgy came to him. "Holy Christ. Holy God. Lamb of Christ. Only Catholics will be saved."

The men picked up the chant and began stomping their feet as they repeated the words. Marcos raised his arms above his head and descended. He led the mob around the square. As the ruffians chanted, some took wooden planks from the cathedral construction site. New men arrived from the side streets, swelling the mob still larger as Pero watched, transfixed.

The mob circled three times and headed west toward the Jewish Quarter, the chant still echoing across the now-empty square, sending a chill down Pero's spine. "Holy Christ. Holy God. Lamb of Christ. Only Catholics will be saved. Holy Christ. Holy God ..."

CHAPTER 37

—m—

SAILING ABOARD THE FOUL-SMELLING FRIGATE, an odd mix of emotions swelled inside Viçente. Salt breezes refreshed his spirit. For the first time in decades, he had no one to protect or to manage, no wars to fight, no brash prince or magistrate demanding this or that. He put doubts aside and imagined Francesca's joyful greeting.

But as they sailed into Naples' harbor, dominated by King Alfonso's massive citadel, blissful euphoria yielded to the tight fist of misgiving.

They took a room in a house near the docks. Viçente dispatched a note for Francesca and then sought out Padre Eugenio, Bishop Barrientos' trusted friend, at a local monastery. He left the holy book and most of his funds with the padre, and then he waited.

In the morning, a message arrived, summoning him to the citadel. His heart pounded a warning as he passed knights with battle-axes and lances beneath flags with vertical bars of yellow and red—dreaded symbols of Aragón, the Iberian state that controlled Sicily, Sardinia, and Naples. In a soaring stone hall, he found Carlo, Francesca's chaperone, again wearing his black goatee, red ribbon across the chest of his white jacket. "Señor Pérez, I welcome you on behalf of King Alfonso."

"Thank you, Don Carlo, but I was hoping—"

"The king is away in Sicily, but he sends his personal greeting. Please." Carlo gestured to a bench, and they sat. "The monarch is naturally concerned. When a man travels across the sea, as you have, to be with a woman … His Highness protects the lady, you understand. There can be no … impropriety."

"I'm sure you'll prevent it."

Carlo scowled. "No prevention should be required, Señor, if, as you write to the lady, you care so much for her."

Had Francesca divulged the contents of his letters? No, Carlo would have intercepted them covertly. Viçente's stomach tightened. "You interfering son of a—"

"No crudeness, Señor. On my king's orders, I'll be as discrete as you allow."

Viçente clenched his teeth and swallowed his fury. In the enemy's fortress, he was defenseless as a dove.

Carlo led him along a bustling avenue near the port and then through a maze of streets that wound uphill. Viçente watched for markers to help him find his way back—a grocer with a display of fresh fruit at one corner, a vine of scarlet bougainvillea climbing to a third-floor balcony at another, a wall of old bricks with a fountain dripping into a carved stone bowl. Carlo turned downhill and up again, following alleys that seemed all alike. The lout was trying to confuse him.

Viçente stopped, gasping for breath, embarrassed. "I'm not as energetic as I was at your age."

"You were wounded, fighting for our enemy at Olmedo." Carlo shot him a shrewd glance. The man knew everything.

"I didn't see you there. I saw no soldiers from King Alfonso's army."

"Our king devotes his time to his Italian possessions," Carlo said casually. "In his absence, his brother, the King of Navarre, and his wife govern Aragón. Aragónese soldiers did not fight because the wife and brother bickered."

Viçente weighed the information. If King Alfonso had little to do with Aragón's aggression, might he be innocent of other offenses?

They followed an avenue lined by poplar trees, yellow-and-cream palaces set close to the street. Carlo veered up the staircase of a manor, three times the breadth of any other. Butlers in golden tunics admitted them. The corridors were lit by crystal chandeliers, air permeated with the odor of burnt wax. Through another pair of doors, out onto a balcony. Carlo gestured toward a bench on the landing. "I will sit here, to be available for you and my lady." He waved past the balustrade. "She awaits you in the park."

Viçente took a moment to catch his breath and survey the formal garden with walkways set off by low hedges. At the far end, lush cypress trees cut a jagged border into the blue of the distant sea. The ocher hues of Naples climbed a far-off hill. At the center of the garden he saw a table and chairs and a splash of golden fabric—a parasol, which lifted as she rose, dark hair flowing to the shoulders of a long cinnamon-colored jacket, a blue skirt beneath. She smiled and gestured with graceful hands to bushes with but a few pink blossoms—rosebushes, the ones she'd written about.

At last, Francesca and her garden.

CHAPTER 38

—⁓—

HE URGED HIS BODY TO walk straight and tall, like a younger man. Francesca came forward, her cinnamon jacket unbuttoned, a white blouse beneath. She stopped half a step away. He took her hand and she stepped into his arms. He ran his hands over her shoulders, down to the narrow waist, up along her side. He kissed her forehead and felt moisture on his chin. She backed away and looked up at him.

"You're crying," he said.

Tears dripped off her lovely chin. "Sorry, and I'm sorry about the lack of blooms. I promised a beautiful garden in my letters, but it's winter." She smiled with those golden-brown eyes, but he knew she was inspecting him. How much did his infirmity show? Her eyes narrowed in the bright light, creating those tiny furrows at the edges. He'd treasured memories of her smile, but how could she be even more exquisite in person?

"Beautiful," he said. "I've longed to spend time with you here."

"You're out of breath. Are you well?"

"It's warm, and Carlo walked me all over the hill." They gazed at each other for a few more moments, and then she took his hand and led him along a path to one side of the garden. They passed behind a cypress. She stopped and turned up to him. He pulled her close, slipping his hands beneath her jacket, kissing, touching, smelling her perfume, feeling her breath on his cheek.

She clutched his shoulders so tightly he winced. "Your wound," she whispered. "I didn't mean to hurt you. I've been wild with worry."

"How much time before Carlo comes running?"

"Very little, I should think." She flashed a lustful smile, sunlight touching her eyes that shimmered the color of dark honey, and she kissed him so deeply, he longed to remove her jacket and set it beneath her on this ground. She eased away, looking sullen, and smoothed her dress. "Better go back."

As they walked toward the center of the garden, Carlo rushed toward them. "He's not a bad man," Francesca murmured. "Just a bit grim." Still, Viçente felt like a child caught stealing sweets.

Carlo charged up to him. "What did I tell you about propriety?"

Viçente swallowed his irritation, but Francesca poked a finger into the chaperone's chest. "Don't be dreary, Carlo."

The chaperone retreated a step. "My lady, I have orders from King Alfonso."

"Did he tell you to assault our guests? Señor Pérez is a distinguished official from Toledo."

"Used to be," Carlo grumbled.

"You're rude." Francesca's frown turned to an impish smile. "Did the king tell you to prevent me from having an innocent kiss with a dear friend?" The kiss had been far from innocent, Viçente thought, but it made no sense to correct her.

"The king, my lady." Carlo was blushing. "He fears your impulsiveness."

"I'm not a maiden, and you can't restore my innocence. A kiss will do nothing but lift my spirits." She took Viçente's hand and pressed it to her cheek.

Viçente felt a tingle of pleasure, but his cheeks burned. Was Francesca trying to have him killed? "Let's sit and talk about this," he said. To his surprise, the other two complied. "Don Carlo, I'm not here to cause trouble."

"But you do."

"Only because you're a twit." Francesca slid her chair closer and took Viçente's hand beneath the table.

"Wait, Francesca," Viçente said. "Carlo is merely following instructions." He turned to the chaperone. "I've taken the long journey here because I want to get to know Francesca, not compromise her."

"Carlo comprehends only baser cravings," Francesca said.

"You trust men too much, my lady," Carlo said.

"Perhaps you think no one would care to know me." She pursed her lips. "You see me as a body with no soul."

"Certainly not, m-my lady."

"Viçente sees more in me." Francesca pressed the back of Viçente's hand against her thigh. Another twinge of delight. But she had spoken so casually of lost innocence. How many others had she thrilled?

CHAPTER 39

—〰—

RABBI BENJAMIN TOILED AT THE side of the narrow street, shaded from the sun by the three-level dwellings at one flank of the Jewish Quarter. Nearby, women and adolescents took rocks from piles in the street, carried them into buildings and up to the third level, where masons sealed the windows that used to look over the Río Tajo and the hills. The beauties of the outside world were no longer safe to enjoy. The evil ones had come for the past two Sundays, like hornets pouring from a buried hive, threatening their sanctuary.

Benjamin's arms ached as he shoved a wooden paddle through gray-brown mortar in the trough. Even his beard felt heavy, its curly, black strands caked with grit. "I'll need more water," he called.

One of the women brought a white pottery pitcher. "You work too hard, Rebe."

"Not so much as the others." Benjamin nodded toward a young man dumping rocks from a cart onto a pile. As the woman poured water into the mortar, he wondered why she used such a fine vessel, with a blue-and-brown painting on its side, but then he saw its rim was chipped.

He stirred the muck, thinking that he, as a mortal, was marred like the pitcher. When it came time to protect his flock, he abandoned erudite arguments and idealistic sermons for this wooden shaft. He sighed and swiped his shirtsleeve across his sweaty forehead.

"Here, Rebe, let me." Jacob, a man of eighteen, held out his hand. Benjamin relinquished the paddle and Jacob stirred easily.

Benjamin fretted about this bright fellow with brown curly hair and beard, and for all the young ones, for history was cycling back on itself. Benjamin's father had told him of the persecutions of the 1360s and '70s and the most horrible in 1391, when Christians decimated the Jewish community. "In 1412, they came again," Benjamin told the young man. "I was too young to fight, so my papa sent me with my mother to the tunnels."

Jacob paddled mortar into a bucket, grinning. "That still makes you pretty old, Rebe." Benjamin swatted at Jacob's arm and the lad dodged. "We're ready for them, Rebe. We've stocked the tunnel with provisions."

Benjamin sighed. "I was your age when the angry ones returned six years later, in 1418. The elders gave me an ax and told me to defend the tunnel entrance while men in their twenties and thirties defended the barricades."

Jacob shifted the full bucket to the side and moved another close. "Did you have a chance to fight?"

"Don't yearn for that. We'd stand no chance. The mobs never broke into our quarter that year, but they captured some unfortunates outside and hurled them from the high bluff above the river."

The young man filled the new bucket with three quick swipes of his paddle. "I'd rather swing a sword at the barricades than stay trapped in the tunnels."

Benjamin heard a sound and tensed. A rooftop sentry called, "Prepare for the devils!"

Benjamin shouted, "Don't provoke them. We'll be safe inside our walls."

"They'd never provoke us," a man grumbled as he helped roll a wagon of stones against the bolted gates.

Women herded children into buildings, bound for the tunnels and caves. Men muttered curses as they took positions in third-story windows and on the rooftops, armed with rocks and spears to hurl. Others waited in entryways with sabers and crude shields. Benjamin retreated to a doorway, hearing the chanting grow louder and the first thuds on the gates. The portals swayed and creaked with the pressing mob. He murmured prayers, trying to let only sacred Hebrew into his ears, reverence for *Yahweh*, not fear and fury. He finished a traditional prayer and whispered, "*Lord, God, protect my people. Save my people.*"

He felt the loud blows and the trembling of gates in his chest, and he couldn't keep out the evil voices. "Holy Christ. Holy God. Lamb of Christ. Only Catholics will be saved."

Lord, God, protect my people. Save my people.

The chant repeated over and over and then subsided, and a man's voice shouted, "*Dirty Jews of hell, putas and pendejos, leave Castile, or die!*" The mob picked up the words and screamed them again and again.

Benjamin tried to listen only to his prayers. *Lord, God, protect my people. Save the chosen people.* He prayed until he felt the evil diminish. The good Catholics of Toledo had not broken in.

CHAPTER 40

—⁓—

MARCOS HEARD THE KNOCK ON his new office door. "Enter."

The middle-aged clerk who skulked in wore the fat cheeks and nervous grimace of a fake Jew-convert. Why did Sarmiento refuse to dismiss these impostors?

"The rabbi's outside," the clerk said. "He'd like to talk with you."

"Do I look like the Jew-lover who used to sit this chair? Send him away."

"Yes. Certainly." The clerk nodded, backed up a step, and smacked his head on the doorframe as he turned to go.

—⁓—

Arriving the next day, Marcos found an ugly creature in a tall black hat and shaggy beard in his anteroom. He let out a snort. "I take it you're the rabbi."

The rabbi rose, holding himself with the stooped posture of a sinner. "I was hoping to discuss the violence. I'm sure you've heard about the last three Sundays."

"Didn't my clerk send you away yesterday?"

"I hoped you'd have time for me today. It's an important matter."

"Nothing about Jews is important."

The rabbi was standing with his head bowed, like one afraid of God's truth. "It can't be good for the city when people are attacked."

"Not people. Not worth my time."

The Jew raised its eyes for a moment to his. "You manage a city now. I thought perhaps you'd see it differently. If the *Guardia Civil* could just visit neighborhoods near our quarter, nights and Sundays—"

"You think I'm like the *marrano*, Pérez, catering to blasphemers and shunning churchmen? Our guardsmen are busy at night. They pray on Sundays like righteous men."

Marcos stepped over to the clerk, who'd been watching wide eyed, and murmured, "Get two guardsman so they can toss this Jew out a window."

The clerk ran out.

When Marcos turned back, he saw the rabbi's eyes flash up to his again for a moment and back down to the floor.

"You dislike us," the Jew said. "I know, but perhaps you could find some compassion."

"Compassion comes from Jesus and only to the worthy."

"We've not harmed you. We do nothing to offend."

Marcos' fists were clenching and unclenching by their own will. The twitch had come back under his eye. "You offend the Lord, Jesus."

The Jew raised its eyes again, longer this time, like one not truly afraid, not ashamed at all. Marcos took two quick steps forward and slapped it hard.

The rabbi stepped back, running a hand down his face. "It's true what they say about you, isn't it?" He was openly assessing Marcos now. "You're the author of this hatred."

"Ha." Marcos grinned. "You presume to tell me what's not good for Toledo, but I'll tell you: it's vermin like you." He pulled back his hand to strike again, but the creature backed toward the door. Marcos shouted, "Where are those damned guardsmen?" But the Jew was in the hallway now, moving toward the stairs.

"You'll be tortured if you return!" Marcos shouted.

He sat behind the clerk's desk, staring at the seat the Jew had defiled, and muttered, "I'll torture every damned one of you."

It was another half hour before the balky clerk returned with two guardsmen. Marcos ordered him twenty lashes.

CHAPTER 41

—⚹—

BENJAMIN BLEW OUT THE CANDLE and lay beside Esther in bed, wearing, as he had for the last week, an old shirt and trousers in place of night-clothes. The sounds of the evil chanting haunted him all the time, but thus far, the mob had contented itself with taunting and hurling rocks. Benjamin did not comprehend their reasons, nor did he understand what kept them from slaughtering the people as they had in 1391.

If they commenced a killing spree, how many would have to die before he urged all to flee? Who among them would feign conversion? Who would die? Would Benjamin be strong enough to defy the mob with a knife to his throat?

He heard the warning bell clang and his heart pounded. "Get up, Esther!" He slid off the bed, took her hand, and groped in the dark for the railing at the top of the stairs.

Down in the street, people rushed from buildings, some in bed-clothes, most, like he and Esther, wearing rumpled clothing. A few carried lanterns, speaking in hushed voices. "What's happened?"

"Men, take your weapons," he called. "Protect the gates. Women and children to the tunnels. Where are the sentries?"

A man hurried toward him. "In position, Rabbi. They report wag-ons approaching."

A whooshing sound. Benjamin tried to comprehend. Thudding, grating, clattering—stones striking somewhere off to his left. Shouts and a woman's scream. Benjamin followed a man with a lantern, rushing toward the sound. They stepped over rocks in the street. He heard scuffling above. "They're on the roofs," someone shouted. Another voice: "Get out of the street!"

From the rooftop, a man called, "Rabbi! They're not up here. But I see them. They have torches and a catapult."

Benjamin joined others stooping over a man in the street. The man moaned and pressed a hand to the side of his face. Dark blood oozed between his fingers. *Oh my God*, Benjamin thought, but said only, "Take him inside. Are there more?"

"Two others. We're caring for them." Esther's voice.

"Esther, you must go below." Of course, she wouldn't. He took one of the wounded man's ankles and others joined him, carrying the man and laying him in the hallway of a building. Benjamin peered out. A shout and another terrible whoosh overhead. Something slammed into a wall outside, bounded to the street, slid, and skipped, sending fragments crashing. He covered his ears and turned away, but he couldn't keep it out. He fought fear and rage and the urge to sob; he, above all others, had to show strength.

When it grew quiet, men with lanterns converged on a flat piece of stone lying in the street. Benjamin saw the Hebrew lettering carved in it: *In memory of.*

The beasts had broken into their cemetery.

He heard shouting from beyond the gates and another terrible whooshing sound. He ran for cover.

How long would this go on?

CHAPTER 42

—∽∾—

NACIO AND HIS BROTHER, HAD departed from Naples, and Viçente now resided in a cubicle on the top floor of the citadel like a prisoner, guarded by mercenary soldiers and spied upon by Carlo. At noon, he was allowed a meager two hours with Francesca.

He couldn't help missing his friends back home and Diego. He thought about the duty that used to possess him. He'd given all those years to it—to his people, even to those others who shunned the true God. He'd given much of his former vigor, sacrificed the free motion of his right shoulder and arm; but something about it had satisfied, too.

He shouldn't feel guilty about taking this time—shouldn't, but couldn't stop.

Still, his dreams were infused with sweet thoughts of the lady, and his mornings with anticipation.

Now, sitting in her garden, he felt exhilarated, but vexed by her reluctance to explain her life here.

Francesca pushed her plate of fruit to the side, sipped wine, and said, "I told you Italy's delightful."

"Would it be so grand if you didn't live in the king's palace?"

"It's not the palace. It's the food, the wine, cypress trees and flowers, the Tyrrhenian Sea." She gazed toward the panorama. "Even the sky is bluer than Castile."

"But you're Lady Francesca of the royal family."

She frowned. "Please don't ask again how I'm related to the king."

"If he's to sever my head for kissing you behind that tree, I should know whom I'm kissing."

"Do you tell me everything about your family?"

Viçente's chest constricted. How could he speak of parents who had been hidden Jews all their lives? "You've met my son, Diego, and I confided in you about Marta and her death."

She laid her hand on his forearm. "Perhaps I'm afraid of driving you off before we're well acquainted."

"When we kiss, you call me 'darling,' and I want to know everything."

"It takes time for a woman." Francesca stood, and her look turned from sulky to lustful. She held out her hand. "I do crave the feel of your tongue inside my mouth."

Viçente glanced up at Carlo on his balcony. "Don't you worry that King Alfonso will punish me when he returns from Sicily?"

"I'm guessing he'll not behead you."

The words made his gut squirm. "You tease as if my life is nothing, while your chaperone threatens the dungeon."

"Your life is very much to me, and the king *won't* harm you. But if you're nervous, we can stay here and look respectable." Francesca slid her chair, facing Viçente so that her body blocked Carlo's view of him. She brushed the fingers of one hand across his cheek, and a pulse of excitement ran through him. "I asked Carlo for more time with you this afternoon."

"He's a disgusting fellow."

"Carlo savors this little authority." She smiled and ran her fingers over the back of Viçente's hand.

"I want a chance to really hold you."

She slid her fingers onto his thigh.

He set his hand on her knee. "You're so beautiful."

"Don't be shy," she said, caressing him closer. She stared into his eyes and murmured, "That's the beauty of having our chaperone; we can want everything, but we can only do so much."

He ran his hand to the inside of her thigh, feeling the supple flesh beneath her skirt, stroking.

She sighed. "It's difficult for me to tell. There was another man whose life I cherished. I was married."

Viçente stilled his hand. "Back in Segovia, you spoke of foolish men. You meant him?"

"He was a marvelous fool." She stared deep into Viçente, and the magic of her golden-brown eyes, together with these confidences, filled his heart. "I'm beginning to believe you are as well," she said. "He was Duke of Savoy. My king arranged the marriage. After a while, we became passionate and devoted. He went to war at my king's side as if it were some grand adventure." Francesca swallowed and Viçente saw a tear trickle from her eye.

"I don't possess a palace. No butlers wait on me."

"That doesn't matter." She cupped his cheek with her hand. "I trusted him, Viçente. I loved him, and I thought every part of me died when he did. Now you want his place." Francesca yielded an embarrassed smile. "I must look horrible."

"You look lovely and vulnerable, like a woman who needs comfort from a man." He took her hand and led her along the path toward the cypress.

"My darling Viçente," she said as they reached the cover of the tree. She rose on her toes to embrace him. Between kisses she whispered, "I asked Carlo to stay on his porch a few minutes before he disturbs us." Her tongue entered his mouth, and he ran one hand down her back and the other up her stomach to her breast.

"How much time?" he murmured.

"Not enough, dear one."

CHAPTER 43

MARCOS SET HIS CHAIR FACING the open window, rested his feet on the sill, and gazed across the square at the new cathedral tower. The office, this chair, and the view had recently belonged to the *marrano*. Marcos had cast the devil out and seized it. *Sangre Pura* was growing. The filthy Jews cowered in their quarter. He chuckled at the memory of their absurd, shabby rabbi begging for protection. After Marcos' head clerk had been flogged, Marcos demanded from him the names of every Jew and *marrano* in city government. The clerk swore there were no Jews and held back the list of *marranos* for two days. Then Marcos had banished him and all the other fakers.

He left his office, strode uphill to the *alcázar*, and marched into Don Ricardo's office. The commandant rose from his desk and stood erect in his starched black-and-gold uniform with the red sash. On the wall, Marcos noticed a framed golden sword—some ridiculous trophy. He stepped close to Don Ricardo. "I suppose you've no word of the *marrano*."

"Correct, sir, we have not located First Deputy Pérez." Don Ricardo looked impassive, but Marcos noticed the way he kept his hands by the front of his thighs, worried for his *cojones,* no doubt.

"Don't call him that. *I* am first deputy."

"Yes, sir."

The son of a whore was solid and half a head taller, but Marcos jabbed a finger into his chest. "Maybe you're only fit to serve a *marrano*."

Don Ricardo held his place, his lips compressed, eyes impassive. "As I've told you, Viçente Pérez departed with two men."

Marcos would slap the commandant but for the strength in those eyes. "You're a policeman. Question them."

"As I've also informed you, sir, they haven't returned—"

"Question their relatives, you dog!" Marcos saw movement from the corner of his eye and turned.

Pedro Sarmiento entered. "Commandant, please leave us."

The officer clicked his heals and obeyed, and Sarmiento closed the door. "Did your shouts impress him?"

Marcos gritted his teeth. "You shouldn't interfere. I'll dismiss him and have Sancho command the *Guardia*."

Sarmiento pulled a document from his pocket and shoved it at Marcos. "You've been reckless, Deputy. Look what you've done."

At the top of the page Marcos saw the embossed red lion and castle of Castile, flanked by two dragons breathing fire at one another. King Juan's crest.

My faithful Sarmiento,

I trust this letter finds you healthy and that you enjoy your new position. As your king and benefactor, I take proprietary interest in your well-being, and serious matters have come to my attention.

You have always served your king honorably, so now I assume that it's inexperience that runs you astray, inexperience and an incautious deputy. I'm sure you know that Marcos García leads parties of ruffians who raid the Jewish Quarter. They hurl rocks over the wall, aiming to kill Jews.

How could you allow such a thing? Jews are royal property, the only ones who seem to pay taxes these days. Jews support my treasury, and my treasury supports all. More important—as Bishop Barrientos reminds me—Jews are among us for a reason. We demean them, but we don't kill them; for one day, they will witness the Second Coming of our Lord Jesus, and they will repent their sins. Jesus will smile upon Christians at that glorious moment and favor us with paradise.

Whoring goddamned Jews. The king only cared about them because of some revenue and the meddling of the whoring red bishop. Marcos felt sweat breaking out on his forehead. He dared not look at Sarmiento.

Protect the Jews, Sarmiento. As I recall, Don Ricardo, the commandant of Toledo's Guardia Civil, is most capable. I'm sure he's up to the task.

Now to the issue of conversos that Deputy García dismissed from city positions. Must I remind you that converts are proper Christians, protected by royal decree? Reinstate them at once.

Aside from that, my dear Pedro, I'm certain your reign in Toledo will succeed and that your abilities will grow to match your responsibilities. I am confident you'll not disappoint me again.

Your King, Juan II of León and Castile

Sarmiento glared. "You see? Don Ricardo has influential allies."

Marcos cast the letter toward the desk and watched it flutter to the floor. "That *pendejo*, Barrientos, is one of the Jew lovers. And the king—"

"These attacks have gone too far, Deputy."

"You knew what I was doing," Marcos snapped.

"You'll not say that again." Sarmiento glowered. "When I was the king's man, I protected his position. Now you're my deputy. You never informed me of your actions, and I never approved."

"But we're partners."

Sarmiento's lips held a strange, sickening sneer. "The word 'disappointment' coming from King Juan is a bad sign. Ending a note with pleasantries is worse. Luna's the cause. He never wanted me here. Cease the attacks and reinstate the *marranos.*"

"You're too easily intimidated."

Sarmiento smashed a fist on the commandant's desk. "The king of Castile is displeased." Marcos cringed, but suddenly Sarmiento's fire disappeared. "I know that the *marrano* sons of whores went to the king behind my back, and we will take revenge. But your rabble catapults gravestones at harmless Jews. How long before they kill?" Sarmiento eyed the king's letter, lying on the floor.

Sarmiento's coolness unnerved Marcos more than his outburst. He retrieved the paper and set it on the desk. "Jews are the roots of the *marrano* tree. We must sever them."

"Talk like a zealot, and you'll be gone." Sarmiento ran a hand through his hair and glanced at the framed sword on the wall.

What was he thinking, this strange Sarmiento who flew from fierce to gentle on impulse?

"Two of the *marranos* I dismissed worked in the treasury. We can charge all of the *pendejos* with theft."

Sarmiento settled in the commandant's chair, hands clasped behind his head. "Imprudent, Marcos. I'll write to the king, acknowledging that my first deputy is new and over-eager. We caught two employees stealing from the treasury. To be cautious, we sent their friends home during the investigation, but we've restored the innocents."

"It's our holy mission to expel them all."

"My mission is survival."

Marcos stepped close. "If the king trusts Don Ricardo and his guardsmen, can we? The men of *Sangre Pura* stand with us. Let them shout and beat the walls of the Jewish section, doing no real harm. Each raid brings more recruits."

Sarmiento opened his mouth, then paused. "Let them march, but be careful. I'll tell the king I've taken personal control of the *Guardia*. I'll say that *Sangre Pura* is a group of simple fellows who resent the godless ones and I've ordered you to restrain them."

"You make me sound a fool."

"Pay attention, Marcos—don't miss my wisdom. As my letter mollifies the king, we'll strengthen our position. You'll recruit brutes for

Sangre Pura and find money in the treasury to increase the *Guardia Civil.* When your *Sangre Pura* and my *Guardia* number in the hundreds, not even Constable Luna will attack this fortress city. We'll undermine *marranos*—remove some from government, eliminate their merchant's contracts, increase the fees they pay to conduct business, all at a measured pace."

It was weak, but workable. Marcos' heart sank. What a disaster if Sarmiento felt confident devising his own strategies. But the magistrate was inconstant, one minute terrified of the king's displeasure, the next fortifying the city against him. *Manipulate the pendejo,* Marcos thought. *Hold out the lure of marrano gold so Sarmiento can feel only greed. Undermine the king's faith until Sarmiento's too fearful to submit.*

"Yes, Magistrate. We'll do as you say."

CHAPTER 44

—ɷ—

VIÇENTE HAD BEEN TWO WEEKS in Naples, sharing lunches, thoughts and dreams, and ardent moments with Francesca, each day embracing in their private place behind the cypress before the ill-tempered Carlo escorted him from the palace. After that, he explored.

One day at sunset, he watched women sitting on the yellow hulls of overturned boats, mending fishing nets. Up beyond the beach stood their homes—two-story structures with tan stucco walls and brown tile roofs, second-floor balconies where laundry hung in the waning light, mountain peaks in the distance. He memorized details to bring back to Francesca and to write in his next letter to Diego, all the while thinking he shouldn't let himself love this woman who'd lured him into the palace of the enemy and wouldn't reveal her relationship with the king. He strode toward the fortress, picturing her face and body. Damn, her body was too much in control of him.

Just short of the fortress, he halted. Beneath the torches at the main gate stood a score of royal soldiers, where normally there were four. A contingent of mercenaries in stiff leather vests and leggings leaned against the wall, battle-axes glimmering in the torchlight. A chill ran through him as he realized Francesca's monarch had returned.

At a nearby inn, he ate a piece of bread and a few scraps of chicken, the food like clay in his stomach, requiring a full pitcher of tart red wine to calm.

Late next morning, Carlo arrived, his face bearing the smug look of a man about to best his rival. "The king summons."

—m—

After leading him up the hill, Carlo allowed him a scant minute to find his breath before taking him into the palace and along a different corridor. Uniformed soldiers opened doors to a magnificent salon. Sunlight streamed through open windows between creamy-yellow draperies. Women in fine, embroidered gowns stood beside a low platform that supported two thrones. A lone figure sat upon one—Francesca. A diamond tiara adorned her long black hair, which flowed onto the shoulders of her red velvet gown. Lord Christ, she occupied the queen's place.

Carlo propelled him forward, but Viçente jerked free. Carlo muttered, "Move into place before His Majesty enters."

"What is her relationship to the king, damn it?"

"Stand here to face him." Carlo prodded, and Viçente backed away, turned to find himself a mere two paces from the steps to the thrones.

Francesca kissed the fingers of one hand and held them out to him. "Did Carlo give you my note?"

The chaperone shrugged. "Misplaced, my lady."

A pair of doors at the side opened with a crack. Francesca sent Viçente a quick, worried frown.

"What did it say?" Viçente asked.

"Quiet," Carlo hissed.

Soldiers strode in, followed by men in dark jackets carrying leather-bound volumes.

"The scholars feel clever with their books," Carlo whispered. "King Alfonso loves his Latin verse."

The scholars took chairs to one side. A short, corpulent man strode forward, bearing a ruby cape and golden crown. He stepped onto the dais and bent to peck Francesca's cheek. Almost Viçente's age, perhaps fifty, with a fair complexion and a nose as round as his head, the king was graceful given his girth. He settled easily onto his throne and nodded to Viçente. "The Lady Francesca seems nervous today, not her natural state. There are matters I would discuss with you, Viçente Pérez. You are Pérez?"

Viçente tried to steady his trembling legs. He bowed low and straightened. From his visits to the royal court in Valladolid, Viçente knew how men sought favor—demonstrate good humor while showing deference. He forced a smile. "Your Highness, I've anticipated the pleasure of this audience."

"It took pluck for a supporter of Castile's King Juan to enter my lair."

Viçente glanced at Francesca, who gave him a subtle nod. "The lady tells me that men who come with good intentions need not fear you."

King Alfonso's pudgy cheeks dimpled with a smirk. "They call me 'Alfonso the Magnanimous,' but it's not always apt."

The *pendejo* was trying to intimidate him—and succeeding. "The king is modest." Viçente shifted weight to the leg that seemed more solid.

"You show spirit, Pérez. And you a *converso.*"

Viçente felt his face flush. He saw worry in Francesca's eyes. That the king would bring up his heritage this way—this king, one of the Royal Cousins—was ominous. But King Alfonso hadn't used the pejorative, *marrano.* "I am called a *converso,* Your Highness, because my parents were once Jewish. I'm proud to say that I've always been Christian. I—"

The monarch raised a hand. "I wish to address this business about *conversos.*" His face reddened and he lowered his voice. "I had no part in the dismissal of Castile's converts. My queen has been regent of Aragón, and my brother, the King of Navarre, is the one who took charge of Castile. They acted not from malice, but to gain approval from a certain faction. A man of your position would understand such political considerations. But still, were I not king, I might apologize for their actions."

Viçente had been ready for a slur, not an apology. "Thank you, Your Majesty. It must be difficult for you to say."

"And you, Señor Pérez." The king chuckled. "You managed to hold office and protect other *conversos* in Toledo. I admire this."

"They're Christians, Your Majesty, deserving the rights of any free man. My superior, Magistrate Ayala, was generous enough to keep us."

"Then he dismissed you when you wouldn't betray your king— poor judgment on his part."

Viçente was shocked. King Alfonso was praising him for loyalty to his enemy. He was far different than Viçente had expected, and Francesca had sworn he wouldn't harm him. He watched the king's eyes, wondering how sincere his 'apology' about converts was. How candid could he afford to be? "My king stood for justice, Your Majesty."

"Implying that I did not." King Alfonso's frown seemed half amused, half incredulous. Viçente took it for encouragement.

"Shall I be honest or diplomatic, Your Majesty? It's not my place to accuse a king."

"And yet you do." The frown grew darker.

Time to retreat. "You're so far away here in Naples. I'm sure you weren't aware of acts carried out in your name." Viçente did his best to smile. "Yet you seem to know everything about me."

The monarch's frown became a scowl. He rose and pointed at Viçente. "I know you took advantage of my sister, Francesca."

Oh, Jesus. *His sister*. Viçente's heart pounded as he took a step back.

The king's chin quivered and his eyes held some inscrutable mix of emotions. "Not only in my garden here at the palace, but in Segovia, in Prince Enrique's chapel, under God's clear eyes."

How could he know about the chapel? The king had apologized to clear his conscience, and now he'd have Viçente slaughtered, not because he was a *converso*, but for kissing Francesca, his sister, in the chapel. *His sister*. But where was the resemblance?

Francesca grimaced as she pulled in a deep breath. "Alfonso, you promised not to call me that. You said you'd give me time."

"He shamed you, sister."

"I didn't, Your Majesty. I—"

Francesca stood and faced the king, looking angry, but still more calm than she should have been. "There was no shame until you divulged all to the court."

King Alfonso looked to the scholars and courtiers. His face grew red. "Get out." He thrust an arm toward the exit and the assembly hastened past the soldiers and through the doorway. But the soldiers remained.

Francesca had laid open their secrets. How could she trust this king, this brother, so much? And King Alfonso had lured him to express himself freely, while planning ... planning what? Why hadn't he recognized the tactic he'd employed with false converts on his staff?

King Alfonso glared. "Step up here, man, and face me."

Viçente couldn't move.

"Pérez, I am king. I command it. "

Francesca took a step toward Viçente, her eyes pleading. "Viçente, this is wrong." She whirled toward the king. "Alfonso. Don't torture him."

CHAPTER 45

—w—

THE KING GESTURED AGAIN FOR Viçente to approach. Francesca stepped toward him, her look anguished. She couldn't have intended this, but intentions be damned.

Escape.

Strapping young soldiers blocked the exits. He felt others close behind. The windows opened to a courtyard within the palace, surrounded by high walls. Even if he could run from the building, where could he hide? He set his jaw and faced King Alfonso. "I did not dishonor her, Your Majesty. I am a Christian as good as any, and I have only respect for the lady."

"I gave you a command."

Viçente stepped toward the platform, his stomach a tight knot.

Tears streamed down Francesca's cheeks. "It's all right. He won't harm you. Tell him, Alfonso. You're torturing this good man."

The king shook his head, his ferocity evaporating. He grinned like a man intoxicated. "Señor Pérez, it's one of those pleasures that accompanies power. Sometimes I can't resist."

Viçente paused on the first step, trying to understand. "This was a joke?" Maybe Francesca hadn't brought him to a fatal trap, but she could have warned him about this lunatic.

King Alfonso's smile sagged. "Any other sovereign would execute you for speaking with his sister, and you kissed mine in a royal chapel … a goddamned *converso*, too. Come on. I won't hack off your ears."

Viçente climbed the remaining steps and stopped before the monarch, his body shaking. He met the king's eyes with a level stare. "A senseless joke." The words were hollow, but he couldn't say what he wanted.

"Forgive me, señor. I meant only to tease my sister. Francesca has been without a man so long and now she acts like a maiden. He's much older than you, Francesca, his hair's more gray than black."

Francesca glanced fondly at her king. "Viçente's prettier than you, even with that crown atop your round head." How could she look at him that way?

The king had a fair complexion and blue eyes, like his cousin King Juan of Castile, while Francesca's skin bore more bronze. She reached for Viçente's hand, but he pulled it away. She whispered. "He calls me 'sister,' but it's not so simple."

"You should have told me."

Alfonso waved a hand at him. "Señor Pérez, you're fast friends with my nephew, Enrique, and now you've bewitched my sister. It makes one wary. What quality in you so captivates?"

"He's kind and honest. He's very kind." Francesca pressed her forehead into Viçente's shoulder. He stood rigid.

"And you, sister, are smitten. But you're mistress of my palace, and in my home we'll have decorum. Carlo will continue his scrutiny." The king extended his hand to Viçente. "Welcome, Señor Pérez. I'm pleased my sister invited you, even if you *aren't* pretty."

Viçente bowed and stood before this mad king, waiting to be dismissed.

How could she have laid him open to such fear and humiliation? A woman who cared would never have done it, only one who played with a man's heart. He marched from the throne room, rushed downhill to the citadel, and ascended the long staircases to his room.

Still panting from the climb, he folded his clothing and began packing the satchel, but where would he go? Neither Toledo nor Segovia would welcome him. And why was he so furious at her? She did love him. She'd shown with her weeping. She'd stolen his good sense and his heart and his will, and now his pride.

He heard footsteps and Francesca appeared in the doorway with Carlo behind. "May I enter, if I promise to be forthright?"

Viçente nodded.

Francesca whispered something to the chaperone, and he backed out of sight. "Do you invite me to sit?"

As he gestured to the simple chair, he noticed that her diamond tiara was gone from her knot of black hair. She lifted the hem of her red velvet skirt, settled in the chair, and watched him.

"You're his sister." His voice sounded harsh; his throat burned with rage. "You told him about our intimate moments."

"Did you consider that 'sister' might be a term of kinship from a man whose family is far away in Aragón?"

"I stood before the king, alone and terrified. You sat upon your queen throne while he threatened me, and you still won't tell me."

"He'd promised he wouldn't."

"Wouldn't tell the truth?" Viçente turned his back to her.

"Promised to let you get to know me first."

"All the time pretending he's not your brother?"

"He's really not."

Viçente whirled. "*Damn it.* If you can't speak truth—"

"You've no right to demand my secrets." Francesca dabbed her eyes with a handkerchief.

"My anger comes from love and frustration, from yearning to know you."

"Love?"

He nodded.

"I'm afraid of that word, but I've longed for you to say it." She reached toward him. He ignored her hand. She sighed and laid it in her lap. "King Alfonso's father was my father, Fernando de Antequerra. My mother was one of his wife's maidens. They weren't married, could not marry, but they loved each other." Francesca covered her face and sobbed. "This is my shame. It's always been my shame."

"Francesca, you're a fine woman. That's all I expected. Not a king's half-sister, not a virgin, not a—"

"Not a *bastarda,* I would think."

The word stung and offended him. How could she shame herself that way? "Better lovely like you than a pompous princess. And they say that Alfonso's son is also—"

"Also improper. It's different with a man. Viçente, don't hold this deception against me. I couldn't believe you would accept my stain." She frowned. "I still don't believe, but just now you spoke of love."

He looked at her pleading, moist eyes. She'd held back for fear of losing him, and she'd not led him into a trap after all. He hesitated and then wrapped his arms around her, feeling guilty because he had untold secrets, too.

PART V

SANGRE PURA

—ᴍ—

"Having forgotten the fear of God ... and the loyalty that he [Sarmiento] owed me ... as his King and natural lord, he rose and rebelled together with some of my disloyal individuals of the common people of that city (Toledo) ... making with them a conspiracy and sworn allegiances and deals and homages and fraternities ... to rebel against me and the royal crown of my kingdoms ..."

—FROM A STATEMENT BY KING JUAN II, APRIL 18, 1450
(SOURCE—B. NETANYAHU, *THE ORIGINS OF THE INQUISITION*)

CHAPTER 46

—⟋⟍—

CLENCHING AND UNCLENCHING HIS FISTS, Marcos paced Pedro Sarmiento's waiting room. Why would the magistrate treat him like a lowly petitioner, especially today, when Marcos had news to astound?

The portal creaked open and Sarmiento appeared in one of his blousy white shirts and russet trousers. He handed Marcos a paper as he entered. "Our king favors us with another missive."

Damn it. The monarch's last letter, a month before, had prodded Sarmiento to meddle in Marcos' operations: the city treasury and *Guardia Civil*. He moved near the windows and read the monarch's scrawl.

My dear Pedro,

How is your health, faithful servant? I trust you are content running the great city. As always, I think of you and consider ways to lessen your burden.

In my last letter, I inquired about your first deputy and this group called Sangre Pura. I was relieved by your reply, that this faction will insult, but will not harm, the Jews. I commend you for taking personal control of the Guardia Civil. I trust your judgment, but worry that you may be overwhelmed by the responsibility of governing Toledo and protecting my property.

And there's the added burden of restraining your first deputy. I've had an inspiration that will reduce your travails.

Constable Luna and I have contacted your predecessor, Magistrate Ayala. He has apologized for his transgressions. The heads of noble houses have spoken on his behalf, and we have determined to return him to the post of chief magistrate.

Naturally, Pedro, you retain control over the alcázar, the Guardia Civil, and the city gates, so your authority will continue. I am certain you will come to appreciate the benefits of this new arrangement. Señor Ayala's reappointment commences on the day you receive this letter.

My wishes for your continued health and long life.

Your King, Juan II of León and Castile

Marcos crumpled the paper, as his gut turned over. "'Reduce your travails.' *Mierda.* The king's mad. And what's this lie about trusting you?"

"He eliminates those he distrusts."

Marcos watched his magistrate to see if he might be about to strike, but Sarmiento walked to his desk and sat on it. "The bastard has gall," Marcos said. "Usurping one of your offices and pretending it's a gift."

"That bastard is king."

"If you let him do this, he'll take your *bolas* and tell you to be grateful you still have teeth." Marcos saw a crooked smile cross Sarmiento's lips. Again this strange calm. "It's Pérez. I don't know by what means, but he's arranged this for Ayala."

"You always blame him," Sarmiento said. "But you don't even know where he's gone."

"He was Ayala's deputy. He's godless and vile, and the king almost made him magistrate." Marcos was pleased to see Sarmiento's eyes narrow.

"When you capture the man, we'll act." Sarmiento swung his hand like a cleaver through the air. "For now I could follow the king's demand and yield to Ayala."

"A mistake, my lord."

"Or appease King Juan by dismissing you."

Marcos turned to the open window, forcing himself to swallow both fury and fear. He saw a vendor down in the square, arranging flowers on a stand. Another set out tomatoes. Ignorant peasants. He faced Sarmiento again. "That would compound your troubles. I have three hundred in *Sangre Pura*. You control Toledo's gates and *Guardia Civil*. If you yield this position to Ayala, the king, as a courtesy, will make your life more comfortable by sending a new commander for the *alcázar* before you can acquire any *marrano* gold."

"I heard your argument about *bolas* and teeth, and I comprehend it." Sarmiento dropped into his armchair and sighed. "Another option—executing you might impress His Majesty."

Marcos throat tightened, but he held his gaze steady.

"Don't worry, Deputy. Your decapitation would earn the wrath of three hundred unruly louts. Their riot would end any chance of regaining the king's respect. Your audacity and crude cunning have brought me the king's distrust, and his distrust makes me depend on you. We will not bow to King Juan's will. I'd decided as much before I let you in. Do we have funds for more *Guardia Civil*?"

Marcos felt confused and elated and nervous at the prospect of a Sarmiento with such insight. Would Sarmiento become a true partner, or might he settle on the absurd notion that he could govern alone? Marcos moved closer and said, "I discharged five more *marranos* from high-paying posts. We'll abolish those positions and the others we discussed and increase the *Guardia Civil* to one-hundred twenty."

"Ah, Marcos, in your own small way, you contribute."

"What grand tasks do *you* undertake?"

"You may know that Navarre has captured Atienza and Torija in the north. Manrique and the Moslems attack Castile's south. The Count of Benavente nibbles from the west. I will ride to Pamplona to offer our assistance to the King of Navarre."

Marcos forced himself not to gloat at the irony; sabotaging his relationship with the king would make Sarmiento more dependent on Marcos and his loyal ruffians. "Wonderful, Magistrate. When will we leave?"

Sarmiento grimaced. "You've already enraged one king. I'll go alone. And don't make petulant faces."

Marcos paced to the wall with its rack of spears. Here it was again, Sarmiento's irrational independence, but at least he was moving in the right direction. "Since we're breaking with the king, let's expel the other *marranos* from office."

Sarmiento was shaking his head, but Marcos continued. "When you return from the north, we'll try them for blasphemy and confiscate their gold. Unleash *Sangre Pura* and let them kill Jews."

"Ignore the Jews, and I'll choose the time to deal with *marranos*," Sarmiento said. "If we limit our actions, the king will hardly notice us among his distractions. Now fetch a lamp and burn this." Sarmiento nodded at the letter. "Regrettable that the king's note was lost. He might have had something interesting to say."

CHAPTER 47

—⟋⟍—

Viçente entered the palace one noon and received a note:

Signor Pérez,
Come to lunch in my garden. Do not tarry.
Alfonso the Magnanimous

With thoughts and questions swirling in his mind—and no longer possessing an appetite—Viçente followed a servant outside, through a maze of hedges to a small garden with a covered wooden platform. He mounted the stairs and found a table and chairs.

King Alfonso arrived with a courtier. He sat and gestured for Viçente to join him. "Francesca's chaperone tells me you're dissatisfied. Is that so?" He shot a perplexed look at the courtier.

Viçente swallowed. "Your Majesty, I—"

"It doesn't fulfill you to reside in a royal fortress and court the king's sister. True or false?"

At dinners he'd attended, Viçente had seen King Alfonso don this imperious mask to coerce his subordinates. But sitting alone with this king, how could one's hands not shake? "It is a great honor to court the lady, but your man Carlo limits my visits to two hours a day, and yes, Your—"

"An enormous honor, especially for a *converso.*"

Viçente looked him in the eye. "I'm a Christian like any other, and, Your Highness—"

The rotund king sat straight in his chair and pursed his lips. "And you want how much time together? Three hours? Four? You want to sleep beside her bed?"

"More time, Your Majesty, but nothing dishonorable. We'd both appreciate it."

"And my sister requests better accommodations for you and harps at me about taking you with us on our retreat to Castellammare in a fortnight." King Alfonso gave one of his inscrutable stares. "You're not fulfilled? You expect me to provide amusement?"

"After my two hours with the lady, I've little to do."

"You talk a great deal. Do you know that, Pérez?" He was silent for a moment. "You've been a city administrator in Toledo."

"I have."

"An able administrator, I'm told. *Conversos* and Jews are masters of finance."

Viçente forced himself to reply only to the compliment. "Thank—"

"Pérez, don't speak every time I end a sentence." The king eyed Viçente, as if waiting for him to put in another ill-advised word. "I have an offer to please you, but only after you perform a service. I've ruled Naples only four years. The old accounts lack order. I appoint you Examiner of the Ancient Accounts. Find some gold for me in this city. And don't ask to be paid. I've already hosted you to two state dinners, and we lodge you at royal expense."

Viçente scrutinized the king, considering the offer. The work could be interesting. Was it a genuine need or a futile task? A ploy to separate him from Francesca those other hours of the day? No matter. If he undertook it, Viçente would be helping to fund Castile's enemies, perhaps helping the Royal Cousins regain control and deny *conversos* their livelihoods. "Thank you, Your Majesty, but—"

"Don't thank me, and don't make more work of this than it merits. If you succeed, you can accompany the royal personage and the lady to Castellammare. Take your lunch here and then my man will introduce you to the royal bookkeeper." The courtier pulled back the king's chair as he rose.

Viçente jumped up. "I'm sorry, Your Majesty, but I wonder if you might—" King Alfonso glared, and Viçente took a quick breath. "If you might assign another task."

"I am king. I gave you this one." The monarch turned to leave.

"I can't. It would be treason against Castile, my lord."

The king's face grew red and his eyes bulged. "You're so loyal to your bungling king. Take this task or face my jailer."

Francesca had told Viçente that King Alfonso wouldn't hurt him, and she'd been right before. Now Viçente forced himself not to blink or back away. "My king may not be perfect, but he's my sovereign."

"Then you don't relent?"

"Your Majesty, if one of your officials went to Castile, would you regard it well if he betrayed you?"

There was silence. King Alfonso's lips twitched. "You're not half as afraid as you should be." He stepped to the edge of the platform and turned back, his mouth twisted in a perplexed knot. "Señor Pérez, I have a question. With you here in Naples, who's protecting your *conversos*?"

A question that stung. A question that had nagged him for weeks.

Despite Viçente's fears, that afternoon no soldiers came to take him.

The next day, the king had Viçente moved from his cold cell in the citadel to a comfortable chamber in the palace.

—⟋m⟍—

BENJAMIN LED THE TEN MEN and three women from the bustling market, through narrow streets toward the Jewish Quarter. The women and Benjamin carried hand baskets of fruit and vegetables. The other men wore halter sacks, hands free to draw their knives. They passed through a square, where boys played with a ball made of thatched reeds. City women stood by, staring at Benjamin's people, the Jewish women's hair covered by cotton shawls, men in thick beards, black hats, and tunics.

His people had to chance these trips to market. The attacks had only come on Sundays or at night—so far. Walking uphill with the heavy basket, Benjamin's knees ached. He paused and turned back to survey the party. "*Hold.* Is someone missing?"

A women called out, "Victorio and Leda. A peddler was trying to sell them trinkets."

Jacob spoke up. "They were flirting. Maybe they stopped in a doorway."

Benjamin headed back down toward the market, his people close around. "I told everyone to stay together," he muttered as he reached the square where the boys played. "We'll split the party." He gestured to three of the men. "Explore that alley." Pointing to some others, he said, "You go on toward the market." Two women and two men turned in that direction. "The rest come with me." He stepped toward the side street.

"Wait." Jacob held up a hand. "We can't rush off so far that we lose contact."

"Right," Benjamin said. "Search only to the next corner, and return. If there's trouble, shout for help."

As they left the square, he noticed the children had ceased playing to watch them. He followed Jacob and two other men along the side street with three-story buildings so close they closed off the sky. A man, shy of fifty, shouldn't be so easily winded. Some men that age—Viçente Pérez, who was a bit older—fought wars. Benjamin turned a bend and found the others waiting. "We've looked a distance in each direction and called out," Jacob said. "There's been no answer."

If they went further and got into trouble, their cries couldn't be heard, and if the other groups had trouble ... *Think of everyone, not just the two.* "We'll turn back and see what the others found."

Back at the square, Benjamin's heart fell, seeing only the seven. "Jacob, take the women back to the quarter. The rest will search with me."

"No, Rabbi. You take the women."

"Victorio and Leda are part of my congregation. I'll not desert them."

"You'll slow us, Rebe." Jacob fixed him with a determined stare—he was becoming a leader.

From the chasm of buildings he heard a rumble and the muttering of male voices. One of the women cried, "They're coming for us!" She turned toward the Jewish Quarter and ran, dropping her basket. Brown onions bounded toward the local boys, who chased and kicked them.

The chanting came louder now, echoing. Approaching from more than one direction? Panic ran cold in his veins. *"Follow her,"* he shouted. "Move fast. Stay together."

The younger men and women ran. Jacob took Benjamin's basket of tomatoes and strode with him. "Slow down, men," he called. "Keep the

Rebe company." He smiled, and though the young man walked easily, Benjamin saw perspiration on his smooth forehead.

The street wound between buildings, so he couldn't see the gate to their quarter, but he knew there were two streets yet to pass. The shouts behind grew louder and more distinct. Benjamin looked over his shoulder to see the first of the shabby band, wooden planks in their hands. He heard the word *Jew*. He stumbled. Jacob dropped the basket and gripped Benjamin's arm. Tomatoes burst on the ground. His legs felt weak, but Jacob shoved him on. Two of the other young men waited and then kept pace.

Shouts from behind: "*Jew bastards. Christ killers. Look, the leader of the Jews. Kill the scum.*" Something hit the wall near Benjamin ... an onion. Its scent burned his nostrils.

Panting and about to fall. There was no hope, the mob close. "Leave me," he gasped.

Jacob and another man half-carried him now. "Save yourselves," he cried, but they kept on. One crooked block to safety. The screaming came close and loud. Something smacked the back of his head and bounced away. A potato. Rocks clattered on walls and paving stones. The man who'd been holding his left arm went down. Benjamin fell to one knee. Jacob lifted him. "Go on, Rabbi. I'll take him." Jacob helped the injured man up and the three ran on.

He saw the gates ahead, halfway open with men ready to close them. New energy filled him even as shards of ice seemed to be slicing deep in his lungs. Sentries on the rooftops watched and archers were poised to shoot. "*No,*" Benjamin called, but his voice was drowned in the evil chanting. If they killed Christians, the attacks would worsen. People would die. But the archers loosed their arrows. He didn't turn to look, but he felt the enemy hesitate. Then they were inside. The gates closed. He knelt on the paving stones, wheezing, pain cutting his knees and lungs, tears running from his eyes.

That night, sentries reported sounds beyond the walls, sounds but no attacks. No Leda and Victorio. Benjamin visited Leda's family and later Victorio's, imploring *Yahweh* to bring the young ones to safety. He returned home and Esther joined him, kneeling on the floor, praying late into the night.

The next morning his people found the mangled bodies of Victorio and Leda outside. They placed Victorio's severed arms atop the torso and Benjamin held his head in place as Jacob wrapped the body in white cloth. Esther and the women cared for Leda.

As the graveyard outside the walls was no longer available, the people brought the two bundles to the tunnels beneath the quarter. Benjamin spoke God's words over them and begged for answers.

—ɯ—

MARCOS COULD NOT COMPREHEND. Two weeks before, Pedro Sarmiento had returned from his trip north, elated with his good news. The Navarese king would support Toledo's independence. A day later, Sarmiento wanted to abandon the quest and plead for King Juan's forgiveness. He ranted that Marcos was to blame for all their troubles. That same afternoon, the magistrate plotted rebellion yet again and praised Marcos for forming *Sangre Pura*, calling it 'our salvation.'

The past week had also been perplexing, though far more tranquil. The magistrate had not left his domicile, demanding darkness and silence. Clearly Sarmiento was falling apart under the strain of rebellion, and Marcos feared his reaction now that they'd killed Jews.

In the *alcázar* chapel, Marcos knelt and gazed at Christ's tortured figure on the crucifix. "I fight your true enemies, the ones who pretend to believe," he whispered. "You have given me this task, and I freely accept." But Christ demanded actions, not useless chatter. "I'm not a swordsman, Lord, but you gave me a mind, and you've allowed me, by my wits, to attain almost enough power. Almost. Now Magistrate Sarmiento loses his will. Still, my men killed two of the godless ones." Up on the cross, Jesus seemed less anguished. "We'll do more, I swear it. We'll go after the deceiver who humbled your vicar."

Marcos' thigh ached where it had broken. He saw the agony in Jesus' eyes, which reflected his own pain and his frustration for

Sarmiento, for the king, for the godless ones. Pain was Jesus' gift to make him resolute.

He heard the Lord's voice inside his head. *Don't offer excuses. Make the others follow or circumvent them, but do not fail.*

—⁓—

He found Sarmiento at his desk, alert again. "Good morning, Marcos. I hear your ruffians have been active." Sarmiento wagged a finger and smiled.

Marcos stomach felt queasy as he sat and leaned forward, resting a hand on Sarmiento's desk. "It's a good thing, Magistrate. The Jews are vile and—"

"I'm not displeased that your men killed those two." The magistrate scrutinized him. "But did you know they were going to do it?"

If Marcos told the truth—that he hadn't known—he'd lose face, but if he feigned foreknowledge, he'd be called out for disobedience. "No."

"Then it's clear, isn't it? You aren't meant for command."

"I was meant to have high ideals, Magistrate, and our destiny is to rule together. Expel the last *marranos* from government."

"They can't harm us," Sarmiento said.

"You'll be gratified, Magistrate. I found a law that demands we eliminate the *marranos*."

"You're ranting, Deputy." Sarmiento ran a hand over his shirt to smooth it.

"From the Fourth Toledan Council in 633. It was never rescinded."

Sarmiento chuckled. "When I was on King Juan's council, we laughed about that eight-hundred-year-old decree. The Moors have taken Toledo, and the Christians taken it back, and yet another three-hundred-and-fifty years have passed and a dozen kings have ruled and died since. They've all employed converts."

"The law—*marranos* have no rights." Marcos pounded a fist on the desk. Sarmiento glared, and Marcos lowered his voice. "We have almost four hundred now in the brotherhood, a hundred and thirty in the *Guardia Civil*. You have Navarre's pledge."

Sarmiento slipped a dagger from the desk drawer and began trimming his fingernails. "Think beyond your hatred, Marcos. Our King Juan will attack either his weakest rival or the most threatening. We're not the weakest, and we will moderate our offenses. Are you paying attention?"

Marcos felt a muscle twitch beneath his eye. "Must we be the king's meekest subjects?"

Still casual, Sarmiento pointed the blade at Marcos. "Against King Juan's orders, and without my sanction, your brutes wet the streets with Jew blood. We discharged most of the *marranos* from office, and we ignore the order to make Ayala magistrate. We are *not* meek."

But we're too meek for Jesus. Marcos strode to the spear rack and yanked one out. "With your knife you whittle at your fingers, when we could wield men's weapons and do God's work." He rammed the spear into the wall, sending plaster chunks flying.

Sarmiento shoved back his chair, his eyes furious. "*Put it down.*"

Marcos returned the pike to its notch. "Ancient law supports us. The people support us. We can torture *marranos* and prove they're secret Jews."

Sarmiento shook his head. "Your hatred for Pérez drives you beyond reason."

"Once they admit their crimes, you can confiscate their wealth." Sarmiento's subtle smile encouraged Marcos. "We'll hold an inquisition, but we'll call it some other name. We'll create a record and hold it up to all Castile, expose King Juan for the weakling he is, and send the *marranos* to the fires of hell. We'll cleanse the blood of Toledo." Marcos stopped, hearing voices outside and a pounding on the office door.

Commandant Don Ricardo entered with a sergeant. "Chief Magistrate, an emergency at Bisagra gate. King's Constable Luna with a squadron of soldiers. He claims royal authority to take command of our gates."

Sarmiento jumped up. "Your guardsmen kept them out?"

Don Ricardo's face flushed. "Our men let him through the outer gate but closed the inner one. Luna and some soldiers share the yard between gates with our guardsmen."

"*Fools. Curse them to hell,*" Sarmiento shouted.

Marcos recalled Luna's sneer that night on the balcony as his giraffes pranced in the courtyard. "Call in your reserves," he said to Don Ricardo.

Sarmiento glared and spoke through gritted teeth. "You don't command the guard." He turned to Don Ricardo. "Send runners to their homes. Assemble and arm. Keep them close but hidden until we decide."

Don Ricardo sent his sergeant on the run.

Marcos followed Sarmiento and Don Ricardo out the door, muttering low so Sarmiento couldn't hear. "Decide what? Attack the *marrano*-loving dog."

Five minutes later, as rain drizzled from a gray sky, Sarmiento, Marcos, Don Ricardo, and a half-dozen officers of the guard looked down from the ramparts. Sarmiento wore a wide-brimmed, black hat, while Marcos' uncovered head was sopped and frigid. He panted from the uphill climb. Water trickled down his back. Below, just outside the city walls, scores of royal soldiers stood in formation. Those, together with Luna's men between inner and outer gates, made up a formidable force. How could Sarmiento seem so impassive?

They descended from the ramparts to the near tower, staying out of view of the bay between the gates. Don Ricardo asked the tower commander, "How many of our men in each turret and in the yard?"

"Four here, sir, and the ones you've brought. Four in the other tower, five of ours in the yard with the constable's twenty."

"The gate at the far end?" Don Ricardo asked.

"Open, sir."

"Our enemy's boxed like a gift," Marcos said. "Close it on his neck."

Don Ricardo jabbed a finger at Marcos. "Five of our men are in there. Attack and they die."

Marcos batted his hand away. "Have your archers shower them with arrows. Once they kill Luna, we'll see who's left."

Sarmiento grimaced. "I want the *pendejo* out, not in."

"You've been waiting for this, Magistrate," Marcos said. "Without Luna, the king's helpless."

Sarmiento's eyes darted as he shook his head. "Quiet, Deputy." Sarmiento walked to the front of the tower and leaned through the crenature between gray blocks of stone. "Constable Luna."

A crisp, happy voice replied. "It's a fine day, Governor Sarmiento."

"There's a bit of a storm, Constable," Sarmiento said.

What was this *mierda* about the weather?

"His Majesty is still concerned that you have too much to do." Luna chuckled. "I bring his greetings and good news. This proclamation puts the city gates under my command."

"Only the gates?" Sarmiento called.

"Yes, Governor Sarmiento. You'll still control the battlements and *alcázar.*"

Marcos pushed aside one of the *Guardia Civil* and poked his head through another crenature. Below, Luna stood with a group of soldiers, the constable's thinning hair matted around the bald top of his head. Luna held a scroll up toward the magistrate. The man was audacious, occupying a trap with no shield or helmet. Marcos wanted to hurl his sword toward the scoundrel's brain, but he pulled back and stepped next to Sarmiento. "Kill him or capture him. We *must.*"

Sarmiento turned to him, his look resigned. "I'm afraid we can't."

"But you hate him," Marcos hissed.

"Not hate, exactly. I just wish ..." Sarmiento looked down and turned back toward the yard.

Marcos grabbed his sleeve and yanked. *"Don't."*

Sarmiento's hat fell off as he spun, his face red and furious. He slapped Marcos hard across the face.

Marcos backed away, holding his cheek, feeling Sarmiento's glare like a blade cutting his chest, and *Guardia* men all around. He stroked his wet, stinging cheek with cold fingers, feeling the guardsmen's eyes on him, his gut twisting with rage.

Sarmiento picked up his hat, moved back to the opening, and called down to Luna. "You're too kind, Constable. I'll come view this paper."

"Weakling. Idiot," Marcos muttered.

"Get out of my sight," Sarmiento growled as he passed Marcos and descended the tower stairs to give it all away.

CHAPTER 50

—ɯɯ—

MARCOS' CHEEK STUNG. TEARS BURNED his eyes, but the guardsmen wouldn't know. His face was already wet with rain. Lightning shot across the sky over distant hills. Thunder rumbled, but the rain came softly here. Down in the courtyard, royal soldiers gathered around Magistrate Sarmiento, Don Ricardo, and Constable Luna. *There's still time*, he thought. *Run him through with your sword.* But Sarmiento hunched over Luna's document, sheltering it from the rain.

After a few moments, Sarmiento ordered the near gate opened and stalked through it into the city. Don Ricardo shouted up to the tower guards. "Yield position to the constable's men." Luna's soldiers entered the base of the tower. Marcos heard their boot steps on the stairs. He followed a *Guardia Civil* man through the portal and up the steps to the high ramparts. Behind him, the *Guardia* sergeant rammed the bolt into place on the sturdy door that would keep Luna's soldiers from the battlements. Marcos hurried away from the guardsmen and then slowed his step.

I've failed Christ, he thought. *The marranos have won.* He trudged to the tavern where the wool carters gathered, consoling himself with a glass of stout, and another. By the time Sancho arrived, Marcos felt woozy. He bellowed out his anger and then laid his forehead on the table, muttering, "One day we won't need that *pendejo* of a magistrate, and then we'll pay him with lashes for this humiliation." Raising his

242

head barely off the table, he looked up at the wool carter "You'll help me with that, won't you, Sancho?"

"Aye, Marcos. It'll be a pleasure."

Long after dark, he stumbled home, flung open the outer door, and climbed the stairs. Halfway up, he noticed the door to his quarters stood ajar. He took another step, puzzled, touching his cheek where the magistrate had slapped him, and panic took him. He stepped backward and missed the stair, falling hard. Pain shot through his leg as a burly *Guardia Civil* entered the door from the street, blocking the exit. Marcos reached for his knife but it slipped away and clattered on the stairs. He groped in the near-dark stairway.

"Don't make us strike you down." Another guardsman lumbered down, grabbed his arm, and breathed foul air at him. "Magistrate Sarmiento commands us to watch you. We'll be agreeable so long as you obey."

His leg throbbed. His thoughts were hazy. "I'm under arrest?"

The brute shrugged and dragged him to his living room, followed by the other man. They stood close, huge, intimidating, and smelly. The shorter one, a hand's width taller than Marcos, observed, "Pretty plain for a first deputy's abode."

Marcos lived in two rooms because he only needed two. He had a bed, a settee, a table with two wooden chairs—no frivolous ornaments. But he wouldn't explain to these fools. His stomach churned. Lurching away from his captors, he rushed through the bedroom door and crossed to his only window. As he jerked open the shutters, the *Guardia* men hauled him back. "Let go. I have to—" Marcos' gut convulsed and he covered his mouth, sending vomit splattering from his hand onto his face and hair and spurting through his nose. The guardsmen released him back to the window so he could retch into the alley.

—∿—

CHAPTER 51

VIÇENTE HAD BEEN IN NAPLES six weeks. He missed Diego, his home, and his work, but Castile had changed. He had no position there. His friendship with Prince Enrique was poisoned. And now word had come that Pedro Sarmiento controlled his city. He'd met Sarmiento just that once on the battlefield, and the thought of that arrogant man governing unsettled him. Would *conversos* be employed? Would the helpless be protected?

There they were again, Jews, and the damned rabbi, appearing unbidden in his thoughts, as if they were his responsibility. He found himself grinding his teeth, feeling guilty for not taking Enrique's of-fer, guilty for the pleasure of these idle days.

King Alfonso had assigned him the task of reorganizing the Office of Licenses and Decrees—issuing condolences to soldiers' widows, congratulations for newlyweds, import permits. Apparently, this drea-ry position was the royal punishment for his obstinacy, but he decided to pretend it was a challenge. It had only taken a week to improve its efficiency, assigning one staff member to track all the requests.

Every few days, he stopped by Padre Eugenio's monastery to see if any letters had come, and here were four, all from Diego. Back at his room, he took out the magnifying lens and opened them, glancing first at the dates—all over a month old. He felt so distant and unin-formed about the changes back home. Damn this business of relying on monks to transport the mail.

He read the letters through quickly and then looked them over again, rereading the most interesting passages:

Papa, I've been settling in here in Valladolid, making friends and learning about the national finances. I think this will interest you— the reason this king supports converts and condemns violence against Jews: half the royal income originates from these two groups. I never realized.

I've only been working in the treasury for a month, and they've already entrusted me with overseeing loans the noble houses have made to the king. I even have an employee working for me! So am I following in your footsteps? I hope so. But I've noticed that much of the treasury's staff is composed of older workers who seem unable to tell the difference between fifteen doblas and fifteen maravedis, so maybe I shouldn't let my promotion go to my head. Don't ever tell anyone what I wrote about the old clerks. They're nice fellows but not very bright. I'm glad we send the mail with trusted monks. Otherwise, I couldn't be so candid.

Papa, you and I may have something in common. There's a pretty señorita named Amanda who works at my boarding house. She's been watching me closely, and I can't take my eyes away from hers. I took her to a concert last week and another last night. She kissed me goodnight in a way that warmed me everywhere, including my heart.

I have a new friend in the Royal Ministry of State, and he tells me that since Pedro Sarmiento took control—and that's only been a few weeks—violence has increased in Toledo's Jewish Quarter. And I hesitate to write this, because I know how hard you've worked for our people, but the city officials dismissed all the converts from their jobs. As I wrote in my last letter, the king relies on Jews for much of his income, so King Juan sent a letter demanding that Sarmiento protect 'his property,' the Jews, and reinstate the conversos to their positions. Perhaps the king thinks that safeguarding Jews makes him seem benevolent, but at least it should help the poor wretches. I'm sure Señor Sarmiento will submit to King Juan's wishes, so please don't worry about your former employees. They'll soon be back to work.

Viçente's heart was thumping inside his chest like a rabbit trying to escape its cage. Violence in his city. Violence he might have prevented if he had chosen duty over selfishness. He thought back to the confrontation he'd had with Enrique while bears howled in the moat. He'd almost died of his wounds, yet the arrogant prince demanded he leap back into Castile's corrupt politics. Not for the public good, but to further Enrique's schemes. Not high purpose—greed.

What he'd chosen was love and a chance to live. How could that be wrong? And why did it always fall to Viçente to protect the weak? Did no other man care?

Viçente reread Diego's last letter over and over. The Jews were in danger, but not the converts, not Viçente's friends and staff members and all those other good people. The king was interceding. King Juan had given Toledo to Pedro Sarmiento, and the king demanded *conversos'* rights—and apparently, security for Jews as well.

But there was another simple truth: His shoulder had been injured in battle, but his soul had been damaged, too. He didn't want responsibilities. Didn't want to think about Toledo. He sought love and nothing more.

There was no reason to worry, as long as Sarmiento owed King Juan his seat of power.

That evening, he stood with Francesca on the balcony beneath a half moon. The palace door stood partway open so Carlo could 'watch and protect the lady.' Viçente told her of Diego's letters, about the evil faction called *Sangre Pura* and how far away and helpless he felt while the king and magistrate quibbled over his people's fate. She shivered and Viçente wrapped an arm around her shoulders.

"You wouldn't think of returning there?" she asked.

"I'll want to some day. I can never govern again, but it's still my city and my nation. I have friends and comrades there."

He felt her quaking against him. "You gave up too much for them already. Look at you." She stroked his shoulder.

"As long as there's peace, you can go with me. If not to Toledo, to Segovia or Valladolid."

"You can do much for Castile by staying here in Naples," she whispered. "I know one of your king's enemies well."

"I couldn't ask you to."

She shook her head. "Not so loud. King Alfonso has authorized soldiers from Aragón to join his brother, King of Navarre, in a new assault."

"Thank you for wanting to help, but—"

"You can use this to regain King Juan's trust. You did snub him when he thought of offering you Toledo."

Of course she was right. At present, he might not be welcome in Segovia or Valladolid, but the king would value this information. "I'll send Barrientos this news. He'll pass it to King Juan."

Francesca gave a hopeful smile. "I'll find out more for you, but you must stay here, where you're safe and most loved." She pressed herself against his chest. Her tenderness warmed him and raised tingles of desire.

How it hurt him to be so far from Castile and hold such scant power, and how deeply this starry Italian night seduced his soul. "I'll stay," he whispered. "Don't cry."

Carlo made a racket by kicking the door, and they had to separate.

—⚉—

CHAPTER 52

FOOTSTEPS IN THE HALL. PEDRO Sarmiento sat up in bed and reached for his knife. Dull light from his window told him it was dawn. Banging on his bedroom door. He threw on a robe, opened the door, and found Don Ricardo with one of the servants.

The commandant, unshaven, his uniform jacket half buttoned, gave a quick head bow. "Chief Magistrate, there's a problem with the *Guardia.*"

"There'd better be a disaster to barge in this way."

"Half of the squad didn't report to the *alcázar* for morning watch, fifteen men. We sent runners to three of their residences. They've gone missing, sir." Don Ricardo's gaping stare was unnerving coming from the laconic commandant.

"Wait in the hallway." Pedro closed his bedroom door halfway, dropped his robe, stepped naked to the chamber pot, and took a piss. "You said there were fifteen missing, but you've checked only three."

"We've no time, Chief Magistrate. With Constable Luna holding our gates, we must consider it a crisis."

Pedro doubted that Luna could capture fifteen men by stealth, but the other possibility was also grave. "How many men are at your disposal, Commandant?" Pedro pulled on a pair of leggings.

"Ten in the *alcázar* and eight in the street outside this mansion."

Pedro slipped on a white shirt, tucked it in, and tightened the laces on the breeches. He pulled on his high black boots, feeling his pulse beat in his temples, fearing one of his terrible headaches was coming on. Taking slow breaths, he strapped on his sword.

At the *alcázar*, they outfitted eight *Guardia Civil* with long swords and chest armor, took two archers from the fortress, and marched the ten to Marcos García's home. The street outside was empty, absent of the two guardsmen who should have stood at the building's entrance. Pedro drew his sword and followed Don Ricardo up the stairs.

García's door stood open. Inside, the deputy sat alone on his settee, watching Pedro with nervous eyes. A muscle twitched in his gaunt cheek.

"What have you done with the *Guardia* men?" Pedro demanded.

García glanced at him. "Magistrate, I didn't order this. My men were outraged that you treated me with contempt."

Pedro eyed his sword. "I could part your hair with this. Tell me where they are."

"I don't know, but I can negotiate their release."

How had Pedro let this coarse commoner cause so much trouble? "Your cutthroats, your beloved *Sangre Pura*." Pedro slammed his sword onto the table, smashing a plate.

García didn't flinch. "You once found them useful."

"You never knew your place, Marcos. You were my inferior, and now you're nothing." García slouched on the settee, so damned sure of his cause, sure that Pedro wouldn't strike. "The mob can't save you." Pedro hauled back and kicked his leg. García screamed and pulled his feet up onto the settee. He looked at Pedro with teary eyes, but the eyes did not repent. Pedro smashed a fist into García's face. Blood spurted from the corner of his mouth. This man had endangered his standing with the king, *his standing with the king*. But Pedro couldn't kill him. He had to show the king harmony in his city, needed *Sangre Pura* on his side and the appearance that he'd brought García under control—if he even wanted to be on the king's side.

Pedro forced himself to hold back. "Feeling more sensible now?"

García was looking past Pedro, and Pedro turned to see a charcoal marking on the white wall—a simple cross that García must have drawn there. García grimaced and stood, trembling but looking Pedro straight on. "You've squandered our gains by giving Luna the gates. If you kill me, *Sangre Pura* will riot. Luna will bring an army to take back the city, and he will slay you."

"My mistake was granting you such freedom." Pedro felt a sadness coming, a headache and a sudden fear of this man, but he had to overcome it.

"You've demonstrated your dominance. Now let's reconcile our differences." Blood oozed down García's chin as he glanced toward the doorway, and Pedro realized that Don Ricardo still watched.

Without looking back, Pedro said, "I'll meet you downstairs, Commandant." He heard the door close. "The rabble gives you leverage, but if I have to, I'll strike you down." He stared hard at García and saw the twitch return to his cheek. "Order the guardsmen released."

García dabbed the corner of his mouth with a knuckle and examined the bloody finger. "Then you'll keep me as first deputy."

Pedro clenched a fist and saw his subordinate cringe. He needed this man for the crude hatred that let him commune with the guildsmen. He needed the mission, too. Ridding Castile of the *marranos* could bring Pedro history's acclaim. "A man in your position can't demand fine brandy, Marcos, and a man in mine can't lose respect. Once you free my *Guardia Civil*, I'll remove the sentries from your home, but you'll not venture out for a week. Accept, or I'll kill you. Your holy mission will die, too."

Pedro savored the look of resignation that displaced his former deputy's arrogance.

From a doorway opposite García's home, Pedro Sarmiento waited for the *Sangre Pura* men to emerge. He approached their stout leader. "You'd be Sancho." Pedro held out a hand.

The balding fellow spat on the street. "And you're the man who bloodied Marcos García."

"We need to speak." Pedro nodded toward the doorway where he'd been standing.

"Not there." Sancho led Pedro a dozen steps in the opposite direction.

"I want to discuss our mutual interests," Pedro said.

"Talk plain." Sancho eyed Pedro and spat again.

"Your men like Marcos García?"

"They don't like the man that locked García up. Marcos told me to release your guardsmen, but I could just as easy capture you."

"We should be on the same side." He thought he saw a touch of curiosity battling the man's surliness. "Your friend García feeds your men's anger, but what about other appetites? Kill a hundred Jews, and your pockets are still empty."

Sancho licked his thick lips and grinned. "You going to give us gold?"

"If you help me."

Sancho looked down at the paving stones and murmured, "Sometimes I think of beating Marcos like you did, but when he talks of the cause, and when we lead our men against the Jews, we stand together."

"Some gold wouldn't hurt." Pedro removed his coin pouch and held it out. He could see the greed in Sancho's eyes, but the wool carter turned and walked away.

CHAPTER 53

—⟶

BENJAMIN FOLLOWED THE YOUNG SENTRY, David, as he edged forward through the tunnel, the flame of his torch skimming the ceiling. Dank air hindered Benjamin's breathing as he thought of the departed members of his congregation buried in side passages further up the tunnels, souls denied the peace of their hallowed cemetery because of the danger.

They came to a stack of wooden staffs leaning against the wall. "No light beyond this bend," David said. He fastened the torch in a wall niche, took a staff, and led on, using the pole to feel the way.

The exit was half-filled with rocks, barely visible in the pre-dawn light. David climbed the pile and pressed his back against a bush, making room for Benjamin to step out.

They leaned against a boulder, taking in the fresh air, half moon overhead, the sound of water gushing in the Rio Tajo down in its chasm.

"I'll accompany you," David murmured.

"Then who would watch your post?" Benjamin detected a glow in the eastern sky. He had to be going.

"You need protection."

"You guard the tunnel to safeguard all the people, not just one faltering rabbi." He took David's hand and kissed it. "Your other duty, young man, is to remain safe, to grow up in the faith, and to raise a family."

The lad smiled. "I thought your role was to see to our souls, Rebe, not to sneak about in darkness."

"Young man, my Esther used to argue as you do, and she was far more persuasive. But she learned that the rabbi cares for the people's spiritual and also corporal needs." Indeed, Esther had accepted sacrifice and peril long ago and overcome her fears through days of dread and sorrow.

He released David's hand and stood. "There's no more time." He pointed and waited for the boy to disappear into the tunnel.

Making his way among the low bushes, he came to a trail that climbed the slope to the narrow alleyways of the old Muslim Quarter. There would be few Muslims here now, but many *Moriscos*—converted ones. Here among these pears from the Muslim branch of *Adonai's* tree, men wouldn't think of trampling fruit from the Creator's other boughs. But always life demanded caution.

An occasional oil lamp lit the streets, but he could proceed only as fast as sore bones and wheezing lungs allowed. Light shone from cracks in shutters of three-story residences. Pots clanked inside. A thump sent him dodging to the shadows, but the noise came from inside a building. Smoke from cooking fires drifted. A door opened. A man stepped out and glanced toward him. He moved on, gulping smoky air, glancing over his shoulder. No one behind. By the builder's home, he hid in the shadows where two buildings came together.

It wasn't long before a man emerged from the house. The proud posture, the goatee—it was the builder. Benjamin hurried forward. "Don Gonzalo, I apologize for this intrusion."

Gonzalo gaped and then touched his arm. "Rabbi, why didn't you knock?" The builder walked Benjamin through the courtyard, into his home, his living room. He retrieved a lantern and set it on the table. "You've come because of the attacks on your people?"

Benjamin nodded, and they sat.

"Perhaps it's finished now," Gonzalo said. "The madmen seem more tame since Luna took the gates."

Gonzalo's wife appeared, dark-featured with a scarf over her hair. She served dried fruit and cups of juice from a tray.

Benjamin sipped the cool liquid. "God willing, they'll let us alone. But these *Sangre Pura* have venom enough to murder us all. The priests now denounce even their own converts. "

"They say Marcos García's behind it."

Benjamin shook his head. "I believe that, but why not blame all mankind or God, who provides new miseries for each generation? What divine purpose is served, letting the evil ones strike Jews or *conversos*?" He'd said too much to one outside his flock and needed to make amends. "When our faith is tested, we must hold it strongest. That's what I tell my people."

"Surely, Jews don't believe that God has malicious intentions?"

"Some other person—not the spiritual leader of his people— might savor the irony of *conversos*, who fled Judaism for the safety of Christianity, finding themselves tormented by their new brethren. I'm sorry, Gonzalo. I seem to be sharing my bleakest thoughts with you."

The builder pursed his lips. "How can I help, Rabbi? You know I'm in your debt."

"You owe me nothing. It was Samuel, the mute, who saved your daughter. Nonetheless, I would take advantage of your decency." Benjamin ran his moist palms over his black trousers.

"Rabbi, my daughter's virtue is a debt I freely pay a hundred times. How can I assist?"

"It's been weeks since the madmen killed two of my people returning from market, and we've not dared return. We have chickens to lay eggs and stores of milled grain, but no fresh fruit or vegetables."

"I can obtain produce, but I can't deliver it to your gate."

"There's an empty warehouse outside our quarter on a little-used alley. If goods can be brought there, we'll retrieve them."

Gonzalo inclined his glass toward Benjamin. "I'll fetch a wagon and give you what I have in my storeroom, then bring another load tomorrow."

Benjamin was tempted to hug this worthy man, but he held back, still rebuking himself for his ill words about God and his creations. "I don't know how to thank you."

Gonzalo opened the front door and morning light shone in. "If you don't mind having potatoes for company, you'll be part of the first cargo."

CHAPTER 54

—◠—

ON THE EIGHTH MORNING, MARCOS answered a banging on his door. A pair of civil guardsmen confronted him. "Come with us," one said. When Marcos hesitated, the man grabbed his arm.

"Give me a moment to put on my boots." The men stood over him as he donned them.

The guard should have made this a request, should have asked if he needed time to prepare, should have addressed him with respect. This crude treatment could only have come at Sarmiento's direction.

Walking before them toward the *alcázar*, his heart filled with smoldering anger and sudden doubt. After a week of quiet in the city, could Sarmiento feel bold enough to eliminate him? Could his dithering mind have conjured new fears that drove him back to king and constable? As he climbed the stairs, he thought, *Can't show weakness. Prove yourself invaluable. Use his hatred of Luna and his greed.*

Sarmiento waited beside his desk—silk shirt, silken brown hair, empty soul. "Marcos, we have a problem."

"It doesn't affect me. I'm not first deputy."

"You forced me to discipline you." The magistrate settled in his desk chair and gestured for Marcos to sit.

Marcos walked to the window and glanced at the vendors in the square. "Now you remember who put you in this office?"

Sarmiento grimaced. "Constable Luna's mad. He demands a loan of a million *maravedis* to fund the king's battles."

"Luna and the king ignore yet another law—Toledo's royal exemption."

"You see my difficulty."

Marcos chuckled. "My four hundred *Sangre Pura* hate you for caging me. Burden them with a new tax and they'll rebel."

The magistrate shook his head. "Luna left his squads at our gates. He'll return in a fortnight for the money."

"You're collecting the taxes?"

"The council gave the order, not I. The taxman begins his work."

The taxman was a thin weasel of a *marrano* named Alonso Cota. "Rally your courage, man." Marcos clapped his hands.

Sarmiento flinched. His eyes narrowed and he stood like a scolded child. "I thought of asking for *Sangre Pura* to accept the tax, but it seemed ... naive."

Sarmiento's words implied that he was about to discover his *bolas*. Marcos pointed at him. "So we act."

"Breaking with the king ... I don't—don't know if my city guards would follow that order, but your men ..." Sarmiento glanced at him and looked away.

No. Sarmiento's *bolas* were still absent. "You want *Sangre Pura* to attack them."

"Don't tell me what you're about to do. Just do."

Marcos stepped close. "If I solve your problem, you'll reward me."

"I thought you didn't care about riches."

"Expel the last *marranos* from government. That's all."

The magistrate nodded. "Once we revolt against the king, there's nothing to prevent it."

"We'll try them for heresy."

"A few of the rich ones," Sarmiento said.

Marcos saw Sarmiento's sly smile and understood. "If you take their gold, Magistrate, you'll cede a share to *Sangre Pura*."

"I'll command the distribution. How much for yourself?"

"God, not gold, is the current that carries me, Sarmiento. But I'll be the one to sack Viçente Pérez' home. And you'll make me first deputy again."

"You were insubordinate."

"I can free you of Luna. If not first deputy, just give me command of the *Guardia*."

"A week ago, I was damned glad you didn't control them." The magistrate pouched his lips and smoothed his shirt with a hand. "You'll control the dungeon, Marcos. I won't offer more."

Marcos could see Sarmiento's point. And there were benefits to the proposal. "I accept." He stepped past the magistrate, yanked a spear from the rack, and marched out of the office.

CHAPTER 55

—⟶

VIÇENTE ARRIVED WITH KING ALFONSO'S caravan at "the villa" in Castellammare—a half-dozen small palaces, their stucco walls washed in pink, with ivory-colored pillars and adornments. The largest rose three stories, with blue-and-white tile murals by the entry—on one side a battle between Roman warriors and a barbaric hoard; on the other, Neptune holding court on a bluff above the sea. At the far end of the property, Viçente discovered a similar bluff. From it, he gazed west toward Toledo, praying the fears he could not banish from his thoughts were unjustified, that King Juan and Pedro Sarmiento worked together to protect his people.

Francesca met him that afternoon wearing a pale peach summer dress with red hibiscus blossoms, black hair flowing halfway down her back. Her eyes shone brilliantly in the sunlight. She took Viçente's breath away, as she often did, and he kissed the back of her hand before strolling with her between palm trees to a bench at cliff's edge.

Francesca cupped a hand behind her ear. "The waves make the pebbles purr like a cat for us." She pointed at a palm tree. "And that yellow-breasted bird sings a love song." Sitting, she reached into a sack she'd been carrying and produced a small green box with a golden ribbon. "A gift."

"You give me too much." He sat, leaving a little space between them so her chaperone wouldn't come running.

"Something you can use this time." As he unwrapped it, she said, "Did you notice, Carlo seems happy this morning? He loves these summer sojourns at the villa."

"Still looks grumpy to me. What is it?" Viçente examined the object—wire loops and round pieces of glass. "Spectacles? I've seen them in drawings. Thank you. People really read with them?"

"Here in Italy, they've been used for a century. Alfonso wears them, but not in public. Someone might think him imperfect." She laughed. "Here, I've brought a note for you."

Viçente put the contraption on, hooking the wires behind his ears. "Everything's blurry, and they pinch my nose."

Francesca plucked them from his face, twisted a bit, and handed them back. "Try them now."

They felt better, but still the blur. She handed him the paper and positioned his hands. "Hold it there."

And he saw: *Welcome to Castellammare. I love you.* Then in smaller letters, *I hope you love me, too. Francesca.* "Now without the spectacles," she said.

Viçente removed them. "It's tiny printing, impossible. Thank you, dear one. Of course I love you." He kissed her cheek and looked over his shoulder at Carlo, watching from a second-floor balcony. "Will we never be rid of him?"

"Maybe for a few moments. Put the spectacles on again and look at me."

He did, and she moved close. Her cheeks had freckles he'd not seen. Tiny flecks of gold danced inside the brown of her eyes. Every new thing about her touched his heart and other more passionate parts.

"Now that you can really see me, what do you think?"

"Lovely."

"You're handsome in them." She giggled. "Your eyes are big as a deer's." She looked down at her hands. "If I were Alfonso's true sister, they would have married me to the king of Portugal or Grand Duke of Brittany."

"Your Duke of Savoy wouldn't have been sufficient?"

"Not for a proper royal alliance … and when my husband died in battle," she paused, "they'd have betrothed me to another royal household. So you see it's good that I'm only half—half proper."

Francesca laid her head against his chest. He stroked her shoulder, caressed her cheek, felt the moisture of tears.

She'd told him so many of her secrets now and given so much. If they were to have a true relationship, he had to divulge his, and pray she wouldn't flee in disgust. "I must tell you something about my family."

Footsteps sounded behind them. The chaperone darted forward, bowed to Francesca, and then jabbed a finger at Viçente. "Pérez, control yourself. You're not to touch the lady."

—⋙—

Viçente's heart pounded. Something had awakened him in the night. A light. Movement—someone with a candle. He found his knife beneath the pillow and rolled off the bed. He heard a woman gasp. "Who is it?" he demanded.

"Please speak softly. It's Penélope."

He recognized her now in the candlelight, one of Francesca's attendants. "What's happened?"

"Quietly, sir. There's no trouble. The lady wishes to see you."

His heartbeat eased as he pulled his sleeping shirt closed and took the robe from its hook by the door. Penélope led him down the curving staircase to the salon. Moonlight shone through the open doorway.

"Sir," Penélope said. "You'll find her at the bluff."

Outside, Viçente felt the balmy breeze. Between the palms by the cliff top, he spotted a lone figure. He strode across the tile patio to the lawn, feeling damp grass between his toes, beginning to hear rocks beating each other with the shifting sea. She stood in a flowing gown, arms outstretched to take him in. He held her, touched her back and sides, felt her breasts against him, her stomach and thighs pressing. Her body—not constrained and stiffened by corsets—felt warm, yielding, inviting. He slid one hand to the small of her back, the other to her breast, supple and full, the nipple turning to a hard pea.

"Another gift," she said. She raised a hand to rub something against his lips. He parted them, and she slipped mint leaves in. They kissed long and deep.

"I love you, Francesca."

"And I love you." She pressed herself up to kiss again.

"Carlo?"

"He's away," she said. The thought brought him shivers of erotic joy. He kissed her throat as she said, "Carlo fancies one of the maidens in this town, and when we come each summer, he steals away to spend his nights with her."

"Hypocrite."

"Be happy for him, Viçente. He is blissful as we are. Be happy for us." She tilted her head, exposing more of her throat.

He shrugged off his robe so only his nightshirt and her gown separated them. She pressed a hand against his chest. "Be easy, Viçente. I've never given myself this way before."

He kissed her forehead. "With your husband?"

"I was given to him and came to love him after. I've never let myself trust so fully."

Sensations—the warm, moist breeze, silken skin beneath her jawline, the scent of blossoms in the air and her perfume, her body melting against his. He thought of what he wanted, of what she'd told him that afternoon. "So you love me, and you're not meant for the King of Portugal."

"Just for you," she whispered.

"Would you be free to marry a lowly Castilian?"

"No lowly Castilian has asked."

Viçente took a step backwards and knelt on the damp sand. "If he did, I imagine he'd do it like this."

She moved to him and pulled his face to her stomach. "Don't tease me, Viçente."

He ran his fingers along her thighs, feeling their suppleness through the thin cloth. He pressed his face into her tummy so hard she gasped. "I'm afraid to ask earnestly."

"Because you think Alfonso would object?"

Just as likely, she'd object once he told her his parents' secret. "I'm a *converso*, undesirable, repugnant, and I've seen the way he acts around you."

"I'm the one who's impure. You're just a lovely, strong man." She slid her hands beneath his nightshirt, gently feeling his shoulder wound. He felt a tingle and braced for pain that didn't come.

"I'm afraid, too," she said. "You were almost lost to me, *querido*. It's such a lovely moonlit night. Touch me, Viçente. Touch me everywhere. Kiss me and stroke me, please. Make me cry out with joy, but keep this gown between us, and don't ask for promises or vows. We will build faith and trust and love one night at a time."

With one hand he stroked from the gentle curve of her stomach to her ribs and breasts. The other cupped her buttocks, the inside of her thigh. His mouth explored, and Francesca sighed with delight. When she joined him on the sand to hug and kiss, they kept their thin garments between. Tears flowed down her cheeks and would not stop for all the kisses he placed upon her eyelids.

Though she'd denied it, the way she'd put off his question of marriage renewed his fears that there was some grand obstacle. He'd speak of it again, and there was still the issue of his heritage to reveal, but this night was for stroking and tasting her body.

—☿—

CHAPTER 56

PERO JERKED AWAKE. LIGHT SHONE through the small window to the stone wall opposite. It was still afternoon, but something had prodded him from sleep—a clatter in the hallway. The door banged open and Marcos strode in. "Pero, it's time to summon the masses." Marcos wrinkled his nose. "Don't you ever bathe?"

Pero took his frock from a chair and pulled it over his head. In the hallway, Marcos took a spear from the floor and marched to the stairs. Pero rushed to keep up. "What's happened? Be careful with that."

"Ring the bells."

Pero wanted to ask again, but Marcos' scowl prevented it. In the dining hall, Pero found three priests and assigned the largest to yank the bell rope. They crossed the alley and entered the cathedral. By the time Pero, Marcos, and the two priests approached the altar, the bells rang out.

"Light candles," Marcos commanded.

There was no need. Afternoon sunlight radiated through stained-glass windows to the eastern walls, but Pero nodded, and the two priests moved to the task. "What shall I do when the people come?"

"Pretend it's Sunday Mass," Marcos said. "Speak to them of secret Jews."

"And then?"

"Introduce me and I'll reveal the *marranos*' latest outrage."

—☿—

Candles burned on the altar table. Chandeliers had been lowered, lit, and raised again. As Pero watched, they poured into the cathedral—men in heavy cotton work clothes and women wearing aprons and scarves tied over their heads. The women stood at the rear as the men slid into pews or loitered by the massive pillars.

The congregation had transformed since the sermons about secret Jews. Noble families and business people now attended other churches, replaced by these lowbred citizens.

Their whispers became a murmur. Like trickles of water from many mouths, it streamed up to the high vaults above and rained back down in a cacophony that sent chills down Pero's back. He saw Sancho, the burly leader of the wool carters, confer with Marcos and walk toward the rear. Marcos nodded, and Pero raised his hands for silence. The babble decreased. Pero cleared his throat and began. "This afternoon—" He swallowed and tried again. "This afternoon, God bless us, we have an important announcement." The cavernous cathedral swallowed his words.

Marcos rolled his eyes toward heaven, stepped up the altar stairs, and held his spear above his head. Men pointed and cheered. Marcos lowered his spear and raised a hand. The crowd grew still.

Pero summoned his strength, thought of a recent sermon, and raised his voice. "The Jews are among us, brothers and sisters. They pretend to be of us. They pretend to believe, and, not believing, they defame Christ." Marcos nodded and Pero rushed on. "They are the evil. They defy and defile our Lord. We, with pure spirit, will conquer them. God will conquer them and burn their souls forever."

Marcos gestured for more, but there'd been no time to prepare. Pero needed to bring this to a good end. "They poison the wells of Christians. They poison our spirits. God grant that they be reviled and punished for their sins. Amen." Pero sighed and stepped back.

Carrying the spear, Marcos came forward. Someone shouted, "García is back! García triumphs!" The mob chanted, "*Sangre Pura. Sangre Pura.*" Marcos took the crucifix from the altar and handed it to Pero. "Hold it high." Pero held it over his head.

Marcos shouted, "Now the pigs steal our money in plain day."

Grumbling from the crowd.

Pero envied Marcos' bond with these men, but he prayed they would soon leave and that his soul would not be soiled by their deeds.

Marcos shook his spear in one hand and clenched the other in a fist. "You've seen the soldiers at our gates. The king's Constable Luna doesn't belong in our city. His soldiers don't belong. Now he demands a million *maravedis* from the people." Shouts rang out and Marcos waited. "Luna and this greedy king steal from common men, this wealthy villain king, this corrupt constable. They impose a new tax to fill their pockets and impoverish the people, but it's against the law."

Pero spotted the two priests who'd lit the candles leaving through a side door.

Someone yelled, "*Pendejos.*" Another, "*Puta Madre.*" Not proper words for this holy place.

Marcos jabbed his spear in the air over and over again as he shouted, "The *marrano* tax collector will come to your home. If you have no money, he'll take your chickens. He'll starve your children to support Jew dogs and heretics. While we were gaining strength, we attacked the Jews who are the root, but we're strong now. We're ready to sever the tree, ready to take *marrano* gold for the people."

The throng was becoming a mob, performing a fierce, sinister dance, stabbing knives into the air, screaming, "*Sangre Pura! Sangre Pura!*"

The swearing and now this mad behavior ... Pero saw that Marcos was red-faced and panting from the exertion. He waited a moment and then tapped Marcos on his shoulder. "Please don't let them kill everyone."

Marcos glowered, but he raised his hand, waited for silence, and spoke less fervently. "We are righteous. We are angry, but we will not murder. We will capture the *marranos*. We will try them before God and expose their blasphemy, with the vicar of god's church to witness."

Pero felt his stomach knot. Marcos seemed to speak of some sort of inquisition, but they'd not received the Holy Father's approval.

Marcos gestured to one side of the cathedral. "Those over here, meet Sancho in the square." He swung his arm across. "You men, follow me."

If this was the beginning of a holy crusade, perhaps Pero should be joyful, but he wished another priest were standing in his place before this angry swarm.

Marcos shouted, *"We will drive the marranos from hiding, and then God will cast them to hell."*

The rear door swung open. Men began to pour out.

Holding the spear aloft, Marcos took a step down and then glanced back, smiling. "It's a joyous moment, Pero. God's soldiers are marching."

CHAPTER 57

—⚋—

THE SUN HUNG LOW OVER the hills beyond San Martín Bridge. Marcos stood beside a two-story, stone-and-mortar dwelling at the western edge of Toledo, anxious for the attacks to begin—the assault of his force on this western bridge and Sancho's groups on the eastern Alcántara Bridge and the main Bisagra Gate. Church bells had struck off two hours since the warriors had departed Cathedral Square—ample time for Sancho to prepare. Why hadn't he sent a runner?

And no quarrymen had appeared on the ridge across the Río Tajo where the road emerged from the forest. They should be descending that road by now.

The brown brick towers at each end of the bridge were manned by Constable Luna's soldiers, formidable in their armor, but *Sangre Pura* spies reckoned only eight or ten guarded each end—half in the towers, the others on the ground. Constable Luna would pay the price of his arrogance, but why no word from Sancho?

There, a horse-drawn quarry wagon with high wooden sides. Horsemen appeared, and more wagons, threading their way down the opposite hill. *At last.* Marcos stepped into the alley, crowded with donkeys and carts. Scores of *Sangre Pura* sat in the dirt, leaning against the walls. Marcos spotted their leader, his short-brimmed cap tilted over his face. "Get up," Marcos said. The man stood, brushing off his breeches. He squinted and rubbed his stubbly chin. Others gathered around. "Choose a good runner," Marcos said. The fellow gestured to a lanky youth and Marcos told the boy, "Dash to our forces near Bisagra Gate. No stops along the way." The lad nodded and Marcos continued, "Tell Sancho to wait for the cathedral bells to chime the hour, then roll his wagons toward the gate." Marcos grabbed his arm to keep his attention. "Sancho must send a messenger to the Alcántara Bridge so all three forces attack at once. Repeat my instructions." The lad succeeded, and Marcos released him to sprint away.

He looked to the others. "Remember, everyone, you're workmen trudging home. Don't hurry, but meet the quarry wagons at the center of the bridge."

They waited. Men broke into small groups and murmured. The bells clanged. Marcos smiled to show confidence. But what if they captured this bridge and Sancho failed? "Roll the carts," he said.

A red-faced fellow took the reigns of the first donkey and tugged, drawing the cart, filled with sand and tools, from the alley. *Sangre Pura* fighters in work clothes followed the cart on foot. A second wagon rolled forth. Soon a procession advanced beside the city walls to the stone road leading down to San Martín Bridge. Twelve carts, with scores of *Sangre Pura* 'workmen' trudging beside, chatting, teasing—a congenial work party tired from the day's toil.

Across the Rio Tajo, the quarry wagons waited on the road near the river. Marcos stood close against the wall, where the soldiers in the towers couldn't see, and unfurled the red flag. The attack would come in minutes. But if one of their forces attacked too soon and the defenders sounded an alarm, the soldiers at the other gates might secure them. Skilled archers would defend.

He heard footsteps and turned. Sancho lumbered toward him.

"I hurried here to tell you," the stout wool carter gasped. "We haven't found the tax collector, but we'll torch his barn once the attack begins."

Marcos seized the front of Sancho's dirty, brown shirt. "You should be leading the assault at the gate! Holy Christ, we're going to fail."

Sweat glistened on Sancho's fat, stubbly cheeks. "My men are ready. They're waiting for the order."

"We're moving on the bridge. I sent a messenger, you fool." Marcos released his grip and looked to the *Sangre Pura* moving on their target, with no way to call them back.

Sancho's face contorted in a grimace, but only for a moment. "I met your messenger on the way here and sent him on to tell Juan Alonso and Fidel."

Marcos trusted Juan Alonso, who was a canon of the cathedral. He wasn't as sure of Fidel. "Both the bridge and gate at the same time. You should be there to direct."

"I wanted to watch San Martín fall with you." The oaf grinned at Marcos like a boy at his father. *Dios!*

Below, the lead wagons rolled onto the span from both sides and plodded toward the center. Sancho pointed. "See, you worry too much."

The men reached the middle and stopped. They appeared to argue, and then to wrestle. Marcos clenched his fists so hard his fingernails gouged his palms. Several of Luna's soldiers ran from the near guard tower toward the melee as the last wagons halted at the gate. Soldiers charged from the opposite guard tower, too. *Glory to God—it was working.*

The 'workmen' approaching the bridge on foot surged forward. At the near tower, *Sangre Pura* men pulled swords from beneath the sand in the wagons and swarmed in. Marcos saw three of Luna's soldiers atop the tower shoot crossbows at the men on the ground. A band of *Sangre Pura* faltered. Some fled, but others hurled rocks at the soldiers. The soldiers retrieved more crossbows, but then two of them turned.

"They're shooting into the tower," Sancho cried. "*Sangre Pura* is in."

At the center of the bridge, workmen stopped tussling, pulled pitchforks from their wagons, and speared startled soldiers. Marcos could hear only the thunder of the water on the spillway. But he saw his men toss two soldiers over the rail into the Río Tajo. In the near turret, soldiers fended off stones hurled by men on the ground and swung swords to fight attackers within. He had to be there!

As he dashed toward the bridge, each footfall shot pain from his left thigh to his spine. He gasped for breath. Ahead, a soldier toppled from the turret, and another. New men appeared on high, wearing work clothes and brandishing swords. Marcos slowed and raised his arms in triumph. Sancho came hurtling toward him, huffing like a beaten mule.

At the bridge, a dozen *Sangre Pura* grabbed him with grimy hands and raised him on their shoulders. The men shouted, "*Victory!*" again and again. "Set me down," Marcos said, but their shouts drowned his voice. *"Marcos García brings us victory."*

They carried him across the bridge and back again, almost dropping him into the river, and finally set him down. Sancho, red-faced and beaming, took Marcos in his sweaty grip and hugged him.

Marcos jerked free. "I must see what happened at the other gates while you neglected your post." He shoved Sancho away and rushed up the hill, through the city, toward Puerta de Bisagra, pausing often to catch his breath, worrying about this motley army he'd raised. Heading down, he rounded a corner and halted at the sight of the gate's near turret. The guards at its crown wore no armor or helmets. *Sangre Pura* had vanquished the corrupt constable.

The sky was growing dark and Marcos' leg throbbed as he mounted the stairs to the magistrate's office. He paused to take in air and prepare.

Sarmiento stood by the windows, his white shirt looking yellow in the torchlight, his eyes watchful.

"We've captured the bridges and gates," Marcos said. "Luna's soldiers have fled."

The magistrate didn't advance to congratulate him.

"Surprised by our success?"

"Pleased, Marcos, pleased." Sarmiento managed a smile. "You've rid us of Constable Luna's unwelcome presence. I would have expected the *pendejo* to leave a more competent force at the gates. Did you suffer many losses?"

"A few dead, a dozen wounded. If we'd failed, would you have handed me over to the *pendejo* for hanging?"

"You speak harshly, Deputy." Sarmiento swept a hand toward Marcos, like a man bestowing a precious gift.

"So you restore my office. And command of the *Guardia Civil*?"

"I gave you the dungeon, and you'd no doubt like the treasury. That's enough."

"The *Guardia* commandant is insubordinate." Marcos circled the big desk and took the magistrate's chair. "Most of his men are sons of Muslim curs."

Sarmiento grimaced. "Don Ricardo shows *me* respect."

"Perhaps this chair should be mine." Marcos leaned back. "You were about to give it to Luna, and I hold the city gates."

Sarmiento sneered. "You lack judgment for the job, Marcos."

"Your position is toothless while my men hold the gates."

Sarmiento reached the desk in three quick steps and stood over Marcos. "Your gates rest between Luna outside and my forces here in the *alcázar*. *You* are now within *my alcázar*. We've already agreed on terms."

Marcos held his gaze. "We still have questions to settle. You'll let me try the *marranos* for heresy? After all, Magistrate, their gold will make you rich."

"I won't have you murder a quarter of our citizens, but finding a pretense to confiscate their possessions with nine shares out of ten for the chief magistrate …"

Elation quickened Marcos' pulse. The greedy *cabrón* was going to agree. "Most of the pigs will flee, so you'll be spared the unpleasantness of killing them, but we'll purify the blood of this city. Five shares of every ten for my men."

Sarmiento straightened and pointed at Marcos. "If you petition the Vatican for an inquisitor, Archbishop Carrillo will oppose."

"We'll call it a '*limpieza*,' not an 'inquisition,' a program to purify the blood of Toledo. The pope is weak. Archbishop Carrillo avoids Toledo. You're the magistrate."

Sarmiento's expression turned thoughtful. "Whatever we call it, we'd want some sort of holy sanction."

"With an absent archbishop, Vicar Pero López de Gálvez is God's voice. We'll prove the *marranos* are false Christians, and Rome will thank us. You'll be justified in seizing the heretics' gold."

"If the pope objects to your *limpieza*, we'll say the vicar gave Rome's approval?" Marcos nodded and Sarmiento said, "Seven shares for me, and I control the distribution."

Three shares would make Marcos' men rich.

The magistrate beckoned and Marcos eased himself from the chair. Sarmiento settled in it. "Since we've ousted the king, we might as well rumple the pope's bonnet, too."

CHAPTER 58

—⧂—

Marcos shivered from the cold as he waited at the *marrano's* house. What treasures would a money-hungry parasite possess after controlling Toledo for years and conniving with the king's constable?

Sancho strolled toward him with a few fellows in muslin.

"You brought tools?" Marcos asked.

Sancho nodded, and one of the men hefted a sledgehammer. Marcos pointed at the door. As the man smashed it, Marcos pictured the hammer annihilating the *marrano's* face, blood spurting from nose and eyes like slivers of wood from his door.

He stepped over the broken boards and walked into a sitting room, his eyes drawn by a patch of color on the wall, a painting of a woman in her thirties—the *marrano's* wife. It was too late to slay the bitch. She'd died years before. He took out his dagger to slice it.

A shout from the back. "There's someone here!"

Marcos found Sancho blocking the doorway of a kitchen storeroom. "She tried to get past me, but I knocked her down."

A woman sat on the floor beneath shelves of earthen crocks, her white apron crammed between her thighs, yellow skirt askew, fat ankles sticking out. "Who are you?"

"*Criada*," She looked up with wide, pleading eyes.

The maid would know things. "Bring her."

Sancho yanked the woman up and shoved her into the kitchen. She was in her forties, Marcos guessed, too fat to be interesting. "Where's Viçente Pérez?"

"I don't know." She backed up until she hit a tall cabinet, slid past it, and wedged herself in a corner of the room.

"No need for fear," Marcos soothed. "Just answer our questions."

"He's been away for months." A tear trickled down her cheek. She shook her head. "I don't know where."

"How do you get paid?"

"I go to the bookseller on Calle de Gracia. Señor Pérez has arranged—"

Marcos was losing interest. He wanted to sift through the *marrano's* secret possessions. "Are you a Jewess?"

Her eyes bulged. "No, Señor, Christian."

"Was your father a Jew?"

Sancho stepped around Marcos and patted the woman's cheek. "Better not lie. We'll find out if you do."

"No. No," she cried.

"Your grandfather?" Marcos asked. "It's hard for me to restrain Sancho."

The maid began to sob and babble incoherent words.

"Take her home and find out. If she's lying, lock her up. And capture the bookseller."

The house held no grand statues or paintings, no golden ornaments, and no indication of the *marrano's* whereabouts—a poor showing for a man who'd stolen from Toledo's till for so long.

The desk in the corner of the library held only a simple pen stand. He slapped it off, the ink jar flying open, blue liquid splattering across the wooden floor and onto a wall. The desk was devoid of interesting papers, but on the bookshelf, he spotted a framed commendation from King Juan for meritorious service to the city of Toledo. He snorted and grabbed it. The damned *marrano* had nearly ruined Toledo, ripped the soul right out of it, and here was evidence of the king's collusion. The commendation that mattered awaited those who struck the evil down.

In the largest bedroom, he found a pencil drawing in a wooden frame atop the bureau of a man and a boy. The *marrano* and his son. He snatched the picture from its frame and held it as he examined a tall mahogany armoire filled with the *marrano's* clothing. He leaned into it, trying to detect the scent of unholy evil. The doors were inlaid with some lighter wood, the cabinet costly. "Remove the garments and bring this."

The men tossed the clothing to the floor and lugged the cabinet to the dining room. Marcos ordered them to fill it with silver utensils and candlesticks.

He laid the certificate on the dining table and listened to metal clattering into the cabinet as he examined the drawing of the smug *pendejo* and his adolescent boy. Marcos knew his name—*Diego*, and he'd learned his whereabouts from Sarmiento's contacts in Valladolid. In his twenties now, he'd begun work at the royal treasury, another *marrano* hoarding money for King Juan and stealing for himself. Marcos pulled his dagger and slit the drawing, pressing hard to gouge the table top, separating the man and boy. He ripped Viçente Pérez in half before discarding him and slipped the boy's picture into his pocket.

The men had finished with the silverware and the cabinet wasn't full. "Add the chandelier."

Back in the sitting room, he yanked the woman's portrait free and tossed it on the floor, then dug his dagger into the plaster wall, carving, "P-U-T-A." *Whore.*

From the floor, the *marrano's* wife smiled at him. She wore a red dress that revealed a triangle of pale skin from her throat to the space between her breasts, like the harlot she was. A ruby necklace rested on that skin—almost pleasing.

Sancho stood watching from the doorway. "You fancy that painting?" the wool carter asked.

"Don't be absurd. Was the maid lying?"

Sancho shook his head. "No Jew ancestors. We captured the bookseller and locked him in a closet at the tavern."

"Deliver that cabinet of silver to Magistrate Sarmiento. Smash the dishes and scatter the pieces around the house."

Sancho frowned. "My wife would like some new plates."

"Give your wife the bed, and leave the garments to the men. Boil them first to get out the stink."

The stocky wool carter rubbed his hands together as if pleased, but his eyes narrowed. "I'll have them fetch the woman's picture to your quarters, then."

"Fine, Sancho, but break the damned dishes."

CHAPTER 59

—✲—

PERO TOOK SEVERAL LONG BREATHS to control his nerves as he focused on the greasy hair of the sinner's head. The man's clothes were raggedy with bloody slashes across the back, like the last penitent Pero had seen. At least this one was able to kneel by his own capacity. Pero avoided looking at the man's back and evaded thoughts of what had slit the shirt, because such thinking had taken him close to vomiting with the last man. "You confess that you practiced Hebrew dogma while pretending to be Catholic?"

"Yes, as I told the jailer, Padre."

"You admit this freely before God?"

The man's shoulders trembled just a bit, and he stared at the floor, clearly too guilty to look a priest in the eye. "Aye, freely."

Another priest might question that word, given the state of the fellow's shirt, but Pero had no such intention. "You repent and vow to practice only the Catholic rites for the rest of your days."

"I do and I will, gladly."

"Why?"

"Because it's right." The fellow nodded and nodded again. "It's what God wants. I understand that now."

Pero thumped the man lightly on the forehead to make him look up. "Now this is important. Have you ever fallen from grace and confessed to a priest before today?"

"No, of course not. I didn't—I didn't realize what I was doing, I suppose. A few days in that cell, I had time to think and pray. Now I see it."

Pero let out a long slow breath and smiled. He was saving another soul without sacrificing a life. "Very well. You will be given a penance, and after you complete it, you'll return to God's grace. In addition to the prayers I command, you will thank Jesus every day for this gift."

—–ᘏ–—

After the man was led out, Pero found himself alone in this grand assembly room of the *alcázar*.

He leaned back in his chair. On the ceiling, he saw a painting of God the Father gazing down between heaven's clouds. Perhaps a king had commissioned the painting back when Toledo was the city of monarchs.

The first two *marrano* prisoners he'd seen this day had sinned by reverting to Hebrew ways. They'd confessed and repented. God in his mercy would accept them back. Well and good for them, but how was Pero to justify this to Marcos?

So many times Pero had followed Marcos' instructions without question—preaching all those sermons, even the difficult ones, to the ruffians of *Sangre Pura*, and this past week, dismissing the cathedral archdeacon because he disagreed with the *limpieza*. Marcos was brilliant and usually right—striving to be in God's service—but not always. It had been wrong to send Pero after that *Morisca* girl all those years ago.

God's portrait on the ceiling comforted Pero because it scared him. *God,* he prayed, *help me know which of these sinners can be redeemed. Help me bring them back to you. Lord, please keep my thoughts from confusion if Marcos urges me to do what is against your will. And Holy Jesus, don't let Marcos beat me.*

God stared into his eyes, not angry but kind, not condemning but determined.

A loud crack. The door swung open. Marcos strode in, followed by a uniformed *Guardia Civil* and a peasant in a spotted, tan frock—*Sangre Pura*. These two dragged an emaciated fellow, shirtless, with a stained cloth draped over his shoulders. Pero saw red spatters on his skin, bloody knees exposed through rips in his trousers, a dark stain below his crotch. Dirt caked the man's face and his eyes bulged. Pero couldn't breathe. The prisoner bore a likeness to one of his former parishioners, a merchant of some sort—a book dealer.

Marcos said, "This man has sins to confess. Don't you?"

The guards held the man up as he mumbled, "Aye, Padre."

"Louder," Marcos demanded.

The man sucked in a breath. "Vicar. I have sinned."

Pero wondered why Marcos had personally brought this sinner. Perhaps he'd offended in some especially grievous way. "Kneel." Pero took a cushion from a chair, leaned forward, and dropped it near his foot.

Marcos kicked the pillow and it careened across the polished wood floor. "The lousy *marrano* has soiled himself. He'd ruin the magistrate's pillow."

"He's hurt," Pero said.

Marcos sneered. "Kneel, you son of a Jew whore."

The *Sangre Pura* pushed the prisoner and he fell to his knees, winced, and hunched forward. "Please have mercy, Padre."

"Speak up," Marcos commanded.

Pero smelled the man's urine. His stomach lurched at the thought of opposing his mentor, but God was watching. "Marcos, this man's confession is between him and God's delegate."

Marcos grunted. "He'll lie to you."

Pero's hands quivered but he swallowed his trepidation. "This is the way it must be."

Marcos stomped to the opposite side of the salon and watched.

Pero sighed and regarded the prisoner. "Speak to the Almighty of your sins."

"I-I have practiced Hebrew rites while a member of the church."

"What rites?"

The penitent grimaced. Tears dripped from his chin. "I ordered my wife not to cook on Saturday. I ate meat prepared in the old ways." The fellow appeared to think for a moment. "I-I called God, '*Yahweh.*' Oh yes, I mocked Jesus, calling him 'false God.'" The man looked over his shoulder to where Marcos stood.

God watched from above.

"What else?"

"That's enough, isn't it? I've sinned terribly, Vicar."

These were mortal sins, but the bookseller might still be saved. "And now you repent? You seek Christ's mercy?"

"Yes. Yes." The prisoner nodded vehemently.

Pero's heart beat faster. He was bringing this man back to the Lord. "You'll atone, take the sacraments, and affirm Jesus Christ?"

"I will."

"I have one vital question. Have you ever done this before—reverted to the vile ways and come back to the church?"

"I don't know what I'm supposed to say." The prisoner glanced across at Marcos again. His shoulders trembled.

Pero touched the *marrano's* arm. "Only the truth before God."

"What's the worst thing I could have done?" The man stared at his clenched hands. "He'd want me to say that."

"The worst is to fall from God, receive absolution, and then blaspheme again." Pero pointed at the sinner. "But only say it if it's true."

"I did it. I did all that you said, and now I seek God's mercy." The prisoner, still shaking, raised folded hands toward Pero.

Pero felt anger tighten his chest, anger at the *marrano's* sins, and re- lief, because now Pero could hand him over to Marcos. For his sins, the heathen deserved the torture they'd given him, and if his repentance was insincere, the torture to come in hell. "You confessed to a priest before? What penance did he impose?"

"Yes. Yes." The bookseller looked pleased. "The priest commanded me to pray for three hours on the stone steps of the church with no shoes on." The man kept nodding and looking at Pero. "And they laid a sack of flour on my shoulders. I swear. The priest was furious and made me pray on a cold day bearing that weight. Just don't let the guards take me back to the basement."

No, Pero thought. *We'll be sending you to God's cellar.*

Marcos strolled back to Pero. "A good day, Vicar: three for the executioner."

Pero's stomach felt like a sea of writhing worms. "I'm sorry, Marcos. I can't relinquish them all."

"*What?* Three sinners confessed."

Pero didn't dare get to his feet with Marcos so close over him. "They're all guilty, Marcos, but, praise Jesus, God is merciful."

"Don't be a fool."

Fool or not, Pero couldn't relent. "This is the holy sacrament. If a man strays once and repents, the church forgives. Only if he blasphemes a second time do we give him over for civil punishment."

"They're *marranos,* not real Christians."

"You can execute the third man." Pero's thigh muscle twitched and his voice quaked. "That's all I can allow. I've consulted my priests and read the words of Saint Thomas. And there was Archbishop Carrillo's letter condemning our *limpieza* and reminding me of these church doctrines."

"Stop ranting, Vicar."

"The church is my haven, Marcos. If a Vatican official questions my acts …"

Marcos took a few steps away and stalked back. "Popes are corrupt. God speaks to *me*, Pero. The Lord Jesus takes my confession."

Pero glanced up at God for assurance. Marcos stepped close, swinging his arm back to strike. Pero turned his head, ready for the blow. "Better not to beat me if you wish my help." Pero saw Marcos' hand still. "Magistrate Sarmiento insists on church approval."

"Don't oppose me, Vicar," Marcos said.

But he hadn't struck. Pero felt relieved and a little bit … powerful. "God speaks to us through popes and saints. God shows mercy because men are flawed. Those men confessed, and they want to believe in Jesus."

"God commands me to cast the *marranos* out of Castile."

"Only in the manner he provides." Marcos was shaking his head, but Pero continued. "You hurt that bookseller. The church only condones torture when there's no other way to the truth."

Marcos gave a menacing grin. "That sinner conspires with our enemy, the *marrano*, and refuses to divulge his whereabouts."

Pero's chest tightened at the memory of that day in Viçente Pérez' office, when Pérez had forced Pero to admit his lie about the mute. Sweat dripped down his sides beneath his cassock. "The book merchant confessed that he had forsaken Jesus more than once. I'll approve his execution."

Marcos brought his face close to Pero's, breathing out the stink of garlic. "I have more *marranos* in the dungeon. I'll expect better from you tomorrow."

CHAPTER 60

—◆—

VIÇENTE RETURNED WITH THE KING'S party to Naples. But his senses trailed back to that bluff above the sea in Castellammare, touching Francesca's body in the sheer gowns she wore—the scents and sounds of the sea lingered in Viçente's dreams. Her scents and her laughter, too, and her luscious contours. Francesca had forbidden him her skin, but its silk through the gossamer fabric had been intimate and thrilling. And now that he'd savored those delights, it was time to reveal his family secret, and, if she didn't cast him away, to speak again of marriage.

He found Francesca the next evening in the dining hall, conversing with some of the king's guests, and he pulled her aside for a moment. "We have to talk."

"I feel the same way, darling, and I'm going to arrange it. You'll see." She squeezed his hand and gave him a luminous smile before turning back to conversation. He was assigned a seat near the center of the long table, between a plump friar and an even-more-rotund courtier. As they dined on a roast pheasant, he watched Francesca, seated at one end of the table, and the king at the other, sending her little smiles each time he shifted his attention from one guest to another.

He yearned to talk to her, nervous about what he saw between her and King Alfonso, what he sensed that he couldn't see. The pheasant was not welcome in his stomach, but he managed.

After dinner, she accompanied some of the guests for farewells at the front portal and then hustled back, skirts crinkling. She took his hand and led him toward the garden. Out to the balcony, hands entwined, the side of her thigh skimming his, down the steps, along the path, murmuring, "Viçente, my love. Oh, Viçente. You want to talk, and I do, too. But Alfonso still has important guests, and he allows me scant minutes with you. Can you wait one more day?"

She was part of his life now, or he hoped she was. He needed her to accept him and his past, to understand him fully and change her life to be with him. "I want to speak of marriage, and I have something to confess, and—"

"We'll speak of everything my love, everything you wish and more."

Her mood and her sparkling eyes seduced. "If I wait until tomorrow?" he asked.

She raised a hand to the sky. "Tomorrow night, the moon will be lovely and full, like this, and we'll discuss it all."

He chuckled, relieved and frustrated at the thought of waiting another day, but enchanted by her joy. "What about this lovely moon?"

"We'll share its light and our love. We'll share exquisite moments. What more could you wish?"

"What any man does." He glanced up at Carlo, watching from the balcony, and then cupped her chin in his hand. "Is this another of your mysteries, and will you reveal it for me now?"

She shook her head. "What fun is a secret told? You must meet me on the island of Ischia, in the town of the same name."

"Does the moon know to look for us there?"

She nodded, pressing her chin into his palm.

"Will it shine on Carlo at some other location?" He couldn't imagine how she'd rid them of the chaperone, but why else would she glow this way?

She frowned and tugged his hand from her chin. "No more questions. Go to your office tomorrow, and make some excuse to leave at noontime. Take the boat to Ischia and find a room at the *albergo*."

He did ask other questions, but she laughed them away, and later he tossed in bed, his slumber filled with joyous anticipation and anxious worries.

—◊—

That morning, before sailing to Ischia, Viçente headed to Padre Eugenio's monastery. As he strode downhill, all of his needs, desires, and fears spun his thoughts like a waterspout at sea.

He could have destroyed the testament or left it in Toledo, but he'd brought it for her. Did that make the least bit of sense? Did some sacrilege permeate his soul, drawing him to it?

Pitch lamps illuminated the dim hallway as Padre Eugenio shuffled toward him. With one hand, the padre adjusted the brown skullcap that couldn't quite cover his baldness. In the other he held the leather-wrapped bundle. He met Viçente's eyes and offered the package. "You seek this?"

How had the padre known?

Viçente took a lamp and the testament into the chapel. Sitting on a pew, he opened the book and turned pages until he came to a picture of Moses receiving the tablets. With his magnifying lens he focused on this powerful figure, wearing, like Padre Eugenio, a brown robe with a rope cincture. The tablets lay shimmering at his feet as Moses' eyes bulged with fright. Lightning, red as blood, filled the sky. Viçente shivered and touched the picture, taking in God's power. This book was impure, scribed in Latin and Hebrew—Christian and profane. But Jesus had come of the Jews. Jewish blood filled the disciples.

Now Moses' anxious eyes brought memories of Viçente's father the night of his thirteenth birthday. Moses and Judah, frightened or guilty because of their sins? So many times after, as he'd grown up in his parents' house, his father's eyes had watched him, Papa not speaking because Viçente had rebuked speech. Maybe Papa's eyes had held not guilt, as Viçente had seen it, but profound regret.

He knelt, gazed at the crude wooden cross on the mortared wall, and whispered, "Lord God, how can my Jewish blood be a sin if I believe in you?" The lightning in the book was red, and there at the front of the chapel was the cross, where Christ had shed red God blood. Had God so loved the Jews that he'd shed his blood, giving Moses the laws, and again from Jesus on the cross? No. God disdained Jews, but he loved those who'd seen the truth. Why, then, should so many Old Christians despise converts?

"Jesus, Son of God, I am so thankful that you came to save my soul."

The book carried the word of God, even if the Jews held it sacred too. If he gave it to Francesca, and if she trusted him, she'd understand.

He re-wrapped the book and returned it to the padre, who handed him a half dozen letters. He sat on a boulder by the waterfront and opened the first, which bore Prince Enrique's seal and was dated less than three weeks before.

My Dear Viçente,

I have not written for all these months because I was angry. I offered you the great city and you fled. I would write of your stupidity, but I seek your agreement.

Sarmiento governs Toledo like a fool. His deputy, Marcos García de Mora, encourages riots in the streets and attacks on the Jewish Quarter. My father learned of this and told Sarmiento to protect them—can you imagine?—defending Jews. Sarmiento ignored the order and Bishop Barrientos counseled my father to divide Sarmiento's power by returning your old mentor, Ayala, as chief magistrate. Father appointed Ayala, but Sarmiento ignores that demand as well. Father seems more bewildered than furious at this treason. He vacillates and makes excuses. He disgusts me. I should be sovereign of Castile. Even as I advise my father, I build my army.

You forsook reason for a woman. I've only twenty-one years, but I've known many wenches besides my deformed spouse. Their pleasure's brief. Surely, you realize this now.

I forgive you and I renew the quest to make you chief magistrate of Toledo. Return and pledge me loyalty. Though Father's irrational and he snubs me much of the time, please believe me when I say I can give you the city. Become my friend again. Become powerful. I miss your steady counsel.

Enrique, your future king

The name 'Marcos García' made his skin itch and his gut sour. How had that *pendejo* gained Sarmiento's trust? And trusting García—who so loathed *conversos*—said much about Sarmiento's intentions. What evil might they perpetrate? Obviously, they'd already begun; those attacks on the Jews, the dismissal of converts from office. And if they were ignoring the king's demands, what more?

His heart was pounding hard, loathing the images that the name 'Marcos García' planted in his brain.

Viçente slid the letter into his pocket, picturing the rabbi for a moment. He gave a quick prayer that the infuriating cleric would be all right. Damn him.

Enrique's offer again—he did not want this. He hated the thought, but could he refuse again with the potential danger escalating?

He looked at the remaining five letters, all from Diego. He checked the dates and opened the most recent, counting on his son to raise his spirits.

Greetings and good health, Papa!

Your last letter amazed and amused me. I am so pleased that I met Lady Francesca, so now I can picture the two of you being tracked around the palace by that suspicious chaperone. I laughed aloud at the irony; you issue death certificates in the government of King Alfonso while I toil to balance Castile's royal revenues here in Valladolid.

As I wrote before, I've been seeing a great deal of Amanda, who serves me breakfast each morning at my lodging and whom I take to dinner most evenings at a tavern. She's the prettiest girl in Valladolid and I know you'd like her. I'm doing my best to fool her into thinking that I'm not a bad fellow so she'll keep seeing me. That should be incentive enough for you to return soon.

I'll write more of that later, but there's shocking news. I've learned from my friends back home that Toledo is racked with strife. Armed men roam the streets at night, attacking anyone who dares walk alone, even in our part of the city. Some of our fellow conversos have barely escaped and one was badly beaten. No one dares venture out past dark. The Jewish section's under siege. They've beaten many of them, including women, and there's a rumor that some have been killed. Of course we're not supposed to care about Jews, but I know you strove to protect them while you were first deputy.

My friend in the ministry tells me the king has written again to Magistrate Sarmiento, chiding him for giving Marcos García too much power. I think you mentioned García to me, didn't you? Some foul rogue? The king lost patience and ordered Sarmiento to give control of the city courts back to Magistrate Ayala. King Juan's still hopeful that Sarmiento will restore peace. We all hope for that, but Sarmiento does not respond, and now Constable Luna's received the king's permission to take some secret action.

I'm sorry to send this news, for I know it will trouble you.

There were two more pages and four more letters, but it was time for Viçente to board his boat.

CHAPTER 61

—⁓—

ON THE BOAT, SAILING TO Ischia, fears and worries assailed him. He'd ignored the events in Castile too long, ignored his duty, pretended he had no duty, kept telling himself there was no real danger for *conversos* back home, telling and telling and telling again, because it was a lie that had to be told a hundred times to make it real.

All because he wanted to remain in this romantic bliss.

But today's letters changed it all. Marcos García was governing with Sarmiento. Converts could be in as much danger as Jews. Staying in Naples would rend his soul. Leaving Francesca would shred his heart.

But what of her? Francesca had evaded questions of marriage, even without knowing his parents' sins. His Jewish ancestry ruined all—her willingness to marry him, Alfonso's disdain, the cursed Bible and his own doubts. How would she speak the words of rejection when he confessed?

All the more reason not to put it off.

For the first time since his wounding, his path was clear. He would tell her all, propose marriage, and ask her to travel with him to the king's court in Valladolid. Would she accept? If not, was he prepared to go without her? Was the situation in Toledo really so dire? And where did the path go from Valladolid? Could he place any faith in Enrique's fantasy about making him magistrate?

—⁓—

He arrived in Ischia and took a room at the inn. As dark fell, Viçente threw open the shutters and gazed down at the deserted square and docks beyond. Still agonizing, he'd come to another question: What emptiness in his soul had let him ignore the threats to his people? And his answer, weak as it might be: *I'm depraved because I'm in love.*

Soft light from lanterns across the harbor shimmered on the water. A figure wrapped in a shawl darted from a side street beneath an awning to the inn's entrance. Hope filled his heart, and he said a quick prayer. A knock on the door. He opened it and Penélope leaned in, her plain features serious. "Come, Signore. Quietly."

They hurried downstairs, past the square to a side street that narrowed to a trail and led up a valley. A cloud drifted to cover the moon and they slowed. Water trickled nearby. A pungent smell came on the wind. The cloud floated on, and the moon shone on a grove of trees. Lamps glimmered here and there in the small forest. The path divided to three tracks entering the woods. He saw figures lurking in the shadows and halted— men wearing helmets but no metal armor— mercenary soldiers?

Penélope touched his arm. "Don't fear. Follow to the left and you'll find her." The maid took another path and disappeared among the trees.

He entered the woods and glanced back. No pursuers. Advancing along the path, he saw a shaft of moonlight through the trees—a clearing. The flowing water sounded closer now, and the odor told him it was a sulfur spring. In the clearing, water glistened in a stream that gushed beside the trail. A form sat at the edge of a pool. The figure slipped into the water.

"Penélope was very slow." Francesca's voice, her music, her moon shining on the side of her face and neck, bare shoulders.

What had plagued his mind all day fell out of it at the sight of glistening skin, at the thought of what they might do.

"Is anyone else here?" he whispered. "What should I—"

"Enter the water, of course." She giggled.

"But ..."

"It's all right. Take off all but a little something."

He kept his under-breeches and watched her as he backed into the water, its warmth soothing his calves and thighs. The bottom of the pool was smooth rock with blocks of stone for seats. He settled beside her, water lapping at the top of his chest. The moonlight revealed her shoulders, her collarbones. He reached out and she caught his hand. "What are you wearing?" he asked.

"You aren't patient about secrets." She grasped his other hand to restrain it, leaned close, and kissed him.

Her tongue met his while she still held his hands. He slid his foot along the smooth skin of her calf. Still kissing, she pressed herself to his chest—her breast, intimate skin. *Oh God, what joy.* She held his hands a little longer, then released. He ran them over her naked back. "You have no secrets now," he whispered, stroking her stomach and breast. But was it true?

She sighed. "What could be more important to reveal than this?"

His heritage was more important, but not more pressing. And what of the events back home and the mercenary soldiers in the woods? He didn't care. He slipped off his underclothes and lifted her to the surface of the water, marveling at the sensuous curve of her spine, her buttocks and thighs.

Touching with his fingers, savoring with his eyes, he wanted her so badly but needed to delight in seeing her and to feel every soft, hidden part.

She moaned and slid on top of him. They made love in the pool, and nothing else mattered, only the explosion of passion and the peaceful holding afterwards.

After a while she led him out. They wrapped themselves in towels, and Francesca spread a blanket on a patch of earth.

She lay on her back, looking up at the sky. "I have more news, my love. Chief Magistrate Sarmiento met Alfonso's brother, the King of Navarre, plotting another rebellion."

"*Madre de Dios.*" The implications dazed him. If Sarmiento plotted against King Juan, the king's protection for *conversos* and Jews would be meaningless. Marcos García and Sarmiento—evil upon evil with no restraint.

"You see darling, you made the right decision, staying here. I bring you information most interesting."

Even after having read the letters, he'd wanted to believe that he could stay in Naples a while longer. But with this news, no illusions remained. He had to leave, not delay for a proper wedding. She'd agree to marry and go or … she'd have to decide.

"Diego and Enrique wrote to me," he said. "Mobs have been killing Jews and attacking converts in Toledo."

She turned on her side to stare at him. "You can't think of going."

"I've tried to ignore the danger, but now I can't. Marcos García, that thug I spoke of who killed the mute, has gained control. And now you tell me Sarmiento's plotting rebellion. My people are vulnerable—the men who worked for me, their families, the lads who fought with me."

"Try not to think of it. You said yourself, you have no power there. And here you have me." She reached to touch his cheek.

"With this information, I'll convince the king to help. Enrique still wants to make me magistrate."

"Enrique's rash. He convinced you to go to war, and look." She glanced at his shoulder. "You *are* considering it."

He started to speak, but she blurted, "This is horrible." She shoved his chest with both hands. "You promised you wouldn't go back to war."

"I'll go to Valladolid, to King Juan. There's no fighting there."

"All of Castile is a damned war. Stay with me."

Shocked by her shove and this angry tone, he took a calming breath before answering. "I hate the idea of returning. I hate the rage that's infected the church and the prince scheming against his father. I despise *Sangre Pura*, but I'm so far away here, so helpless. I can't imagine how far this has gone since my son's letter."

"You didn't mention that you hated leaving me."

"I hope I won't have to." He took her hand. "Come with me, dear one."

She was staring at him hard, shiny tears running down her cheeks.

He wrapped his arms around her. She held back and then allowed him to draw her in. "Don't answer yet," he said. "There's something I must divulge first, but if you agree, we'll marry right away."

"Don't speak as if I can accept this."

He felt the gentle heaves of her body as she sobbed.

They lay that way for a few minutes, and then she pushed herself back, wiped the tears, and looked into his eyes. "I'd pictured a longer courtship." She gave a mirthless chuckle.

"If we go to Castile together, you can make sure I'm careful," he said.

She cuffed his chin with a hand. "Before you hugged me just now, I was devising a plan."

"Oh."

"I'd ask Alfonso to put you under guard so you couldn't run to danger."

"You wouldn't."

"Just a dozen years or so, until you were too old to travel."

"I don't think I'd like that."

She wiped at her eyes again. "Then I thought about why I admire you so much. You're serious—far too serious. But you stand for something that's better and more noble than all the men they call 'noble.' When you came here, you were wounded and beaten, and even then you needed more to do than laze in the Italian sun and dine with me. My king had you run one of his bureaus, and you put it in order so quickly that now *it* bores you. Every day you grow stronger, coming back to the true Viçente. I've known this. You can't be content issuing marriage licenses to aristocrats. But I was hoping to put it off.. You must achieve for the good. You must protect people, your people. I can't overcome this."

Staring at her, Viçente was thinking what an amazing woman she was, seeing all of this in him. But did it mean she'd go, or was she about to cast him aside?

"Now," she said. "I've been serious like you, at least for a few minutes. We were having a joyous evening, and then it went sour. This next disclosure of yours, you said you've been putting it off, so it must be dismal as well."

"I—"

She unwrapped herself from her towel and lay back on the blanket, naked in the moonlight. "I'd appreciate a little more joy first. I'm chilly. Please take off your towel and warm me."

They coupled again and held each other. He felt her heartbeat against his chest, but it didn't comfort him, knowing what he had to say. He eased off her and sat up. Moonlight cast her body in a soft glow, dark nipples, shadows beneath her breasts, along her ribs, where her pelvis rose beside her abdomen, black tangle below. What he'd longed for all these months, what he'd just found, he had to risk for truth. "You put me off when I spoke of marriage back in Castellammare. Is it because King Alfonso would oppose it? I'm sorry. It's presumptuous."

"I do, Viçente, I want to share your life." She pressed his hand to her stomach.

"Alfonso looks at you as if you're a possession, and some of the things you said ... does he ask more of you than to hostess his dinners?"

"No, Viçente, no longer, but I'll tell you." She took a breath. "When I was fifteen, Alfonso visited my mother and me in Sardinia and stayed at our house. Our father—Alfonso's and mine—had urged him to care for us and always to treat me as a sister, but he didn't always live up to the promise. He seemed so gallant then, can you believe?" She let out a harsh little laugh as the shiny streak of a tear ran down her cheek. "The way he looked at me made me feel like ... a woman. The way he kissed me, too, many times during that visit, but that was all. Maybe that's another disgrace. My soul has many. Now you know them all."

He stroked her side. "Your soul is very special. Does he still nurture that passion? Would he try to prevent you leaving with me?"

She flinched. "Of course not. He's protective as a brother would be. Hug me again, Viçente." She settled back on the blanket and covered herself with a towel.

"Not yet. I have to tell you about my disgrace." He lay close, watching her worried eyes. "You know there are different kinds of converts. Some grew up Jews and converted by choice."

She skimmed a hand through his hair. "It's not important. I haven't resisted because you're a convert."

"I need to say this, Francesca. Some Jews converted out of fear or pretended to convert. The pretenders are vile. Because of them, Old Christians mistrust us all." He hesitated. "And then there are *conversos* like me."

Francesca touched his temple. "But you've prayed and taken Communion with me."

He kissed her hand. His gut felt queasy, as it had that terrible night in his father's library. "My parents raised me Christian, but on my thirteenth birthday, they confessed." His voice broke. "They'd pretended all those years."

"Viçente."

"They never asked me to follow their godless ways, but they secretly denied the Savior."

"But you …"

Tears ran down his cheeks, and he brushed them off. "My family was contemptible. I'm a seed spawned in disgrace."

She searched his eyes. "If we only accepted lovers whose ancestors were pure, we'd be alone. We're here, in love, and we both believe."

"I have an old Bible written in both Hebrew and Latin. A rabbi in Toledo gave it to me."

"A rabbi—was he trying to convert you?" Francesca shook her head.

"He gave it out of gratitude after I ordered the Toledan guards to protect Jews."

"That was your duty. You said you believe."

"I carried the testament all the way to Naples because it's precious. I wanted to give it to you."

"In Jesus?" she said. "You believe in him?"

"In Jesus, yes."

She wrapped her arms around him. "Throw the Bible into the sea, Viçente. It can only bring harm. Hold me, and don't think of it any more."

Viçente swallowed to steady his voice. "My papa cut out a piece of my heart the night he told me."

She held him tight and whispered. "I love you and I think you're perfect."

They embraced, not speaking, as tenderness seeped from her bosom into his.

There was so much more to speak of, but she had said enough; she wanted to share his life. He'd give her a little time to think this over, and then tomorrow night, back in Naples, he'd press for an immediate nuptial.

They parted before dawn. Viçente followed the trail back to the square and slipped into the *albergo*. After breakfast, he took the boat for Naples, feeling so full of love and longing, he wanted to shout. Instead, standing at the prow as the vessel skimmed past the tower into Naples harbor, he silently thanked Jesus for this new chance at love.

The boat docked near the citadel. He jumped off and strode to the monastery. He didn't know if he could destroy the old Bible. It was God's word, even if part was in Hebrew.

A monk admitted him and left him to wait in the vestibule. Hearing footfalls, he looked up. Instead of the gaunt Padre Eugenio, a large priest lumbered toward him in a white linen robe. The man passed a pitch lamp, and Viçente recognized Bishop Barrientos. The sight of his beloved priest should have delighted him, but ... "Bishop, why are you here?"

"A fine greeting." Barrientos embraced Viçente and then stood away, his expression somber. "My son, the wickedness in Toledo requires that we travel to Rome. Come to my chamber and I'll explain."

PART VI
POPE NICHOLAS

—⁂—

In the Roman Court where His Holiness resides, I saw that everyone present did obeisance to money. They all honored it with due solemnity and bowed down before it as if to His Majesty.

—FROM *LIBRO DE BUEN AMOR*, BY JUAN RUIZ.

If any one abide not in me, he shall be cast forth as a branch, and shall wither, and they shall gather him up, and cast him into the fire, and he burneth

—JOHN 6:15.

CHAPTER 62

—◊◊◊—

Viçente followed Bishop Barrientos along the corridor. "Your news, it's not about Diego?"

"No, Viçente, but we mustn't talk here."

So the evils in Toledo had worsened still further, or the Royal Cousins' armies had attacked, or worse. They entered a stone cell barely two paces wide with a narrow bed, wooden chair, and small table with a lit candle. Barrientos bolted the door.

"What's happened, Bishop?"

"Marcos García and his men have ceased catapulting stones at Jews and begun torturing converts. They seek confessions of heresy in a travesty they call '*limpieza.*'"

"My God. How could Archbishop Carrillo allow it?"

"His eminence doesn't dare enter Toledo. There's no church sanction, only some rogue priests."

"How far has it gone?"

"I see from your face, my son, you already imagine it. Some *conversos* fought back. They were slaughtered and their leader hung upside down in Zacadover Square. Now Sarmiento and García arrest whom they want." Barrientos grimaced. "Before I left Castile, they'd caged several city officials and affluent tradesmen. They claim that some admitted performing Hebrew rites."

Viçente bumped the table and grabbed the candle to prevent it from falling. "You can't believe their confessions, Bishop."

"Taken under torture, I'm sure. We must beseech Pope Nicholas to intervene, or other cities might follow."

"Why would the Holy Father involve himself in King Juan's crisis?"

"This *limpieza* is in fact an inquisition, and only God can commission one, that is to say, His Holiness. If Toledo confiscates converts' wealth, the pope receives nothing. If God commissions an inquisition, the Vatican takes a share. Also, we will bribe His Holiness. I'll explain later."

Viçente pictured Francesca in the moonlight, their intimacies and promises, his proposal of marriage that she hadn't answered. If he left now, as Barrientos asked, that would have to wait. "Bishop, it's a terrible time for me to leave."

"We need a symbol, my son, a voice of the persecuted. You are that man, the only one who can do it. And the pope is the only person who can halt this travesty without bloodshed." The bishop swung the door open and gestured for Viçente to step outside. "I'll change my robe. Then we'll fetch your clothing from the palace and speak to your lady."

Waiting in the hall, Viçente tried to think of some way to delay this long enough to marry Francesca, if she agreed. But what reason could outweigh the lives of Toledo's *conversos*? His people needed him, and he was in a position to act.

Francesca met them in a salon wearing a simple, cream-colored dress that revealed little. Her hair, still damp from bathing, shone a brilliant black upon her shoulders, and Viçente found her lovelier than ever. She listened in silence as Barrientos explained. He finished with, "I'll grant you privacy," and stepped out. Carlo entered.

Francesca pointed at the chaperone. "Turn your back."

Carlo opened his mouth to reply, but Francesca's glare allowed no opposition. Carlo moved to a window, parted the curtains, and looked out.

"Do you understand?" Viçente asked. "Now I can really make a difference."

"I want to say no, but I do. You've missed Toledo and longed to do something for your people." She stepped into his arms and he held her. "I almost wish you weren't such an admirable fellow."

"I was afraid you'd beg me not to go."

"I've had all your time these past months, and this is crucial." She pressed herself to him and kissed him long and hard. He felt her damp hair between his fingers and felt his desire, and hated the idea of leaving. "And it's a relief," she said. "Rome's far safer than Castile."

She backed up a step, and he saw the misgivings in her furrowed brow and tight smile. "We've removed all obstacles to our joy, and you run away. If I didn't see such regret on your dear face, I'd think you'd drunk your fill from my cup."

"I want to drink it every day. Marry me when I'm back from Rome."

She hugged him again, fiercely, and whispered, "God protect you. Come back soon." She turned and walked out of the salon.

—⟡—

Two mercenary soldiers rode ahead and three behind, traveling through a long valley between low mountains. The early evening sun blazed on Viçente's shoulders. Barrientos' brown robe was darkened by moisture on its back and sides—his face red, white hair matted beneath a wide-brimmed hat.

Instead of dwelling on their separation, Viçente should savor the freedom of riding in the open air with his beloved bishop and the opportunity to help his people. But would his presence really make a difference?

Barrientos glanced at him. "You have inquiries, my son."

"You plan to bribe the pope. Are those saddlebags filled with gold?"

The horses clopped down into a streambed, their hooves grating on rocks. Barrientos leaned forward, keeping balance. "King Juan's Vatican ambassador will bring the funds."

"But this seems unlikely to—"

Barrientos raised a hand. "This pope's sympathetic to the Dominican cause, which is to say the conversion of Jews. He's learned and intelligent, establishing a Vatican library, supporting the sciences and arts. But many good causes flutter into Rome on lofty wings, and not all are heard. Thus two bribes are required; one for admission to his holy presence, the second for suitable results. One of my fellow Dominicans will accompany you to emphasize that torturing converts subverts the church's efforts. *You* will speak of your people and their piety. Pope Nicholas will listen because we pay for the hearing, and he'll agree because you'll convince him."

"You're not coming?"

The bishop leaned across and touched Viçente's elbow. "My son, I must return to keep king and prince from slitting one another's gullets. The Dominican master general, Bartholomew Texier, will be more effective than I, and you'll have King Juan's ambassador, not to mention that friend of yours who works at the Vatican. What was his name?"

"Ralducci. But Bishop—"

"Viçente, I've always been proud of you. You've stepped away from it these last months, but you can't forsake a life's work. You're a first-generation Christian who's well spoken and pious. You've helped build God's cathedral and defended your rightful king. Who could better speak for converts?"

Viçente felt the blood come to his face. "Before I *stepped away*, I gave a great deal. Didn't I deserve a few months of peace?"

"Certainly, son—"

"And don't you think I agonize over their plight?"

Barrientos took in a breath. "The king was poised to give you power, extraordinary for someone not born to nobility."

Viçente snorted. His birth to false converts was far from noble. "I was wounded, my body and my heart."

"Healthy now. Time to pick yourself up."

"Enrique still imagines he can secure Toledo for me."

"I can't think how. He antagonizes his father at every opportunity."

"When I received Enrique's letter, for a minute I dreamed of it. Not out of ambition, but for Toledo's *conversos*. Either way, I want to wed Francesca and return with her to Castile to see what I can do."

The bishop beamed. "I approve, my son."

Barrientos' arrival now seemed like a gift—this trip to Rome, a chance to protect his people, an end to his impotence.

They stopped at a roadside *albergo* near the village of Caianello, and though he'd denied having gold inside his saddlebags, Viçente noticed that Bishop Barrientos held them tight. Their room on the second floor had whitewashed walls, one small window, and three beds beneath a slanting wooden ceiling.

"Would you keep watch while I bathe?" Barrientos gestured to the bags and departed. After a while, he returned, his balding head pink and glistening. He sat on a bed and nodded toward the saddlebags. "Did you look inside?"

"Of course not."

Barrientos reached into a bag and brought out a leather-bound packet. "I hope you'll contribute this to our cause."

"Open it."

Barrientos complied and Viçente's eyes confirmed. He felt his face flush with anger. "I didn't ask you to take this from the monastery."

"We can not fail with the pope, Viçente. The testament assures access."

"It raises suspicions."

"You doubt your belief, my son?"

"The pope will doubt if a convert presents this."

Barrientos turned pages until he came to the picture of Jonah in the whale's belly. "This most rare of books holds God's words, and

God inspired the artist. It will buy us an audience with this pope more surely than any statue or gold scepter."

How could Barrientos not understand? Marcos García, or even King Alfonso, could use the testament to condemn Viçente, the result possibly fatal. "I *don't* give my permission."

"You could wear a rabbi's beard and the pontiff would embrace you for this gift, but we'll not say it came from you. Bartholomew Texier, the master Dominican, will help us."

"If your master believes it's vital—"

"Thank you, Viçente." Barrientos looked down, turning pages as if admiring the book. "We'll bring the testament and seek Master Texier's guidance."

"No *converso* can be part of an audience you purchase with a Hebrew text. I return to Naples in the morning."

"Just a moment, Viçente. I'll find my shawl and take your confession. You can speak to God of the murders these sinners commit in Toledo and confess that you refuse to intervene because someone might suspect your piety."

Viçente fled the room, ran downstairs and out, strode through the hamlet of Caianello with its humble stone houses and up a trail to the top of a low mountain. He sat on a boulder, cursing the bishop until his anger turned back on himself.

CHAPTER 63

—ⴰⴰⴰ—

A GRAY-HAIRED MAN RODE TOWARD Viçente on a black horse, leading another by a rope. The fellow had deeply furrowed cheeks and wore a scarlet silk tunic that clung to his paunch. A limp, green velvet cap flopped atop his head. This showy courtier couldn't be Ralducci, Viçente's affable twenty-year-old friend from thirty-five years before. But there *was* something familiar in the man's grin as he dismounted and spread his arms. "Viçente, is that you?"

"Good to see you, old friend." He hugged Ralducci and stepped back. "We must talk about events in Toledo."

"I've heard about the inquisition." Ralducci wore the gleeful smile of a man who'd thrown a good round of dice in a game of *Marlotta*. "I can help you with Pope Nicholas if you offer inducements."

Inducements. Viçente swallowed what he wanted to say. "Let's go. The Dominican master expects us."

"Don't fret, Viçente. Even a master waits for the pope's man." Ralducci grinned, baring yellowed teeth.

They mounted, and as they rode, Ralducci gestured at the refuse-strewn street. "Rome's a pig wallow, but my pope will get the filth off the streets and bring fresh water. Romans had good water during the Empire, so we modern Italians should be able. And see how dilapidated St. Peter's has become." Viçente spotted the old church. He'd thought it huge in his student days, but it was far smaller than Toledo's new cathedral. The main pediment stood askew and he saw wooden patches where roofing tiles had fallen away. Ralducci continued, "Pope Nicholas plans a grand replacement."

They crossed a bridge over the *Fiume* Tevere and rode between stalls shaded by cloth canopies. Old women hawked their products—olives, plums, and apricots, jewelry made from shells and glass beads, trays of butchered meat. They passed shabby buildings washed in faded pinks and golds. Ralducci pointed. "We're close now. There's the bell tower of Santa Maria sopra Minerva. We can see the sights tomorrow and toast the pope's health in my favorite tavern."

They left their horses in the monastery courtyard and Ralducci led up the stairs. "They have trouble these days deciding." He chuckled. "Some Dominicans want to return to vows of poverty. Others cling to their privileges. Who knows, they might even consider chastity."

—⟊—

They waited around a large oval table in a wood-paneled meeting room. To Viçente's right sat Ralducci in his pompous finery. At the end, Bishop Barrientos wore a white gown and skullcap. Behind him, a fireplace bore two carved marble statues of St. Dominic's dog.

Across from Viçente, King Juan's Ambassador Ortega, a sharp-nosed man of forty, chatted with Barrientos about the long trip from Castile. To Viçente, he said, "King Juan sends his regards, Señor Pérez. He sent me here because I have experience in matters such as these."

"Reminding me that I do not?"

"Precisely, which makes silence your best course."

Viçente saw the door swing open and suppressed his response. A priest entered. He wore a brown cassock and walked with a cane, his face wrinkled, shoulders hunched. Settling at the head of the table, he looked around. "I'm pleased to see that the pope has graced our meeting with Signor Ralducci, and welcome, Ambassador Ortega." He eyed

Viçente. "You would be the *converso* that Bishop Barrientos praises so. I'm Master Texier, young man."

Texier's tone, speaking the word '*converso*,' sent a shiver down Viçente's spine. "The bishop's kind."

"He tells me you raised money for Toledo's cathedral." Texier pursed his lips. Wrinkles creased the pale skin around his mouth. "I should have such assistance. You see, Signor Pérez, in my years as Dominican master we've restored the Order's integrity and forged agreements to assure that the holy church will never experience another ruinous schism. There is, and must always be, only one pope. I'm an old man who does not wish to be forgotten, so I establish a legacy."

Viçente gaped. This 'champion of asceticism' was making a brazen appeal for funds.

Ambassador Ortega spread his hands on the table and said, "You deserve such a tribute, Master Texier, and Castile's King Juan will contribute. Do you plan a monastery?"

The old man's eyes brightened. "A library. It's under construction."

"Something of a coincidence, with the pope founding a Vatican collection," Ralducci said.

Viçente caught a movement from the corner of his eye and saw Bishop Barrientos produce the testament from under the table. "And I've brought this rare volume to present to the pope." Barrientos slid it toward Ralducci. Viçente's heart pounded.

Texier rose. "Why didn't you tell me about this?"

"It's for Pope Nicholas," Barrientos said. "It's vital that he support our cause."

"This *cause*." Texier sneered. "It involves some sort of rogue inquisition?"

"These men in Toledo betray the king," Ortega said.

"They persecute converts," Barrientos added. "Señor Pérez will join you with the pope as an example of a *converso* who contributes much to the church."

"And did you also contribute this testament, Signor Pérez?" Texier hobbled closer to Ralducci, his eyes on the Bible.

Viçente's stomach knotted.

"No," Barrientos said. "I received it from a new convert who wanted to be free of his Hebrew past."

Texier leaned on his cane, eying Viçente. "You know, Bishop Barrientos, with so many false Christians about, many of your brother bishops feel the need to root them out."

Viçente blurted, "Bishop Barrientos is nothing but honorable, and I am true as any Catholic." Regretting the outburst, he lowered his voice. "What these men do in Toledo isn't sanctioned by Rome."

"He speaks truth." Beside Viçente, Ralducci leaned back in his chair. "The church can't allow low-order priests to initiate these actions."

"Or to ignore their God-sanctioned king." Ambassador Ortega shot an angry look at Viçente.

Ralducci pulled the testament near and turned a few pages. "Remarkable."

Master Texier stared over Ralducci's shoulder. "I've seen illuminated versions in Latin or Italian or Castilian, but never Hebrew and Latin together." He leaned on the table, gawking. "Even the Cataluñan Bibles are not this fine. I will take it for safekeeping until we meet Pope Nicholas." He reached for the book.

Ralducci clung to the testament, looking up at the Dominican. "We agree it's for His Holiness?" Their eyes held and Texier nodded. Ralducci released it.

Texier clutched the text against his side as he hobbled to his chair and dropped into it. "It would be fatal to your meeting if Pope Nicholas took up the absurd notion that this was the testament from which Signor Pérez worshipped."

Barrientos slapped the table. "Master Texier, the situation is too urgent to slander a man for your own ends." He paused for a long breath. "There's no reason for the pope to believe that." He folded his arms and glowered.

Texier smirked at Ralducci. "The pope agrees to have this meeting?"

"Provided you bring the prize."

—〰—

Outside, Viçente turned on Barrientos and Ralducci. "This is the Dominican master who'll help us save Toledo? He's stealing the testament."

Barrientos shook his head. "The old master has changed. I don't—"

"Why in hell did you show it to him?" Ralducci snapped. "This is Toledo's problem. Pope Nicholas has no interest unless you bring that book." He poked a finger at Viçente's chest. "And mind this: Do not anger that old man. If his Dominicans spread the word that you're a despicable Jew, your audience is doomed."

This meeting had been a disaster, but it had opened Viçente's eyes to a truth: besides Barrientos, Viçente was the only one in Rome who cared about Castile's *conversos*.

CHAPTER 64

—⚹—

MARCOS STOOD ON THE PLATFORM in Cathedral Square, surrounded by prominent Old Christians. Across the square, another platform bore the execution spikes. A banner above read, *THE DAY OF GOD'S VENGEANCE.* A huge pile of dry branches lay nearby. Beside him, Pero, in a black cassock, sweated like a roasting hog and glanced at the sun as if willing it to disappear. No clouds came to relieve the heat. So much for the vicar's newfound rapport with God.

The rabble filled the triangular plaza from city building to archbishop's palace to cathedral and up the streets to the north. Men passed wineskins and squirted red spirits into gaping mouths, receiving plaudits from their fellow drunkards. Marcos saw women, too, gathered in circles, scarves or lace kerchiefs on their heads. Children darted among them, but only gruff male voices rose above the murmur.

Pero gestured to the execution scaffold. "I wish you'd not placed it so near his palace."

"Don't spoil this day with idiotic fussing," Marcos growled. "If not for petty church rules and Sarmiento's spinelessness, we'd burn forty, not four."

Pero gave Marcos a nervous but steady look, a gaze he wouldn't have dared a month before. "Archbishop Carrillo disapproves the *limpieza.* Our acts defy his instructions and defy again by placing *that* before his residence."

"Pigs must die to feed the masses. A true Christian wouldn't object."

Pero squinted like a hurt child, and Marcos said, "When the church sees what we accomplish, they'll make you archbishop."

Sarmiento stepped to the podium. He grinned and waved, and Marcos' stomach knotted. Sarmiento, who last month threatened to scuttle the *limpieza*, now wished to lead. What wonders a cache of confiscated *marrano* gold could achieve.

The magistrate raised his arms for silence. Men in the crowd shook their fists and yelled, "*Bring the pendejos out. Burn them! Skewer the pigs!*" Voices echoed around the square as the mob pressed against the platform. Marcos felt it tremble and sway.

"Sarmiento, give us their blood, *Sarmiento, now.*" A man shouted, "*García!*" The call became a chorus. "García, García!" The platform wobbled and Marcos felt a shiver of fear. Sarmiento looked around, bewildered, then beckoned him. The mob chanted, "*Sangre Pura. Sangre Pura.*" Marcos' pulse surged with power, exultation … and terror. He stepped forward and put up a hand to quiet them.

"Today we annihilate four sinners," Marcos shouted. "Next week, we'll capture more. In a year, Castile will honor us." He waited for quiet and called out, "If you topple this platform and crush me, who will lead you to this great victory?"

Laughter broke out. Tension eased. Sarmiento hissed in Marcos' ear, "Now, back to your corner."

Sarmiento shouted, "In a moment, our guards will bring the prisoners. As chief magistrate, I remind you; this is an official gathering, a serious occasion."

"My ass—" Another voice from the crowd, followed by, "*Guardia Civils* are pigs, too," and then a chorus of insults for the civil guard.

A woman shouted, "My son, José, is one of the guardsmen. You *cabrones* better not attack them."

Guffaws erupted and Sarmiento shouted, "We are all here for one purpose and we have cause for jubilation. Men of *Sangre Pura*, your brothers, participate in today's ceremony. Tomorrow, you'll receive a share of the heretics' stolen wealth. Now bring the prisoners."

A dozen *Guardia Civil* stepped forth, then pairs of guardsmen dragging the first three captives. Each wore a brown sackcloth robe and tall, conical hat, with their hands tied behind them. The fourth prisoner strode, as if he were leading, as if the flesh beneath his robe were not disfigured with welts. He blinked and glared toward Marcos and the nobles on the stage. More guardsmen formed up behind. The troop marched before the archbishop's palace and up onto the execution platform.

Sarmiento called, "Face us, evil ones."

The guards prodded until all stood upright.

"Before we execute these defilers, our esteemed vicar will attest to their transgressions."

Pero plodded forward and Sarmiento nudged him to the rostrum. Pero cleared his throat, straightened, cleared his throat again. "These four men have profaned God not once, but many times. They cannot be redeemed on Earth."

Pero's voice had come out loud and resolute for once, but now he halted, looking to Sarmiento. Sarmiento whispered to him and Pero nodded. "On God's behalf, I relinquish them to civil authority." Pero raised his hand high and made the sign of the cross.

The magistrate, his arm around Pero's shoulder, shouted, "The church has declared these men heretics and surrendered them for punishment. As lawful head of the tribunal, I sentence all four to death."

Pero touched the magistrate's elbow and spoke to him. Sarmiento added, "The vicar reminds me that one of the prisoners sincerely seeks God's forgiveness. We'll treat him with mercy. Guardsmen, follow your orders."

Guards shoved each prisoner up three steps and tied them to the stakes. The first three prisoners were vile, scrawny men, comical in their pointed hats, eyes bulging from sallow, detestable faces. The bold *marrano*, strapped to the pole at the right, stood taller. His eyes blazed. With a quick shake of his head, he flipped the pointed hat off.

It tumbled over the edge of the platform. A boy grabbed it, evaded the guardsmen, and scurried back beneath the cordon. The rabble cheered.

A guard approached the first prisoner, removed his hat, slipped a hood over his head, and replaced the hat. This was the *marrano* for whom Pero had demanded mercy, the damnable bookseller who'd helped Pérez.

Three leaders of *Sangre Pura* came forth, carrying torches and buckets of pitch. A fourth followed at a distance, a fleshy, dim-witted fellow with a huge round head. He pranced onto the platform in a green-and-red smock and a mischievous leer, waving a scimitar. Skipping across the stage, he jabbed the blade at the air. The crowd applauded. The man poked the scimitar toward the bold *marrano*. The prisoner ignored him. The *Sangre Pura* clown turned to the crowd and barked like a dog. He grinned, skipped to the next prisoner, and menaced him. This *marrano* jerked in his bindings to avoid the blade that jabbed near his groin. The tormentor leapt back and forth between that captive and the next, jumping high so the blade flashed close before each *marrano's* face. Men in the crowd leaped, too, thrusting knives into the air.

The wild man sprang up the stairs to the blindfolded prisoner on the left, swung behind, and ripped the scimitar across his throat. Marcos heard a grunt and saw blood spurt toward the crowd. The *marrano's* body jerked and slumped. Women screamed and a man bellowed, "Pig blood! We got spattered with goddamned pig blood."

Marcos barely heard. He was thinking back to that night when he and Sarmiento had killed the soldiers in Simancas Castle, feeling the warm fluid between his fingers. He sniffed the air now for the smell and taste of it, imagining Viçente Pérez had just been slain instead of the bookseller.

Men in the mob raised wineskins and squirted red spirits at one another. Shouting, "Blood, blood, everywhere blood," they erupted in stupid laughter.

When they calmed, Sarmiento shouted, "We showed mercy for the repentant. Now we burn the worst alive. Stand back, citizens of Toledo. Guardsmen, *Sangre Pura*, do your duty."

Civil guardsmen piled dry branches around the poles and added pitch. The two prisoners in the middle thrashed at their ropes, trying to kick the branches away. *Sangre Pura* men pressed lit torches into the brush. The flames burned low at first, but when the pitch took fire, dark smoke rose. The *marranos* in the center bawled, "*No! No, God, No!*" as the flames grew, but the bold prisoner kept silent. *Marranos* wriggled and writhed on their poles, gasping and coughing and screaming long and loud. Flames ignited the dead bookseller's robe as the two in the center screeched. Their garments took fire and they danced a fiery jig. Then, one at a time, they fell silent. Marcos watched the defiant one on the right, his clothes aflame, body twitching, face contorted in pain. Finally he shouted, "*Jódese, Todos.*" His body shuddered and slumped.

The rabble jumped and danced. Crackling fire blackened the *marranos'* legs and licked up their bellies, rising. The banner above caught fire. The wind shifted and smoke blew toward Marcos. "*God, it stinks,*" someone shouted, but odors were a triviality.

Something touched his arm and he jumped, turning to see Sancho, a slack wineskin slung across his chest. "Can't I enjoy this one triumph without interruption?"

He intended to turn back to see the last of them consumed, but the wool carter beamed at him. "You should be glad to see me. I've brought wonderful news."

Marcos glanced back at the fire. The post tops still showed above the flames, but the four *marranos* and their pointed hats had disappeared. Sancho, as usual, had robbed the final bit of joy.

CHAPTER 65

—∭—

VIÇENTE'S STAY IN ROME STRETCHED to a month without an invitation from Pope Nicholas, the delay caused by Master Texier's refusal to yield the rare Bible to His Holiness.

Finally, King Juan's Ambassador Ortega offered a sufficient bribe, and Texier consented. Their meeting would take place in two days. Along with this news, Viçente received an invitation from Cardinal Juan de Torquemada for the next day.

Perplexed but hopeful, Viçente presented himself in the reception hall of the Dominican palace, where a monk informed him that, "Father Torquemada attends the Princess of Naples in the chapel."

Viçente felt blood rise and his spirits soar. Could it be?

A monk brought Viçente to a salon with furniture the color of gruel; the room's sole adornment, a plain wooden cross.

The door swung open and she entered, wearing a black lace mantilla over her hair and a pale yellow blouse, tight about the bodice, with a neckline that showed the silken skin of her shoulders and sensuous collarbones. Her chestnut eyes glistened.

A priest in a white robe and bonnet followed—about Viçente's age, round-faced with thick, gray eyebrows and a bulging nose. Francesca stepped beside Viçente, wrapping her arm through his. "Viçente Pérez, this is my kindly confessor, Cardinal Juan de Torquemada."

The cardinal touched his elbow. "Señor Pérez, welcome. I understand that Rome has been less than hospitable. My servants will bring refreshments to compensate."

Francesca stepped away and settled gingerly on a sofa, spreading her green skirt wide, petticoats crinkling. The cardinal sat beside her and Viçente took the chair.

"While we were in Cardinal Juan's little confessional box, I had time for more than penance," Francesca said. "He'll support your cause, Viçente."

Cardinal Torquemada shook his head. "We don't reveal the confessional's secrets. I'm sure you understand our sacraments, Señor Pérez."

Shocked, Viçente blurted, "I'm a Christian."

A thin monk and a short, dark woman in a flowered apron entered and set small tables before them with tea and little cakes. When they left, the cardinal said, "I apologize, Señor. I've offended you, and now I compound my transgression by telling you to be wary of your friend, Ralducci."

Viçente bristled, but Francesca set her teacup down and slid closer to Torquemada. "Trust the cardinal, Viçente. Hear what he has to say."

"There's another group seeking papal audience," Torquemada said. "Prominent men representing the city of Toledo. I see from your expression, you weren't aware."

"The *false* government of Toledo," Viçente said.

"Those who hold the city and undertake their inquisition desire approval from His Holiness."

Viçente stood and turned away, trying to understand. "How can they? The king's opposed to them, and Toledo's archbishop—"

"Don't blame Cardinal Juan, Viçente. He wants to help." Francesca patted Torquemada's hand. Viçente tried to ignore his emotions and focus on Torquemada's gentle smile and soft blue eyes.

"Clearly, Ralducci didn't tell you about the Toledans, Señor Pérez," the cardinal said.

"Ralducci must not know."

"I was with Pope Nicholas and Señor Ralducci five days ago when they learned of the Toledans' arrival," Torquemada said. "Ralducci speaks of a precious testament in Hebrew and Latin. He advised the pope to meet with the Toledans if they offer something of similar worth." Viçente set his half-eaten cake back on its plate, feeling ill. If Ralducci was bargaining with his enemies, what might he imply about the Hebrew testament?

"Señor Pérez, these men say that scores of *conversos* have confessed grievous sins, and others are implicated. Many have fled Toledo. I only speak of this to protect you."

"Innocents." Viçente shook his head. "I'm to meet with Pope Nicholas to tell him the truth."

The cardinal nodded. "I can assist."

"Ralducci's arranging a meeting." By the time Viçente finished speaking, he knew the words foolish.

"Ralducci can be generous with his own praise," Torquemada said. He turned to Francesca. "Now, my lady, I have imparted my information and offered my assistance. How else can I please you?"

Francesca, blushing, looked straight at the cardinal. "You could offer us a bit of privacy."

—⟊—

As soon as he'd gone, Viçente snatched the table and set it against the door.

"Dearest." Francesca wrapped her arms around his neck and pulled herself up, pressing her lips to his, her body to his, opening her mouth to him. His fingers caressed her sides, her buttocks, her breasts. Love and joy and passion drove his heartbeat.

"We meet with the pope tomorrow," he said. "Then I'll hurry to Naples and we'll marry."

She drew back just far enough to murmur. "Wonderful, darling. Did I mention that Penélope's an inventive seamstress?" She kissed him again, her tongue tickling the inside of his mouth.

He chuckled. "That's a strange remark."

She backed up a step and gazed at him, her eyes shiny with lust. "We've little time. Cardinal Juan would do much to please me, but soon he'll become concerned about my virtue." Francesca reached under the bottom of her blouse, moving her fingers from side to front to side. The top of her skirt edged lower. Her hands disappeared behind her. With a crinkling, the skirt and petticoat skirts dropped.

She stepped over the heap of fabric, and the sight of her smooth, supple legs sent a new excitement through him. His eyes followed up her thighs. "You took your confession without under clothing?"

"Do you think Jesus would mind?"

"Not at all." He kissed her. He was sure that the petticoat was supposed to continue above the waist but for Penélope's creative stitchery.

"I looked proper, didn't I, with Cardinal Juan? Even now, my under-blouses are laced tightly about me, my breasts tucked in."

He cupped a fully-clothed breast in one hand as he ran the other downward.

She reached to unclasp his belt and he skimmed his fingers over her, stroking, pressing. She pulled him onto the settee, and they kissed, caressing one another … loving her… filling her.

"We mustn't cry out." She moaned.

"I've missed you so," he sighed.

CHAPTER 66

—⟪⟫—

VIÇENTE WAITED WITH MASTER TEXIER and Ambassador Ortega in the pope's antechamber. The Dominican master wore a brown robe and skullcap and the scowl of a man on a distasteful mission. The ambassador's cloak was the color of persimmons, with yellow-and-brown lions embroidered on the sleeves. He held a neutral expression, but he tapped his fingers incessantly on the arm of the settee. Viçente fidgeted, too, feeling ordinary in his simple wheat-colored jacket and brown leggings. He glanced at the tapestry on the wall of the Last Supper. The image of Christ and his disciples should comfort, but the supper had led to crucifixion, which led Viçente to thoughts of Toledo's innocent converts.

The grand door opened and Ralducci emerged in a rich blue tunic. Texier levered himself up with his cane. Viçente whispered to Ortega, "Will he cooperate?"

"Our king pays a small fortune for it."

"Did the old weasel bring the testament?" Ralducci muttered.

"We've not seen it," Ortega said. "But he's agreed."

They entered an opulent hall. Sunlight streamed through windows on one side. Ahead, a golden canopy floated over a carved wooden throne. The man seated there, Nicholas, appeared small. His ruby robe, bordered in white, spilled over the throne's arms. His high-pointed bonnet was of the same colors, and he held a jeweled scepter.

"Magnificent, isn't he?" Ralducci said.

Viçente could hardly breathe.

"Trust me. Remember your role, and don't try to tell him how to run the church." Ralducci chuckled, but trust was no longer imaginable.

They halted before Pope Nicholas and Viçente took in his thin features and straight, aristocratic nose. His calm hazel eyes probed Viçente's. Reverence for this successor of Christ on Earth filled him with respect and ... love? How could such feelings arrive without exchanging a word between them? The pope lifted a hand with a large ruby ring. Texier kissed it. Ambassador Ortega followed, and then Viçente, kneeling, kissed the ring. The pope withdrew his hand. Viçente stepped back.

Ralducci gestured to the visitors. "Your Holiness, I believe you've met Ambassador Ortega, representing King Juan, and this is Don Viçente Pérez. They kindly offer a priceless book for your library, and they've a serious matter to discuss."

Courtiers pushed chairs forward and they sat. Pope Nicholas looked to Master Texier. "I believe you're keeping this volume for me, Bartholomew."

"Yes, Holy Father." Texier sat back in his chair, his expression neutral.

"Pope Nicholas has many duties and little time," Ralducci said. "Ambassador Ortega, please explain your purpose."

The lion on Ortega's sleeve rippled as he gestured. "Your Holiness, I'm sure you've heard about the villainy in Toledo. The king's former butler, Sarmiento, was given charge of the city, and he's revealed himself a scoundrel. First, he and his deputy terrorized the Jews. Now they've turned to torturing good Christians."

Pope Nicholas gave a dismissive flip of the hand. "We know all of this, Ambassador. These *scoundrels* claim they've found impostors among our flock." The pontiff glanced at Viçente, and Viçente's breath caught. The pope moved on to Master Texier. "Is not torture one of the Dominican's valued tools for rooting out pretenders?"

Texier sat back, looking smug.

"Master Texier, you're still among the living?" Ralducci asked.

"The pope asked me a question to which he well knows the answer. I pledged to endorse the ambassador's assertions, and to oppose this *limpieza* in Toledo, so I withhold comment."

Ambassador Ortega grimaced. "Sarmiento and his henchman call their persecution '*limpieza*,' but in practicality it's an inquisition. They are not priests, nor bishops, and are performing an unauthorized church rite."

Pope Nicholas leaned on his scepter and shifted in his seat. "Doesn't a vicar support them?"

Ortega looked to Master Texier, but the old man seemed to be asleep. Ortega said, "A vicar is hardly enough. Your Holiness, please."

Ralducci nodded toward Viçente. "Signor Pérez understands the implications of this *limpieza*. He's an exemplary citizen of Toledo and prominent church member."

Viçente took a deep breath and began. "These traitors, who pretend to do God's will, torture good men and women who worked with me in Toledo. Their sons fought for King Juan. They're descended from Jews, but they're loyal Christians who helped build God's cathedral. Holy Father, what would any man confess when he's beaten or when they threaten his wife or child?"

For an instant, Viçente thought of what Papa had told him on his thirteenth birthday about the torture Jews had suffered. He fought for focus.

"And *you* are descended from Jews," Pope Nicholas said.

Sweat broke out on Viçente's face. "Yes." He couldn't tell if there was malice in the pontiff's words, but the hazel eyes lured him to say more. "García and Sarmiento prove that Christians can be less honorable than—"

"Than Jews?" The pope asked.

"They've killed defenseless people," Viçente said. All their eyes were on him, and now they'd all suspect that he was referring, in part, to murdered Jews. He had to stay with converts. "Pope Nicholas, I despise my Jewish ancestry. Sarmiento and García torture men to obtain false confessions. The church can't desire that." Ortega was staring at Viçente, grim-faced. Ralducci looked away. Master Texier, eyes still closed, smirked. Viçente wished he comprehended the meaning of the pontiff's still-gentle gaze. "I've said too much. I didn't mean to offend."

"No, Signor Pérez," the pope said. "I'm pleased to hear your views. It appears that you have some sympathy for the Hebrews."

Viçente lifted his hand from the arm of the chair, saw it tremble, and gripped the chair again. "They're pitiable, but their fate should be left to God's judgment."

"What's your position, Ambassador Ortega?" the pope asked.

"The pope's power and the king's power support one another, Your Holiness. In the reprehensible church schism, which, praise God, has ended, the pretenders to the Holy See sought the kings' support, and so did the rightful popes. Now we seek yours."

Pope Nicholas clapped his hands. "An interesting argument, but these miscreants in Toledo can hardly spark a church crisis. They're fortunate they found a few priests to stand with them."

"It would be a welcome gesture if Your Holiness reconfirmed King Juan's sovereignty," Ortega said.

"Welcome, but how prudent, while King Juan's cousins covet Castile's throne? One is my neighbor, King Alfonso of Naples. Why support your king and anger my neighbor?"

Ortega opened his mouth to respond, but Pope Nicholas waved him to silence. "I understand your position, and I'll pray for guidance." Ralducci stood. Master Texier clutched his cane.

But too much had been omitted. Viçente looked to Ralducci for help, but his old friend merely waved toward the door. If Master Texier wouldn't defend his order, Viçente had to raise the point. "Holy Father."

All motion stopped, and Pope Nicholas frowned.

"Before Sarmiento came to power in Toledo, I was first deputy there."

"Commendable," the pope said.

Ortega glowered. "Señor Pérez, this is hardly the time to list accomplishments."

"You're a man of God, Pope Nicholas," Viçente said. "But also an administrator, as I was. I once directed our tax collector to gather business taxes and report shopkeepers who refused."

Ralducci jabbed his thumb toward the exit. Viçente's heart hammered, but he went on. "Instead, the tax collector beat a shopkeeper who couldn't pay. The man was crippled and lost his business."

A smile crept into the pope's eyes. "You're about to tell me how you punished the tax collector for disobedience."

"For disobedience and for assaulting an innocent man," Viçente said.

"You liken my vicar in Toledo to your tax collector? What's the vicar's name, Ralducci?"

"Pero López de Gálvez," Ralducci answered.

"So it's a slight on my authority," Pope Nicholas said. "If this Gálvez initiates an inquisition without my sanction?"

"Far worse, Your Holiness," Viçente said. "This vicar and his allies usurp your role. They pretend to seek your approval only after they've committed murder, against the instructions of church law and human conscience."

"Thank you. I can always use the advice of another manager." Pope Nicholas stood. Texier began tottering toward the door. There were more points to be made, but Viçente couldn't go further. He and the ambassador followed the old man.

"*One Moment.*" The pontiff's voice echoed in the chamber. The men turned, and Pope Nicholas said, "Master Texier, did you think you'd leave without further mention of the testament?"

Texier grimaced and held his cane up. "I came alone. I wasn't able—"

Ralducci called out, "You have a coachman outside and dozens of monks who could have carried the book."

Texier lowered his cane and glared. "Your Holiness, you don't—"

The pope thumped his scepter on the floor. "If you think to make the testament part of your patrimony, Father Texier, compare the legacy of a defrocked priest possessing an old Bible to that of an honorably retired Dominican master."

While Texier stood open-mouthed, Ralducci added, "Provide it by day's end."

Texier's angry scowl cheered Viçente for an instant but no longer.

CHAPTER 67

—⁓—

OUT IN THE HALLWAY, AMBASSADOR Ortega turned on Viçente. "You had a role to play, Pérez. You should have kept to it, but you exposed your goddamned Jew-loving soul."

Viçente *had* spoken too much of the Jews, but the pope's sympathetic look had led him on. "Pope Nicholas needed the truth."

"Don't try to explain." Ortega charged ahead, swinging his arm backward toward Viçente, speaking over his shoulder. "Ralducci should have excluded you as I requested."

Viçente waited as the ambassador disappeared into the stream of monks and scribes strolling the corridor, and then he moved on, stepping out into bright sunshine, halting at the top of a marble stairway. Three men climbed toward him—two in formal dress and a large priest in brown vestments. Viçente recognized the priest and one of the others—a man with a thin mustache and graying hair—Rui García de Villalpando, a respected Castilian. This was the group Cardinal Torquemada had mentioned; Toledans come to meet Pope Nicholas.

The priest pointed at Viçente and spoke to his companions. Then he and Villalpando mounted the steps and walked past. The shorter man, a powerfully built, dark-featured stranger, paused just below Viçente. "We thought we'd have to seek you out in Naples, Pérez."

"I don't understand, Señor—"

"My name's not important. Your son's name is *Diego*." The man climbed the final step and stood so close that Viçente smelled the foul exhalation from his fat-lipped mouth.

Viçente's stomach knotted. "What of it?"

"Foolish lad returned to Toledo."

God, what was he talking about? Diego was in Valladolid, many days ride from Toledo. But what this man implied ... Viçente felt sudden fury and shoved him backward onto the paving stones, then straddled him and grabbed his throat. "Tell me."

The man clutched Viçente's wrists and grinned. "Your boy told us about your tryst in Naples."

"*God damn you.*" Viçente tried to choke him, but the man pried his fingers away. Something pressed against his back, gouging the old wound. Arms reached around, squeezing and lifting him. He glanced up to see the priest's large head above. Pain burst in his stomach. The vile stranger had struck him from below. Gasping for air, he saw the thick-lipped man swing again, smashing a fist to Viçente's crotch. His body wanted to crumple with sickening agony, but the priest held on.

The stranger stood and brushed himself off. "You can resolve this matter for your son, Pérez, some question about his heritage."

"How dare you fight in the shadow of the Vatican?" The voice was familiar, but it came from behind. The priest freed him. Struggling to keep his balance, Viçente turned to see Cardinal Torquemada in a white robe and red bonnet.

"They've taken my son," Viçente wheezed.

"Is this true?" Torquemada demanded.

The priest bowed. "Revered Cardinal, the authorities in Toledo detained this man's son. When my companion informed Señor Pérez, he attacked."

"I know your purpose in Rome," Torquemada said. "You persecute Christian converts, and now you abduct Señor Pérez' son?"

The priest's mouth moved without sound for a moment. Then he managed, "No, it's—it's the city authorities. They hold Diego Pérez over a legal matter."

"Cardinal, he said that it has to do with my son's heritage. They've captured Diego for their inquisition."

"Why would you persecute Christians, Priest, and why lie to me about it?" Torquemada asked.

Rui García de Villalpando stepped forward. "Cardinal Torquemada, perhaps you remember me?"

Torquemada scowled. "Señor Villalpando, you once had an honored name."

"Cardinal, we come to Rome on a holy mission."

"One that will damn your soul." The cardinal touched Viçente's shoulder. "Are you all right?"

What if this was true? It must be true. How else would they know about Naples? Viçente stepped toward Villalpando, wanting to drive his fist into the aristocrat's jaw, but the priest and the stranger intervened. *"What have you done with my son?"*

Villalpando spread his hands in a gesture of innocence. "Your son worked for Constable Luna in King Juan's treasury. Luna tries to impose an illegal tax on Toledo, so your son bears responsibility."

Beside Viçente, Torquemada stood rigid. "If you hope for any standing with the pope, send word to Toledo to release Diego Pérez."

Villalpando bowed. "Alas, I have no power in the matter. Señor Pérez must deal with this personally."

"The pope will hear of this matter." The cardinal tugged at Viçente's arm. Viçente resisted for a moment, feeling spent and helpless. Then he followed Torquemada into the building, where the cardinal took him to a small dining room.

Viçente's stomach was turning over with pain and despair. "I must go to Toledo."

"These men are deceivers, Viçente. They may not have your son."

"Without delay, and I need to write a letter."

Torquemada took Viçente's hand. "Try to hear me, son. It's scant comfort, but those men just gave me the wedge that will keep them from seeing His Holiness."

Torquemada brought paper and envelope, quill and ink, and placed them on the table. Viçente's hand shook as he wrote:

My dearest Francesca:

It cleaves my heart to write this.

I promised to return when I finished here in Rome, but I cannot. I've received word that they've captured my Diego in Toledo.

My heart won't let me believe, and yet I must go. All that my son wanted in life was to be like his father. The danger he faces is my danger. They hold him out of hatred for me.

How can I write of this? I long to be with you in your rose garden. I yearn for your beauty, your warmth, your kiss, to be together for the rest of our lives. I can only pray that God grant us more moments together. I despair that he may not.

Casting about for something to ease Francesca's fear, he added:

I see your face in my thoughts. I hear you saying, 'Don't go. Don't let them capture you, too.' I see the tears in your eyes. All I can say is that thoughts of you will make me careful. I pray that the king or prince will help me, and I will avoid entering Toledo, but I must free my son.

I send you my love forever.

Viçente

He enclosed it in the envelope, wrote her name on the outside, and dripped candle wax on the closure. His body throbbed and he longed to lay his head on his hands on this table for just a few moments.

No. He had to begin this long journey. Without removing his ring, he pressed it into the wax, feeling the heat, using the pain to spur himself to stand.

PART VII

THE PRISONER

—⚭—

*Those [conversos] proceeding from their damaged lineage
are adulterers, sons of incredulity and infidelity, fathers of
wickedness, sowers of all discord and division, abounding in
all malice and perversity always ungrateful to God, contrary
to his commandments, putting aside his paths and courses.*

—Marcos García de Mora, "Memorial," as
translated in *A Network of Converso Families
in Early Modern Toledo* by Linda Martz

CHAPTER 68

—✺—

When Marcos learned that King Juan's army was marching on Toledo, panic crawled up the inside of his gut, but it spilled back out in eager waves of anticipation.

Hunched over his desk with a candle, he wrote a list of 'requests' for his majesty. As hours passed, he fumed over royal ineptitude. He rubbed his eyes, paced to the window, and opened the shutters. In the dim morning light, the cathedral tower dominated the dark square, but he was able to make out the black smudge on the paving stones, site of the glorious execution two months before.

He allowed himself a moment to savor their progress: Prominent *marranos* had fled the city, but *Sangre Pura* daily rousted petty tradesmen and their families. All of them should burn, but Pero, in his smug righteousness, and Sarmiento, with his single-minded greed, prevented it. The guilty were forced to sign confessions, absolved of their sins, and expelled from the city. Sancho, the guildsman, and Sarmiento, the magistrate, divided the spoils, passing a portion to *Sangre Pura*. Gold pleased the men, but Marcos knew that hatred and holy duty were their passions.

He visited the taverns often to remind the men of their lofty goals and revel in memories of *marranos* hanging in the square after their futile revolt. One evening, he'd arrived with marvelous news. "Men, we're winning," he'd told his unshaven followers. "In Ciudad Real they've executed a score of *marrano* pigs." The men had shouted and drunk as he'd added, "Soon all Castile will follow our example."

He slammed the shutters closed now, returned to his desk, and started over, making every request a demand—the final one: Expel Constable Luna, the *hijo de puta* who protected heretics. Expel and execute, or your kingdom will fall.

As Marcos climbed the hill to the *alcázar*, sunlight touched the tops of the brown stone walls. Cool air revived him. Thoughts of the *marrano* confessions he had locked in his desk buoyed him. The king could not deny the truth when Marcos presented this evidence.

Inside the *alcázar*, he paused to catch his breath and descended to the cellar; the smell, a mixture of burned pitch and human waste, was disgusting. In the hallway, two guardsmen dozed beneath a lantern. Marcos heard the guards' snoring and a woman moaning in one of the cells. He kicked a guard in the knee. The man yelped and jumped up, then stood to attention.

"Lazy scum," Marcos said. "Get me a torch. Unlock this cell." With the other guardsman now awake, the two hurried to comply.

He grabbed the torch and entered. The cell was three paces across, enough for a half-dozen prisoners, but Diego Pérez was permitted only a crock of waste for company. The young *marrano* sat rigid in a corner, his leg chained to the floor. "Very good, young Pérez. You sit at attention for me."

Pérez's shirt was tattered and blood-stained, his soiled trousers pushed up to reveal grimy calves. One might pity this handsome young fellow, with his brown curly hair, a lithe form, and a vulnerable look. But he was a vile pretender; his comeliness—like a prostitute's— a seduction from the devil, like the count who'd harbored Marcos in Barcelona all those years ago. Marcos chuckled and swung the torch close over the prisoner's head.

The *marrano* raised his arm to defend himself and flinched with the movement. "Kill me if you're going to, García. You won't trap my father."

The fear and pain in the creature's eyes thrilled Marcos. He had to restrain himself and keep this animal alive. "You weren't so confident when my men flogged you and you confessed your disdain for the Lord Jesus." Marcos jiggled the torch in front of the prisoner, watching him cower. "Your back is healing, and you crave another lashing."

Sweat ran down Pérez' face, and his hand, still shielding his eyes, trembled. "I'm not a Jew. You forced me to say that."

"How brave can you think yourself after you disclosed your beloved papa's location?" Marcos wondered if his men had reached Viçente Pérez in Naples. When he found out about Diego, he would come. Family loyalty was a Jew weakness.

Tears ran down the prisoner's face. "My father's a great man."

"If we beat you, you'll oink for us. You'll call your father a sow's ass. Do you crave a bit more fire?" Marcos swung again, angling the torch toward the prisoner's forehead. Young Pérez thrust his hand out, screeching in pain as torch and hand collided. He brushed hot embers from his hair and tried to crawl at Marcos, but the chains stopped him. "Now make a noise like a hog."

The beast glared. Marcos decided to leave, lest he use the flame in earnest. On the way out, he handed it to a guard. "Twenty lashes, and I want to hear his squealing all the way up in the street. Then salve his wounds. We need him alive."

Marcos climbed to the landing, savoring the erotic sounds of whip striking and *marrano* screaming.

He found Sarmiento slouching behind his desk.

"Take a chair, Marcos." The magistrate hadn't shaved and his white shirt was mussed. His eyes flitted from Marcos to the window and back. One hand remained still on the desk, while his other disappeared beneath to scratch his leg, then moved up to smooth his hair, then down for more scratching. The man was suppressing panic.

"This is a good development, Magistrate. The king must finally consider us."

Sarmiento sat upright. "*Consider?* Is that your word for 'attack?' From Fuensalida, his army could be here in hours. Or perhaps you mean 'strangle' or 'decapitate.' Where's the damned Royal Cousins' army?"

"You're the one who arranged their aid."

Sarmiento slammed his fist on the desktop and glared. "Damn your smug condescension. The Kings of Navarre and Aragón pledged action. Do you think I can put pikes up their asses and play them like puppets? There's still Prince Enrique. He just hasn't—hasn't come yet ..." The magistrate's voice trailed off.

"We can succeed without them. This king abandoned his siege at Benevente to come here. Last year, he lost cities in the north, and Granada's nipping from the south. If we hold firm, he'll negotiate."

"Perhaps a hangnail will divert him." Sarmiento barked a laugh, slouched again, and sighed.

"Magistrate, our storehouses are full. We have your civil guard and my *Sangre Pura*. Ciudad Real follows our example, cleansing themselves of blasphemers. The king can't risk our rebellion spreading further." Marcos touched Sarmiento's shoulder, feigning comradeship. "We'll use this moment to eliminate Luna."

The magistrate grunted. "The king will offer an assault, not an advisory role in his monarchy."

"The constable let *marranos* bankrupt the treasury. Nobles and city governors hate him. We can expose Luna's evils. You hate him, don't you, Magistrate?"

Sarmiento nodded, his eyes becoming more shrewd than confused.

Marcos pulled the document from his vest pocket. "This is my letter to His Majesty. Read it over and we'll talk later. Tomorrow, I'll present it to King Juan."

—◊—

At supper that evening, Sarmiento wore a fresh white shirt and a keen expression. A score of candles blazed on the wrought-iron chandelier overhead. Over egg-and-garlic soup, Sarmiento said, "Marcos, I'm intrigued by your plan for Luna, but we'll change one particular."

"Then you accept my main points?"

"King Juan knows your role in our rebellion, so you can not present the letter." When Marcos frowned, he continued. "Don't protest. I do this to protect you."

"You want to go?"

"Don't be foolish." Sarmiento swiped a hunk of brown bread around his bowl, bit off a piece, and chewed.

"We can't send a groom or a servant girl. It's our best chance to rid Castile of the demon," Marcos said.

"I know this king. He'd slice you and read the letter as you bleed." Sarmiento skimmed his knife through the air.

A manservant brought a platter with four stewed partridges and a dozen potato halves and set it before them. The scent of cooked meat and garlic infused the air.

"We'll demand a truce before I go."

"A truce won't govern Constable Luna. If he doesn't gore you, his archers will take you down." Sarmiento brandished the blade again. "The king can read our demands for himself, and I have the perfect man to deliver them." He dropped his knife. It clattered onto the serving plate and Marcos flinched.

Damn Sarmiento. Marcos had provided the inspiration, but now he was waiting for the magistrate's pronouncement, as if that *pendejo* were the clever one.

"The vicar," Sarmiento said.

Marcos would have laughed but for his magistrate's hard stare. "Pero would agree to anything the king says."

"The vicar is ... unsteady," Sarmiento conceded. "But we won't authorize him to speak. His Majesty won't arrest a church official for delivering a message."

Marcos searched for another idea, but preoccupied with the image of his head replacing the partridges on the platter, he found none.

"Look at you, Deputy, not such a confident fellow after all." Sarmiento eyed him, speaking softly. "You treated me with disdain this afternoon. I experience moods sometimes, Marcos, a malady. You have a fine mind and a vision. I need your ideas and your *Sangre Pura,* but also fealty."

For once, the magistrate was confiding instead of acting the pompous ass. Marcos felt almost touched. "Sometimes, Magistrate, you lose sight of our holy mission."

Sarmiento gestured at the document. "I'm sure you haven't forgotten it. Now let me show you how to make your letter more articulate."

CHAPTER 69

—⚇—

PERO RODE TOWARD BISAGRA GATE with his fellow priest, Juan Alonso; the commandant, Don Ricardo; and a nobleman whose name Pero couldn't remember. Alonso was taller than Pero, fair featured with a thin face and wispy eyebrows. The commandant appeared imposing with his sleek, black hair and bushy mustache, his black-and-gold uniform with a red band and gold epaulets. Even the businessman had an air of discernment. His Majesty would look them over and wonder why Toledo had let the fat, stupid priest lead this delegation!

Pero still felt dazed from the morning's meeting with Marcos and Chief Magistrate Sarmiento. The magistrate, who'd seldom spoken with Pero, had called him '*nuestro promotor*' and praised him for his devotion to God and to justice. Next, as Pero's bowels climbed into his throat, the magistrate had told him about a vital mission to meet the king, and Pero had consented to lead it.

As he rode, the confusion in Toledo's streets unnerved him—men pushing carts of boxes and sacks, women with baskets of goods strapped to their shoulders, families riding wagons filled with their belongings; even a half-dozen Jews with long scraggly beards, all bustling out of the city. But while some fled the approaching army, others flooded in for the protection of Toledo's walls.

—⚇—

Three hours later, the four men stood in the hot sun on a dusty street in the village of Fuensalida. Five royal soldiers watched them from the steps of the stone town manor. A dozen more sat on the porch of a general store across the street. Church bells struck for the third time. Sweat trickled along Pero's side beneath his black robe.

A man gestured from the manor entry. As they climbed the stairs, Pero recognized the fellow—balding around the temples but vigorous in his bearing—Constable Luna. The constable held the door open but blocked the entrance. "Who's the leader?"

Pero, holding the envelope by his side, forced his unsteady legs forward. "I am Vicar Pero López de Galvez."

The constable smirked. "Of course, Sarmiento lacked the *cojones* to come. Is that for me?"

"For the king." Pero gripped the envelope tighter.

Luna extended his hand. "I represent him."

"I-I'm to give it to the monarch."

"The archbishop's inside. I could have him demand it."

Don Ricardo moved beside Pero. "Constable, I am commandant of Toledo's civil guard." He took the envelope from Pero's hand. "We bring this matter directly to the king."

Pero's heart eased a bit.

"You were once loyal to your sovereign, Don Ricardo." Luna glared, deep furrows etched between his eyebrows and beside his down-turned mouth. "As royal constable, I demand the document."

"You can't, sir," Don Ricardo answered. "Toledo's charter grants independence."

A voice boomed from inside. *"Damn it, Luna, bring them in.* Let them disrespect their king in person."

They entered a vestibule, two stories high with walls of gray stone and a staircase that arched up one side. King Juan, wearing a loose-fitting shirt the blue of a clear sky, sat beside the gaunt, gray-headed Archbishop Carrillo. The churchman glared, but the king seemed more curious than hostile. Soldiers stood to the rear, and courtiers in persimmon costumes waved Oriental fans over the pair.

Pero handed the envelope to King Juan and backed away. "As instructed, Your Majesty."

Archbishop Carrillo grunted. "One wonders where the vicar gets his instructions. Certainly not from the church, and I think not from our Lord in heaven."

Pero kept his eyes down.

The king handed Luna the envelope. Luna ripped it open as the king asked, "Where *are* you receiving direction, Vicar?"

"I am working for the Lord, Your Majesty, rooting out false Christians."

Luna, burst out laughing, waving the document in the air. "This will entertain you, my king. These upstarts invite *you*, the monarch of Castile, to enter Toledo, but only with a handful of weaponless men."

"*Impudence.*" King Juan frowned—still, not the fierce look of a man about to order an execution. "What else?"

"Sarmiento fears losing his post and seeks assurance. And he wishes to keep the loot he's stolen from the converts. Your Majesty, I hesitate to mention this, but the renegades declare that I'm a dangerous man." Luna pointed a finger toward his chin and smiled innocently. "I mustn't enter Toledo with you." He glanced back at the paper. "Now this is comical: The city will secede from your realm, unless Castile's wrongs are righted." Luna sniggered.

King Juan chuckled, too, but there was no humor in it. "Which wrongs? I've many on the royal conscience."

"The ones inspired by me. My love of converts offends them. They want *conversos* out of government, and they want me out, too. If Your Majesty wishes to return to their good graces, you will hold Cortes and invite all city magistrates to rectify these *grievous offences.*"

Pero's heart beat wildly. Was the magistrate trying to have them killed?

Carrillo's scowl grew fierce. He stood. Pero backed into Juan Alonso. "Who's this other priest?" Carrillo demanded. "We'll need the proper name to pursue excommunication."

"Savor this farce, Archbishop." Luna said. "You won't find a better set of fools." The constable looked toward King Juan and his smile disappeared.

The king glowered and summoned a soldier. Luna spoke with the warrior as King Juan pointed at Pero. "Approach, Vicar."

Pero glanced at Don Ricardo, who stood rigid, his face red and angry. Pero advanced, his legs wobbly, fingernails gouging his palms.

King Juan stood and pulled a knife. He was half a head taller than Pero. "I could lop off your head, you insolent *cabrón.*"

Pero willed his body to remain upright. From the edge of his vision, he saw the soldier depart from Luna and move past him. The boot steps circled behind, and, thank God, moved on out the door.

"Your pope can decapitate your soul," the king added.

"My l-lord, we do God's work," Pero stammered. "We seek the pope's sanction."

"I know that Sarmiento conspires with my cousins against me."

Droplets of the king's spittle coated Pero's face, but he dared not move. He gestured toward the document in Luna's hand. "Magistrate Sarmiento would be loyal. He seeks assurance, that's all … he will, and, and the issues of the realm, and perhaps the letter's unclear."

"Should we *behead* you, Vicar, or incinerate you as you burned those converts?"

"I didn't write it. I only—"

"No, you're just a minion, bedazzled by evil nonsense about secret Jews. *Get out,* and pray that you live through the day." The king thrust a hand toward the door.

Juan Alonso and the nobleman rushed through the exit. Don Ricardo waited for Pero and followed. Outside, armored soldiers flanked the steps—huge, fierce men with drawn swords. Juan Alonso and the businessman reached their horses, while twenty paces away, a score of royal archers aimed crossbows at them. Pero stood frozen.

Don Ricardo hissed, "If it's our day to die, we will," and shoved Pero. He stumbled down between the warriors, tripping on his robe but staying upright, pulling himself onto his horse and smelling the animal's dusty sweat as he stared at the metal tips of the archers' arrows.

Don Ricardo angled his steed ahead and spoke through gritted teeth. "We go at a steady pace, two by two." He scowled at Pero. "You knew what was in the letter, you *pendejo*."

Pero's knees trembled against the leather saddle. "You saw the magistrate give it to me. I knew only what he said then."

Don Ricardo prodded his horse to a faster walk. "Metal-tipped arrows slice through a man as if he was a gourd. In your back, out through your naval. García's a madman, goading the king to attack."

Pero resisted his need to bolt, glancing back for pursuing riders, imagining the feeling of an arrow ripping into him and appearing, bloody, beneath his ribs.

He spotted mounted soldiers atop a bluff, aiming crossbows, something sailing through the air. He ducked low. An arrow punched into a tree ahead. Panic rising, blood pounding in his ears—what was pride to a man's life? He spurred his horse past Don Ricardo, galloping, holding on with all his strength, concentrating on the dirt road ahead and praying for deliverance.

CHAPTER 70

—⚜—

FRANCESCA APPROACHED HER GARDEN TABLE and found dew on her chair where the sun hadn't yet cast its warmth. She flicked it off with her fingers and drew the white woolen cape around her shoulders. A yellow-breasted bird landed on a rosebush, watching her with its shiny, black eye. She bid the bird good morning, opened her book of poetry, and sighed. Thinking of Viçente and their rendezvous on the Isle of Ischia and in Rome made heat swell from that place in her abdomen. When he returned, she'd find a way to end Carlo's meddling.

Penélope came running down the stairs from the portico. The maid carried an envelope, and her playful grin implied that it came from him. Francesca felt a mixture of anticipation and disappointment. Why must the pope delay their meeting, forcing Viçente to stay in Rome?

"A lovely morning." Penélope sang the words. She handed her the letter and stood watching.

Francesca opened it, unfolded the note, and read: *It tears my heart to pieces to write this.* She moved hurriedly down the page, her stomach knotting and tears coming.

"What is it my lady?" Penélope asked.

She lowered her face into her hands and wept.

—⚜—

A strange queasiness germinated inside her, as if worms were eating their way from her stomach to her chest, devouring all that was good and happy and human. This emptiness reminded her of the despair she'd felt when her husband had died. Viçente was alive, but if he were captured by the Toledan authorities ...

She couldn't spare time for self-pity. She rinsed her face, straightened her dress, and strode to the throne room. Two soldiers opened the double doors. Light shone in through the windows. Yellow curtains rippled in the breeze. Alfonso slouched upon his throne, belly protruding beneath his gold-embroidered emerald robe, crown tilted to the side of his head. Two men stood before him, holding hats to their chests as one spoke. Alfonso turned toward Francesca and straightened. The supplicants paused.

"My lord, I need a moment," she called with a shaky voice. Alfonso's stare made her wonder how awful she looked after so much crying, her dress wrinkled, hair loose about her shoulders. She smoothed it with a hand.

"I'm occupied, sister." Alfonso looked vexed, but his narrowed eyes showed concern.

"I apologize, my lord."

"If you'd joined me at breakfast, you could have told me then. Go ahead. Speak."

"It's personal, brother."

Alfonso scowled at her and then at the petitioners. "Leave." The men rushed toward the exit. He flipped his hand. Clerks and sages shuffled out and then the soldiers. The doors closed, and she stood alone.

"I imagine you wouldn't have come if it weren't serious, sister." Alfonso gave a wry smile. "But I must retain the people's reverence. Come, sit beside me."

She climbed the steps and settled. "Viçente's been forced to go to Toledo—where they torture good converts."

He patted her forearm and waited.

"You don't approve of him," she said. "That doesn't matter. He's the man for the rest of my life, and he's in danger." Her voice cracked.

A startled smile crossed Alfonso's face. "No one calls my opinion unimportant."

"You know I love you, Alfonso. You're a wise and generous ruler, mostly. I request protection for my trip to Castile."

"I forbid it." His blue eyes flashed in anger.

"You speak as if I'm royal but treat me like a servant. I'll hire my own escorts."

Alfonso pushed himself up, grabbing his crown to keep it from falling. "I'll imprison you."

Were she not the one he called *sister*, she'd quake with fear. Were this not such an awful day, she'd laugh at his resemblance to a fat fish. But this was the day she'd learned of Viçente's mortal danger. She watched her half-brother drop back onto his throne and fold his arms. He glowered, sulked, looked down at his lap. "You love him this much?"

"Yes, Alfonso, and you can't lock me up. What would your subjects think if their *magnanimous* king put his sister in chains?"

"I don't care that they call me that. I think of your safety."

"You want to keep me here for companionship." She could tell from his look that he grasped her meaning. Despite his bluster, she was his true confidant, the one he dared not lose. "Send as many guards to protect me as you wish."

"Castile's in more jeopardy than you imagine."

What was he saying? "What more have you perpetrated now?"

"I ordered troops from Zaragoza to join Navarre's against Castile's King Juan, but thus far my wife and brother ignore the command." Alfonso snorted. "You're not really a queen. You can't save him."

She felt the blush of shame rise in her face.

"Maybe I can assist," he said. "Tell me what's happened."

"They've captured Viçente's son in Toledo." Her throat constricted. "Men he met in Rome told him. He's gone to rescue Diego."

"The proposition sounds uncertain." Alfonso nodded thoughtfully. "We'll strike a bargain, sister." He removed his crown and hung it over the corner post of his throne, his graying hair mussed like a boy's. He took her hand, offering a weak smile. "Toledo's Magistrate Sarmiento welcomes my ambassadors."

She tugged her hand away "Supporting Sarmiento, you condone murder."

"I try to spare you these unpleasant practicalities."

"Go with me and help prevent a tragedy."

"My offer's generous, sister, not absurd. I'll send my minister of state, Guido Tivolini, to Rome to meet with these Toledans. If young Pérez is really imprisoned, my minister will negotiate his freedom."

She shook her head. "Send your minister with me, straight to Castile."

"You must choose, Francesca. Go alone and fail, or remain here, and let Tivolini resolve this."

Tears flowed down her cheeks. Not now—she couldn't let her weakness show. Alfonso's jaw was set in obstinacy, the cleft in his chin in shadow. "I don't understand why you oppose my journey." She searched for an argument, but he wasn't about to yield, and Tivolini would have a better chance. "You promise your minister will do everything to save Viçente and his son? He'll leave for Castile tomorrow."

"Tivolini will have the weight of my authority, but I'll not send him on a vain errand. He leaves for Rome tomorrow, to Castile if necessary. And you'll stay here."

What hell it would be waiting so far away while a diplomat decided Viçente's fate. But she nodded and fled to her chambers.

CHAPTER 71

MARCOS PEERED BETWEEN THE MERLONS of the high battlement and listened to the clamor of the distant army. Hundreds of paces away, down in the open space between the city's walls and the orange groves, smoke rose from cook fires, surrounded by ranks of brown tents. He could make out the glint of sunlight on armor as soldiers moved about. At the center stood a huge white pavilion with a yellow banner flying, the king's red lion and castle. Figures gathered outside, some in armor and some without. The king and the damned constable would be among them. Let them besiege this fortress city with its hundreds of armed men, storehouses of food, cauldrons of oil to boil and rain down on them. Toledo's righteous power would prevail against a mad constable and depleted royal treasury.

Further along the parapet, something caught his eye—a black metal cannon. He approached. It was two paces long, set on a cart with an opening large enough to take one of the balls mounded nearby, each the size of a large orange.

The clatter of hooves on paving stones. Two riders emerged from the alley and rode up. One wore a gray riding jacket over a white tunic—Sarmiento. The other had a ruddy tan, black hair, and military bearing, but he wore the rich green tunic of a prosperous merchant. "Captain Sanchez, at your service."

"What's this about?" Marcos asked.

"Be civil, Deputy." Sarmiento smirked.

"Whose captain are you?"

The fellow laughed and Sarmiento said, "Isn't it obvious? He's Prince Enrique's man, arrived with welcome news. Tell him, Captain."

"The prince's army is in Alcalá, ready to march on Toledo."

"Enrique sent me this excellent letter." Sarmiento plucked a document from his jacket pocket and unfolded it. "Here are a couple of the prince's best phrases: 'I am prepared to mediate your misunderstandings with my father, King Juan.' I like that one, don't you, Deputy? And here: 'I offer to support your dominion in Toledo as long as you return loyalty to me.' I'll happily grant fidelity to a man who rips the serpent from my throat."

But Marcos understood this prince, a *marrano*-lover like his father. "Does he have the *cojones* to rid us of Constable Luna, or will he connive with the devil? And what's his position on *limpieza*?"

Sarmiento waved a dismissive hand. "You complicate everything. I take 'mediate' to mean 'boot the king's army out of our orange grove.' Correct, Captain?"

"Yes, sir. Our force is greater."

"But what of our holy purpose?" Marcos asked.

"Stop scowling," the magistrate commanded. "We're being saved before the king unsheathes a sword."

Marcos reached for the letter. "What are the conditions?"

The magistrate held it back and turned to Sanchez. "Give us a moment, Captain." The officer strolled away, and Sarmiento said, "The prince did write something about the *marranos*."

"Damn it, what?"

"Quietly, Deputy. The prince doesn't mind imprisoning thieves if they happen to be *marranos*, but we must refrain from killing them for the present."

"We can't trust that dog." Marcos grabbed the paper. "You saw him with Pérez at the battle of Olmedo."

Sarmiento leveled a finger. "Careful of that document. It's his commitment."

That damned twitch was back under Marcos' eye. "Magistrate, we can hold the king off and force him to back down. If we surrender to Prince Enrique, he'll demand our loyalty, then our strength, and finally our pride."

"Did you fail to notice the army preparing a goddamned siege? Enrique will honor my command. And my second priority involves not the *marranos*, but their gold. I'll retain mine, and so will *Sangre Pura*."

"The movement," Marcos said. "The holy cause—to save Castile's soul. It's your moment in history, Magistrate."

"When you're dealing with royalty, you don't rave about causes. I'll write back to the prince with words like, 'It is vital that we be allowed autonomy to deal with the issue of *conversos*.' Grand, isn't it? The *converso* issue might involve confiscating their gold or continuing the *limpieza* or whatever the prince thinks it means. Once he dislodges the king and returns to Segovia, we'll do as we wish."

"No. Make the prince commit to the *limpieza*." Marcos saw Sarmiento's look grow distant. He was going to agree and relinquish their advantage. Again.

Cursing under his breath, Marcos leapt on his horse and rode to the *alcázar*. He entered and stomped down to the dungeon, thinking of the pieces of *mierda* who obstructed God's work—King Juan; Constable Luna; Viçente Pérez, who'd subverted Prince Enrique's morals; even Pero, the spineless vicar.

He took a lighted torch, entered the cell, and saw young Pérez slumped in a corner. Marcos brought the torch close. The creature cringed, wrapping its arms around itself and shivering. Marcos felt a clenching in his chest—something like pity. He backed away. Emotions distracted. Emotions deceived. They could not be allowed to undo a man on Jesus' mission. The Savior demanded logic, and logic told him to keep this one alive to lure the father. "Guard, fetch some broth. Salve those wounds. Give it another blanket. Don't let him perish."

CHAPTER 72

———⟶⟶⟶———

ANGER AND FRUSTRATION BURNED MARCOS' gut as he departed the dungeon. The *marrano's* son was dying, and Sarmiento was moving toward alliance with Prince Enrique. How to prevent it? If the king could be lured into battling his son for Toledo ... by what means, damn it? Provoke the *pendejo* to attack the city before the prince arrived.

In the arsenal, Marcos found the gunnery sergeant, a stubby man with a thick, black mustache, the top buttons of his uniform undone, showing a tangle of dark, curly hair. They walked together to the high ramparts, both huffing like winded nags by the time they arrived. Sentries stood watch at every third crenel in the wall. Marcos led the sergeant to a vacant space. He gulped a deep breath and pointed at the king's army. "That big white tent belongs to King Juan." Marcos gestured to the cannon. "How far can that weapon send a ball?"

The sergeant stroked his chin with a calloused hand. "I call this my *lombarda*." He patted the weapon. "Its reach depends on wind and height to the target and whether it's fog or clear."

Marcos wondered about the man's senses, calling the cannon a red cabbage. "This is the height and that tent the target."

"My God, you want to shoot King Juanito?"

"We aren't aiming at the king. We're warning him." Still, killing the king would be a glorious achievement. Prince Enrique would have to battle the Royal Cousins for power, keeping him occupied and out of the way. "Pay attention, Sergeant, and answer me. If we'd shot at mid-morning today, could it have reached?"

"No fog today. No rain, and the wind was down." The sergeant puffed out his cheek and shook his head.

Marcos grabbed the man's arm. "Will it shoot that far?"

"Farther, shorter, depends on the slant we set to the barrel."

"Sergeant, can you make your cabbage hit the goddamned white tent?"

"Two minutes to reload. How many tries do I get?"

"The *cabrones* will be out of the tent before that. Do you have more cannon?"

"Another near Bisagra gate." The sergeant looked up, as if appealing to God. "I don't know, First Deputy. We'd have to be awful lucky."

"Don't tell anyone, Sergeant. Tomorrow morning, bring your second cannon. When our enemies gather in that tent, you'll fire those two big *pollas*. If you hit that tent and take off Constable Luna's head, I'll make you the richest man in Toledo." Taking off Luna's head was the only outcome that would prevent Sarmiento's rage, but as always, Marcos would deal with him.

Next morning, the cannons sat ready on their carts at two of the crenels in the wall. Civil guardsmen observed as Marcos and the gunnery sergeant watched distant figures enter the king's tent. The sergeant measured the slant of one gun with a marked stick and looked up to a banner on a nearby pole, barely moving in the scant breeze. He knelt and sighted along a steel rod that was attached to the barrel, then stood and leveled a hand over the weapon as if saying benediction.

"Ready?" Marcos asked.

"This one's right. I'll check the other."

"You've checked it twice. Fire the *canallas*."

"We'll have to be damned lucky," the man said for the fifth time.

One of the civil guards handed the artilleryman a lit torch, and he held it to the tar-soaked rope at the back of the weapon. A flame edged up the rope. The sergeant watched, looking satisfied.

"Light the other one, damn it."

The gunnery-man stepped around as a thunderous boom shook Marcos. Smoke filled the air. The cannon leapt backward on its cart and struck the rotund sergeant, knocked him into the air, his torch flying, sparks and embers showering the stone pavement.

The sergeant lay on his back, moaning. Marcos shouted to a guardsman, "Light off that other weapon!" He looked out toward the king's tent, trying to see the projectile, praying that the shot was well placed. But why hadn't the second one fired?

Marcos glanced back to see the guardsman holding the blackened staff and shaking his head. "Fire's out, First Deputy."

Down in the encampment, he saw motion to the left of the king's shelter. One of the brown tents collapsed, then another. Soldiers scattered.

"I'll run for some fire," the guardsman said.

Marcos saw figures streaming from the royal tent, scurrying into the orange grove. "Don't bother."

—w—

Marcos sat at his desk, rereading his draft of a law banning *marranos* from government with the cannon's boom still reverberating in his ears. Two civil guardsmen entered. Marcos jumped up. "You can't barge in here."

"Chief Magistrate Sarmiento's orders." One came at him as the other stepped around his desk. "Give over your knife, sir." Marcos heart beat fast and hard. The guardsman held out a hand. Marcos looked him over for a moment and complied. The other guard grabbed his wrists and bound them. He felt panic rising with the pulse in his veins, but this was just Sarmiento giving him a scare. They were rough, these two, grabbing him by the elbows to shove him up the hill.

"Slower. Let me take a breath."

The men gave him a minute and then continued to the *alcázar* courtyard. They gripped Marcos hard then and yanked him down the stairs. *God, no, the dungeon.* "Stop," he called, but they hauled him past the six cells to the torture room door. Sweat poured off his forehead. One guard rammed back the bolt and led them in. The other wrapped burly arms around his chest, pressing the air out of him and pinning him on a table. "Don't move." He lay, looking up at the man's pock-marked face. Light from the torches shone on the dark stone ceiling.

Sarmiento appeared beside the guard. "An unpleasant place, isn't it, Deputy? Makes you consider the consequences of disobedience."

"You're angry about the cannon?" Marcos heard the tremor in his voice and hated it. He searched for a suitable explanation.

Sarmiento chuckled. *"Angry's* a feeble word. You shot at the god-damned King of Castile. We were trying to negotiate with the man."

"I thought we were negotiating with Prince Enrique." Marcos tried to turn on his side, but Sarmiento jabbed him in the chest.

"You opposed my dealings with the prince," Sarmiento said.

"But accepted your decision, Magistrate. Please let me up."

Sarmiento glared. "Don't think your *Sangre Pura* hooligans will save you now. They're not as enamored with you as they once were."

Whatever Sarmiento pretended, he couldn't risk enraging the brotherhood. If Marcos could only get him to calm down. "We fired the cannon to show the prince that we're finished with the king. I thought you'd be pleased."

"You know about this equipment, Marcos?" Sarmiento pointed to a metal frame hanging from the ceiling. "We could cinch that body truss around you and let you dangle with the spikes piercing your skin." Marcos recognized grim fury in Sarmiento's eyes, but the incon-sistent fool couldn't maintain this mood long. "Sharp blades sliding in and out between your ribs every time you breathe."

Sweat ran from Marcos' torso. He felt a mad sensation that it was blood dribbling out of holes in his chest. Trembling shook his limbs. "Think of my service, Magistrate. Think how *Sangre Pura* would react."

"You helped place me in power, and you've given us purpose. But I can't let you endanger my rule. You will end your disobedience."

"I wanted to show the prince—" Trying not to think of the goring, Marcos glanced away and saw a wooden contraption with the screw handle protruding from the top.

"You like the head vise?" Sarmiento chuckled again. "Excellent. Or there's the rack, if you'd like to be separated from your arms."

His stomach turned over as he imagined his skull compressed until his brains splattered across the cold stone floor. "Our holy mission, Magistrate. We've almost cleansed Toledo of the *marrano* filth. We're spreading our vision to other parts of the realm." If he could continue long enough to cleanse this one city, that might be enough to make God smile on him. Please, Jesus, let it be so.

"Holy mission that robs you of all sense."

Sarmiento was calming, but he'd require a show of regret. "Magistrate, I understand my error. I'll ask your permission before giving any more orders."

"You won't have to. The *Guardia* will ignore you from now on."

"I must control the prisoners to get their confessions and document their blasphemy."

Sarmiento ran a hand through his hair and pouched a cheek. "Prince Enrique does seem skeptical of our inquisition."

"My evidence will prove our claims."

Sarmiento nodded slowly. "If I let you live, you'll direct the questioning and nothing more." The magistrate watched him for a while, then turned and trudged out, followed by the guards with their torches. Marcos let out a long breath, already thinking of the celebratory wine he'd drink that evening after dinner.

The door slammed shut and Marcos flinched. The chamber disappeared in darkness. He could feel the presence of the torture devices, like demons lurking. He felt his way to the door and tried to push it open. It wouldn't budge. "Magistrate, please," he called.

Sarmiento's voice. "You need to ponder your transgressions."

He felt his way back to the table, wondering if the magistrate was still outside. He lay down and cold began seeping into his bones. More and more cold. Could he sleep in this horrible place? Of what would he dream? Maybe he'd envision flames and the four evil ones burning. That should warm him.

His teeth began to chatter.

A clunk. The doors swung open and a guardsman beckoned. So once again, the magistrate had hurled empty threats and then relented for fear of *Sangre Pura*. Marcos smiled and sat up.

For the next few days, Marcos observed the king's army from vantage points around the city. To the east and west, across the Rio Tajo, battalions blocked access to the bridges of San Martín and Alcántara. The siege had begun, but why didn't the damned king attack?

Several days after the cannon shot, the royal army removed the blockades, broke camp, and marched away.

CHAPTER 73

—⟶

VIÇENTE SPENT TWO WEEKS ON a smelly, pitching ship, suffering seasickness and heart-sickness and agonized nightmares. Finally, the ship docked in the fortress city of Cartagena, and there he gained hopeful news. The king laid siege to Toledo.

Exchanging horses along the route, riding to exhaustion for four days, he reached a promontory close to the city. Below, he saw part of the castle of San Servando, the Alcántara Bridge, and the city beyond. His stomach churned at the sight of Toledo rising on its bluff—the cathedral tower and the *alcázar* where Diego must be captive, if he was alive.

Down on the road, he saw no signs of a royal blockade, but to the far side of the city, dust clouded the air—a strong eddy of wind, or a large movement of men. He halted a horseman coming from the city. "I heard that Toledo was under attack, but I see no sign."

The man wiped his brow with a sun-browned forearm. "Young prince made some bargain with the magistrate and booted Papa out." The stranger gestured to the dust cloud. "Prince's army moving into the groves."

Bargain with depravity, Viçente thought. But this could save Diego. He rode upriver and hired a boat across the Tajo, then headed for Enrique's encampment. At a guard station, he identified himself first to a corporal, then a sergeant, and finally a captain. Each led him deeper into the bustling camp full of men carrying gear and hammering tent posts, setting pots and racks of venison over cook fires, coarse laughter resounding. A man in a golden turban ambled toward him, wearing a silk robe with swirls of blue and green—Juan Pacheco. "V-Viçente, how good to see you." Pacheco had filled out a bit, a handsome, robust man in his mid-thirties. He glanced down at his robe and said, "As you see, we dress for the adventure."

Viçente wrapped his arms around the prince's counselor. "I need help, Juan, for my son. Sarmiento has him captive."

Pacheco pulled back and stared. "Are you certain?"

"Not completely, but Sarmiento's men in Rome swear to it."

"Better Sarmiento than some other knave."

Pacheco gestured and Viçente followed between tents. "I don't understand, Juan, are you collaborating with the cur or planning an attack?" Pacheco glanced back, and Viçente saw the truth in his eyes. Anger tightened his throat. "How could you support his persecutions?"

"We've convinced him to curtail them." Pacheco stepped over a shovel that lay on the ground, halted, and looked at Viçente. "I see the hurt in your eyes. You're naïve. Sarmiento helps us gain power. It's Enrique's obsession."

"That's why he wanted me to govern Toledo. Is he still furious that I refused, Juan?"

"Just don't anger him with talk of right and wrong."

They came to a huge yellow tent with a red lion stitched on one entry flap and an orange pomegranate opposite. Inside, Oriental silk screens angled them one way and another until they arrived at the open center, cast in a yellow glow from the canvas. Viçente spotted Enrique, sitting cross-legged on the carpeted dirt floor, wearing Arabic garb like Pacheco's. There were several chairs, and two chests holding cups and bowls.

Viçente's hands shook as he bowed. "My humble greetings, Prince."

"You used to call me *Enrique*."

Viçente tried to think what he'd say if he wasn't desperate. "The last time I saw you, you shoved me onto my buttocks."

"The bears would have preferred I toss you over the edge."

Viçente made out Enrique's features as his vision adapted—the keen eyes and familiar flattened nose. "I'd be prudent to apologize, but I can't think of pleasantries. I seek your help."

"Too late to govern Toledo."

"Still, Viçente's a friend," Pacheco said. "And Sarmiento carries the persecutions too far. Viçente thinks he's imprisoned his son."

"On what grounds?" Enrique stood and picked a pear from a bowl on the chest.

"Sarmiento's men approached me in Rome. They say Diego's being questioned about his devotion." Viçente's voice cracked, and he cursed himself for it.

"We're in delicate negotiations with the magistrate." Enrique bit a chunk from the pear and started pacing. "What made the boy wander in to be captured? If he really is captive."

Viçente looked for some sign of the old Enrique, the lad he'd befriended, but found only hard calculation. How could he value Diego's life so little? "García detests me. He's lured my son."

"Viçente can hardly enter Toledo and ask." Pacheco poured liquid into a cup. "Have some pear juice, Viçente."

Viçente waved it away. "The king was about to attack, and you drove him off. Sarmiento owes you a huge debt. You can request Diego's release."

"He already gave me the *quid pro quo*. Toledo pledges me loyalty. I represent the city in negotiations with the Royal Cousins." The prince watched him for a moment, his look intense. "And to please us, they've stopped attacking converts."

"Pacheco told me." Viçente stared at him, waiting.

Enrique turned and flung his pear against the wall of the tent. "Goddamn it. I've not marched my army here to content myself with one freed lad."

"He tortures my boy, Enrique, my innocent. Can you imagine?"

"I don't have a son, Viçente." The prince's tone softened. "If I didn't have to produce a successor, I never would."

"Then think how your father would react if you were prisoner."

The prince took a long breath and turned to Pacheco. "Is there a way to help him without jeopardizing our position?"

"Request Diego's release solely as a gesture of good will."

"Didn't you hear what I told Viçente? Their gesture was to cease the executions."

"You won't even ask for my son's life?" Viçente saw Pacheco's warning glance and lowered his voice. "I don't understand, Prince."

"We're trying to forge an alliance with Sarmiento. I have to think of a whole city."

"The city, or the power of controlling it?" It crept out, foolish words that only hurt his cause.

Enrique scowled. "I've already helped your people, but for every compromise Sarmiento grants, I concede something. I can not make a priority of one careless lad."

Viçente bristled at the word, even as he recognized a new maturity in the prince. He was no longer a hasty youth, but a man in his middle twenties, one who might actually consider Toledo's well-being. "I have properties in Segovia," Viçente said. "I'll sell them and pay a ransom."

"Good," Pacheco said. "Let me go to Sarmiento and find out if he has the boy. I'll mention possible recompense if they grant his freedom."

Enrique nodded. "The greedy *pendejo* might welcome a bribe."

"And freeing Diego that way wouldn't jeopardize your alliance."

Enrique stepped close. "Go outside and wait while Pacheco and I discuss it." He patted Viçente's cheek. "Despite what you may think, I've not forgotten our good days."

CHAPTER 7 4

—𝔪—

THE NEXT MORNING, WHILE PACHECO rode to the city, Viçente strode beside the orange grove and followed a footpath that meandered along the bluff. At a promontory over the Rio Tajo, he sat and listened to water flowing over the weir in the canyon. Church bells chimed the hour. He tried to conjure images of Francesca in a sundress, sitting in her garden, but the pictures kept turning back to his son. The bells rang again … and again. Could Pacheco have returned already with Diego? *No. Don't let yourself hope.*

Back in camp, a half-dozen soldiers stood guard by the prince's pavilion. A sergeant confronted Viçente.

"Has Juan Pacheco returned?"

"Aye." The soldier pointed a large, gloved hand at Viçente. "You can't approach here."

Viçente's pulse pounded. "Did a younger man arrive with Pacheco?" *Jesus, let it be so.*

A tent flap drew back and Pacheco stepped out. "It's all right, Sergeant."

Viçente saw Pacheco's glum expression and his heart sank. Pacheco took his arm and led him into the grove.

"Is he there?" Viçente clenched his fists as he walked. "*Speak,* Juan."

"I saw him, Viçente. I'll tell you everything." Pacheco moved faster and Viçente kept pace.

"Why not talk in Prince Enrique's tent?" Viçente saw the answer in Pacheco's shame-faced frown as they halted between the lush trees with their undeveloped, green fruit. "Diego's captive, but Enrique denies us help? Damn it, Juan, tell me how he is."

"He looks … unwell, my friend, hag-haggard, but he's alive and able to bear the weight of his chains."

Chains. "You demanded his release?"

"I couldn't demand. I asked for his freedom and reminded them that we'd liberated Toledo from the king's army. Magistrate Sarmiento seemed to consider it."

"My money—did you offer it?"

"Yes, and I was prepared to add my own, but García argued with the magistrate about his loyalty to Enrique. García shows him little respect, and Sarmiento seems embarrassed by it. He sent me from the room." Pacheco's lower lip quivered.

"You're a good friend, Juan."

"When they invited me back, García inquired whether you'd returned to Castile, and Sarmiento asked about your relationship with Prince Enrique."

Viçente remembered García's eyes that day in his office years ago—like black marble, shiny with loathing. Now, Viçente returned the hatred. "If Enrique approached Sarmiento, they'd free Diego, wouldn't they?" He tore a small, green orange from a tree and squeezed it until his palm hurt. "Enrique must give me the respect of a meeting."

Pacheco shook his head. "He avoids you because he feels badly about this. As he explained, we can't barter away our advantage while we forge this pact."

"I'll go to the king." As Viçente said the words, he knew they were hollow. The king had fled at Enrique's approach. "Or …" As Viçente searched for other ideas, he dropped the orange to the dirt and crushed it with his boot. There was only one possibility: "I'm the one they want, not him." He lifted his boot, exposing the squashed white pulp of the fruit and a wet spot in the dirt.

"Señor García spoke of an exchange, but I didn't want to mention it. He said Diego had confessed crimes against God that originated with his family." Pacheco shook his head. "You can't do it, Viçente."

"Don't you understand? They torture Diego." Viçente's voice broke. Of course Pacheco knew. He'd seen Diego. "García hates me because I foiled his plan to incarcerate a poor, mute Jew. After we freed the mute, García murdered him."

Pacheco stared at him, his jaw tight. "You can't accept the offer. We've only begun our negotiations with Sarmiento. In a fortnight, perhaps, Sarmiento will need some boon, and we'll be able to bargain for Diego."

The squashed orange seemed to Viçente like his dreams for a future with Francesca—the sweet promise stolen, the bitter juice of regret all that remained. "As you bargain with me now, to delay while they kill him slowly. If you're my friend, Juan, arrange the trade."

—m—

The hoof beats thudded in Viçente's chest, his horse taking him away from life, away from Francesca, forever. He rode beside Pacheco beneath the outer towers of the Bisagra gate with its *Guardia Civil* watching from above, through the inner portal, up the cobbled street to the summit, leveling out by the high-walled *alcázar*.

From the courtyard, a guardsman he recognized led them upstairs, along a hallway, suffocating with the scent of burnt tallow, to a familiar meeting room with a long table lit by two lamps.

Marcos García strutted in, followed by four guardsmen. Pacheco stepped beside Viçente, and García halted a pace away, scowling. "You've come to face the reckoning for your sins."

García and guardsmen, no one else. Viçente swallowed, his heart pounding. Did the madman plan to betray the agreement and keep Diego, too? "Where's my son? Where's Chief Magistrate Sarmiento?"

"Do you think he'll save you?" García cackled.

"It's part of our agreement," Pacheco said.

Sarmiento entered and stood beside his deputy. His impassive blue eyes lingered on Viçente. "So you've captured your adversary, Marcos."

"You remember your promise, Magistrate," Pacheco said.

"Of course, Señor Pacheco." Sarmiento grasped Pacheco's hand and smiled. "We'll turn over the young *marrano*."

"And Viçente will have a chance to see his son."

More guards entered, and Viçente moved close to the table, up on his toes, trying to look past them.

Sarmiento said, "Let the prisoner pass."

The guardsmen moved aside, and Viçente saw his son—gaunt, hollow-eyed, but he wore a clean shirt and his face was unmarked.

He reached Diego in three strides and wrapped his arms around him. Diego flinched and Viçente pulled his hands away. "The *cabrones* beat you."

Diego hugged him. "Papa. Oh, Jesus, you shouldn't have come."

"My dear son, of course. My beloved boy." He pulled back to look at Diego, so thin and sad but such a fine young man.

Tears ran from Diego's eyes. "I came to Toledo in stealth, Papa. I merely walked by our house, but a spy informed on me."

"It's all right. Juan Pacheco will see you to safety."

"Take that *marrano* away," García commanded.

"I'm proud of you, Diego." Viçente felt hands clutch his shoulders. "Write to Francesca. Tell her I love her. Tell her I had to." Pain erupted in his old wound as a guard yanked him back.

"One minute," Pacheco said. "You've promised not to harm Viçente."

"But we must question him," Sarmiento said. "You understand." The guards lifted Viçente and he struggled for another glimpse of his son.

"I love you, Papa."

The door slammed shut, and the *Guardia Civil* dragged him to the stairway.

CHAPTER 75

—⚭—

THE STENCH OF HUMAN WASTE filled Viçente's pores. Marcos García de Mora sat on a stool outside his cell, staring between the bars. The gaunt man bared his teeth, his tongue darting like a snake tasting the air. The vision sent a wave of nausea through him. A guard held a lighted torch over Viçente, following García's order to 'illuminate the prisoner.'

The first time García had come, Viçente had dared look away, and on García's orders, a guardsman had pursued him with the flame, threatening to set his hair afire.

So now Viçente eyed García and tried to think of anything besides his thirst and hunger, the filth of his body, the pain in his limbs with his ankle chained to the stone floor. Had this been Diego's cell? Was his son's blood part of the detritus that Viçente touched no matter where he laid his hands?

"Wanting to say something?" García grinned.

Viçente shook his head.

"Answer me."

"No." Viçente's voice came in a grating whisper.

García stretched. "Enjoy these comfortable moments, *marrano*. Think of that Jew whore in the red dress and the power that one-eyed old man gave you. Contemplate your errors, like that day when you tormented my vicar—so reckless. Magistrate Sarmiento shows restraint because of your powerful friends, but after I make the case against you, God will have his justice."

Viçente noticed García's look of distaste as he said Sarmiento's name. The man abhorred his superior and detested the command for restraint. "If I die of hunger, you'll not have the pleasure."

García departed, and a guard brought a bowl of tasteless liquid with bits of brown pulp floating in it.

Viçente tried to divert himself with small things—the murmured words of prisoners in other cells, the arrival of new guards and the sounds of the dice games they played outside his cell. He reminded himself that he'd saved Diego from this horror and tried to fill his thoughts with Francesca. She'd have received his message weeks ago, would have imagined his tortures as he'd imagined Diego's, would cry out in her sleep. It wounded his heart to think of her, but it pleased him, too, and he would not stop until he died. His prayers were long conversations with Jesus, seeking salvation, healing for Diego, and an easing of Francesca's torment.

The guards removed two ragged men from another cage and brought a woman. The word passed that it was Saturday. He'd been imprisoned for four days, with nothing but gruel, a crust of moldy bread, and a few sips of water. At least the stomach cramps had ceased.

García appeared again. Two guards entered, placing a basin near Viçente on the floor, filling it with water from a pitcher and setting another pitcher nearby.

They filed out and García said, "Clean yourself. You're going to see the magistrate."

Viçente sniffed the liquid, raised it to his lips, and drank, letting it pour down his neck and chest. He took slow breaths, then sipped, cupped a hand, dipped it in the basin and splashed it over his face, drank again until his stomach cramped. He lowered his face into the basin, relished the soothing coolness, raised up and flicked water off his face with his fingers. Outside, García watched like a bird of prey. Viçente turned his back, removed his shirt, poured water over his chest and under his arms. He sighed and murmured, "Oh, Jesus. Thank you, Lord."

"*What language is that?*" García banged something against the bars. "Guards, you heard him. Shackle his hands and bring him."

Viçente's heart hammered. He pushed himself up, feeling weak and unsteady and pulled on his shirt. A guard manacled his wrists as a shorter guardsman leaned close and whispered, "I'm sorry, Señor Pérez." Viçente nodded, recognizing the man by his stature and his curly, brown hair, trying to remember his name.

The sympathetic guard unchained Viçente's ankle and the two led him, stumbling, up endless steps.

In the second floor dining room, candles blazed in a chandelier above the long table. Their scent helped clear the dungeon's stench from his nostrils. Magistrate Sarmiento lounged in a chair at one end of the table, wearing a crimson robe—some sort of judicial garb? "At last, our honored guest."

The guards shoved Viçente into a chair at the opposite end.

"Be easy," Sarmiento cooed. "He's our prince's friend. You look wan, Señor Pérez, but you'll soon have a fine dinner." Sarmiento turned to García. "Report on the prisoner's comportment, Deputy."

"He displays his Jew-swine practices shamelessly. We gave him water, and he performed ritual bathing and Hebrew chanting."

"It's a *lie*. I've never been a Jew and don't know Hebrew. Magistrate Sarmiento, I prayed to Jesus."

Sarmiento raised a hand. "You'll be able to demonstrate your innocence shortly. But watch your tone, Señor. Your high-placed allies aren't present to grant favors."

García pulled a paper from his jacket with a flourish and pointed to the taller guardsman. "Did you witness the Hebrew ritual I described?"

Viçente saw the guard blink, seemingly confused. Then he spoke in a gruff, military tone. "Aye, your honor."

"And you?" García gestured to the guard who'd whispered to Viçente.

The man shrugged. "I didn't hear, my lord, can't say it was Hebrew."

"Naturally, this guardsman couldn't recognize that perverse language." García laughed and waved his document. "The second charge—it's illegal under the decrees of 633 for a *marrano* to hold office. Pretending to be first deputy was a criminal act."

Sarmiento shook his head. "Señor Pérez, my counselor's expertise extends to the ancient, dusty laws of bygone eras. Tell us something relevant, Deputy."

García grimaced. "While illegally acting as first deputy, he ordered the *Guardia Civil* to interrogate good Christians and protect Jews. Against the pleas of church officials, he released a mute Jew who'd stolen sacred property."

Viçente thumped the table, making the chains rattle. "García and the vicar fabricated the charges after the mute saved a women they planned to rape."

Sarmiento shrugged. "A dead mute can't testify."

"Listen to the way he defends a Jew criminal." García sneered. "Even his clerk reports that Pérez prayed in Hebrew in his office."

"Bring the clerk," Viçente demanded. "Let him say it to me."

"We burned the sinner at the stake." García dropped his papers onto the table. "This man held high office while no other city in Castile employed a *marrano*. He subverted our prince's good sense through guile."

"Magistrate Sarmiento, does your justice defend rapists and punish the innocent?" Viçente called. "Do you accept the lies of this *deputy* who disdains you?"

"Señor Pérez, it's a long list of offenses, but I'll grant you a chance at redemption and also a fine meal. It's a simple test. Everyone knows that Jews refuse pork." Sarmiento clapped his hands and servants entered.

Viçente sat back in his chair, feeling a little hope. He'd often eaten pork since his university days. But false hope was worse than none. These men didn't intend justice.

Two serving women entered and brought plates to the head of the table. Viçente caught a scent of cooked meat and began salivating. A third maid carried a plate to him, but a foul odor arrived with it.

García laughed. "Enjoy your feast, *marrano*." He slid a knife through his own food and lifted a rib bone, thick with meat.

Viçente regarded his meal, a clump of fat covered in brown ooze.

"I trust you like the meat of pigs." Sarmiento took a lusty bite.

"I don't see any meat," Viçente said. "Can I have a knife to look for some?"

"No weapons." García spoke with his mouth full. "Pick it up."

Viçente poked the slimy mass and lifted it. It jiggled in his hand. There was no solid meat here, but he was famished. When he'd been a boy, his mother had removed the fat, the meat probably prepared in forbidden ways. Even as an adult, Viçente didn't enjoy fatty meat, but when he dined with others he consumed fat and meat together. It was expected.

"Eat," García commanded. "Or confess you're a Jew."

Viçente held the hunk aloft and felt something inch across his finger. Where his thumb had penetrated, white maggots wriggled from the fissure. "It's full of worms." He felt bile rising. He dropped the wad of fat onto his plate and vomited to the side. Retching and remembering that terrible night—the sumptuous dinner with Momma and Papa and then the awful truth.

Sarmiento laid down his meat and said, "I'm sorry, Pérez, but you've proven the charges against you. Deputy, in your list of accusations, did you note that Señor Pérez has charmed the lady Francesca of King Alfonso's house and plundered her virtue?"

Francesca ... When these men ceased tormenting Viçente, they would kill him and rob her of his love. *"Pendejo.* The lady has more goodness than you could imagine."

García jabbed a finger at Viçente. "The Jew-lover speaks of virtue, but he subverts Christ's church."

"Enough," Sarmiento barked.

Viçente tried not to look at the hunk of fat as he grasped it with both hands and flung it. His chained hands clattered down, smashing his plate. The putrid mass flew to the center of the table and bounded forward, careening off Sarmiento's red robe.

A brawny arm wrenched Viçente upward, crushing pressure on his throat. He saw the magistrate stand and gawk at the brown slime on his chest. Viçente clawed at the guard's arm, but couldn't gather any breath. Sarmiento approached the exit, speaking over his shoulder to García. "All right, Marcos. Obtain his confession as you wish." Viçente's vision began to blur.

The magistrate hesitated. "Release his throat." The pressure eased and Viçente dropped to the floor, gasping. Sarmiento jabbed a finger toward García. "Marcos, we must still justify ourselves to the prince. Obtain the vicar's sanction." Then he strode out of the room.

—ɯ—

CHAINED IN HIS CELL, VIÇENTE tried to push aside terror and think of a way to exploit García's hatred for Sarmiento, but thoughts eluded him.

García appeared. "You were foolish to soil a vain man's cloak."

A *Guardia Civil* unbolted the door with a clank. Guards unshackled Viçente and led him out, turning toward the open door to the torture room. His legs felt feeble. "Don't do this."

"When you were first deputy, surely you knew this chamber," García said amiably.

Mary, Mother of God, make me strong. Francesca, forgive me for leaving.

"But you would have tortured Christians and freed Jew swine," García said.

A cold darkness and the stink of burned flesh. The shorter guardsman, the one who'd spoken to him that morning, lit torches on the back wall as three others shoved Viçente toward the rack. At either end, spoked wheels held shafts with ropes attached. Blood pounded in his temples. He ripped one arm loose and tried to twist free. A guard punched him in the stomach. He gasped, still trying to propel himself away as two men lifted and slammed him down. "In the name of Jesus, no," he wheezed. One restrained him as others tied his wrists and ankles to the machine.

"Bare chested," García commanded.

Viçente smelled the guard's body as the man ripped his shirt away, leaving Viçente shivering on the table. A loud clacking sounded from above and below. Ropes cut into his wrists and ankles, tighter and tighter still, now trying to tear his arms and legs away. He fought not to scream as his shoulders, then his torso and buttocks rose off of the slab. The clacking stopped, and he hung like a roasting carcass.

García's eyes lingered on Viçente's face, then moved down his body. "I reserved this mechanism for you, Pérez. If we leave you this way for an hour you'll feel pain like you've never known. Two hours might kill you, but we won't kill you, until you've confessed. Crank the arms."

Three rapid clicks and cramping agony erupted in his wrists, elbows, and shoulders. He tried to picture Francesca, but his mind filled with blinding, red fire. He looked to the cold stone vaulting of the ceiling for respite, but none came.

—⁊⁊⁊—

He must have gone unconscious, but now his senses were coming back, and with them, the horrible memory. He opened his eyes and saw the madman grin.

"It would entertain these guards to rip off your arms, but I'm willing to stop." García spoke quietly, as if they were conspirators, and Viçente noticed a twitch beneath his eye. "Confess your Jew practices."

Viçente wanted to spit at the *pendejo*, but his mouth had gone dry. He'd confess almost anything to end this, but would never abandon God. "I'm Catholic," he rasped.

García shook his head. "We merely whipped your son, and he told the truth."

"God *damn* you."

"No, you perfidious swine, may God damn you." García's eyes bulged and his face turned color. He inhaled and breathed out slowly. "I must be careful, *marrano*, and not kill you before you confess to my vicar. Do you know about inquisitions? If you were Christian, you would."

Viçente swallowed, trying to think through the agony. "You don't care about that."

"But I do. I'm a pious man, trying to cleanse Toledo's soul."

Viçente took several quick breaths. "You despise me … for exposing the vicar's depravity."

"You did far more than that. You're the worst of the heretics. God commands me to pursue the *limpieza* and rid Castile of the vile blood." García nodded to the guards.

Two clacks sounded from the lower end of the rack and two from the top. Viçente's body was stretching apart. Another click.

—⟋⟍—

He was dreaming. They wanted him to confess, but what was it about, Jesus? Something tore in his thigh, sending a spasm through his groin. He screamed and warm urine gushed into his trousers. He had to stop screaming, had to think. God, what could he say? He couldn't deny Jesus, couldn't disappoint him.

—⟋⟍—

From somewhere in the darkness, García spoke, but Viçente could only hear his blood pounding. "The pain," Viçente wheezed. "I can't …" He heard a clunk and felt himself drop onto the platform, head thudding.

"I was telling you about the church," García said. "It only permits torture for known blasphemers, which of course, you are."

The release of his limbs made Viçente giddy with relief. Something about the word *blasphemers* made him want to laugh, but the pain wouldn't allow it. He needed words to avoid more torment. "If I say I'm a Jew, you'll stop?"

"And confess to the vicar in the correct manner. Our vicar reads the works of Saint Thomas." García wrinkled his nose. "He thinks even Satan capable of redemption."

Viçente's shoulders felt numb. His legs and wrists burned, but his thoughts were clearing. He would die on this cold piece of machinery, but if he could help save other converts ... If he could build on García's disdain for the vicar and Sarmiento ... "Saint Thomas and the vicar are too kindly for you?"

"Do you admit your sins?" García nodded at a guard and spun his hand in the air.

The wheel turned with the awful clack, clack, clack. Ropes tugged at his ankles and wrists, clack, clack, cutting into him, joints on fire. His stomach clenched, muscles trying to resist the irresistible. Something in his shoulder popped, ripping his old wound. Tears streamed down. Bright pain exploded.

"*Oh, God. Oh, God. Oh, Jesus. Dear Jesus.*" Was it his voice screaming? No matter. The world went black and wicked.

—⁓—

Sweat trickled down his chest. Shivers rippled through him. He opened his eyes and stared at one of the torches. A guard swung a bucket and he wanted to duck. Icy water shocked him alert.

"Your endurance is pathetic." García stood over him, the twitch returning beneath his eye. "Magistrate Sarmiento demands that we preserve you until you meet the vicar's conditions. Don't make me rip you apart."

"The vicar balks at murder?" His voice came out a hoarse whisper.

"The vicar's weak. I give him purpose. And you're a Jew *pendejo*. Tighten the ropes."

Viçente heard the terrible clacking and closed his eyes. He begged Jesus for blessed unconsciousness. The noise ceased. A slap stung his cheek.

García glowered. "Look at me. You will not die until you speak the truth. Admit that you are a perfidious secret Jew, and have done with this."

"What could Jesus want with a lie?"

"*I know what Jesus wants.*" García's face contorted and he raised a fist.

Viçente had seen that fanatic look before in crazed men who believed in a cause beyond reason. "Does Sarmiento know you're mad?"

Marcos García smashed the fist into Viçente's chest. It made a hollow thud but hurt little. "You want to goad me into killing you without church sanction, but you *will* confess to the vicar, and you *will* die and go to the fires of hell. Untie him. He's too weak for another try."

CHAPTER 77

—⁓—

FRANCESCA'S MONTHLY CYCLE HADN'T COME since her visit to Rome two months before. Nausea plagued her mornings. At first she'd doubted, but now she knew. Viçente's child flourished in her womb.

It should have been a blissful time, but fear stole all joy. Three weeks ago, one of Alfonso's emissaries had returned with confirmation: Diego Pérez was captive. Minister Tivolini and his party had departed from Rome for Toledo to negotiate Diego's release. But Viçente was unaware of this help. He'd act to save his son, no matter the consequences. How spineless she'd been to let Alfonso keep her here.

At night she woke to visions—her love chained in a cell, bleeding, feverish, terrified. But then she dreamed that he and Diego had been rescued. As her room brightened with the first glow of dawn, she thought she heard the babe in her womb whisper, *Only trust in yourself. Go save my papa.*

Awake now, trying to clear her mind, how could she decide between staying in Naples to protect this life inside her and going to him? She cursed her foolish indecision. Her unborn baby knew the answer.

Penélope attended her as she bathed and wrapped her hair in a scarf. The maid helped her don a modest, flowered, white dress and sat with her in silence. When the noon bells rang, she descended. In the small dining room, their usual places were set by a window looking out to the rose garden. Something moved inside her as she sat. Not the kick of a baby, not yet—pieces of her heart churning.

Alfonso strutted in, wearing a robe the color of a ripe lemon. He stood beside his chair, a frown settling in above his humped nose. "Sister, you look miserable."

"You expect me to stop fearing for him?"

"Tivolini's in Toledo by now. He'll settle the matter." Alfonso sat, pulled a towel from the table, and spread it across his belly. A maid laid down plates of roasted vegetables.

A tear defied Francesca and trickled down. She looked away, hoping he wouldn't notice. "It's been weeks since Tivolini left."

Alfonso plucked a piece of red pepper from his dish and popped it in his mouth. "We settled this, sister." He chewed with bulging cheeks.

She couldn't worry about crying or about seeming weak. She *was* weak. "I made a mistake. I must go to him."

"I generously sent my minister and you agreed to stay."

"And I suffer here, don't you see? Don't you feel for me?"

Her half-brother observed with the same detachment he showed the marinated mushroom he held between his fingers.

She'd avoided the disclosure, but what else might move him? "I have his child in me."

The mushroom slipped from his hand and fell to his lap. "You stupid ... Francesca, you bring scandal to my house."

"A baby, Alfonso, a baby born of tenderness. Can you say as much for yourself?"

He stood and heaved his plate against the wall. It shattered, leaving an oily splotch. "I tried to prevent you from being like your whore mother, Francesca."

What he'd called her mother, she had been, a whore. All her life Francesca had despised the word. But here was her half-brother, possessed of another empty royal marriage, his wife residing in distant Aragón and Alfonso's favorite, his son Ferrante, a bastard, too. "You think you have the right to judge? Viçente and I are in love."

"Love—a woman's excuse for wantonness." He gnawed on his lip and observed through narrowed eyes.

She had foolishly come to Alfonso as a supplicant, but supplicants were subject to their benefactor's whims. "And a man needs none. Who keeps you company, brother? Who would grace your table and converse with your guests if I were gone? What friend would listen to your troubles?"

His look became uncertain. "Ferrante listens to me, and Lucrezia. You threaten to desert me?"

"If your son and your lover aren't sufficient, you have a palace full of nobles whenever you summon them." Francesca took a deep breath and raised a finger. "It's true, isn't it, that you trust your secrets only to me? You rely on my companionship, as I rely on your generosity."

"We're friends, really, aren't we, brother and sister?" He stepped behind her and laid a hand on her shoulder. "You really are expecting? You're fragile then. A voyage would harm you and the child. For your sake ..."

She looked up at his chubby face, full of mock concern. "It's best for me and my child to be with him, no matter the risk."

"But you rely on me to—"

Francesca pushed her chair back, butting it into his belly. He grunted and retreated. Anger knotted her stomach, at herself more than Alfonso. She always did what he wished, and he counted on it. "If you think my life too scandalous and don't want me to return, tell me now." It could be a relief never again to face his gentle tyranny.

Alfonso's face crumpled as if he would weep. "You'll come back if I help you?" She nodded and Alfonso said, "Give me a day, sister. Let me consider."

CHAPTER 78

—⚸—

A GUARD OPENED THE CELL door and set something close. He crawled to the limits of his chain and used both hands to pick up the scraps of meat and bread. Back in his corner, he sniffed and devoured them. Fighting to keep his humanity, to remember his name, to think of something beyond survival. *Jesus. Jesus and Francesca.*

He lay on the cold floor, trying to remember how many times they'd put him on that terrible stand—three? Each time, he'd refused to parrot García's confession, and each time he'd been tortured to unconsciousness. How could he speak against the Lord God, Jesus? Later, the guards had pulled him from the table, twisted his limbs and his torso into excruciating agony to put his joints back in place, only to make them more raw and every moment dreadful. Arms and legs refused to lift him, fingers no longer clutched a bowl to drink from it.

Whenever García came, Viçente tried to learn about the scrawny man's relationships with Sarmiento and the vicar, to conceive the depths of his captor's madness, devise a way to use it. No matter what he did, he would die a vain death here in the bowels of the *alcázar.* If García killed him before he confessed, would it infuriate the magistrate and cause a rift? Or was Viçente mad as García to think there was a chance?

And now they came again.

CHAPTER 79

—⟡—

THEY'D TORTURED THE *MARRANO* AGAIN without a confession. Marcos bolted from the stone chamber, past the cells, up the stairs toward the court-yard. He inhaled cool air, panting like a man twice his age. But clean air couldn't relieve his disgust. He'd halted this morning's session with Pérez after only a few minutes. A few minutes had wounded the *mar-rano* badly, his shoulders releasing readily now. Marcos told himself that he ended the torture to avoid killing Pérez. In truth, strange, repulsive emotions churned his gut. Pérez had looked so *human*, his features agonized, eyes pleading like a Christian's, a Christian affirm-ing the Savior no matter the pain.

But Pérez had humiliated the vicar and protected hundreds of Jews.

The dungeon's stink still hanging over him, he muttered, '*Marrano, marrano, marrano,* impostor and traitor to God,' but he couldn't rid himself of the nagging pity and shame for this crippling weakness in his own nature.

In the *alcázar* courtyard, Marcos stopped at the sight of Pedro Sarmiento standing by two wooden chairs. Sarmiento stepped forward and touched his hand. "Are you feeling agreeable, Deputy? Come, sit with me." Marcos complied, but what was the devious *pendejo* planning now?

"We shall consider a change of strategy to court our fine prince."

By the entry gate, Marcos saw a pair of guardsmen and two more near the stairway. Sarmiento planned to capture him if he opposed. "This has to do with the *marrano*?"

"I will speak," Sarmiento said. "And you will hold your anger."

"*Dios mío*. You want to free the swine?"

"Not what I want, but there's a new interest at stake. This morning they summoned me to Enrique's camp."

Marcos gut tightened. "You should have taken me."

"They wanted me alone, and I complied to demonstrate good will."

"*Good will*," Marcos spat. He saw Sarmiento's glower and lowered his voice. "Can't you see? We must defy this prince. What kind of *mierda* did they feed you today?"

Sarmiento gave Marcos a pitiful half-smile. "The prince and Pacheco had a stranger with them, fat and ugly, like a frog—King Alfonso's Minister of State, Tivolini."

Marcos grabbed Sarmiento's forearm. "King Alfonso was to send troops, not some minister."

Sarmiento eyed Marcos' hand until he let go. "Prince Enrique welcomed this Tivolini, so I didn't object."

"That's the damned problem. You grovel before him like a pet hound."

"Remain civil, Deputy."

"Tell me what they want."

"Tivolini asks to see the prisoner. I told them he was ill. We must wait for him to recover."

"He's a heretic."

Sarmiento sighed. "I reported that we treat Señor Pérez well and we don't plan to punish him unless the church confirms his guilt. Enrique said that Bishop Barrientos arrives in days to see the prisoner."

The damned red Jew-loving bishop.

Sarmiento stood and pointed at Marcos. "Prince Enrique can aid us or destroy us. I tried coaxing and explaining, Deputy. Now I command. Find a physician for Pérez. See to the making of soup and nourish him."

Marcos had thought Sarmiento a weak fool blinded by his fears and greed. But what if he was actually a clever schemer, complicit with the devils? No. That couldn't be.

He felt that twitch in his cheek and his hands trembled. His heartbeat raced, but he remained silent as Sarmiento climbed the stairs toward his office. The magistrate turned back and said, "You're upset, Deputy. Stay away from Pérez for the rest of the day."

Soup be damned. The pig would confess to the vicar and die. Even if it sparked war between Marcos' *Sangre Pura* and Sarmiento's *Guardia Civil*, Toledo would eradicate this evil.

CHAPTER 80

—w—

VIÇENTE COULDN'T SEE THE BUGS in the dark, but he felt them crawling. He swatted his arm. No matter how he lay, the hard floor tormented his bruised thighs. Elbows and shoulders burned. Vermin crawled inside his ears and licked his chest. He felt their sticky tongues.

Father, why have you forsaken me? It's dark. Is it night? Am I alive? Why have you forsaken me? The pain—he must be alive to feel it. *Father, answer me.* Who's speaking? Speaking to God or to Viçente's papa, or to his Father who is God?

Viçente is thirteen years old in Papa's study, and Papa tells him the awful secret. *No, God, it can't be.* Viçente crying. No, it's Jesus weeping. Jesus is here with Viçente in this filthy, putrid place, the Lord calling to Papa, *Don't forsake me. You pledged your love, but you stayed a Jew. Father."*

Viçente opened his eyes, trying to see the insects. Perhaps God had sent a message with them. Trembling, pulling the threadbare blanket against his chest, his arms, his stomach and knees burning with every movement. There—he saw Jesus floating above him, wearing the crown of thorns, trickle of blood running into one eye, tears mingling with the blood and running down Christ's cheek. Papa had wounded Jesus. *Damn, Papa, stay out of my cell. Stay out of my heart.*

A moan echoed and then a shout, *"Why have you forsaken me?"* Viçente covered his ears and felt his mouth moving, breath escaping. He opened his eyes and saw a man in uniform watching from outside the bars, a man who looked familiar, but the light was dim. Somehow

Viçente knew that the guard wanted to help, but how could he, when even God condemned him?

Turning on his side, Viçente saw Jesus lying on the floor nearby, curled up in pain like Viçente, shivering like Viçente. His eyes were so blue even in the dark. Each one contained the sea and was lit by the sun. Jesus stared into Viçente's heart and whispered, "Now you understand crucifixion. I forgive your transgressions." Was Jesus talking to Viçente or to his papa? Jesus' lips moved again. "I will forgive you, Vicentito." The name Viçente's mother had called him as a boy.

Jesus vanished.

Viçente understood the terrible truth; God had left him, but Jesus still cared. Jesus shared this torture and would forgive Viçente even if he made a false confession.

His arms cramped as he pushed up to his knees, trying to set one foot under him, toppling onto his side. "Guard. Call your master. I'll confess what he wants."

Keys clanked. Cell door swung open. Viçente's pulse pounded as a guardsman entered—the shorter man, the one with curly hair, carrying a bowl. Remembering his offer to confess, Viçente's stomach knotted. He was about to deny the Savior.

"Deputy García sends broth to nourish you."

Smelling meat and onions, he raised it to his lips and drank. The warm vessel comforted his hands. The liquid soothed.

"Slowly," the guard whispered.

Sometime later, the man returned with more broth and stale bread. Another guard brought water and fresh clothing. "You'll be presentable for the vicar," the kindly guard said. "He doesn't abide torture."

Viçente drank and struggled to remove his tattered shirt. He dipped a rag into the water and rinsed his torso.

The second guard ordered, "Put on the clothes and stand."

Viçente managed to pull on one arm of the shirt and drape it across his back.

"He can't," the kind one said.

"Up." The gruff-voiced guard nudged Viçente's buttocks with his boot.

The shorter guard touched the other's arm. "He tried to stand before. We'll lift him together."

Viçente wished he hadn't agreed to confess, but how could he face the rack again? To distract himself, he tried to recall this guard's name from years ago. *Think of anything besides denying Jesus.*

The one grabbed his arm and yanked. Viçente groaned. The shorter guard wrapped his arms around Viçente's waist and pulled him up. "Be easy. Remember, he used to be first deputy."

"García is now."

The shorter guard pulled Viçente's shirt on and buttoned it.

Viçente's thoughts had begun to clear, but with this movement, his throbbing joints radiated confusion again.

The kind guard patted his shoulder. "I remember, Señor Pérez."

Two others came, and the four hoisted him. He felt better now, being carried, more able to think. He was about to lie to God, but Jesus had said he'd be forgiven. His parents had lied, pretended not to be Jews, because Christians were killing Jews. Papa pretended to be Christian to save his boy, Diego. No, not Diego. His father had done it to save Viçente. What else had Papa said that night?

The men turned a corner and mounted more stairs. A stab of pain in his shoulder, but he understood pain now, when it would make him lose awareness. The granite blocks of the ceiling looked close overhead, cleaner air, chandelier bright with lit candles. He squinted. They set him on a chair and he held on hard to keep from falling.

García strode in, his black hair slick and glossy, mouth twisted in a smirk, but his eyes were set in dark circles. His grin faded quickly.

"So you finally tell the truth, *marrano?* I sent nourishment to make you alert when you speak to God."

So many things seemed odd today, and this another; Viçente no longer imagined he could set García and the magistrate against each other. It was in Jesus' hands. "You expect me to be grateful?" he rasped.

García frowned. "You're the worst sinner, but I'm glad this ends today."

"You relish the torture," Viçente said.

García spoke softly. "Your death will cleanse Toledo. When you speak to the vicar, remember—you practiced your religion in secret, confessed once before, and received forgiveness from the church. That's what you must say."

Viçente couldn't think why García gave such instructions, but it seemed unimportant. "Find me a true priest instead of the vicar."

"Pero's head of our church. Your words go straight to God." García pressed his lips tight in a wry smile. "And my magistrate will be mollified." He glared at one of the guardsmen. "Don't let him fall off that seat."

—⁂—

Trying to hold himself upright, wondering why García had seemed subdued rather than jubilant … thinking. Viçente had despised his parents for their deceptions, but now he was about to deny Jesus, and his false confession would go straight to God. Even the disheveled rabbi and his people risked death to uphold their ill-guided beliefs. Viçente tried again to remember Papa's words on that terrible day—so difficult.

The door opened, and a priest entered in a black cassock—the vicar—more obese than Viçente remembered, almost bald around the edges of his skullcap. He regarded Viçente with wary brown eyes. "Kneel for confession."

"If I try, I'll collapse."

Vicar López gestured to the guards. They grasped Viçente's arms and eased him down. He groaned, and the priest glanced away. "Get him up on his knees and leave."

"He's in pain, Padre," the gentler guard said. "Would the Lord be satisfied if he sat against the wall?"

"Set him there and go." The vicar pulled a chair near, settled on it, and leaned close.

Viçente said, "You seem to have sympathy for me."

"I don't like violence, but the church allows a man to be tortured once to expose the truth."

If not for his pain, Viçente would have laughed. "Once is a deadly amount on that rack. You think Jesus approves?"

"Don't speak of Jesus as if you know him."

"They put me on that machine four times, maybe five. I'd be on it again if Jesus hadn't allowed me to confess."

"*Don't say that.* The Lord cannot be an excuse for your sins. To be forgiven, you must admit and repent."

Viçente pressed his hands against the floor, easing his painful back by the power of feebled arms, unclear now what Jesus had wanted him to confess. Speak lies or state his true transgressions? His body hurt a little less in this position, and his thoughts seemed clearer. The priest watched with a look of distress as tears ran from Viçente's eyes. "My sin is … my true sin is that I hated my father, not God the Father, but the man who raised me. Papa was a Jew who pretended."

The vicar leaned close. "Speak to me and through me to Jesus, son. Accept responsibility for what *you've* done."

"I am responsible. Papa only pretended to be Christian to save Mother and me from violent men like García, and I despised him for it." Tears flowed freely now. Viçente's voice cracked. "Jesus, please help Papa understand."

The vicar let out a loud breath and shook his head, his eyes watery. "This makes no sense. You must tell me how you strayed from the Lord."

"If I strayed, it was never from Jesus. He lay with me on the floor of my cell. He spoke to me, Padre." Viçente realized he had called the vicar 'father' as if speaking to a real priest, but wasn't there a bit of the Christ's compassion in that plump face?

Vicar López stared for a time and then said quietly, "You blaspheme to speak that way of Jesus."

"Padre, you see the truth in my eyes. Jesus didn't desert me, and I won't desert him." Viçente glanced up at the chandelier, hoping to see the Lord. The light hurt, and he turned away. In his mind, Papa appeared as he had on Viçente's thirteenth birthday.

"Let me save you. Repent or face damnation." Vicar López crossed himself, and Viçente saw doubt in his frown.

"I remember now. I see Papa's face. I hear him. This is what he says, Padre. 'It is depraved and evil to harm another person for his beliefs.' That's the sin I've committed Vicar. I harmed Papa." Viçente sighed. "I don't understand everything Jesus said, but I think he told me that he forgives my father. Can Papa forgive me?"

CHAPTER 81

—ᴍ—

WATCHING THE PRISONER MADE PERO feel sick. Wounded, emaciated, struggling to focus his thoughts, Pérez murmured the prayers of penance Pero had commanded. He needed to interrupt and make the man confess what Marcos wanted. But sitting below him on the floor, tormented by unimaginable pain, Viçente Pérez had spoken with gravity and courage. How could Pero disbelieve what his heart and soul witnessed? And what kind of inquisition would torture an innocent so?

He walked to the door and unlatched it. Marcos pushed in past him. "You approve the execution?"

"What did you do to the man?"

Marcos eyes darted from the prisoner to Pero. "Not a man, a blaspheming *marrano*. Do you think I took pleasure, wounding him?"

Pero did, but wouldn't say it. "He claims to love Jesus—"

Marcos shoved Pero back against the wall and dug a fist into his stomach. "That lying *pendejo* is forcing us to ..." Marcos eased his hold, but his knuckles still pressed Pero's gut. "Use your senses, Vicar." Marcos' breaths and his words came in bursts. "This *marrano* is so deceitful ... he has you babbling. Try again, Vicar. Better for him to confess than to continue this."

Pero tried not to let Marcos' unusual breathing distract him. "He told me about his father and he wept."

391

"Our men from Rome ... they say that Pérez gave the pope a Hebrew Bible. He even tries to convert the Holy Father ... Listen." Marcos grabbed Pero's arms.

Pero could see now. Marcos and Viçente Pérez were both sincere. Marcos tried to pursue God's work, and he'd been right so many times, but now his zeal blinded him. He tensed, fearing that Marcos would beat him. "You're wrong, Marcos."

"Think of that day we first met Pérez. He released the mute Jew who stole the crucifix."

Pero felt more confident now that Marcos hadn't struck. "The mute was blameless."

"Pérez humiliated you, the vicar of the holy church ... He's fooled you, Pero. He's Satan. I'm taking him to a cave for more questioning." Marcos stepped toward Pérez.

"A cave? Why not the dungeon?"

"Sarmiento wants to surrender him to the prince."

Pero grabbed his arm. "He's pure after his confession. Killing him would be a sin. Let me speak to the magistrate. He trusts me."

Marcos whirled and glared. "Protect blasphemers like Pérez and Jesus will question *your* faith."

Pero felt as if the wind had been kicked from him. "Marcos, you can't think that."

"Come to the cave tomorrow and observe the swine's confession."

"No. I can't condone it."

"You're spineless, Vicar. Send Juan Alonso ... or some other priest with the courage for God's work."

CHAPTER 82

—⚭—

HOW ODD. VIÇENTE HAD GIVEN up his notion of creating discord between García and the vicar, and now they argued.

The vicar departed and García paused, watching Viçente, as if taking a moment to gather his strength. Then he marched forward, a powerful fury concentrated in his spare body. He halted a pace away, and his boot swung back. Viçente rolled onto his side, pulling in his legs. The boot struck and pain stabbed his side. He groaned and tensed for more.

"Are you pleased, you *hijo de puta*?" García glared, his moist eyes ringed in dark circles. "Our vicar is weak and gullible." García paused for breath, his face pale. "Tomorrow, Pérez, we will speak of the Hebrew Bible you gave to the pope. You will confess to a different priest who will recognize your lies. We'll end this tomorrow. The cities and the king will learn. The notorious Viçente Pérez was a secret Jew." He shook his head, looking more spent than angry, and summoned the guardsmen.

Viçente was carried back to the basement, past his cell, but not to the torture room. A guard with a lantern and a key opened a door in a dark corner—one that Viçente had never noticed—and led them along a tunnel. They laid Viçente on the stone floor. Lantern light cast shadows on the rough ceiling. Cold seeped into his bones. As a boy, he'd visited the tunnels—old cisterns for water storage, caves that held stores, a wondrous place to play with his friends. Looking up, he saw the shorter guardsman regarding him with troubled eyes.

García appeared with three men who wore coarse workers' clothing—*Sangre Pura.* "Return to your duties." García gestured to the *Guardia Civil.* As they marched away, García bent close. "I've listened too long to my pathetic magistrate and vicar," he said between gasps. "I take you where your precious bishop and the prince will never find you. Your son and your whore in Naples will learn that you died a heretic."

Francesca. Diego. God, give them courage.

They carried him from one tunnel to another, pausing a few times for the wheezing García to catch up. They laid him inside a cave, where Viçente listened as García spoke to the stout leader of the *Sangre Pura.* "Keep this place secret. If I don't return tomorrow, bring Padre Juan Alonso. Force the *marrano's* confession to the priest … cut the pig's head off, here in the cave. You swear to obey?"

Viçente heard the way the madman was gasping as he spoke. And he'd been doing it earlier. Why?

The *Sangre Pura* man's stubbly cheeks bulged in a stupid grin. "It will be my honor."

"Where are you going, Marcos?" the barrel-chested man asked.

"To see if Sarmiento has the *cojones* to continue the *limpieza.*"

CHAPTER 83

PEDRO SARMIENTO SLAMMED HIS FIST on the desk. García had defied him again. Pedro stalked out of the office, but in the hallway he halted—his former deputy was walking toward him. "Where have you taken Pérez?"

"Would you be unhappy to learn he was dead?" García asked.

Pedro clenched a fist and held it near García's chin. "Have you forgotten that vice for crushing heads?"

He saw that twitch in García's cheek, but the fellow didn't back away. "If Pérez were alive, you might not want to know, Magistrate."

Pedro slammed the heel of his hand into the deputy's chin, sending him staggering against the wall. "Return him to his cell and nurse him to health. *Now.*"

García, wide-eyed, cupped his cheek in a hand. "Magistrate, think of the good counsel I've given you. Recall how you received this office."

"I ordered you." If Pedro swung again, the man would crumble.

García raised a protective arm and gasped, "The prince championed Pérez to be chief magistrate ... before you were given it. I wounded Pérez ... so you could take the post."

The sight of his former deputy panting with fear raised Pedro's spirits. "That's all past," he said, but he was thinking about García's words. He didn't want to admit that Pérez could challenge him, but the king was peeved and Enrique impulsive. Both had favored Pérez once. Instead of swinging again, Pedro ran his hand down the front of his shirt. "I have more to offer the prince than he does."

"You always had more … but the prince prefers the *marrano*. Keep him alive … and Prince Enrique will demand his release." García touched Pedro's elbow. "You comprehend my point, Magistrate?"

Pedro did understand. García longed to kill Viçente Pérez. If the man lived, some day the prince would demand his freedom.

García patted his arm and murmured, "Imagine Pérez sitting with the prince, wearing a silk robe, swearing that your place as magistrate is rightfully his … using guile and his beloved bishop … bribing Prince Enrique with promises of *marrano* gold."

Pedro could picture it, and it soured his stomach. He was annoyed by the way García perceived truths before he did and repelled by those greasy fingers on his clean shirt. He hated the thought of giving in yet again. "Enrique wouldn't turn on me."

"You know otherwise. I see it in your face."

Pedro was about to say something inane about promising that Minister Tivolini could visit the prisoner. He bit his lip and held his tongue.

"If the *marrano* dies of his illness, they can't blame you," García said. "He was a blasphemer. God sickened and slew him." The deputy grinned, his eyes keen and confident. "Killing him will please *Sangre Pura*."

So here García was again, threatening him with the brotherhood. The deputy was blinded by his cause and didn't understand; *Sangre Pura* loved their gold far more than killing Jews. One could take advantage of a fool with too little fear. One could blame that fool and claim innocence for Pérez' death and a host of other sins. Pedro pursed his lips and smiled. "I'm sorry to hear of our prisoner's demise. Bury him promptly so the disease doesn't spread to Enrique's camp."

PART VIII

THE BULLS—1449

—ᗰ—

Many of the inhabitants, especially among the conversos, he
[Sarmiento] robbed and arrested under manipulated charges
of heresy; he laid violent hands on clerics; he expelled members
of the religious orders from the city; and he committed other
criminal offenses, which ... not only work to the detriment of
the faith, but also pose a danger to the state of the kingdom.

—FROM THE PAPAL BULLS, 1449 (SOURCE—B.
NETANYAHU, *THE ORIGINS OF THE INQUISITION*)

O, illustrious Prince and powerful Señor Don Enrique! How did
the bad friar [Bishop Barrientos] deceive you and make you forget
the oaths and promises you had given to the holy city of Toledo?
... [why do you wish to] bring about a rise in the tyranny of that
tyrant [Constable Luna] and enable the heretics to increase the
mendacity [which they practice] against the Catholic faith ...

—FROM AN ENTREATY TO THE PRINCE, WRITTEN
BY MARCOS GARCÍA DE MORA, 1449 (SOURCE—B.
NETANYAHU, *THE ORIGINS OF THE INQUISITION*)

CHAPTER 84

—〰—

VIÇENTE WOKE IN NEAR DARKNESS but not in the cell. This was more like a cave. He shivered and began to remember as he edged onto his side. Two men sat on chairs several paces away, men without uniforms—*Sangre Pura*. There were no bars, but none were needed for one who could barely crawl.

He closed his eyes and drifted.

Thudding sounds. Voices echoed. Figures moved toward him. "Over here," someone said. They wore no uniforms, so they had to be the mad ones. They brought a lantern close and they gathered, five pairs of boots. The iciness of the stone floor invaded his stomach and bowels.

A voice whispered, "Señor Pérez, it's Nacio. We traveled to Naples together." Viçente looked up, seeing a young man with thin, dark eyebrows and a strong chin. He recognized this Nacio, who beamed at him. Viçente tried to smile.

"We must lift you. Be careful, men." It had to be a dream, but he felt their strong hands and the pain that came with motion. "We've been waiting for a chance to help, Señor Pérez."

"Be careful of *Sangre Pura*," Viçente gasped.

"Rap them on the head and they fall like any man." The fellow beside Nacio chuckled, and Viçente noticed a resemblance between them.

"One of my brothers was a guard in the dungeon," Nacio said. "He felt ashamed, but he couldn't help you there."

Viçente tried to remember the trip to Naples, arranged by the builder. "Your uncle is Gonzalo."

"We'll take you to him, Señor."

CHAPTER 85

—ጢ—

"MOVE FASTER, SANCHO." MARCOS BURNED with fury, heartbeat pounding in his throat as he strode beside the bungling guildsman into a residential building, down the narrow staircase to the old cistern carved in the city's base rock.

He rested as Sancho lit a lantern. The wool carter looked at him, shamefaced. "I don't know how it happened."

"It happened because you and your men are dumb as cattle."

Sancho climbed steps cut into the cistern wall, over the top, and ducked low into the tunnel, which was lit every twenty paces by a torch. Inside the cave, three *Sangre Pura* stood by a body on the floor.

"Fidel was a good man," Sancho said. "A leader when we captured the gates from the constable."

Marcos looked at the twisted body and blood-smeared face, with its close-cut beard and staring dead eyes. Fidel had performed well that one time, but what Marcos saw on the floor resembled not a hero, but a slaughtered sheep. "They let the son of a whore escape." Marcos glared at the three *Sangre Pura*. "Who was the other guard who bungled this?"

A strapping young man glanced at him, and Marcos saw a purple bruise on his forehead. The fellow mumbled, "I wish they'd killed me instead."

Marcos spit on the floor, glared down at Fidel's body, and booted it in the chest. Pain erupted in Marcos' leg. He balanced on his aching leg and kicked the corpse's head with his other foot. The body jerked and Marcos looked up to see shock on the men's faces. He was breathing in sharp gasps, and the cave felt desperately small. Stepping beside Sancho, he muttered, "Grant the fool his wish. Kill him."

Without waiting for a response, Marcos stalked out to the tunnel. Instead of heading back along the passage, he moved toward darkness. Too furious to reason, he paced, breathing hard, working to slow his breath, slow his thoughts, moving deeper into the gloom.

A lightning bolt of pain shot up his left arm, and he cried out.

Pressure on his chest, no air, tumbling to the floor, trying to breathe, but the weight on his chest overwhelmed effort and will and extinguished the light.

CHAPTER 86

—⚏—

VIÇENTE WOKE ON A STRAW mattress covered in blankets. Overhead, he saw thick beams, no windows in the whitewashed walls.

A man descended the stairs, not tall, but his straight spine made him seem so. Tears came to Viçente's eyes as he recognized the dark features and goatee. "Gonzalo, oh my God."

The builder smiled. "I'm delighted to see you safe." He sat in a chair beside the bed and reached toward Viçente's arm, but didn't touch it. "How badly have they hurt you?"

Viçente raised himself a bit, wincing. "I have arms and legs, but I'm not sure they work."

"Lie back. You'll recover soon, because you're a fine man and the Almighty wills it."

"You've repaid whatever debt you thought you owed me many times over."

"Your gift to me, my daughter's virtue, is never-ending."

Viçente knew by now, there was no point protesting that the gift came from Samuel, the mute.

"Gonzalo, I heard they were attacking the Hebrews. Have you news of Rabbi Benjamin?"

"He's safe. There was great danger for a time. Then *Sangre Pura* acquired a taste for converts and lost sight of the Jews." Gonzalo shook his head.

"So they survived."

"All but a few."

Viçente felt relieved and surprised that he no longer thought it shameful to care about Jews. "What place is this? Is it safe here?"

Gonzalo patted his shoulder. "The safest place I know. You've been bellowing in your sleep like a cow giving birth, so we put you in our cellar."

CHAPTER 87

—✺—

IT HAD BEEN SEVERAL DAYS since Marcos' life almost ended in the tunnel, but he was alive. Last night he'd even ventured out for a few hours on one of the patrols, searching deserted *marrano* houses for Pérez.

But stories had been told of men who'd suffered similar pains and died soon after, and he still felt that twinge in his left arm where God had pierced his body with lightning for losing the *marrano*.

He took a few deep, reassuring breaths and pulled off his night-shirt as the cathedral bells struck eleven o'clock. After rinsing his face in the basin, he began dressing. A knock on the door startled him. He pulled on trousers and fastened the clasps as he went to open it. Sarmiento stood in the hallway, wearing one of his white blouses, his wavy, brown hair shiny, his look cheerful. "Aren't you going to welcome the most important man in Toledo?"

Marcos swung the door wide and stepped to the window to open the shutters for light. Turning back, he found Sarmiento inspecting the bare brown walls, the three worn, padded chairs, the plain wood table with its unlit, blue pottery lantern and two wooden seats. "I was here once before," Sarmiento said. "But I was distracted. Is this all my first deputy possesses?"

Marcos ignored the mockery. Austerity was his virtue. The men of *Sangre Pura* respected it. "I don't live for gold as some do."

Sarmiento poked between the armchairs. "A picture?" He brought out the portrait from Pérez' house. The smiling face of the *marrano's* woman on the canvas taunted Marcos. The cut of her red dress and the rise of her breasts enticed and infuriated. Sarmiento set it on an armchair. "This woman with the ruby necklace doesn't despise wealth. Your mother, Marcos?"

Damn him, his mother might have been a housekeeper, but she was no Jew-loving whore. He turned to the window, resisting anger, calming his pulse. "No one, Magistrate. You've come for something important? Have they captured Pérez?"

Sarmiento chuckled. "There's no word of that fellow. I have to admit I was vexed when your pure-bloods lost him, but it doesn't matter any more, thanks to my astounding progress with Enrique and Bishop Barrientos."

God, what had the fool done now? "We agreed not to meet with them until we found Pérez." Marcos sat in an armchair.

"You agreed with yourself, Deputy." Sarmiento brushed off one of the wooden chairs and sat. "The bishop invited. I accepted. You haven't seemed your energetic self lately, so I didn't trouble you."

"What did they say about Pérez?"

"They questioned me about his condition, which means that they're unaware of his escape. I said he has a fever, and the physician demands isolation. Poor devil is so ill." Sarmiento put on a sorrowful frown, but the devious, hooded eyes darted, and the narrow lips betrayed a faint smile. "Stop making those grotesque faces, Deputy. I have wonderful news. Prince Enrique gave me a written pledge. I am perpetual magistrate of Toledo. Even if Enrique allies himself with his father, he'll insist on my autonomy."

Marcos slammed his fist on the arm of his chair. "*Hijo de puta.* Prince Enrique speaks of turning the city back to the king?"

Sarmiento gave a dismissive wave. "It's possible, if the king grants Enrique control of another worthy city, like Burgos. Be still, Deputy. Accept my judgment and listen. On Sunday, the prince will march his army into Toledo to display our mutual trust."

"*Holy Mother.* What you do when you act without me. They'll seize the city."

"My life's work is assured here." The magistrate rose, frowning as he regarded the portrait of the *marrano's* woman. "When Enrique becomes king, he'll grant still greater riches. Did I mention, I'm giving him control of the Bisagra and Alcántara gates?"

"You're acting the fool." Marcos blurted the words, and Sarmiento glared. Marcos softened his tone. "Magistrate, you'll enrage *Sangre Pura*. They fought for those gates."

The magistrate stroked his chin, his glower turning to the grin of a disobedient child riding a forbidden horse toward a precipice. "You're such a gloomy fellow, Marcos, really. Our citizens love Enrique. They cheered when he drove his father away."

Marcos took a deep breath and then another. "We planned to spread our movement to other cities—to destroy the *marranos*. It's our cause."

Sarmiento picked up the unlit lamp and scrutinized it, twisting the knob that adjusted the wick. "We've accomplished much by burning those four and driving the others out. And we'll complete the work with that law you've drafted."

"But how will that ..." Before he finished the question, Marcos understood. "You think that if we adopt our law forbidding *marranos* from office, other cities will follow?"

"Now you're beginning to think, Deputy. We'll summon Toledo's Council of Governors to ratify it."

So Sarmiento would surrender Toledo to Prince Enrique, secure his wealth, and declare that he'd vanquished the godless ones. *Marranos* would reopen their jewelry shops and return to the churches to feign devotion. The prince would hand Toledo to King Juan. The cities of Castile would see Toledo's *limpieza* as a failure that none would dare emulate. Marcos' gut clenched with impotent fury.

Sarmiento stepped toward the door. "Ingenious, isn't it? I couldn't have accomplished this without you, Deputy. Forget those other notions, Marcos. This is what we're going to do."

Marcos watched him leave, wondering how the magistrate had become so devoid of conscience and reason. Marcos had put him in power and created the brotherhood. He would rest and grow stronger. Then, with *Sangre Pura*, he'd send this *pendejo* of a magistrate to hell.

CHAPTER 88

—✺—

Viçente's new bedchamber on the ground floor of Gonzalo's home suited him well. Leaning on a cane, he hobbled out to the courtyard and paused, admiring the tile scene on the wall, a pond in a garden. It reminded him of Francesca's garden and how badly he wanted to recover, to spend some time with Diego, and then rush to Naples. He dropped into a cushioned chair.

Gonzalo came out and set a plate of pastries on a table. "It's good to see you moving on your own, my friend."

Viçente smiled. Gonzalo had called him 'Señor Pérez' for most of a week, then used his Christian name these past three days, but this was the first time he'd called him *friend*. "You've been too kind." Viçente heard a strange distant thumping and stopped.

The builder nodded. "The city's astir. Prince Enrique's soldiers parade through the streets near the cathedral, beating drums to celebrate his alliance with the magistrate, but they shun this humble neighborhood."

Viçente reached for the cane. "I must go to him."

Gonzalo restrained Viçente's arm. "Too soon."

"It's my opportunity."

"The prince's men don't venture to this quarter, but the angry ones do."

"My son's in the prince's camp. I must see him."

Gonzalo shook his head. "Nacio didn't risk his life so you could hobble back to jail. I'll inquire about Diego, but you must recover before attempting this."

Of course, he was right. Viçente had barely been able to walk out to this courtyard. He eased back in his chair, feeling ashamed. "I'm sorry. You've done so much for me. When I was desperate in prison, I thought God had forsaken me, but you proved I was wrong."

Gonzalo observed him, his lips pressed together. "The Almighty puts us into this world proud and fearless. Every day he challenges us to reveal our weakness and imperfections. Those who accept his lessons are rewarded."

"Then Marcos García is a *challenge?*" Saying the name soured Viçente's stomach.

"In every generation, men use the Almighty's name to defy what's good and holy. God placed that evil in men and it's difficult to justify. Still, I know God is good." Gonzalo gestured to the plate. "He sustains us with food and faith."

Viçente examined the pastries—a tart with red jam in its center and a flaky cake stuffed with dried fruit and drizzled in honey. "I'm glad to be alive. When Jesus visited me in the dungeon, I thought he was preparing me for death."

"You were delirious."

"Don't you think he comes to people in need?"

"They say so."

"I remember you had a picture of Jesus on your wall that first time I came here," Viçente said. "Surely, you pray to him."

"Strange to remember such a detail after many years."

"I knew you were descended from Muslims, and I came to your home to meet the rabbi. It comforted me to have Jesus watching."

Gonzalo held a hand palm up, as if testing for rain. "Now you see an arabesque design on my living room wall and speculate about my piety."

A small brown bird flitted into the courtyard and settled on a fruit tree. Viçente thought that God was watching from that tiny black eye. "I'd never judge you, Gonzalo, after everything you've done."

"Sometimes we put up Jesus' picture, but we don't prefer portraits of people."

"It troubles me," Viçente said. "Jesus was there in my cell, but not God."

The builder stiffened. "God's always here."

"There's the Holy Trinity. I understand now. Jesus is the human face of God. The Holy Spirit is what gave me peace when I saw him with me."

Gonzalo tapped his fingers on the table. "I believe in Jesus, of course, but still it's peculiar, the idea of praying to him, rather than to the Almighty."

"Sometimes we don't need the Almighty. We need compassion. We pray to saints or to the Virgin. Why not pray to God's son? Don't you believe?"

Gonzalo stood. "A great prophet, a man of tenderness, but you say yourself, he's different from the Almighty. My father taught that there's only one."

"I can't worship power without grace or compassion. And your father considered himself—" Viçente watched Gonzalo's face but saw no sign of offense.

"Catholic, naturally. We've been Christian in this quarter for three hundred years. My sons and nephews work for the *Guardia Civil,* and I lay stone for the cathedral. We prosper as Christians, but our Muslim ancestors brought irrigation, new crops, sciences, and philosophy to this backward land." Gonzalo gave an ironic smile. "Do you think those fat priests know everything of God or display his nature in their tirades against converts? Are they better than other men?"

Viçente thought of the foolish vicar. Then his throat tightened, re-membering the love his mother had showed, preparing lamb for that

thirteenth birthday. "My parents called themselves Christian, but—"
The rest of his sentence was frozen by the habitual fear of the *converso*.

Gonzalo frowned. "Didn't they protect you and raise you as a moral, productive man?"

"They fed me meat that was prayed-over in a blasphemous way. I never would have eaten it." Viçente stopped, remembering the Savior lying by him on the prison floor, saying he forgave Viçente's parents. But Viçente was no saint. How was he to get past the revulsion he'd held in his heart these forty-five years?

And here was Gonzalo, a Muslim who thought he was Christian, safeguarding him. How could he fault the man's virtue?

CHAPTER 89

—◊◊◊—

WHILE MARCOS RECOVERED HIS STRENGTH, Sarmiento pursued his plan. He summoned the pompous, impotent Council of Governors and convinced them to approve the law Marcos had drafted a month earlier. The *Sentencia Estatuto,* 'Sentence and Law,' documented *marrano* confessions, decried their perfidy, and barred converts and their progeny from holding office or testifying in Toledo for all time.

This should have been a triumphant moment, but Marcos' stomach burned with disappointed fury. No other city would follow Toledo's model. This just law, this cherished principle, would perish because of Toledo's surrender to Prince Enrique. Sarmiento was turning their noble cause to *mierda.*

—◊◊◊—

Conserving his energy, Marcos entered the great cathedral, with its high-arching vaults and stained glass. He spotted the two priests in their brown, hooded robes in pews near the front, and the other man kneeling before the altar. Marcos settled behind the priests, Pero and Juan Alonso.

"So you've enlisted our friend." Marcos nodded to the lone man, who stood now, staring at the crucifix.

Alonso's smile revealed crooked, yellow teeth in his narrow mouth. "He won't commit until he hears your assurances."

The man, Fernando de Avila, commander of the Calatrava Gate, stepped toward them along the central aisle. He was youthful with wavy black hair that ended at the collar of his dark green tunic. His chestnut eyes flashed a soldier's confidence.

"Fernando, welcome to our conspiracy," Marcos said.

Pero raised a hand to his lips. "Please, keep your voice down."

Fernando clicked a heel on the stone floor. "Good day, Señor García. It's difficult to believe what I've heard—Sarmiento surrendering Toledo to King Juan?"

Marcos savored this feeling, revealing secrets to change men's fates. "That's his plan, unless we thwart it." Fernando watched with keen eyes as Marcos continued. "In a matter of days, Prince Enrique expects to control Toledo. Then, he'll trade it to the king for the city of Burgos."

"But why? And how will they—"

"Sarmiento will acquiesce so long as the king lets him keep the *marrano* gold and govern the city."

"This is hard to swallow," Fernando said. "My magistrate, he was our inspiration. Where did you learn of this?"

"Sarmiento himself. And I foresee your next question: the king will absolve Sarmiento of sedition, but no one else." Marcos gestured to Fernando and the two priests. "We who organized the *limpieza* and ousted Constable Luna from the gates are unprotected."

Pero gasped. "But I don't see why—"

Marcos poked the vicar's chest. "When you brought our demands to King Juan at Fuensalida, you became his enemy, Pero, but we can bargain for his favor."

Pero pushed off his hood, revealing his pink, hairless scalp. He mopped his brow with a dirty cloth.

"Listen now," Marcos said. "This is complex. For the king to gain Toledo from his son, he must forfeit Burgos. If he could gain Toledo without that sacrifice, how grateful would he be? We can make that happen. I've sent a representative to Constable Luna to arrange our triumph. The key is this—before the prince can react, we'll admit a regiment of the king's forces through Calatrava Gate. They'll come in stealth at night. Fernando, your control of the gate is vital, and you'll be well rewarded."

Fernando smirked. "The good men I command wouldn't want to see my head stuck on a pike. Ironic, isn't it? We open our gates to the king to save ourselves from him?"

Pero slumped back into the pew. "I'm not a warrior, but give me a role and I'll serve you."

"Good," Marcos snapped. "Charge the prince and pin him to the wall with your fat belly." Marcos' jest gave him no pleasure. His stomach turned at the thought of this desperate bargain with their enemies. And there was so little time now to capture Pérez.

—⟶

BISHOP LOPE DE BARRIENTOS WATCHED Marcos García pace from the window of Sarmiento's office to the far wall and back, sending malevolent glances his way. Where was Pedro Sarmiento? Lope's stomach fluttered and his palms perspired. He risked much, coming here alone to pronounce Sarmiento's doom, but if he did it skillfully, the magistrate might thank him for it, and Lope might get a chance to see Viçente. So he wore his white robe and skullcap to emphasize Christ's purity, rather than elaborate vestments of authority, and he kept a benign countenance.

Sarmiento entered, greeted Lope, and sat in his desk chair. He ignored his deputy, who kept pacing, and said, "Bishop Barrientos, you've come with urgent news?"

Lope feigned reluctance, clearing his throat and fidgeting. "I'm afraid this will be difficult. Pope Nicholas has issued three bulls condemning your inquisition." Lope hid the glee that sought to show at the corners of his mouth as García stopped mid-stride and gaped.

"*Dios.*" Sarmiento slumped in his chair. "This can't be true. Bishop!"

Lope gave Sarmiento a sympathetic frown. "A Vatican messenger delivered the document to the bishop of Siguenza. It denounces Vicar Pero López de Gálvez for usurping control and dismissing the cathedral's archdeacon."

Sarmiento grimaced and scratched his leg beneath the desk. "What's the vicar's penalty?"

"Excommunication." Lope folded his hands across his stomach. "All Christians will shun him."

García spat on the floor. "Does the pope ignore our charges against the *marranos*?"

"The bulls accept that some converts are duplicitous. 'Sowers of weeds in the wheat field,' he calls them. But Pope Nicholas disavows confessions taken under torment. He calls your inquisition 'heretical depravity.'"

"It's a *limpieza*," García shouted. "We expel Toledo's impure blood." He stepped to the spear rack and grasped one of the weapons.

Sarmiento scowled at the deputy, and Lope tried to ignore the tingle of fear running down his spine.

"Prince Enrique will use this to renounce his sworn alliance," García said.

Sarmiento jumped up. "Your suspicions don't belong here, Deputy. Prince Enrique and the bishop are our friends."

García jabbed a finger in Lope's direction. "Then let him explain how the pope's decision affects us."

Sarmiento clenched his fists, but Lope waved a hand. "It's a sensible request. Nothing will change immediately. Church procedures dictate that the bishop of Siguenza, having received the papal bulls, will formulate orders to implement them."

"I'm asking if the prince will honor his commitment," García said.

"Of course he will." Sarmiento turned to Lope with a pleading look.

Lope couldn't imagine how this nasty pair had governed a city. He set his hands on his thighs, still trying to appear sympathetic. "I've not wanted to offend you, Magistrate, but I can not avoid the rest. The prince will do what he can for you, but the pope condemns your actions as well."

"Enrique promised me control," Sarmiento whined. He reached toward his desk as if he planned to bring out the prince's certificate, and then let his hand drop.

Lope sighed. "I'm afraid you've also been excommunicated, Magistrate, as well as all who supported your false inquisition." He glanced at the deputy.

García jerked a spear from the rack and leveled it at Lope. "Popes," he snarled. "Popes trample God's will beneath embroidered slippers. You deceive the pope, you false, *marrano*-whoring bishop." He moved forward.

García's eyes bulged as he stalked closer. Lope saw Sarmiento snatch his sword from beneath the desk. Oh God, both were on the attack.

Lope stepped behind his chair, but Sarmiento moved the other way, menacing García. "Put it down, Marcos."

The deputy halted, and Lope breathed again. Sarmiento took another step toward García and the deputy's expression turned from fury to indecision to loathing. He dropped the spear with a clatter, retreated to the window, and leaned on the sill, breathing heavily. "You goaded me to that, Barrientos."

Sarmiento set his sword across his desk with a meek smile. "Could you grant me a kindness, Bishop, and not tell Prince Enrique about this ... disagreement?" The magistrate sank into his chair. "Excommunicated. My God, how could we not be distraught?" He leaned forward, covering his face with his hands.

Later, when he reported this to Enrique, the story would prove amusing, but a lie now served God's purpose. "Of course I'll speak kindly of you. But I would shirk my responsibility if I didn't mention that the pope's order denies you all church sacraments, all properties, and all civil offices." Lope looked down to hide his glee. "His Eminence did restrain himself in one area. He didn't mention the men you murdered in flames before the archbishop's palace."

"The vicar declared those men blasphemers."

"Magistrate, consider God's judgment," Lope said. "Your vicar usurped holy authority to accommodate your wishes. You must repent these murders. I'd take your confession, but sadly, it's forbidden."

The magistrate stared at the sword on his desk, a tear running down his cheek. "You said the prince would do what he can, that it depends on the bishop of Siguenza."

Was it possible that Sarmiento couldn't foresee the implications? "Consider Enrique's situation. The pope excludes you from office, and there are other penalties."

"Don't tell me." Sarmiento looked toward the ceiling, tears flowing freely now.

"Very well, but Enrique has asked me to visit Viçente Pérez. I'm sure you desire to please the prince."

Sarmiento was about to speak, but a loud rattle turned their attention. García had kicked the spear rack. He stood beside it, beaming. "It's a shame, Bishop. The Jew-lover died this morning of the fever."

Lope dropped back into his chair. "Holy Jesus, no."

"We'll show you the grave if you'd like to pray over it," García said.

CHAPTER 91

—ɯ—

WORD HAD COME THAT DIEGO was recovering in the prince's camp. Viçente imagined their reunion and then the voyage on to Naples. *Francesca.* He murmured her name as he stepped forward, balancing with two canes. He made a circuit of the courtyard, set one aside, and made another round. Enrique's army had departed the city, making escape more difficult, but they would find a way soon. He took a step, halted, and shifted the cane to his other hand. Another step—better.

A thud. The outer courtyard door swung open. A dark-featured stranger in coarse-spun clothes entered. *Sangre Pura?* Viçente's heart pounded. The man eyed him, and Viçente tightened his grip on the cane.

"I'm Gonzalo's brother, Ignacio," the man said.

Viçente saw little of Gonzalo's nobility in this man's prominent eyebrows, wide nose, and thick lips, but Ignacio's smile reassured him. "I have news for you."

Gonzalo came out and hugged his brother. "I thought I heard voices. Viçente, this is Nacio's father."

"Wait until you hear, brother." Ignacio looked from Gonzalo to Viçente. "Señor Pérez, my sons in the *Guardia Civil* overhear whispers about a plot among the guards at Calatrava Gate—that's one gate not controlled by the prince. Deputy García is involved, and the gate commander, Fernando de Avila. At Calatrava, the guards had been directed to exclude all royal soldiers, but no longer. Now they're ordered to admit King Juan's forces into the city."

"*King Juan!*" Viçente felt his pulse beat fast as he tried to comprehend. "This is vital news, Ignacio. But confusing. You say García—is he in charge?"

Ignacio nodded.

"He must feel threatened by Enrique, but why unite with the king?"

Gonzalo shook his head in befuddlement. "King Juan's a good man, is he not? But if that *pendejo* García is involved ..."

Ideas swirled in Viçente's mind. If the king seized control from inside, he could try to expel his son. Whatever prize the prince hoped to gain from controlling Toledo would vanish. But Enrique held two gates, and he'd fight to keep them. "This is more important than the fate of one knave," Viçente said. "If the king leads an army toward one portal, the prince will charge in through the others. They'll destroy Toledo. Gonzalo, now I must go to Enrique."

"You're not ready, Viçente. The streets are full of evil ones searching for you."

Viçente clutched the builder's forearm. "Do you understand? This is no longer about me and my son. It's about preventing war."

"Ignacio's son risked his life for you," Gonzalo said. "I'll deliver your message to the prince."

"Enrique wouldn't meet an unknown builder, nor trust you. If you won't help, I'll slip out tonight and make my way."

Viçente stood, watching the builder's eyes until acceptance dawned in them.

Stonemasons from Gonzalo's work crew backed a horse-drawn wagon into the courtyard. Two of them boosted Viçente into the back, and he curled up in corner, supporting his head on a pile of sand.

Gonzalo stood over him. "Prepare for a rough journey, my friend. Ignacio and I will ride atop, and four men will follow on horseback." Workers covered Viçente in burlap, then shoveled sand around him and set tools on top. *Like a corpse in a tomb,* he thought.

The wagon jolted uphill. They halted. "What's your cargo?" A strange voice.

"What's your authority?" Gonzalo's voice.

"We're *Sangre Pura*, ordered by the deputy to search all cargo."

Viçente pulled his legs in close and prayed.

"Sand and tools, nothing more." Ignacio.

"What's beneath?" The cart tipped. Someone had climbed on. Viçente held his breath.

"Get off and stop wasting our time," Gonzalo snapped.

A whip cracked. The wagon lurched forward. The man who'd jumped on yelped. "Damn you. *Stop.*" The voice was further away—the wagon's surge had toppled him.

They gained speed, wagon jostling, wheels grinding and bumping, clomping hooves, rolling uphill. Viçente curled in a tight ball, pressing his throbbing shoulders against the burlap to fend off the tools that pounded him with each jolt. Gonzalo called, "We're at the hilltop, heading down for Bisagra gate. They tried to follow, but my men are holding them off." The wagon tilted and bounded downward on and on and on. "Easy," the builder called to the horses. Viçente heard a drone—brake-wadding bearing on wagon wheels. Finally, they slowed, brakes grinding.

"*Halt.* What's your business?" A harsh voice—prince's guard or enemy?

"Just a work party leaving the city," Gonzalo called.

"Two men on a wagon?"

"Aye," Ignacio said.

"One *maravedi.*"

So it was Enrique's soldier, demanding a toll. Viçente sighed. From behind came hoof beats and a shout. "*Don't let them through!*"

"Here's your payment," Gonzalo said.

"*Wait.*" Horses closing in. "*Those men ran from our inspection.*"

"We avoided some ruffians," Gonzalo said. "They have no standing, no uniforms."

"We're *Sangre Pura*. They have contraband in the wagon."

"I got no orders about contraband, and you got no uniform." The soldier laughed, but Viçente heard more horses coming.

"Look," the *Sangre Pura* called. "These *Guardia Civil* have uniforms. They'll tell you to check the wagon."

Someone jumped on board and ripped back the burlap. An immense, helmeted soldier stared down at him.

CHAPTER 92

—⚭—

THE SOLDIER GRABBED VIÇENTE'S ARM and yanked. Pain tore from his shoulders down his back. As he was dragged from the wagon, Viçente spotted two men in work clothes standing with their horses—the *Sangre Pura*—and three uniformed *Guardia* men climbing down from their mounts. A pair of the prince's soldiers stood near, and others watched from twenty paces away. There'd be archers at the crown of the gate with crossbows to cut Gonzalo and Ignacio down if they fled.

Gonzalo shouted, "Easy with him. He's injured."

"Silence, you."

One of the *Guardia* men asked another, "Is it he?" The second nodded and looked away. His superior addressed the soldier. "He's an escaped prisoner. Give him over so we can return him to his cell."

Viçente's chest felt hollow. He straightened and caught his captor's eye. "I must see your commanding officer."

One of the soldiers stepped forward. He wore the gold sergeant's insignia on his sleeve.

"Please," Viçente said, "Take me to Prince Enrique."

The sergeant snorted. "Why listen to a dirty thief who hid in a pile of sand?"

"He's not a thief." Gonzalo called. "He used to be first deputy."

One of the *Sangre Pura* spat on the ground. "A confessed sinner."

The sergeant prodded his chin with a knuckle. "Back at camp I heard something about a first deputy."

424

"Ask the prince or Juan Pacheco," Viçente said. "We fought together at Olmedo. I bring them vital news."

"He lies," the *Sangre Pura* shouted.

One of the *Guardia Civil* shook his head, and the sergeant asked, "You got something to say?"

The *Guardia* man muttered, "He was first deputy years ago. I served under him."

"Louder," the soldier demanded.

"He tells the truth. He was wounded at Olmedo. That's what I know."

—⟶⟵—

Viçente, Gonzalo, and Ignacio sat on tree stumps in the prince's camp as soldiers gawked at them. Moments later, the troops gave way, and Viçente saw Bishop Lope Barrientos stride forward, wearing a robe and skullcap the color of new oak leaves. Viçente stood. Barrientos beamed and threw his arms around Viçente, stretching and bruising his sore torso. "My son, we heard you were dead." He touched Viçente's cheek and frowned. "Minister Tivolini departed for Naples with the sad news."

Francesca! "Tivolini was here? But I don't—we have to tell Enrique about—"

The bishop held up a hand. "One matter at a time. Tivolini came to negotiate your freedom, but García told us you'd died of the fever." The bishop seized him for another hug, laughing, his belly bouncing against Viçente's. "You've been resurrected, my son."

"Bishop, can't you see how this will affect Francesca? Tivolini must be intercepted. And I have to see the prince."

"Minister Tivolini departed days ago, and Enrique's off hunting." Barrientos backed away and spoke to a captain. "Would you offer an old priest a boon and send riders after Tivolini?" The captain nodded. "It's done, Viçente," Barrientos said. "Now you'll want to see your son."

"And I want to see him." Diego entered the circle, gleeful, fit, and handsome. "Holy God." Diego kissed Viçente's cheek and hugged him hard. "I never surrendered hope, Papa, but I didn't imagine you'd appear like an apparition."

Viçente gasped. "Be gentle, son. And wait." Clinging to Diego, Viçente looked to Barrientos. "This is urgent. Bishop, Captain, we must get word to the prince. The king's army may be advancing on the city."

The captain questioned him and then dispatched a courier to Prince Enrique. Gonzalo and Ignacio went off to find refreshments, leaving Viçente and Diego settled on a thick stump.

"Have you heard, Papa? The pope excommunicated Sarmiento, García, and that foolish vicar."

Viçente let out a little whoop of joy. "When?"

"We heard last week."

"I don't understand. They're still running Toledo."

"It's the church, Papa. Barrientos will explain. They have some archaic procedures. Prince Enrique will wait for the church order. Then the *Guardia Civil* will abandon Sarmiento, and he'll have to go."

"Doesn't sound like the Enrique I know." Viçente ran his hand down Diego's back, feeling the rippled welts beneath his shirt, and tears trickled down his cheeks.

—⁂—

Viçente woke, grabbing for the hand that jostled him.

"You can't sleep all day, Papa."

It was Diego. Viçente relaxed.

"Put on these clothes. The prince wants to see us."

When he and Diego entered the pavilion's great room, they found Gonzalo and Ignacio sitting with Barrientos and three of Enrique's officers in a half-circle of chairs. Enrique and Pacheco occupied a divan, facing them.

Enrique eyed Ignacio. "Men will be slaughtered for this. If you lie, you'll be two of them."

Ignacio swallowed and said, "It's true, Majesty. I swear."

Enrique noticed Viçente and beckoned. "We thought Saint Peter had you." He stood and kissed Viçente's cheeks. "Sit over there."

Viçente and Diego took chairs by Barrientos.

"You've interrupted my hunt, Viçente. I should be angry, but if this man's tale is true …"

"Ignacio and Gonzalo risked their lives to bring me here," Viçente said. "They wouldn't lie."

Enrique pounded a fist into his hand. "*Hijo de puta*. Barrientos convinced me to take the city from Sarmiento peacefully, but we have no time. Bishop, the church must strip the *pendejo* of his office now."

"I'm afraid it will take some—"

Enrique blew out a puff of air. "Of course not. Good, we'll attack."

"We wanted to avoid—" Barrientos said.

Enrique made a brushing off motion. "How many men defend Calatrava gate?"

"Ten or twelve *Guardia Civil*."

"How difficult to capture?"

"We could ride in through the gates we control," an officer said. "Advance within three hundred paces without being seen, and charge."

Viçente imagined the gate's defenders' dead bodies strewn on the ground. "That's a dangerous plan. Ignacio, you've not mentioned Chief Magistrate Sarmiento. Is he one of the conspirators?"

"No, Viçente. They didn't mention him."

The prince laughed. "We'll take the gate and decide later who to hang."

"Don't be so quick." Viçente said. "If Sarmiento's blameless, there's another way."

"You'd deny these fine soldiers a chance for blood?"

"Civil guards would be little sport for your titans."

Enrique nodded to Ignacio and Gonzalo. "You've delivered Toledo from misfortune, Señores. My sergeant will see that you're fed. Viçente and Diego—"

"We'll stay," Viçente said.

"All right, my friend. You know the city best. Pacheco, Bishop, you've dealt with Sarmiento. What do you recommend?"

"Sarmiento dislikes García," Viçente said. "Act as if he's innocent, and he'll cooperate."

Barrientos patted his arm. "Viçente's idea is sound. Sarmiento's distraught over the excommunication."

"If he's so troubled, why hasn't he de-departed?" Pacheco asked.

"Until the bishop of Siguenza issues his edict, Sarmiento's still magistrate," Barrientos said.

Prince Enrique grimaced. "Allowing him to plunder Toledo's treasury at his leisure."

"He and García were about to stab one another in my presence," Barrientos said. "It was quite enjoyable, but Sarmiento desperately wants your favor, Enrique."

Pacheco cleared his throat. "I support Viçente, too. When seeking the Toledans' allegiance, better not kill a dozen of their sons."

The prince frowned. "I assume you have a plan to separate the guilty from the simple fools?"

"I do, my prince."

CHAPTER 93

—⚬—

FRANCESCA, CARLO, AND THEIR PARTY landed in Barcelona, in the kingdom of Aragón—the kingdom ruled by her half-brother, Alfonso. The unceasing nausea of the voyage had drained her. The carriage ride to the king's palace made her queasy.

After settling in, she was summoned to an ornate salon where the palace's red-faced butler awaited on a saffron-yellow armchair. Beside him sat Carlo, the meddlesome twit.

The butler stood and bowed too low and too long before straightening. "My lady, how can I make your stay comfortable?"

"We leave for Toledo tomorrow. Please arrange horses and provisions."

"And a carriage for you, my lady," the butler said. "But surely you'll need days to recuperate from your voyage. If it's not too bold, may I presume to arrange a meeting with Queen María? She's here in Barcelona with her entourage."

Francesca saw a knowing look pass between Carlo and the butler. "If the queen can dine with me this evening."

The butler's jaw dropped.

Carlo blew out a loud breath. "Lady Francesca, we must be practical. It was a long voyage, and you've been ill."

And such a tedious journey because of your whining, she thought. "We'll depart tomorrow, gentlemen."

Carlo stroked his goatee. "A brief delay won't be such a hardship."

She clenched her fists, about to tell the butler that she would ride a horse rather than occupy a carriage to speed the journey, but she had to think of the precious life inside her. "The king made it clear, Carlo. You'll see to my safety, but not hamper my journey."

Carlo's jaw was tight, brows set in that stubborn, hateful look as he addressed the butler. "The king also demanded that I protect this woman, who is with child. We'll stay three days, more if needed."

She blushed at mention of her pregnancy, and she fumed, but seeing the relieved look in the butler's eyes, she recognized the inevitable. The butler resented her, and Carlo provided an excuse. She would accept the delay as respite for her baby.

That afternoon she learned the wonderful news—her nephew, Enrique was negotiating with Chief Magistrate Sarmiento to rule Toledo. Surely Enrique would rescue Viçente and his son.

—⁂—

Their third and final afternoon in Barcelona, Penélope entered her chamber without knocking. "Lady Francesca, Minister Tivolini has arrived."

Francesca's heart flew and plunged at the same moment. "*Viçente?*"

Penélope shook her head. "I don't know."

Francesca found the minister in the salon, sipping tea with Carlo. Tivolini stood and bowed, and Francesca noticed his deeply creased forehead, his wide, fat lips compressed in a look of regret. The minister looked away, but Carlo watched her, his eyes gleaming with ill-disguised triumph. She fought the need to vomit.

Tivolini finally met her gaze. "The news from Toledo is not favorable, my lady. Prince Enrique camps there with his army. He's forging an alliance with the magistrate."

"Tell me about Viçente."

"Dear lady, I wish I had other news." Tivolini sighed. "His son was rescued ... but Señor Pérez died in prison of the fever."

430

Tears ran from her eyes, and her breath caught. Tivolini touched her shoulder, but she pulled away. "You're wrong."

"No, my lady."

She jabbed a finger at him. "You never wanted the task of rescuing him."

Tivolini's look became cool. "Bishop Barrientos told me this himself."

"Then what's this deception about a fever? You mean they tortured and—" The words 'killed him' would not pass her constricted throat. "The truth, Minister."

Tivolini shrugged. "There could have been torture. We have no proof."

She sank into an armchair, weeping. Carlo cleared his throat. "She's distraught. We'll rest a few days before sailing home."

"*No.*" The strength of Francesca's voice surprised her, and the men stared. "King Alfonso ordered you to aid my journey, Carlo. We leave for Toledo in the morning."

"But, my lady." Carlo looked at her with that smirky frown he used in other men's company.

She wasn't sure yet why, but she had to go. Despite Tivolini's word, she couldn't imagine Viçente was lost. And if he was? Then she'd find a place where something of his spirit remained, locate his grave if she could, pray for his soul.

What meager solace that would be.

—ᴍ—

Wʜᴀᴛ ᴀ ᴍɪsᴇʀᴀʙʟᴇ ᴛᴇɴ ᴅᴀʏs these had been for Pero. First, word of his ex-communication had crumpled him to his knees, sobbing and praying for forgiveness. But the news had set Marcos ablaze with curses for the pope, the 'red bishop,' and degenerate *marranos.* Marcos planned to fight on, but how long would it be before some church order stripped Marcos and Magistrate Sarmiento of all authority?

Then yesterday, he'd been in Marcos' office when word came that Viçente Pérez had escaped the city. Marcos had smashed crockery and screamed before dropping into a chair, gasping, his face pale and dreadful.

Now Pero climbed the stairs to Marcos' home to deliver yet more horrifying news. Marcos opened his door and Pero blurted, "Have you seen the notice?"

"What are you talking about?" Marcos admitted him and closed the door.

"They nailed it on the board outside the cathedral. The prince—" Pero heard footsteps and then a rapping. He stepped toward the bed-room, thinking to hide in a closet.

Sancho, the guildsman, barged in, flung his gray cloth cap onto the table, and said, "*Goddamn it.*" He looked at Pero, crossed himself, and eyed Marcos. "Did you hear? The prince commands the citizens to help him root out 'betrayers who would open the city to the king.' He's hunting us, Marcos."

Marcos' jaw tightened and his eyes narrowed. He strode to the window and whirled back. "This isn't bad. Prince Enrique will bring Pérez, and we'll have a chance at him. Sancho, assemble the men. Pero, we'll plead our cause to Sarmiento. *Sangre Pura* and the *Guardia Civil* must barricade the streets and hold the city for King Juan."

Holy God. Marcos' schemes had gotten them excommunicated, and now this. Pero scrutinized Marcos, hoping to find a spark of respect or caring in his eyes, but Marcos turned away, took his sword from a post on the wall, and strapped it on.

Sancho snatched up his cap. "Does Sarmiento support our pact with King Juan?"

"Doesn't know about it," Marcos snapped. "I'll convince him."

"My men must hear from Sarmiento."

Marcos grabbed the wool carter's collar. "Rally them, you coward. Tell them we haven't finished our work until the last *marrano* dies." Marcos pushed Sancho aside and strode into the bedroom. He returned with another sword with its scabbard and belt and thrust it at Pero. "Strap it on."

The cold steel repulsed Pero. He wanted to protest, but Marcos and Sancho were out the door. "Come, Vicar."

The sword was so heavy, the belt too short. When they reached the street, he slipped the strap over his shoulder. They parted from Sancho and followed narrow streets that should have bustled with workmen, but Pero and Marcos moved alone past the marketplace. Entering the alley beside the *alcázar,* their footsteps echoed off brown stone walls, echoing the rhythm of Pero's fearful heart.

Marcos halted at the corner, breathing hard for a while before peering around. Pero eased forward, too, seeing the usual contingent of *Guardia Civil* near the *alcázar* entrance, but also helmeted heads—the prince's soldiers standing where they didn't belong. Marcos' eyes bulged. He knelt on the ground, gasping and muttering.

Pero rested his rump against the wall, set his hands on his thighs, and bent forward. "The soldiers there, what does it mean?"

Marcos scowled, but it seemed his thoughts were on something else—on his breathing, on gaining control. Finally he said, "Sarmiento betrays us for Prince Enrique. The *Guardia Civil* and the prince's troops oppose us. The *marrano* caused this."

Pero didn't believe Viçente Pérez was the devil, but he kept silent.

Marcos nodded, his look growing confident again. "We'll escape through Calatrava Gate, and I'll organize *Sangre Pura* from outside the city." He straightened and walked slowly with Pero through the winding streets, until they were halted by the sight of a lone figure in a black jacket with gold medals on the chest—Fernando de Avila. He stepped from a doorway and marched straight to Marcos. "They tricked us! Sarmiento ordered a change of the guard. Once his men were in position, their captain sent my men to the *alcázar* 'for discipline.'"

"*Pendejo*," Marcos muttered. "*Estúpido.* You ran like a child?"

Fernando glared. "My men fled and I hid nearby until Prince Enrique's soldiers arrived."

A numb sorrow filled Pero. How had things come to this? He'd only meant to be a simple priest, and God had given him Marcos, who'd helped him understand things, gain status and power … and enmeshed him in this horror. "We were going to escape through Calatrava Gate."

Marcos crossed his arms, glowering. "Everything's changed, Vicar. We'll shelter in the city and organize *Sangre Pura* from within."

Pero felt an instant of absurd joy. He could at last help Marcos. "Stay with me in the rectory."

That evening, priests guarded the rectory doors and the underground passage to the cathedral. Pero and Padre Juan Alonso listened while Marcos and Fernando made plans for *Sangre Pura* to seize the city gates. While Marcos proclaimed that tomorrow they would capture the devil, Pérez, and cleanse the city, Pero tried to remember why he'd followed this man, more lunatic than leader, now that he considered it.

In the morning, the few remaining priests set out bread, dried meats, wine, and water on a side table in the dining hall. One of the loyal fathers was dispatched to summon Sancho and the men. As they waited around the rectory's massive dining table, Pero heard the muffled clatter of hoof beats and the sound of hammering outside the closed shutters. When it grew quiet, Padre Juan Alonso pulled up the hood of his brown robe and ventured out, returning grim-faced with a torn paper. "A new notice from the prince." Alonso laid it on the table and read.

Royal Order to the People of Toledo
Shun the Conspirators
Report their Locations to my Soldiers
Together, We'll Return Peace to the City
Be it known hereby that I, Prince Enrique, declare these men guilty of treason.
Surrender at the alcázar, treacherous dogs, or face harsh justice.

Pero felt a chill run through him. "Please, Juan, whose names are on the list?"

Fernando gave a weak smile. "For one who's been excommunicated, you're eager for bad news." The word 'excommunicated' brought Pero to the verge of sobbing.

He noticed that muscle twitch beneath Marcos' eye as he said, "The prince is beguiled by Viçente Pérez' and will indulge the Jews, but hundreds of *Sangre Pura* will come."

Padre Juan Alonso looked from man to man. "We four are listed on the notice, along with several of the *Guardia Civil* and a few priests."

Thudding in the hallway. Sancho entered with five lean, young men in brown caps and work clothes, bearing swords and crude shields. The guildsman dropped his shield on the table with a clank that rattled Pero's bones. Sancho took a sausage from the counter and bit off a piece. "A priest unlocked the door for us, Marcos. Now your army's made up of idlers in brown robes?"

Marcos thumped his glass on the side table. "Where are the rest of our men, Sancho?"

"They bow to Sarmiento, the man who shared plunder with them. You gave them nothing but fancy speeches." Sancho chewed open-mouthed. "I warned you."

Marcos shook his head, a peculiar, sickly expression on his face, a tick under his eye, unceasing.

"A few more may come, if they can fight their way past your priests." Sancho gestured at his men standing near the entry. "Eat. At least there's decent food." The five set down their armor and moved to the sideboard while Sancho pointed to the document. "Is that the prince's order?" Padre Alonso slid the paper toward him. The wool carter shoved it back. "Is my name there?"

Alonso shook his head. A smile flickered on Sancho's full lips and rounded his stubbly cheeks.

If only Pero's name could disappear.

A priest rushed into the hall. "Vicar, soldiers and citizens are massing out in the square."

Pero's gut clenched. Sweat trickled down his sides beneath the robe.

"We'll go to the cathedral." Marcos strapped on his sword.

Of course, Pero thought. *The sanctuary of the church will save us.* He took his weapon and followed through the passage to the cathedral's basement crypt.

Pero was last to climb the stairs from crypt into cathedral, his heart beating fast, eyes assailed by light streaming in through the sacred glass. The others explored the huge vaulted space, opening the outside portals a crack to peer out. Fernando returned, his jaw set. "Surrounded."

Beside him, this great man, Marcos, Pero's inspiration, seemed small and absurd, but Pero still longed for a sign of caring. Marcos' eyes flitted around the church. "The rest of the *Sangre Pura* wait outside. We'll climb the tower and order them to attack the soldiers."

Sancho strolled over, shaking his head. "You'll be shouting at the wind, García. You were always shouting at the goddamned wind." The wool carter took a quick step forward and slapped Marcos hard across the face.

Marcos reeled toward the steps but caught his balance, holding his cheek with a hand. "Apologize, *mierda*, before the men arrive."

"*There are no men,*" Sancho bellowed. His voice echoed off the high pillars and descended from the vaulted ceiling. It reverberated to the chapels on the walls, reaching the saints' statues, and the saints whispered back, *there are no men.*

"Up the bell tower," Marcos shouted. "I'll call out to *Sangre Pura,* and they'll heed."

Juan Alonso opened the heavy door and stepped through, followed by Fernando, Marcos, and the five *Sangre Pura.* Pero paused, wondering where his priests had gone. He should stay behind and demand that the soldiers not violate this sanctuary, but then he heard the cathedral's west door slam open. Pero leaped into the stairwell and bolted the door.

Climbing the stone steps in near darkness, Pero's lungs burned. As he approached the first platform halfway up the tower, he heard Marcos gasping as he shouted, "*Sangre Pura. Marcos García … summons you to fight.*" Pero turned a corner and saw Marcos and Fernando peering out the window as Juan Alonso and the five *Sangre Pura* watched. Pero squeezed in next to Fernando to breathe fresh air. He squinted in the light. Below, he saw a crowd with a smattering of black-and-gold *Guardia* uniforms and scores of soldiers in helmets and chest armor.

"*Sangre Pura,*" Marcos rasped. "*Attack the soldiers.*"

Pero watched for signs of the struggle. Instead he heard laughter, a few curses, and shouts. "Look at the fools in the tower. Come down, First Deputy, and face your brotherhood."

"Sancho, call the men," Marcos commanded.

"Sancho isn't here," one of the *Sangre Pura* said. "*Pendejo* brought us and sneaked off."

Thudding sounds from below—soldiers chopping down the door. Pero backed away and began climbing. Fernando passed him and Juan Alonso. Light filtering from above told him he was close to the bell platform. He rested, hearing the awful echo of the chopping, wondering why the *Sangre Pura* men hadn't come past. Marcos stepped into view, his face contorted. He settled on a step and muttered, "My men aren't coming, Pero. The *marrano* escapes us."

Pero's pulse throbbed in his temples. He should be furious, but Marcos had only tried to do God's will. Pero stroked the hair by Marcos' forehead, thinking that soon their souls would be consigned to heaven or hell. Marcos patted his hand, then stood and trudged upward. Pero followed, savoring that bit of warmth.

At the top, sunlight shone through arched openings, twice as tall as any man. In the center, behind a railing, the bells hung from a huge metal brace—large and dark and shiny. Pero surveyed the platform. The width of three men shoulder to shoulder, it ran around the four sides of the tower between the great bells and outer low walls. Padre Juan Alonso stood on the left flank, a sword dangling from his hand, his eyes sorrowful. Beside him, Fernando de Avila tipped his sword and bowed to Marcos and Pero.

The chopping ceased. Pero heard faint shouts and screams. "Our five fighters," Marcos said as he drew his sword. "I ordered them to defend the tower."

How could the soldiers attack? The cathedral was sanctuary. But from the stairwell, Pero heard boots tromping. He backed into a corner, and Padre Juan Alonso retreated to his side. Marcos seemed to be gaining strength, the color returning to his face. He and Fernando stood near the stairs. As the pounding boot steps grew intense and terrifying, Marcos and Fernando backed toward Pero, their weapons leveled.

Two soldiers burst from the stairwell, brandishing battle-axes and bellowing. Another pair stepped forth, followed by men dressed in workmen's clothing, carrying spears. How could Pero's heart pound so hard in a chest gone hollow? He dropped his weapon and slid to the cold stone floor, the bottom of his robe pulling up to expose his thighs. Marcos and Fernando retreated along the platform, pursued by two soldiers and some workmen. A soldier stopped near Pero and kicked his thigh. Pain shot up his leg and he screamed. The soldier snarled, "Sit out the fight on your ass, Padre, and I won't poke you with this." He slid the blade of his shiny battle-axe forward between Pero's legs as Pero's heart beat wildly. The blade stopped a finger's width from Pero's crotch and he lost control. His urine streamed across the floor.

Metal clanging—Pero looked up to see Fernando taking a stand halfway along the platform, swinging his sword side to side as if swatting gnats. He steadied it and lunged. A soldier countered with his ax. Marcos yelled, *"God will defeat you,"* and darted at the soldier, his sword repelled by the man's body armor. Marcos retreated as another warrior swung an ax at Fernando's shoulder. Blood spurted, showering the huge metal bells. Fernando shrieked and spun. As he fell, something wet splattered Pero's face. He lifted his hand, his fingers spotted crimson. He covered one eye with the other hand but couldn't stop watching. Marcos, his face ghostly white, his left arm stiff, grasped his weapon in the right hand. The blade wavered as he pointed it at one of the working-class men behind the soldiers. The soldiers watched for an instant as Marcos called to the workmen, "I know you. You're *Sangre Pura*. Help me."

Pero couldn't comprehend the meaning of the blood, like some holy sacrifice. He regretted the words he'd never said to his remarkable friend. And then one of the rough-looking men stepped close behind the soldiers, leaned across the railing by the huge bell, and thrust a spear at Marcos' belly.

CHAPTER 95

—⚊—

Marcos saw Fernando writhing on the floor. Pain ripped up his left arm and constricted his chest.

Pain—God's punishment for failure.

He had to stand, to defend, to turn the fight around. And now he saw the means, a *Sangre Pura* coming up behind the soldiers. His men *had* come. "I know you. You're *Sangre Pura*. Help me!" But instead of attacking the soldiers, the *Sangre Pura* leaned past and Marcos saw the metal tip of a spear dart toward him. Fighting his pain, he tried to dodge.

He felt a prick as the weapon sliced into him and thought, *that's not so bad*, but his sword flew from his hand and he fell, crashing into the wall behind. His gut erupted with searing agony. The shaft was buried in him, its handle swaying just above the stone floor, blood and something else gushing, and a horrible stench. He covered the wound with his hands and felt the oozing fluid.

A soldier stood over him, his lips moving but the voice coming from far away. "No more. Rip the spear out and we'll take him to the prince."

The *Sangre Pura* yanked the spear. Something shifted in Marcos' bowels and he screamed as pain knifed up his body through his head, blotting it all away.

—⚊—

He felt a jostling motion and agony boiling inside. *God help me.* Dying, dying without destroying the *marrano.* Marcos closed his eyes. He would curse God for allowing the evil ones to foil him, but if he did, he'd have no chance for heaven. Instead he begged Jesus to forgive his failure.

Four soldiers carried him into the cathedral. He wondered if they might stop for Pero to give him the rites, but they moved on into bright sunlight. On the cathedral entry porch, they tilted the litter and he caught a glimpse of thousands of men in drab clothing in the square, shaking fists, waving sticks—and scores of soldiers by the cathedral stairs. They cheered him, but he couldn't get up to acknowledge it, and then he heard their words. *"Cut the hijo de puta open. García, you treacherous mongrel."*

The soldiers dropped him on a table. He screamed even as he tried to understand. How could *Sangre Pura* betray him? He couldn't see them now, only the blue sky. Their shouts didn't matter. This cramping, burning pain was everything, that and the judgment. *Jesus, I tried to complete my duty, but fools let our enemy escape.*

More shouts. "Hail, Prince Enrique." Two men stepped close, each in chest armor with no helmet. One wore a breastplate etched with a gold lion—the blue eyes and fair hair, square jaw and ugly, flattened nose—the young prince and the one beside him, his lackey, Pacheco.

Prince Enrique raised his hand, and the mob silenced. "Señor García, I warned Magistrate Sarmiento that you'd betray us, but he valued your cunning beyond reason. Now you've hatched a plot to refuse me Toledo. Do you deny it?"

"Who—" Marcos' voice was too low. He struggled to take in air. "Who told you?"

The prince gave Pacheco a knowing glance. "It was Viçente P-Pérez," Pacheco said.

Marcos clenched his fists, feeling his abdomen burn. *How could the fiend have known?* "He's evil."

Prince Enrique jabbed a finger at Marcos, making him cringe and pain flare again. "If Viçente hadn't brought the word, you'd have lured my father's army to Toledo and ignited war."

Marcos thought of a way to gain God's approval, if only he could muster the cleverness he needed. "Please listen." He took another breath, putting all of his energy into speaking. "The only way Pérez could know ... he's Satan. Prince. He's Satan."

"Who told you this, your excommunicated vicar who sits in the dungeon?" The prince smirked.

"The *marranos* ... revere Pérez." Marcos gasped. "They confessed. They despise Jesus ... Pérez admitted it, too."

"You crippled him with torture," Pacheco said. "Viçente will recover, but you won't." Pacheco flipped the back of his hand at Marcos and turned away.

Prince Enrique wrinkled his distorted nose, his features grotesque. "You reek. Your intestines dribble out like slop from the slaughterhouse. Since you regard Viçente Pérez so, you can bid him farewell."

Could this be true? The *marrano* had come, as Marcos hoped, and the square was filled with *Sangre Pura*. It was still possible. A bit of strength pulsed in his veins.

CHAPTER 96

—᎗᎗᎗—

A COLD SHIVER RAN UP Viçente's neck. He stood at the foot of the cathedral steps with only a dozen soldiers between him and the mob. A shout from close behind. *"Give us García. We'll hack him apart."*

The west cathedral portal swung open and soldiers brought out a litter. The mob shrieked, their harsh shouts setting Viçente's heart racing. There, as the guards carried the bloody litter down the steps to the entry porch, Viçente spotted García, the man who'd tortured Diego. Was he alive? Workmen set a table on the platform and soldiers dropped the litter onto it. García let out a howl that chilled Viçente but also thrilled him. García's hand dangled from the table. Crimson beads of blood dripped from it.

Enrique and Juan Pacheco mounted the stairs. Enrique grinned as the mob shouted for García's death. Seeing the blood, feeling the mob's fury, Viçente felt a depraved craving to gore the man who'd tortured his son. He fought the need to vomit, even as he tasted joy and despised the depravity in him that did.

Enrique leaned over the prisoner, as if taking his confession. Viçente couldn't hear their words, but then Enrique beckoned. It was foolish and dangerous, but Enrique had brought him, and now he couldn't resist. He made his way slowly, concentrating on the cane and the stairs ... and the blood dripping from those fingers.

Now he steadied himself and stared at García—the soiled, mangled guts spilled out, slimy and purplish, on his abdomen. Viçente forced down the bile in his throat.

"You can be the one to give him last rites," Enrique sneered.

"What of the mob?" Viçente asked.

"They're mine now." The prince's confident nod gave Viçente a little courage.

"Don't forget to anoint him. Use his feces for oil." Pacheco followed Enrique to the side.

García watched him with dark, malevolent eyes sunken in his cadaverous face. "Like a pig to the slaughter, you come." His voice was a weak rasp, but he looked certain.

"You're a madman, García. You're the one dying." Viçente begged Jesus to make it true. The mob could overcome Enrique's soldiers and take him.

García smiled and bloody drool spilled out of his mouth. "An army of *Sangre Pura* came to support me."

"Shouting for your death."

"They revere me. When they kill you ... it will assure my place in heaven. I recognize you, Satan."

"You're the beast who tortured and killed. You whipped my son almost to death." Viçente clenched his fists, but couldn't bring himself to strike this defenseless hulk.

García's face contorted. He gasped and wheezed, and the wheezing went on and on. Viçente thought he was dying, but García sucked in a huge breath and shouted, "*Sangre Pura*." Again he gasped and screamed, "*Kill the marrano*."

Viçente heard men's voices from down in the square. He stood rigid, dreading an attack, but he couldn't let his terror show. He glanced at Enrique, ten paces away, arms folded across his chest, looking amused. The prince waved at the mob, and the murmur faded. Viçente stepped to the end of the table, grabbed García's hair in his fist, and twisted his head toward the crowd. "Look at your adoring thugs."

García shrieked and flailed his arms. Viçente dropped his head onto the table. "They're too much like you to revere you, full of blind envy and loathing."

García lay still, eyes darting. Then he whispered something. Viçente kept his hand on the dagger at his belt as he bent closer.

García's depraved smile returned. "My *brotherhood* could have attacked ... but they grant me the honor of killing you." García clenched his jaw and seized Viçente's tunic, moaning, pulling Viçente close, growling and whimpering.

Viçente lost balance. He dropped his cane and grabbed the table with both hands. He stared straight into García's eyes, smelling the stench, feeling desperation and loathing. García glared and growled and Viçente said, "What do you plan to do now, you soulless dog?"

García released one hand from Viçente's tunic and tried for the knife. Viçente pulled back, the weapon out of García's reach. García tried to rise, his face a glowering, agonized horror, but he collapsed and Viçente slapped him. García lost hold with the other hand and reached with claw-like fingers, but Viçente stepped away.

Marcos García lay on the table, eyes closed, wheezing. "*Sangre Pura*, I need you."

"You have nothing to give them anymore. I pity you."

Juan Pacheco came over and retrieved Viçente's cane for him. "Those two will take care of García." Pacheco nodded to a pair of soldiers with battle-axes.

Standing at the edge of the platform, Viçente looked at the crowd of hateful men, and tried to understand how such awful emotions thrived, even in his own soul, side by side with noble visions.

CHAPTER 97

He pictured Francesca as he paced through the orange groves with Diego, each day a bit further. As he drifted off to sleep at night, he worried for her and longed to hold her. Traversing the encampment, seeing the high walls of Toledo, memories of the dungeon assailed him, but with García's death, Viçente was no longer hunted. The people of Toledo seemed devoted to Enrique, and the prince had issued orders of protection for Viçente and his son.

When he felt strong enough, he and Diego returned to their home. Viçente paused in the doorway, stricken by the sight of this lifeless shell—shattered yellow dishes strewn around the salon and dining room.

Diego moved on, but Viçente lingered, looking for Marta's picture. In its place, a profanity had been gouged in the bare wall. His flash of anger dissolved to empty sorrow.

In the dining chamber, his boots crunched broken plates. A dozen holes had been gouged in the plaster wall, as if a frenzied man had jabbed it with a spear. *García*, Viçente thought. *Like a rabid dog.* In the kitchen, a pile of broken boards that had once been cabinets. "Where are you, son?"

Diego entered, his eyes fierce. "They pretend to be righteous, but they're *cabrones* and thieves."

Viçente cupped his son's cheek in a hand and gestured. "I have trouble bending. Could you clear that rubble?"

Diego stared. "The hiding place, do you think they missed it?" He tossed broken boards aside and brushed dirt from the flooring stones. He pried one up with his knife. "They're here." He removed more stones, pulled out a metal box, and handed it up.

Viçente opened it and drew out a cloth pouch. He handed the box to Diego, untied the drawstrings, and lifted out Marta's ruby necklace. A chill ran through him as he remembered their tenth anniversary, when she'd closed her eyes for a surprise and he'd looped it around her neck. "You recognize this?"

"From her portrait."

"There's more of your mother's jewelry." Viçente's voice trembled. "I want to give you some of the pieces."

"I'll cherish them, Papa." Diego gave Viçente a sad smile. "So this is what brought you to the city."

"Not just this. I'm taking you to meet a rabbi. Don't look so worried, son. No one's hunting us now."

Though Viçente had governed the city, he'd never approached this substantial building of brown stone and mortar, with brickwork about the doorway and Moorish, arched windows above. He and Diego entered and found a room almost as tall as the cathedral, but not nearly as wide, with Arabesque plaster carvings and Hebrew writing across the upper walls. Light shone through windows set just beneath the ornate, wooden ceiling. Viçente paused, letting his feelings take him. His parents had worshipped here before Christians attacked, forcing them to choose life over faith. A feeling of reverence crept over him.

They followed a passageway and found Rabbi Benjamin in his office. The rabbi stood behind his desk—disheveled beard, the crinkled skin around the eyes that widened with a surprised smile. Viçente had tried to push the thoughts aside, but he'd feared for the rabbi during all these months of violence. Now he resisted the impulse to touch the Jew.

"Oh," Rabbi Benjamin said. "I would have never expected ... And this young man—I see a resemblance." He stepped around his desk and held out a hand.

"My son, Diego."

The rabbi grasped Diego's hand and scrutinized him. "A fine-looking fellow. Has he told you of your ancestry, young man?"

Diego looked confused and Viçente said, "Only a bit."

"Your father's been ashamed." Rabbi Benjamin's dark eyes sparkled above his large, crooked nose as he gestured to a chair. "Sit, young Pérez. Should we let your shamefaced father stand?"

A gentle jibe or condemnation? No wonder the rabbi had always made him uncomfortable.

"No, Papa's been hurt."

"You're a good son. We'll all sit." The rabbi took a chair, folded his hands on his lap, and waited.

Viçente settled beside his son, feeling his palms sweat, searching for words. "They tortured me for being a convert." Not what he'd meant to say, not the steady voice he'd desired.

The rabbi nodded, his beard brushing his black trousers.

"Do you remember our meeting at the Roman Circus several years ago?" Viçente asked. "I ridiculed you for saying Old Christians wouldn't forgive my Jewish ancestry."

"You held power then. You hadn't experienced the way men make a religion out of hatred."

"I shouldn't have been so naïve."

Rabbi Benjamin gestured to Diego. "Heed this lesson, young man. Old Christians distrust converts. They think you've cheated the executioner."

"That's lunacy."

"Never expect rationality, lad. And you, Viçente, your failing is having a just soul, but that's the finest thing I can imagine. But you didn't come to tell me how you've misjudged your Christians."

Viçente had been prepared for a pompous lecture, not praise. He heard a sound and realized he was tapping his foot on the floor. He stilled it. "I want to thank you for your Hebrew-Latin Bible. You'll be surprised to learn that it rests with Pope Nicholas."

Rabbi Benjamin's eyes narrowed. The hand he held out toward Viçente trembled. Viçente thought, *Now he'll harangue me about the Hebrew God, and we'll fight.* The rabbi opened his mouth but paused and said softly, "I don't understand. I cherish that book."

"It's in safe hands. The pope is founding a library, and it's a rare volume. I gave it up to convince the Holy Father to meet with us."

The rabbi ran a hand over his mouth, his look growing tender. "You took a great risk. They might have used it as a sign of your corruption."

"We had to gain an audience. Pope Nicholas accepted."

Rabbi Benjamin nodded. "Then your venture was well rewarded. The pope cast his holy curse on Sarmiento. Marcos García is destroyed. Soon converts will return to Toledo. I approve."

The rabbi's words shouldn't have been important, but they eased Viçente's mind. "I had time to think in prison," he said. "About how wrong it is for men to harm others for their beliefs, even just to disdain them."

The rabbi leaned closer. "Then you came to speak of your father, Viçente. You wounded him with your contempt. Do you expect me to absolve you, like one of the haughty priests?"

Viçente's throat tightened with anger. "I just wanted to see if you're well. We'll go now."

"We met in secret a few times, your father and I," the rabbi said. "That was before I became chief rabbi. I felt honored, because he was a ha-Levi, related to the great Samuel who built this synagogue. Be proud of that heritage, both of you." The rabbi glanced at Diego and back to Viçente. "Your father, Judah, confided his shame and grief for denying Judaism and over a son who couldn't abide his failings."

Viçente gripped the arms of his chair and felt blood color his face. "I was wrong to judge him, I know. I'd beg his forgiveness if I could."

Diego placed a hand on Viçente's forearm. "Papa, I only met Grandfather a few times, but Rabbi Benjamin reminds me of him."

The rabbi's eyes gleamed. "You honor me, young man."

"No," Viçente blurted, but he knew Diego was right—the similarity not in appearance, but in the way they perceived life. "Yes. That's why we quarrel, Rabbi."

The rabbi stroked his beard and then beckoned. "Then speak to me as to your father. Is there something else?"

The unkempt beard and slouchy posture repelled Viçente, but the cleric's smile drew him in. "I've met a woman."

The rabbi fanned his face with a hand. "You've come to speak of your flirtations?"

"He's in love." Diego glanced at Viçente and lowered his eyes. "Sorry, Papa."

"You seek my blessing. This is very good." Rabbi Benjamin's eyes still flashed humor. "And why did you not bring her here?"

"She lives in Naples," Diego said. "And she's beautiful."

Benjamin pursed his lips. "You may be tempted to live in Italy now that Toledo's treated you ill, but you should stay and help your fellow converts."

Viçente tensed, thinking of the cold *alcázar* dungeon. "I can't, but maybe I'll ask Francesca to move with me to Segovia."

"Better here." The rabbi shrugged. "But you're a symbol to the entire nation. Tell this dear lady that your converts have suffered too many indignities to see their finest man run to Italy like a frightened squirrel."

Viçente didn't want to be a symbol or hold office or struggle ever again. If she agreed, he'd marry Francesca and live somewhere in peace. "I don't come to seek your blessing," Viçente said. "But I was thinking about my father, and—"

"I can't offer his blessing. But I knew him, and he would have been delighted if you'd asked. It would have meant that you felt a small part of the reverence a son owes his father."

Along with his guilt, thinking of Papa brought Viçente a nostalgic tenderness that pleased and saddened him at the same time. He was finally coming to accept his parents' memory. "That's all, Rabbi. Thank you."

CHAPTER 98

—⚊—

FRANCESCA GAZED AT THE LOW, gray mountains in the distance, then leaned out the carriage window and looked through the cloud of dust that rose from the horse's hooves and wagon wheels to the soldiers riding behind. Dust was all that remained of her dreams. No, she told herself; there was life growing in her womb.

The carriage jolted along a dirt track as it had for a week with its incessant creaking, the clomping of hooves, filth and discomfort. They climbed a winding track from rolling wheat fields to an oak-studded hill. Opposite her, Carlo crossed his arms, his features set in that sour frown he'd adopted so often since Viçente had come into her life.

Francesca mopped her brow with a handkerchief and gritty dirt smudged the cloth. She focused again on those fields and mountains. It was her duty to view this country, the country of Viçente's life. She wouldn't travel here again, but one day she'd tell their child about his father's homeland and the city he'd governed. Oh, God, how could she believe he was gone?

She heard the driver speak to the horses. The carriage slowed. Dust enveloped them as they rolled to a halt at the top of the rise. The driver came to her door. "Lady Francesca, if you'd like to step down, we're in sight of Toledo."

Francesca's heart pounded in her chest. Climbing down, she saw no city, only a patch of dirt flanked by oak trees, but she followed the man to a promontory where the view opened. There across a canyon, a city sat bold upon its bluff beneath white fluffy clouds. As Viçente had described it, Toledo rose from the canyon walls, a compact unity neatly enclosed in the river's arc. And dominating the near side, a massive fortress with arched windows and square turrets—the *alcá-zar*. Her stomach cramped. They would have tortured him there. His blood had dripped into the bowels of that hulking structure until it was all dried up, his heart and spirit and life's warmth gouged away by his enemies. She shivered and clenched her fists, loathing those men, Pedro Sarmiento and Marcos García. What distorted minds could hate so much that they'd annihilate love and life for some perverted notion of God's will? She shook her head, knowing there could be no answer. But building her own fortress of hatred would destroy her. She would surround their new son or daughter with love.

Somewhere near the city, her nephew, Enrique, had set up camp, and there she would find Diego, their baby's half-brother.

As the clouds drifted, light shone on a tower—the cathedral. Viçente had helped to build that holy center. He'd described the way the men raised this tower that he loved, like a needle piercing the sky, the sun bright upon it. There was something of her love in Toledo, even if he was lost. She would pray at the altar he'd helped build, and if God willed it, she'd find a bit of his soul in his formidable city, something for their child to hold dear.

She rested her palms on her swelling belly as the clouds shifted and the cathedral fell to shadow, but now her hilltop brightened. The sun's warmth touched her. It wasn't impossible … *Lord, please let me find him alive.*

End of *Soul of Toledo*

HISTORICAL CONTEXT

—⁓—

Soul of Toledo is a work of fiction, but its background is factual, based on my research and meetings with professors in Spain. The most detailed history of the era is *The Origins of the Inquisition* by B. Netanyahu, and I have relied heavily on this work.

Written history is always open to other interpretations. The 'facts' of Toledo, 1449—even though 550 years past— are still controversial. Details are lacking. Specifics can be disputed, motivations never truly known. Opposing theories persist.

Viçente and Francesca are fictional characters, moving through this historical landscape. To aid my lovers in coming together, and to move the action along, I let time pass more quickly than the historical record permits. I filled in missing details, as you'll see.

The pogroms of 1391, the year of Viçente's birth, slaughtered many Jews and drove thousands, like Viçente's parents, into exile or forced conversion. The face of Castile changed, but many former Jews retained their positions and their fortunes through true or feigned conversion. Doubts and resentments about the 'converts' festered.

The dramatic events of the 1440s—King Juan's capture in 1443, his escape in June 1444, the Battle of Olmedo in May 1445, and Sarmiento's

1449 rebellion in Toledo—follow history. But history sometimes disappoints in a dramatic sense. Things move slowly sometimes. Kings vacillate when we crave decisive acts.

Though a 'pivotal battle,' only twenty to forty men died at the Battle of Olmedo (depending on the account), and approximately two hundred died later of their wounds, including the 'Royal Cousin' known as the Master of Santiago. The lack of casualties seems remarkable given the fact that thousands engaged in mortal combat.

Also astonishing to the modern reader is King Juan's forbearance in the face of repeated treasons. He pardoned Chief Magistrate Ayala (for the second time) despite his support of the 'Royal Cousins,' only to have Ayala refuse to fight for him in the Battle of Olmedo. Likewise, the king dawdled in dealing with Pedro Sarmiento. After installing Sarmiento in Ayala's place as magistrate, ruler of the *alcázar* and city gates, the king reversed himself and ordered that Ayala be returned to his judgeship. Sarmiento ignored the king's order, and King Juan negotiated with Sarmiento for more than two years before allowing Constable Luna to step in and assume control of the gates. I modified the reason and timing, but not the sequence, of these events, giving Marcos García de Mora and his '*Sangre Pura*' a role in the king's displeasure.

It's difficult today to appreciate such timidity, but this was a particularly faint-hearted king, and, during this period, Castile's king held power by a tenuous thread, which depended on alliances with cities, the church, and with noble families. King Juan II's cousins, who possessed more than their share of power in Castile (secured for them by their father, Fernando, when he'd been regent before King Juan II's accession), made sure that his control was ineffectual.

So isn't it refreshing to find one character who is neither tame nor indecisive? The historical Marcos García de Mora was Pedro Sarmiento's chief advisor during Sarmiento's rule in Toledo. He likely authored the city's demands to King Juan during the city's siege and the *Sentencia Estatuto,* which stripped Jews and their progeny of their civic rights. Marcos García's earlier life is not well known, so I invented a role for him in the events prior to 1445. Marcos needed comrades, so I created *Sangre Pura,* based on B. Netanyahu's argument that the *común* (common folks of Toledo) must have been organized prior to Toledo's revolt against King Juan. I ran far with that idea, letting Marcos' band of bigoted guildsmen kill the mute, Samuel. To satisfy *Sangre Pura's* bloodlust, and also that of my readers, I let the mob attack the Jewish Quarter, repeatedly over a period of years. I confess to vengeful motives in allowing Marcos to break his leg and later to suffer a well deserved—though fictional—heart attack. And I created discord between Marcos and his magistrate, Pedro Sarmiento, to keep things simmering.

The events in the final chapters of *Soul of Toledo* took place over a period of about a year, beginning with Constable Luna's taking of the city gates in December 1448 and his demand for a loan of 1 million *maravedis* from Toledo on January 25, 1449. These actions brought on the rebellion on January 27 by the *común,* encouraged, if not led, by Pedro Sarmiento and Marcos García de Mora, which ousted Constable Luna's men from the city gates.

Now in firm control, Sarmiento and García initiated the *limpieza,* torturing and forcing confessions from many converts. García and his minions took detailed notes of the confessions to support their argument that converts were blasphemers. No one knows how many were persecuted, but much of the *converso* population of Toledo was forced to flee, and at least four were executed. I allowed Marcos to set those four ablaze before the archbishop's palace.

Again at this juncture, history plodded rather than sprinted. King Juan had other matters to attend in his rebellious kingdom, and finally arrived at Toledo four months later, in May 1449. And yes, the single cannon shot was fired at the king. The king, ever meek, departed as Prince Enrique approached with his army late that month. Although the prince was allowed to bring his 1,500 men into the city in June, negotiations between the prince and Sarmiento continued for six months, determining the converts' fate and the conditions for delivering the city to Enrique.

The pope issued the bulls condemning the Toledan rebels on September 24, 1449. That October, Prince Enrique agreed to turn the city over to the king within one year. In mid-December 1449, Marcos Garcia's plot to allow the king's entry through Calatrava gate was discovered, and the prince did indeed return from a hunting expedition to deal with it. Marcos García and Fernando de Avila were killed, drawn, and quartered after trying to escape from the cathedral tower. Vicar Pero López de Gálvez and Padre Juan Alonso were captured there and later executed.

LATER EVENTS

Following the death of Marcos García, the prince's demands on Sarmiento, delivered through Bishop Barrientos, became more forceful. On February 6, 1450, the bishop of Siguenza, following the instructions of the papal bulls, commanded all Christians to shun Sarmiento. With Prince Enrique's acquiescence, Sarmiento sneaked out one night with 30 million maravedis and wagons of confiscated loot. Sarmiento was executed in the town of Zamora in 1451.

Alvaro de Luna, having been many times dismissed by King Juan II only to be reinstated as the king's constable, was executed upon King Juan's orders in 1453. The king's second wife (Isabella of Portugal) was apparently disenchanted with the master manipulator, even though Luna had helped convince the king to marry her. (No good deed-doer goes un-slain.)

The man who fired the cannon at King Juan during the siege of Toledo was beheaded to appease His Majesty.

The Bible I created for Viçente to give to Pope Nicholas would have been a rare book, indeed. Illustrated bibles were created in Spain during the fifteenth century, and the Jews of Toledo had, in centuries past, worked with monks to translate Hebrew bibles into Latin, but I'm not aware of any testaments printed in both languages simultaneously. Pope Nicholas V would certainly have coveted such a volume, since he did establish the Vatican library.

Lope de Barrientos, bishop of Cuenca, was the advisor and tutor of kings (Juan and Enrique), a strong advocate for *conversos* and a key participant in the events of Toledo 1449. He died in 1469 at the age of 87.

Prince Enrique succeeded King Juan upon his death in 1454, but he inherited his father's difficulties and almost lost the throne when Juan Pacheco and archbishop Carrillo turned against him, dethroned him in effigy, and rebelled. Though he remained king until his death in 1474, Enrique was unable to pass the throne on to his daughter, Joana, who was thought to be illegitimate. (By this time Enrique was known derisively as *el impotente*.) Incidentally, Enrique underwent successful cataract surgery in 1469, performed by a Jewish surgeon.

Enrique's half-sister, Isabella (King Juan II's daughter by his second wife, Isabella of Portugal), married Ferdinand, King of Aragón (another cousin-to-cousin marriage), and ascended to the throne of Castile and León, thus unifying Spain. In 1478, at Ferdinand and Isabella's request, Pope Sixtus IV authorized the Spanish Inquisition. In 1483, Tomás de Torquemada, a prominent Dominican (nephew of Juan de Torquemada, who appears in *Soul of Toledo*) became the Royal Inquisitor.

Oh, yes, in addition to creating the Inquisition and unifying Spain, Isabella and Ferdinand cast the last of the Muslim rulers from Granada, expelled all remaining Jews and Muslims from Spain, and sent Columbus on his famous voyage. To modern sensibilities, the revered 'Catholic monarchs' seem morally a mixed bag.

ADDITIONAL NOTE

Another vexing aspect of history was the royals' habit of using and recycling names. Enriques and Juans, Marías and Isabellas abound—yes, Juanas, too. (Think of all the Henrys in European history, remembering that *Enrique* is the Spanish translation.) One of the 'Royal Cousins,' the King of Navarre, was named Juan, as was Castile's king. A second of the cousins was another duplicate—Enrique. To avoid confusion, I referred to these two cousins as 'King of Navarre,' and 'Master of Santiago.' Similarly disconcerting was the royal habit of cousin-to-cousin nuptials, often with more duplicate names. All of history is made more confusing by the royalty's lack of imagination in naming their offspring.

THE BENEFITS OF A SPARSE HISTORICAL RECORD

Without detailed accounts of the Battle of Olmedo, King Juan's takeover of Toledo on behalf of Pedro Sarmiento, Constable Luna's ouster from the city, or many other events, I've been free to create details. In the case of the battle, I set the scene on the Río Adaja rather than the plain nearby. At least today, Adaja's a rather unimpressive stream, without much of a canyon, but it made the battle more fun. After all, this *is* fiction.

TRANSLATED TERMS

—⁂—

Albergo – inn

Alcázar – fortress

Cedula – royal order

Converso (a)- a Jew who converted to Catholicism/Christianity or a Catholic descended from Jews

Cortes – A meeting of all nobles/administrators called by the king

Criada – maid

Dios! – God!

Doblas – currency in fifteenth-century Castile, larger than *maravedis*

Guardia Civil – Civil Guard, the local police

Huevos – eggs (slang for testicles)

Limpieza – a sacramental cleansing of the blood

Lombarda – red cabbage, a nickname for the cannon fired from Toledo at the king

Maravedis – currency in fifteenth-century Castile, smaller than *doblas*

Marlotta – a dice game

Marrano – swine; a derogatory term for *converso*, implying that the person was a false Catholic who consorted with Jews and kept their profane ways.

Morisco(a) – a Catholic converted from Muslim, or Catholic descended from Muslims

New Catholics – *conversos* and *Moriscos*

Nuestro Promotor – our promoter/advocate

Old Catholics – Catholics not descended from Jews or Muslims within
the recent (500 year) past

Pontagos, portagos, bartascos, bulas – types of fees/tolls/taxes levied by
the church in Toledo

Puerta – door, city gate

Querido(a) – a term of affection meaning 'dear one'

Sangre Pura – 'pure blood;' the fictitious organization made up of
those who hated converts and Jews

Seguidilla – an early Spanish dance

Signor – Italian for mister, equivalent to Señor in Spanish

ACKNOWLEDGEMENTS

—⁕—

MY WRITERS' GROUP, HOSTED BY Les and Es Cole, had the integrity to criti-
cize and the insights to do it well.

Rebecca Mahoney, my editor, poured through drafts, finding scores
of inconsistencies, awkward passages, and out-and-out mistakes. She
helped immensely in making this work coherent and grammatically as
perfect as I would allow.

Kristin Bryant who designed the cover of the book, using a background created by the painter El Greco (1541-1614).

Carlos Rubio, Professor, Universidad de Castilla—La Mancha, Toledo,
created a two-day curriculum for me, including a lecture by the fireplace in his lovely home and a walking tour of historical sites in Toledo.
Professor Rubio even convinced the guards in a bank (formerly Chief
Magistrate Ayala's palace in the city) to allow me a view of the patio
where Vicente met with the magistrate after his 'gentle incarceration'
at Segovia. He revealed many elements of fifteenth- century Castilian
life, and I am grateful.

István Szaszdi, Professor, Universidad de Valladolid (Valladolid and
Segovia campuses), helped me research many of my characters and
escorted me to several of King Juan II and Prince Enrique's historical

locations, including the palace holding the lovely Moorish fountain which soothed Viçente after his wounding at the Battle of Olmedo.

My wife, Marguerite, my intrepid companion for our visits to Spain and in life, has been my joy and my understanding companion for 46 years. She encourages me always and cheerfully leaves me for long hours researching and writing.

ABOUT THE AUTHOR

—꠲꠲—

EDWARD D. WEBSTER IS THE author of an eclectic collection of books as well as articles appearing in publications such as *The Boston Globe* and *Your Cat* magazine. Ed admits to a fascination with unique, quirky, and bizarre human behavior, and he doesn't exempt himself from the mix. His acclaimed memoir, *A Year of Sundays (Taking the Plunge and our Cat to Explore Europe)* shares the eccentric tale of his yearlong adventure in Europe with his spirited, blind wife and headstrong, deaf, sixteen-year-old cat.

In his historical novel, *Soul of Toledo*, about Spain in the 1440s, the diabolical nature of mankind stands out as madmen take over the city of Toledo and torture suspected Jews thirty years before the Spanish Inquisition.

Webster also likes to tinker with fictional characters, putting strange people together to see what they'll do with/to each other. He is the author of the novel *The Gentle Bomber's Melody*, in which a nutty woman, bearing a stolen baby, lands on the doorstep of a fugitive bomber hiding from the FBI. The result: irresistible insanity.

From the happily unusual of *A Year of Sundays* to the cruelly perverse in *Soul of Toledo*, Webster shines a light on offbeat aspects of human nature. Webster lives in Southern California with his divine wife and two amazing cats.

See Ed's website, www.edwardwebster.com for more information.

Photo by: Patsy Wright